Cooktown Christmas

A North Queensland Cadet Adventure

C.R. Cummings

Also By
CHRISTOPHER CUMMINGS

Cooktown Christmas

A North Queensland Cadet Adventure

C.R. Cummings

DoctorZed
Publishing
www.doctorzed.com

This 2nd Edition published 2024 by DoctorZed Publishing

DoctorZed Publishing books may be ordered through booksellers or by contacting:

DoctorZed Publishing
10 Vista Ave
Skye, south Australia 5072
www.doctorzed.com

ISBN: 978-0-9756145-2-5 (sc)
ISBN: 978-0-9756145-3-2 (ebk)

A Cataloguing-in-Publication entry can be found at the National Library of Australia
www.nla.gov.au

Cover design © Scott Zarcinas

Printed in Australia, UK & USA

DoctorZed Publishing rev. date: 20/05/2024

Dedication

This book is dedicated to my mother
Cynthia Adelaide Cummings (Nee Wickham)
Licensee
Of
The 'Lion's Den'
1963-1983

A loving mum, always caring and full of good advice and
tolerance; a hard worker, efficient organiser, sensible and
good person and always a lady.

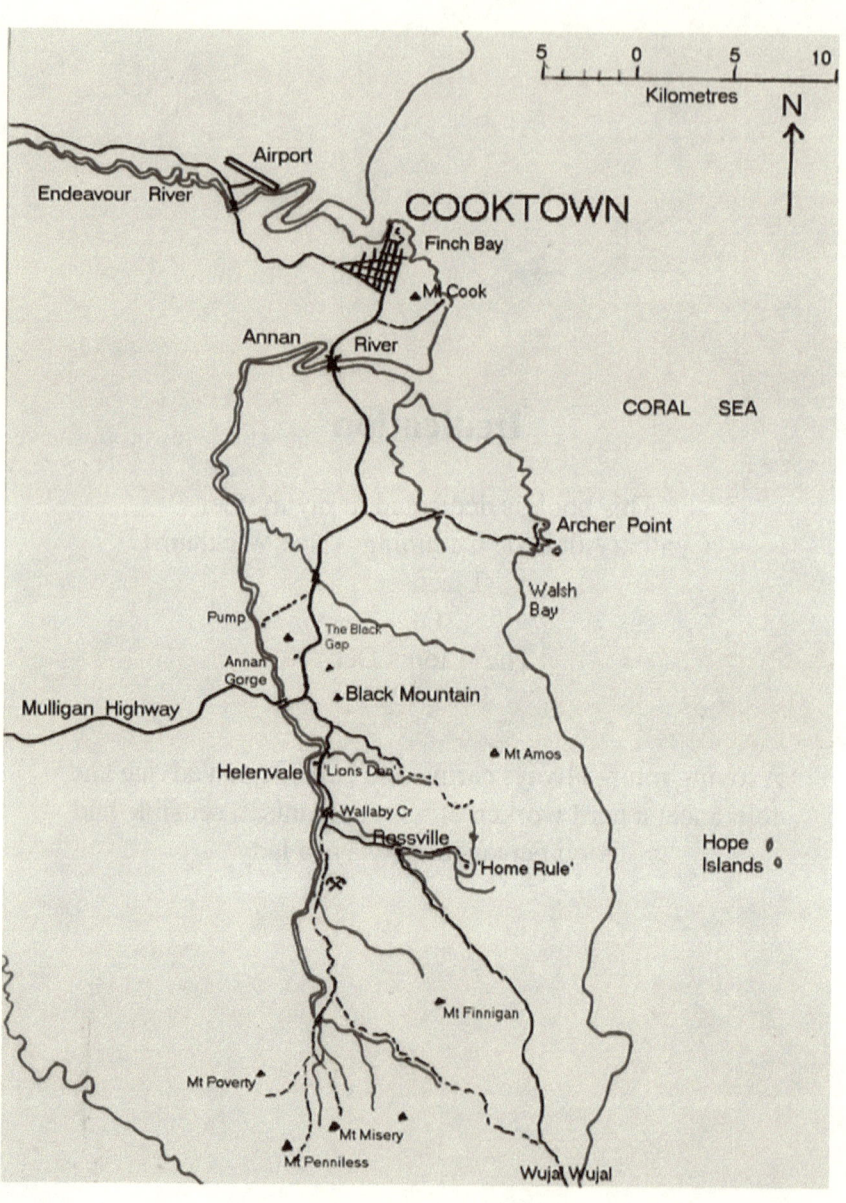

Chapter 1

TAKEN FOR GRANTED

Australian Navy Cadet Petty Officer Andrew Collins, 16 years old, fair-haired and blue-eyed, did a last check of his uniform in the full-length mirror on the wall of the cadet depot in Cairns. What he saw pleased him greatly. He believed he was good looking and his reflected image seemed to confirm this. But it was anxiety rather than vanity that caused him to critically study himself. This was a special occasion and he really wanted to look his best. In a few minutes he would be on public display as the petty officer of the Port Division of T.S. *Endeavour* during the unit's annual Passing-Out Parade.

Andrew smoothed his white shirt and adjusted his peaked cap to exactly the regulation angle. He liked that cap with its glossy black brim and white top but in his own mind it was only a step along his chosen path. The cap he really wanted to wear was the navy officer's cap with the gold braid and crown and anchor badge. His ambition was to be an officer in the Royal Australian Navy.

But first I will be a cadet midshipman, he told himself.

That was a goal he knew he was close to. Already his big sister Carmen had achieved it and the next promotion course was to be in January. That thought added to his anxiety. He knew that only two cadets from the unit would be sent on the 10-day course at the RAN College at Jervis Bay, and there were three potential candidates. The unit had one cadet chief petty officer, Mike O'Leary, but Mike had already finished Year 12 at high school and had applied for 'general entry' to the navy. The four cadet petty officers who might be candidates were himself, his arch rival Dick Carthew of the Starboard Watch, his friendly rival Kit Walker, and his friend Luke Karaku who was the unit coxswain.

As all four were just finishing Year 11 and had at least one year to go, both at school, and in cadets, the choice could fall on any of them.

I hope I am one, Andrew thought, adjusting his cap again and turning to view his profile. The school year had only one week to go and he was feeling that life was pretty good. *Except for my love life,* Andrew thought.

For two years he had been going steady with a female cadet of the same age: Tina Babcock. For the first year or so it had been true romance and they had done everything together as friends. But not as lovers. Tina had been very firm about that. She had allowed a lot of pashing and petting but nothing serious.

Mostly Andrew agreed and happily accepted her policy even though there had been times when his teenage body had been driven by stronger urges. He had coped with his frustrations with good humour and affection. But last night, while giving her a kiss and a cuddle, she had reacted.

"You are just taking me for granted!" she had snapped.

Andrew's protestations that this was not so had only made things worse. She had angrily accused him of not loving her and of just using her. It had hurt and left him floundering for a sensible answer.

"But I do love you!" he had assured her.

"You don't! You act as though you are doing me a favour, and you are just treating me as though my feelings don't matter, like I am part of the furniture," Tina had retorted.

"I am not!" he had cried, his feelings stirred at what he perceived to be injustice.

"You are! And you look at all the other girls as though you are regretting being my boyfriend. At times I get the feeling you are just going with me until you find someone better," Tina replied.

That barb drew mental blood and the feeling of guilt added to Andrew's emotions. He had been looking at other girls and he knew it! But he denied this.

"I have not!" he snapped angrily.

"You have!" Tina had retorted. Then she had shaken her head and said, "Well, maybe we aren't suited to each other. Maybe we have been sticking together out of loyalty and we might not really be suited to each other at all. I think we should stop seeing each other for a while."

Andrew had been shocked by that and had only been able to mutter a feeble denial. Tina had pursed her lips and shaken her head and then said, "I think that is for the best. I think we should both date others, if only to see how we really feel."

That had almost stunned Andrew and he had felt a swirl of emotions which had choked him up. First was hurt pride as the realisation sank in that Tina was dumping him. That had been followed by jealous suspicions.

Has she met someone else? he wondered.

It had hurt, he had to admit that. And the trouble was he didn't know if she wasn't right!

Maybe we should go our own way? he had thought.

Tina had looked stony-faced. "Goodbye then," she had said, before turning and walking away.

Andrew stood there feeling hurt and upset. When he thought about it, he realised that he had been taking her for granted and that he had not been as loving and as thoughtful as he might have been. He was also surprised at how much her rejection hurt. For a while he had struggled to think of what to say to change her mind, and he had been tempted to hurry after her and to plead for her to give him another chance.

But he had not done that and had finally gone sadly home, wondering if he would ever find true love.

Now, the following afternoon, he was still hurting but put on a brave face to hide it. Partly this was injured pride as he did not want the other cadets to know that he had been dumped. The knowledge that his rivals might jeer at him for not being good enough to keep a girl happy added to the unhappiness.

At that moment, Tina came into the room. Their eyes met in the mirror and Andrew felt a spurt of hope and then hurt as she quickly looked away and turned her back. Before he could ask her for another chance, she had walked away.

Sadly, Andrew shook his head. Then he glanced at the clock, braced his shoulders back and marched out, determined not to let his personal upset interfere with the parade. Apart from his loyalty to the unit, he was also motivated by a strong desire for the parade to go well for his sister, Carmen. She was the parade commander, and as a navy cadet it was her final moment of glory. As soon as the parade was over, she was leaving cadets. In January she would be starting at the Australian Defence Force Academy as a real RAN Midshipman.

The Passing-Out Parade now took up most of Andrew's attention. There were 14 cadets in the Port Division and he formed them up in two ranks ready to march on. Next, he inspected them. That brought him face to face with Tina as she stood in the front rank. After the briefest meeting of eyes, she looked directly to her front and ignored him. Andrew felt another surge of hurt but also a profound sense of loss.

She is very attractive, he thought, noting Tina's short-bobbed brown hair, bright hazel eyes and pretty but freckled face. Her build was slightly shorter than his and was also somewhat stocky, but because her breasts were so big he rarely noticed that. In her white cadet uniform she looked very smart. Tina was the same age and was also a 4th Year cadet but was a rank lower, being a cadet leading seaman.

To avoid any embarrassing incident, Andrew quickly moved on to the next cadet in line. The inspection completed he stood the division at ease and stood waiting. The parade was conducted at the ANC depot in Cairns, T.S. *Endeavour.* The depot is in its own fenced yard between the RAN naval base HMAS *Cairns* and the bulk sugar terminal. It backs onto Trinity Inlet, giving access for boats. The main building is a large shed with offices and accommodation at the front. A front veranda faces the gravel parade ground. On the veranda and in the shade beside the main building were seated the official guests, parents and families and friends.

Seeing his rivals and friends from the Army Cadets and Air Force Cadets among the crowd of fifty or sixty people watching really put Andrew on his mettle.

We don't want to muck up and give them any ammunition for bagging us out later, he thought anxiously.

A bellowed command from the Chief Bosun's Mate, Cadet Chief Petty Officer O'Leary, brought both divisions to attention. They then marched onto the parade ground and lined up facing the building and watching crowd. The 'Buffer' then 'right dressed' the ranks. Andrew had to make sure his division was lined up and he did this efficiently but found he was sweating more than the November tropical heat warranted.

The Buffer then handed command of the parade over to Andrew's sister, Carmen. She was the senior Cadet Midshipman and parade commander. Just looking at her caused Andrew to fill with pride and affection. In her white uniform and uniform cap and with her sword shining in the afternoon sunlight, he thought she looked amazingly attractive and smart.

That will be me next year, he told himself.

Carmen called them to attention and then had the armed guard marched on. This was commanded by the unit's other cadet midshipman, also a girl. The guard wore ceremonial whites and had white web belts and gaiters and carried rifles. Having been in such a guard several times

Andrew knew just how they felt, and just how much extra effort had gone into getting their drill perfect. At the rear, cutlass shimmering in the sun, was PO Kit Walker, a rival of Andrew's since their first year. Kit looked very much the part, despite his compact build. Andrew met his eyes and gave a brief nod of approval, which Kit returned.

The RAN Captain who was the reviewing officer then took his stand on the dais. Seeing a real naval officer with his crisp white uniform, bright medal ribbons, gold rank rings and officer's cap again fired Andrew's ambition. The captain inspected them, Andrew having to call his division to attention and then salute the captain when he arrived. He accompanied him on the inspection, anxious that no fault be found. After the inspection, Andrew stood the division at ease. He then resumed his position in front of them.

But he found that standing at the front of other cadets was not an easy thing to do. Andrew had always been self-conscious about the other cadets looking at him and possibly criticising his drill or appearance, but now he found he was acutely aware that Tina was just behind him. In his imagination he could feel her eyes boring into his back. It made him sweat even more.

There was a march past and then the unit stood at ease for speeches and the award of prizes and promotions. This time Andrew scanned the audience, noting his proud parents and the parents and siblings of other cadets. He also noted his History and Geography teacher seated among the VIPs. Mr Conkey was wearing his army cadet uniform as a captain, and when his gaze met Andrew's for a second he gave a smile and an encouraging nod. That sent a glow of pleasure through Andrew, who really valued the teacher's interest and support. The fact that Captain Conkey also wore medals for active service in the army added to his admiration.

Behind Capt Conkey sat four army cadets in uniform. All went to his school and were both his friends and his rivals. Seated on the right of the group was Cadet Warrant Officer 2nd Class Graham Kirk. Graham had once been a navy cadet and he and Andrew were good friends and had shared several adventures. When Graham met Andrew's eyes he grinned and gave a thumbs-up. Andrew gave a slight smile and a faint nod and felt pleased.

Then he remembered that Graham had once dated Tina; had even crept in to kiss her during a field exercise.[1] That had been a year and a half ago, and now the worrying and jealous thought crept in that perhaps Tina might be resuming that relationship.

A fortnight earlier, Andrew had attended the Army Cadet unit's Passing-Out Parade and he knew that Graham, and two of the three beside him: Peter Bronsky and Stephen Bell, would be attending a promotion course the following week for promotion to Cadet Under-Officer, the Army Cadet equivalent of cadet midshipman.

It was that knowledge which added to Andrew's anxiety. He really wanted to keep up with his friends. As the awards ceremony commenced, Andrew's worry ratcheted up another notch. The first few prizes did not concern him. They were for the Best Cadet, and Best Junior Rating. But the award for Best Senior Rating was one he hoped to win. As Lt Cdr Hazard, the CO, read the award, Andrew tensed.

"The winner of the Best Senior Rating for this year is Cadet Petty Officer Andrew Collins. Fall out, Petty Officer Collins," Lt Cdr Hazard read.

Andrew came to attention and called 'Sir!' As he marched over to the Reviewing Officer he felt himself tremble with relief. Very conscious that the army and air cadets were watching Andrew made sure his drill was as good as it could be. He made a snappy salute and stood rigidly to attention in front of the captain. The captain saluted and then shook his hand and handed Andrew the trophy. For a minute or so they posed for photographs. As he stepped back to salute again, Andrew felt a surge of pleasure which partly offset his hurt feelings. As he marched back to his place he also wondered if that might mean he was being considered for attendance on the cadet midshipman's course.

He was. After Carmen had been awarded her prize for Best Cadet Midshipman, Lt Cdr Hazard announced that the unit's selections for the next course were Andrew and Dick Carthew. Hearing that made Andrew glow with pleasure and relief but also made him feel sorry for Luke Karaku. Luke was a Torres Strait Islander and a good friend, and Andrew felt he deserved the promotion more. To Andrew's pleasure, Luke was next awarded the prize for seamanship and also for winning the sailing competition. Luke was then called out a third time and was promoted to the rank of Cadet Chief Petty Officer. He was to be the

---

[1] Read *Cockatoo* by C. R. Cummings

Chief Bosun's Mate for the following year. That seemed a very suitable and satisfactory solution to Andrew and made him feel better. But Kit Walker had missed out and did not look happy, which caused Andrew a little niggle of guilt.

After the parade, Andrew hurried to congratulate Luke. As he did, Dick Carthew joined them. He put out his hand to Luke as well. While they shook hands, Andrew made an effort to overcome his dislike and in turn held out his hand to Dick.

"Congratulations on being selected," he said.

There was a noticeable pause before Dick nodded and took his hand. "Same to you," he said. "But my division will be the best again next year."

Andrew snorted, "Oh piffle! The only reason the Starboard Watch won Best Division is because my sister was the leader."

Dick coloured with annoyance. "We had the best people all round," he retorted.

There was a moment's tense silence, broken by the arrival of Carmen and Hayley Page, the attractive cadet midshipman who was Andrew's divisional officer. Carmen hugged Andrew.

"Well done little brother," she praised.

Their parents arrived and joined in the congratulations, insisting they pose for more photos. This ended the situation and Andrew was able to relax, until he noted Tina talking to her parents. Just once she glanced in his direction and then hastily looked away. That brought Andrew out in another sweat of anxiety as he did not want his social failure exposed at such a public event.

To his dismay Carmen took him aside and said, "What's wrong between you and Tina?" she asked.

Andrew shrugged and blushed. He did not want to admit anything was wrong to her. All his life he and Carmen had been very close and he knew it was hopeless to try to hide the truth from her. After swallowing to moisten a suddenly dry mouth he shrugged again and said, "She has broken up with me."

As he said it, Andrew felt his throat tighten up and tears prickled his eyes. There was no way he wanted Carmen to see that so he struggled to hold them back.

Carmen looked at him hard and then said, "Why? Oh, that's not a fair question. Don't tell me. If she wants to discuss it she will, but I have to say I am not surprised. You haven't been treating her very well recently."

"W... what do you mean?" Andrew asked, blushing fiercely as he did, his guilty conscience biting at him when he remembered trying to pressure Tina into a more physical relationship.

Carmen made a wry face and said, "Well, you have been taking her for granted. Girls don't like that. They want to feel loved and special, not like they are just there for your pleasure and convenience like a piece of furniture."

Andrew blushed again and thought, *If Carmen has noticed then maybe I haven't behaved very well.*

He said, "Do... do... do you think I... I might be able to make it up to her?"

"That's up to you, little brother. But if she has said it is over then it is probably over. Maybe you should both meet new friends."

"But... but!" Andrew muttered. He was now baffled. "What about the holidays?" he asked. It had been arranged weeks before that Tina and another friend were joining the Collins family for two weeks of the Christmas holidays.

Carmen frowned and then said, "She might decide not to come. That's her choice, but she is my friend too, don't forget. She might want to. I will ask her."

That got Andrew both hopeful and anxious. *It will give me a chance to make it up to her if she does join us for the holidays,* he thought.

But he could also imagine it being potentially very embarrassing. The 6-week summer vacation was something he had been really looking forward to. Most of the first week was to be spent at sea on a Royal Australian Navy patrol boat. For the following four weeks the family was going to be running a small country hotel, the famous 'Lions Den' near Cooktown. For the last 10 days he was now to do his cadet midshipman's course at the Royal Australian Naval College at Jervis Bay.

As he walked with his parents to their car after the cadet parade Andrew looked back at Tina and tried to work out how he felt. *Do I really love her? Or was it just that I like her and she liked me and was good company?* he wondered. He wasn't sure but he knew that being dumped hurt. *But maybe it is an opportunity?* he thought, remembering his father's advice that every situation had both good and bad in it and he should always look for the positives. *Maybe she is doing me a big favour and I might be free to meet the girl of my dreams!*

Then another thought crossed his mind and he smiled. "Anyway, it should be fun meeting new girls and I can make the most of the opportunity!" he told himself.

Chapter 2

AT SEA

Despite Tina telling Andrew it was over, he found himself standing next to her 8 days later as they stood on the deck of the Royal Australian Navy Patrol Boat HMAS *Armidale*. The patrol boat was driving at full speed into 2-metre waves on a bright sunny December day. As this was in the Coral Sea 100 nautical miles off Cairns in Far North Queensland, conditions were not too bad. There was a fair amount of spray but the water and wind were both warm. December in North Australia is the end of the hot, dry summer and the start of The Wet, that period of three months of high temperatures, extreme humidity and frequent heavy rain storms.

School had finished three days earlier and the holidays had now begun. That was enough to put the cadets in a good mood. When this had added to it the experience of being at sea in a real navy vessel on such a bright sunny day it made it even better. As they were now quite unexpectedly involved in a drama on the high seas, that should have been enough to make even Andrew feel excited and glad to be alive. And he was, but the emotion was tempered by the knowledge that Tina was standing beside him, stiff with disapproval and ignoring him in a way that made it very obvious to the others that they had broken up.

There were nine cadets on the patrol boat, plus two Officers of Cadets: LT(ANC) Ryan, the unit XO, and SLT(ANC) Mullion, a female officer. The nine cadets were Andrew, Dick Carthew, Kit Walker and Luke Karaku, Tina, Davidson (a leading seaman from the Starboard Watch), Arthur Blake (Andrew's friend and a leading seaman from his watch), Cadet Leading Seaman Nancy Blackett from the Starboard Watch and Cadet Leading Seaman Sarah Creswell (from Andrew's watch and also Tina's friend).

Andrew was particularly pleased to be aboard *Armidale*. The patrol boat was one of the newest ships in the navy. He had once been aboard a patrol boat of the old *Fremantle* class but had not had the opportunity before to visit one of the new boats.

She is a big improvement, he thought, noting how well the *Armidale* handled the conditions. *If this was one of the old patrol boats we would be hammering into these waves and would all be soaking wet,* he thought, remembering a particularly rough trip on the HMAS *Townsville* the previous year.

The reason for the superior sea-keeping ability was very obvious: *Armidale* was much bigger, nearly 12 metres longer than the type her class were replacing. As well she had higher freeboard and a better shaped bow, plus the superstructure was higher and further aft. That was where the cadets and their OOCs stood in a group just aft of the wheelhouse.

Facing them was a Royal Australian Navy Sub Lieutenant dressed in mottled grey and black camouflage overalls, DPNU. He wore a baseball style cap with the patrol boat's name embroidered on it in gold and seemed to Andrew to be very efficient and competent. Helping him were two ratings. He was busy instructing the cadets on how to don anti-flash hoods and gloves. As Andrew had qualified as a Cadet Quartermaster Gunner two years earlier, this was something he had often done but he made no comment and did exactly as he was instructed.

While they were adjusting the hoods and gloves, the captain of the patrol boat, Lt Commander McDowall, came out of the enclosed bridge. He swept his eyes over the cadets, then said to Lt Ryan, "I have been in contact with the Fleet Commander and he has said we may proceed with the mission, as long as I am satisfied that there is no danger to any cadet."

At the word 'danger' Andrew felt a tingle of excitement and could hardly believe his luck. What had begun that morning as just a routine cruise to test some newly installed machinery after a short refit had suddenly turned into a real adventure. The patrol boat had been ordered to intercept a vessel acting suspiciously out in the Coral Sea. For the last three hours *Armidale* had been rushing east at over twenty knots.

Lt Cdr McDowall paused then went on. "I have been instructed to say that the decision is up to you people. This is an operational naval vessel and we may have to use force. That could mean us using our armament and it could mean us being fired on if the vessel resists. If any of you feel you do not want to be in this situation, or if you cadet officers feel that parents must be consulted then we will abort the mission and they will try to get *Cessnock* to take it over."

The last thing Andrew wanted was for them to turn back so he said, "Sir, isn't *Cessnock* still in Cairns?"

"Yes, she is," Lt Cdr McDowall answered. "She won't be able to get under way before about 1600 hours."

Andrew did a quick mental calculation and said, "So she won't arrive in this area until well after dark tonight."

"That's right."

Blake now spoke. "So we might lose contact and the ship might escape," he said.

Lt Cdr McDowall shook his head. "No, we won't lose contact. We have a 'Coastwatch' patrol plane keeping an eye on this fellow. It will keep radar contact. But the ship might move outside Australian waters before *Cessnock* can get here."

Lt Ryan nodded and said, "I think we are happy to proceed. I am sure you will make sure none of us comes to harm sir," he said.

Lt Cdr McDowall nodded. "You can be sure of that. If there is any risk you will all be placed below as far out of harm's way as possible."

As the captain turned and made his way forward all Andrew could do was grin with delight. "This will be good," he said to no one in particular.

The others seemed to agree. Andrew settled into a comfortable position, his eyes scanning the horizon for the first sign of the ship they were hurrying to intercept. As he sat there Andrew began to conjure up exciting daydreams to make the event even more interesting.

We are actually a cruiser in World War 2, not a patrol boat on the 21st Century. And we are about to start a battle with... with.

His mind flipped through ideas and images from things he had read and pictures he had seen. The most exciting scenario he could think of was that the 'enemy' ship was one of the German 'Pocket Battleships'.

Some of them came near Australia, he mused. He knew that one named the *Scheer* had been in the Indian Ocean but then he remembered a movie he had once seen, an old British film called 'Battle of the River Plate'. *No, she is the 'Graf Spee'.* he thought.

From the depths of his memory he dredged up some details of that ship, relishing the thought that it had carried six 11-inch calibre guns. *They will be able to fire from twenty kilometres away, as soon as she is visible on the horizon,* he thought. For a few seconds he imagined the grey monster showing dimly on the distant horizon, then the tiny pinpoints of bright flame as the great guns fired. *Would they have much chance of hitting such a small and manoeuvrable target as a patrol boat?* he wondered.

For a few minutes his mind pondered what he had read about the complexities of old-fashioned naval gunnery. Then he shook his head.

"No, a pocket battleship is not realistic enough. It would more likely be one of the so-called Auxiliary Kruisers," he muttered.

Tina looked at him. "What did you say?" she asked.

Andrew flushed with embarrassment. "Nothing," he answered.

He did not want people to know he was such a romantic daydreamer. He looked back at the horizon while trying to remember which of the German 'Merchant Raiders' had come to the waters off eastern Australia. He could picture a map he had once seen in a book on naval history that showed the track of one such German ship coming right into the middle of the Coral Sea but he could not remember its name.

Pinguin? Or was it the Atlantis? he wondered. He knew it wasn't the Kormoran. *She sank the HMAS* Sydney *off the west coast of Western Australia,* he remembered. But a few moments reflection about that disastrous action in 1941 convinced him that he could imagine the ship they were going to intercept as a merchant raider with all the drama he needed for his daydreams.

They were dangerous ships, he thought. Even though they were only converted merchant ships they carried as many as six or eight 6inch calibre guns. *Plus smaller guns and torpedoes,* he thought. He even remembered reading that several of the raiders had carried naval mines which they had laid off the coast of New South Wales.

At that moment, he spotted the tiny shape of an aircraft to the east. *They even carried aircraft,* he thought.

He pictured the 'Arado' floatplanes those ships had carried and converted the rapidly approaching Coastwatch plane into one in his imagination. As the aircraft got closer that became more difficult to do as it was a twin-engine, high-wing aircraft painted red and white, not a single-engine, low-wing floatplane painted dark green!

The Coastwatch plane circled them for a few minutes, then turned and went back eastwards. There it began circling low above the horizon. One of the navy gunners came past carrying a .50 calibre machine gun.

"Won't be long now," he said, jerking his thumb towards the east.

Andrew had been trained to operate that type of machine gun on his QMG course and he had even fired one. Now he watched hungrily as the gunner fitted it onto its pintle mount. He itched to be allowed to take part. Just seeing the machine gun pointing out sent a thrill through Andrew. He was even more thrilled when another rating came aft carrying an ammunition box. When the rating opened this and drew out the long belt of shiny bullets another shiver of thrill ran through Andrew. They were real bullets and this was a real situation. He knew he was enjoying every second of it!

A muttering and pointing attracted Andrew's attention to the eastern horizon. *Yes! There she is!* he thought, as a tiny black mast broke the skyline. Now he returned to his daydream, imagining that the distant vessel that was quite rapidly appearing was indeed a German raider.

Because the two vessels were approaching on converging courses it was only a matter of minutes before the superstructure of the other vessel became visible. The hull seemed to heave itself up over the horizon. In what felt like no time at all but was actually about ten minutes the tiny shape on the horizon resolved itself into a grimy, rusty looking freighter close up. Details quickly became visible; the puffs of white spray from the ship's bows, the grimy funnel and the obvious rust streaks and patches around her bows and below her anchors.

Close up it was harder for Andrew to imagine the ship as a German raider. For one thing it was much too small. He knew the raiders had all been large ocean-going freighters of about 8,000 to 10,000 tons and this ship was quite obviously only a few hundred tons.

A coaster or inter-island trader of some sort, Andrew decided.

He took in the details. The ship had its superstructure aft with a well deck and raised focsle. Two cargo masts with derricks stood at either end of the well deck. A single small funnel with a wisp of smoke streaming from it indicated a diesel motor ship.

Having fought an imaginary battle against the ship, Andrew switched his mind back to reality. But as the patrol boat swung round to run parallel to the freighter's course and about a hundred metres from it he could not help thinking that it was just such a manoeuvre that had brought the HMAS *Sydney* undone.

The German's were able to fire their torpedoes and then drop their disguise and open fire at point blank range, he remembered.

A glance fore and aft reassured him. The automatic 30mm cannon was trained on the suspicious vessel and so was the starboard .50 cal MG. Its crew had now loaded it and even as Andrew watched the gunner cocked the weapon and braced himself into a firing position. The sight of those two gunners in their helmets and anti-flash gear, standing at their gun ready to fire caused Andrew another shiver of excitement.

On the bridge Lt Cdr McDowall was visible calling orders and studying the freighter through his binoculars. Andrew knew that a radio operator would be calling the ship and that they would use loud hailers if that failed.

That will be me in a few years' time, he thought.

He turned to study the ship. Close up it was sorry looking thing. It was obvious that maintenance was not a priority of the owners. The paintwork was worn and peeling, showing numerous patches of rust. Streaks of rust ran down the sides from every fairlead, pipe opening, porthole and fitting. The anchors were completely covered in rust and the ship's name, originally painted on each bow in white paint, could barely be read. The paint was grimy and rust-streaked.

"*Kanar Matu,*" Andrew read aloud. No flag was visible at the stern but just below the taffrail and only just legible, was the ship's name and below that the word MAJURO. "Marshal Island's registration," he added.

The ship was about 60 or 70 metres long, Andrew estimated. The first 10 metres were the focsle. This had the usual collection of winches, bollards and fairleads. The next 30 metres was the well deck where the cargo hatches were. The last 20 or 30 metres housed the superstructure. This was three stories high and painted a nominal white. The lowest level of the superstructure had a working space around it and was overhung by the second story which looked like it contained accommodation. The third level had the wheelhouse at the front, then the funnel and boat deck aft. The lifeboat that Andrew could see looked very old-fashioned and the white paint was so old it was a flaky grey.

Andrew studied the ship, still thinking about German raiders with concealed guns behind drop-down screens, but he could not see any place where such weaponry could be concealed.

He shifted his attention to the crew. Five or six men were visible although even as Andrew studied them a tall, thin character with a beard and scruffy long hair limped off through a doorway. The others matched the ship. The expression 'motley crew' flitted across Andrew's mind. He could see a Chinaman, a Melanesian, a brown-skinned man of indeterminate race, and several rough looking white men. All wore dirty old clothes and had a scruffy appearance to them.

The freighter was ordered to heave-to and at once did so. The patrol boat came to a stop about 50 metres to port of it. Another flurry of orders had an armed boarding party assemble on the aft deck of the patrol boat. They wore camouflage overalls and helmets, webbing over life jackets and carried pistols and Steyr rifles. Each one had a small radio earpiece and microphone on his head and the radio on the left shoulder strap. Andrew watched with jealous interest as they checked their weapons, then boarded a Rhib, a 'rigid hull' semi-inflatable boat. This was hoisted out by crane and lowered to the water. Andrew counted them.

"Six in the boarding party and two as boat crew," he muttered.

The Rhib powered across the short strip of water and pulled alongside. One of the crew of the freighter tossed a Jacob's ladder over the rail but then made no attempt to assist the boarding party as they climbed aboard.

There was then a half hour delay during which Andrew could only watch. There was a search and a lot of radio messages but the cadets did not get any of this. Only later did they get an outline briefing. The ship had not informed the Australian authorities that it was heading to Australia. Nor did it have any obvious reason to do so as it carried no cargo.

Lt Cdr McDowall said, "They claim they are heading to Cairns for repairs and fuel and to pick up some stores but no bookings have been made at the shipyard there, or with any of the fuel companies or chandlers. Their ship's papers are not in order either. It is all mighty fishy so we are taking her in under arrest."

That was the end of the excitement. The guns were kept manned and trained on the ship but with an armed boarding party on it no-one expected further trouble. Nor was there. Instead, there were ten hours of slow plodding as the patrol boat paced the freighter as it was taken to Cairns. During this time the cadets were teamed up with ratings and did minor duties in various parts of the ship. For Andrew, this meant 4 hours in the galley helping the cook and 4 hours in the engine room assisting with cleaning the parts of a stripped-down pump.

It was after midnight when the freighter was tied up at the Cairns wharves. During this manoeuvre the patrol boat lay in the inlet nearby with her engines just stemming the outgoing tide. Andrew and the other cadets were allowed on deck to watch. Border Force officers and Commonwealth police took over from the naval boarding party.

As soon as this was done the patrol boat edged alongside and the boarding party returned to the patrol boat. Lt Cdr McDowall went the other way to talk to various officials and to the Customs and police officers. When he returned, he had the cadets assembled in their messdeck. The *Armidale* class patrol boats had extra accommodation for carrying Customs or Immigration officers or parties of soldiers when patrolling the more remote parts of the northern Australian coastline. The cadets and their OOCs were berthed in this.

When all were assembled Lt Cdr McDowall said, "We are now proceeding to sea again to continue our trials. You people have the choice of staying on board and doing training with us; or you can contact your parents and go home. So, who would like to stay?"

Andrew's hand at once shot up. So did all the others. Seeing this caused a grin to crease Lt Cdr McDowall's face. He nodded and said, "Good, then we don't have to waste time berthing. We can just get under way. There is a report from some fishermen of a suspicious object on the Hope Islands up near Cooktown. We have been ordered to investigate. But I don't think it will be as exciting as today. OK, if you are not on watch, then get to bed."

Andrew was not on watch but he was too excited to sleep so he waited till the captain had left, then made his way aft to stand and watch. On the way he had to pass Tina and she just stood stony-faced and seemed to look right through him. That hurt but the procedure of casting off the lines and warps and of the patrol boat easing clear of the freighter held his interest and took his mind off the pain.

As the patrol boat swung her stern clear on a spring Andrew saw movement at a port hole in the hull of the freighter. A face appeared, looked out at him, then quickly withdrew. It had been a bearded face topped by a mop of tousled mousy coloured hair, but it looked familiar.

Where have I seen that character before? Andrew wondered.

He could not remember so just shrugged and resumed studying the seamanship involved in casting off and getting under way. But he could not stay there. The ship's Standing Orders did not allow personnel on the upper deck at night except when a particular evolution such as action stations had to be carried out. A petty officer ordered him inside. Instead, he found a port hole to look through. For the next half hour he stood and looked out at the lights of his hometown as they receded into the night. Only when they were well down the channel did he finally make his way to his cabin and to bed.

That was a good day, he thought. *I wonder if tomorrow will be as interesting?*

Chapter 3

ONLY AN RUSTY OLD ONE!

A ndrew knew the Hope Islands, about 150 kilometres north of Cairns and about 10 kilometres offshore, were named by Captain Cook in 1770 when the *HMS Endeavour* was damaged on Endeavour Reef. The two main islands were sand cays a few metres high. Around them were extensive coral reefs, formed in the same way as many similar islands. Coral sand had built up in the shallow lagoon inside the reef until it was high enough to be above water much of the time. Mangrove and other plants then colonised and further stabilised them. East Hope Island now has a dense clump of trees and bushes on it.

The patrol boat arrived off the largest island at 0730hrs. By then the cadets had finished breakfast and Andrew was standing on the superstructure, studying the scene.

About half a kilometre long, he decided after studying the place for a few minutes. He had seen it before when passing in the barge *Wewak* the previous Christmas holidays. Thinking about those voyages gave him some real twinges of nostalgia and anxiety as they had been high adventure.[2]

The patrol boat moved into the lee of the reef and then edged into the lagoon through a gap in the fringing coral reef. But it did not approach any closer as the water between the reef and the island appeared to be very shallow and also thickly studded with coral outcrops. Andrew could see dozens of these quite close to him and he knew from experience the dark brown areas in the water were coral. The lighter colours of yellowish green indicated a sandy bottom.

As the patrol boat turned into an area of sandy bottom, Andrew looked around, imagining himself as the captain and giving the orders to bring the vessel to anchor. His eyes met those of Tina, who was standing aft near the inflatable boat. For a fleeting moment their gaze locked and then she hastily looked away. In that instant Andrew felt a flash of hope, to be immediately followed by a stab of pain.

---

[2] Read *Coasts of Cape York* by C. R. Cummings

Was that regret I saw in her eyes? he wondered.

But the pain of rejection quickly turned to the sharper sting of jealousy when he saw her smile at Carthew. She even laughed at something Carthew said and then she lightly placed her hand on his forearm.

Carthew! That did hurt. *What could she possibly see in that drongo?*

The jealousy grew during the morning. When the cadets and a landing party of seamen went ashore in the inflatable boat, Tina very pointedly made sure she did not go in the first boatload with Andrew. Instead, she came ashore in the second and she sat next to Carthew when she did.

Once ashore, Andrew stood in the shade of a tree at the back of the beach and watched this with growing despair.

Is she just doing that to annoy me or does she really like him? he wondered. *And do I still love her?*

He wasn't sure but he certainly knew he hurt. The pain in his heart seemed too big to contain in his chest. Confused he thought that perhaps Tina was right.

Maybe I should find another girl? he mused.

The XO of *Armidale* called them all to a short briefing in the shade. There he split them into two teams, each of one OOC and four cadets plus a crewmember. All wore their navy camouflage work uniforms and boots and had caps or hats and many had sunglasses as the glare off the sparkling tropical sea could be quite fierce. Each person had a water bottle and small backpack with lunch and other items. Each team leader had a small hand-held radio and the XO had one as well.

"I will stay here with the boat party," he said. "If you find anything give us a call and we will come and have a look."

"What exactly are we looking for sir?" Blake asked.

Andrew had to resist rolling his eyes at this as they had been given a briefing only half an hour ago. The XO raised an eyebrow and said, "Anything that is not natural. We are actually looking for a suspicious object but you can clean up the beach as you go. It is a Marine Park so pick up all the rubbish. Use these plastic garbage bags."

The concept of parking marines crossed Andrew's mind as a silly joke and he was about to ask if the marines were Royal or US when he saw Tina turn and give Carthew a smile. That really nettled him.

"Come on, grab a garbage bag," he snapped, reaching for the bundle held by the navy PO.

Andrew was even more annoyed a few minutes later when he called on his team to start walking and found that Tina did not follow. Instead, she turned and went the other way with Carthew. As Tina was in his watch, he opened his mouth to call her back and to order her to join his group. But he found he was unable to call out. The words seemed to stick in his throat and he just felt a sinking feeling of despair.

This was made worse by Blake saying to him, "Hey Andrew, Tina has gone off with that mob of slugs in the Starboard Watch. Why is she with them?"

"There have to be four in each group," Andrew replied.

But he knew that there were actually more than that when the two OOCs and two navy crew members were counted. Not having the courage to tell the truth as he saw it also rankled. But luckily Blake accepted the argument and did not do any head count to check.

Just once as they walked away Andrew glanced back. That did nothing for his temper as he saw that Tina had fallen behind her group and was walking with Carthew. That made him want to stride out but grumbles from the others soon slowed him down. It was now 0915hrs and the sun was well up and the air in the lee of the trees was sweltering. Sweat began to ooze from every pore and then drip or soak.

The beach was made of fine coral sand and shell grit. This made walking difficult as it gave way readily on any sort of a slope. Small clumps of dead coral rock protruded and the high tide line was littered with driftwood, dead seaweed and small amounts of rubbish. The litter included old plastic bags and drink bottles, a few rubber thongs and even a tiny yellow plastic bath toy.

Andrew began picking up rubbish and putting it in the garbage bag. Most of the others did as well but Blake did not bother and kept on walking, getting steadily ahead of the group. That irritated Andrew and he twice called on Blake to wait. Blake did so, but just stood and looked around. Then he walked across to a clump of seaweed. From out of it he pulled a polystyrene ball the side of a soccer ball. This was attached to a length of rope.

"What's this?" Blake called, holding it up.

"The float from a fishing net," Andrew answered.

The navy Petty Officer with them grunted and said, "We see them a lot. They are attached to drift nets."

Sarah Creswell reached out to touch the ball. "What are drift nets?"

The PO answered. "They are long nets that a laid by a fishing boat. The fishermen put these floats on it every few metres so that the top of the net stays on the surface but the bottom is held down by lead weights."

"How long are these nets?" Blake asked.

"We have picked up a net that was two kilometres long," the PO replied.

"Two kilometres! That's impossible," Blake cried.

The PO shook his head. "Suit yourself," he replied. "But we often see them, particularly in the Gulf of Carpentaria. They are not as common in the Coral Sea. Sometimes they break loose and just drift around. We call them 'Ghost nets' then."

Sarah looked troubled. "They must catch an awful lot of fish."

"They do. They catch everything: turtles, dugongs, tuna, swordfish," the PO answered.

"That's disgusting!" Sarah cried. "It should be against the law."

"It is," the PO replied. "But these nets are set by foreigners like Indonesians and Taiwanese, and we have to catch them at it. That is one of our jobs."

That comment bothered Andrew. He asked, "Surely we know what ships are near Australia, like that one we arrested yesterday?"

The PO made a wry face and shook his head. "In theory yes. But in reality they often slip through without being detected."

Blake took up the theme. "But can't ships just be detected on radar?"

"Yes, if the radar is operating or if a ship or aircraft is deployed to search that area. But that costs lots of money and isn't done as often as we would like," the PO answered.

"The government should," Andrew said.

The PO nodded. "I agree, but that is a political decision and is up to the government. Now, let's get on with looking for this thing."

The group resumed walking. Andrew kept looking out over the shallow, coral studded reef and then on across the rippling waves of the dark blue deeper water beyond. The sight of that always gave him an uneasy feeling, having floated for 18 hours two years earlier after a floatplane crash.

But it is pretty, he thought, noting the waving palms, green trees, white sand, and the varied blues of the water and sky.

Out to his left was a long line of steep mountains. They were, he knew from a study of the chart, at least 20 kilometres away. The beaches at the base were hidden from view by the curve of the earth's surface but they were close enough for him to see that they were clad in dense tropical rainforest. The mountains were just far enough away for details to be obscured by haze.

For several long minutes Andrew studied that coast with a sailor's eye. He knew that back in 1770 *HMS Endeavour,* commanded by Captain Cook, had run on an isolated reef about 12km to the South East.

He must have been able to see these mountains, Andrew thought. Then he shook his head. *This bit of coastline doesn't look very inviting.* There were, to his eye, no sheltered bays or deep inlets. *All a lee shore too,* he thought, knowing that the prevailing wind was from the South East.

He studied the highest peak in sight and tried to recall the map. *That is Mt Finegan,* he thought. *And Helenvale is somewhere on the other side of those mountains.* The 'Lions Den' hotel was at Helenvale and he tried to picture the place. Then his gaze swept on north and he named the key features from memory. *That is Cedar Bay opposite us,* he remembered.

To the North West he saw a tiny white block on a bare cape. *That is the lighthouse on Archer Point. And that conical mountain in the distance is Mt Cook. Cooktown is on the other side of that,* he noted.

Having done those two voyages up and down the coast the previous Christmas holidays he was reasonably familiar with this part of the coast of Cape York Peninsula.

Blake had hurried on ahead and was leaving large pieces of rubbish behind. Andrew called out to him and then Sarah.

"Blake, pick up some litter," she called in annoyance. She bent and picked up a rubber thong. "Another left one," she said.

"I wonder where the right one is?" Sub Lt Mullion commented.

"Not here," Luke Karaku said. "I've heard that the ocean currents separate the right thongs from the left and that they never end up on the same beach."

"That's right," the Navy PO agreed. "Up at Chili Beach near Portland Roads there are several trees with hundreds of thongs nailed to them, and from memory they are all right thongs."

The group wandered on, Blake drawing further ahead by the minute until he was a couple of hundred paces in front. Sarah next drew their attention to tiny starfish in the shallows beside the beach. They stopped and studied these and then looked at the sea slugs.

"Beche-de-mer is one name for them," Sub Lt Mullion explained as they studied the brown, slimy slug about 20cm long.

"Trepang the Malays and Indonesians call them," the PO added.

The group resumed walking. Andrew noted that Blake had gone out of sight and that got him mildly worried. He wondered if he would get into trouble for not keeping the team together but decided that as Sub Lt Mullion had not said anything it was not important.

Anyway, it is an island. We must end up back where we started and so must Blake, he thought.

The beach curved slowly to the right and the anchored patrol boat went out of sight behind them. Andrew kept looking around and checking their progress. It was very hot and there was very little breeze and he continually wiped perspiration from his face. Salt from his sweat began to sting his eyes. He had a drink and checked that the others were not starting to suffer from heat stress.

They are all red in the face, well, not Luke. He is black in the face, and they are all sweating freely so they are alright at the moment, he noted.

Another five minutes steady trudging brought them to the northern end of the island. As they rounded this, the breeze began to increase as they came out of the lee of the vegetation. *Southeast Trade Winds,* Andrew told himself, sighing with relief at the cooling effect of the wind.

The windward side of the island was much more pleasant but the view less interesting as all they had to look at where the shallows of the fringing reef, the low green of the smaller island inside its reef, and then the whitecaps and waves of the deeper ocean. A few distant cumulus clouds completed the scene. It was a scene Andrew was very familiar with having been born in Cairns and been on frequent trips to the Great Barrier Reef and various offshore islands.

Andrew looked out to the east, hoping to see some sign of the Great Barrier Reef or one of the isolated reefs that studded the area of sea between it and the coast but he saw nothing to indicate a reef. He knew that the Great Barrier Reef was in fact thousands of reefs in a two-thousand-kilometre-long chain. Two years earlier he had almost died when diving on the wreck of the *Merinda* at an isolated reef near Bowen. The previous Christmas he had twice been diving at reefs further north. That had been during the search for World War 2 aircraft wrecks and it had been one of the great adventures of his life. Then there had been the terrifying encounter with the Russian drug smugglers at Yule Reef the previous April. As he strolled along, he thought back to that experience and smiled with satisfaction. Having survived such adventures gave him real confidence.

The group continued walking, rounding a small point of sand and coral rocks. This brought them out onto the east side of the island. As they did, so more of the shallows and fringing reef came into view. The shallows were studded with coral outcrops and the edge of the reef was clearly defined by a line of white surf where the waves were breaking. Beyond that was the dark blue of deep water.

Then Andrew saw something which left him puzzled for a few seconds. But when his mind registered what it was, he was looking at his whole being quickened with excitement.

It was Blake, and he was sitting on top of a large spherical object about 1.5 metres in diameter. The object was covered in marine growths: barnacles, oysters and seaweed. It was only its curved shape and the half dozen spiky protrusions that made it obvious the object was man-made. Part of a weed-entangled blue nylon fishing net was caught on the horns on the other side and a length of rotten rope trailed out of the tangle.

That is a naval mine! Andrew thought, his interest quickening.

He was not the only one who recognized the thing. Even as Sarah called to Blake asking, "What's that?" the naval PO uttered an oath and cried, "Bloody hell!"

As Andrew hurried forward, he noted that Blake was sitting between two of the horns, which he was holding with his hands. His feet were resting on two more.

That looks unsafe, Andrew thought, but said, "Blake, that's a mine."

Blake grinned and nodded, and kicked it with his heels. "Yeah, I know."

The PO called loudly and hurried forward. "Sit still and don't move!"

"It's alright," Blake called cheerfully. "It's only an old rusty one."

The PO's face went very red and he seemed to gobble for a few seconds before he shook his head and snapped, "Don't move! Don't touch those horns!"

Only then did it really occur to Andrew that there might be real danger. Not so Blake. He shook his head and thumped the side of the mine with his boot heel before placing his boot back on one of the horns.

"It won't go off," he said. "It must be donkey's years old."

"You are the bloody donkey!" snapped the PO. "That thing could explode at any minute if you bend one of those horns."

"Oh bull!" Blake answered, but with much less assurance. "I broke one off when I was climbing up and one of them is bent anyway."

Andrew lsaw that this was so. Halfway up was a hole 5 centimetres in diameter. The hole was ringed with rust flakes. Hanging out of it were some wires and attached to them was the broken off horn. It dangled against the side of the mine. Around on the far side was a badly bent horn.

"Don't move kid!" the PO snarled. "That looks like a World War Two mine and we blow one or two of them every year. They still work. Worse still, as they get older the chemicals in the explosives deteriorates and becomes unstable so even a slight knock can set them off."

Blake now looked anxious but still not convinced. Andrew shook his head in exasperation and said, "Blake, he means it. He's not making it up. Sit still and take your boots off those horns."

"Why? They are made of steel aren't they?" Blake asked. But to the PO's evident relief he lifted his boots clear and sat astride the mine.

The PO let out an audible sigh of relief, then said, "How the hell did you climb up onto it?"

"By these things poking out," Blake said, indicating one of the horns.

"Oh bloody hell! Sit still and take your hands off those two. You others get out of here. Back off around the point," the PO said. He then moved forward and bent to peer closely at the protruding horns that Blake had used as steps.

Andrew looked around anxiously and saw that both Sub Lt Mullion and Sarah were looking scared and that Luke was wide-eyed. He said, "What are you going to do?"

The PO looked at him and shook his head. "I'm not sure yet. But you lot need to get right away from here for safety."

Sub Lt Mullion asked, "You think it might explode?"

"It could if one of these horns is bent," the PO explained, pointing to one that had obviously been stepped on, the seaweed being scraped on the upper surface.

"Would it make much of a bang?" Sub Lt Mullion asked.

The PO seemed to shudder. "Much of a bang!" he cried. "Ma'am, these things were made to sink battleships. There must be a couple of hundred kilos of high explosive in this thing. It could blast a hole ten metres in diameter in a ship's side. We blew one up last year up at the Home Islands and we had steel splinters landing around us and we were a nautical mile away. Nowhere on this island would be really safe, not according to the book."

By now Blake was looking very anxious as well. He said, "But what do the horns do?"

"They detonate the mine," the PO explained. He pointed to the nearest one. "They are actually made of soft metal so that they bend easily. Inside them are two glass phials or containers. The inside one has electrical wires in it and they lead to a detonator or exploder in the main charge. The outside one has a chemical in it. When a ship bumps the horn the metal bends and the glass tubes get broken. The chemicals then mix to make electricity. The electricity travels along the copper wires and makes the detonator explode."

Andrew nodded. "Like one of those 'cyalume' glow sticks."

The PO nodded. "Something like that. There are a dozen different types and modern mines don't work that way at all, but these ones do. So don't move boy, and can you others please move away."

"But what about Blake?" Andrew asked. "How will we get him down?"

The PO tugged at his chin and shook his head. "I will call the ship and get help," he suggested. "Now back off please."

But Andrew stood his ground. He did not want to leave his friend in danger and he also thought of Tina and her group coming the other way. "We need to send someone on ahead to warn the group coming this way," he pointed out.

The PO nodded. "Yes, good idea. Now let's move away."

At that, Blake looked alarmed. "Hey! Don't leave me!" He began to scrabble with his boots on the weed and barnacle encrusted sides of the mine.

"Blake! Sit still. Stay calm!" Andrew cried.

Chapter 4

MAYBE?

Andrew stared in horror as Blake managed to get his feet up onto the top of the mine. Once there he then wobbled precariously in a crouch.

"Blake, stay still!" Andrew called again.

"I'm not staying here to get blown up!" Blake cried. "I'm going to jump off."

"Wait!" the PO snarled. "Sit still, lad. You are quite safe as long as you don't bump one of the horns."

To Andrew that appeared to be exactly what Blake was liable to do. He wobbled and slithered around on top of the mine, his legs and hands in between three of the horns. Andrew now felt quite scared but did not want to show it. Pretending to be calm he turned and said, "Luke, Sarah, you both go away, quickly!"

The PO agreed. "Two of you go on along the beach the way we were going and tell the other group not to come here. Tell them to go back to the ship."

Sub Lt Mullion looked nervously at the mine and licked her lips, then said, "Andrew, you and Luke go on ahead. Sarah, you come back with me."

"Alright," Sarah said.

She looked very pale but had herself under control again. As she moved over to join Sub Lt Mullion, she unslung her carry bag and took out a camera. Using this she took several photos.

The PO began calling the ship and the other party on his hand-held radio but soon gave up in disgust. "Not working. Batteries must be flat," he said.

Sub Lt Mullion stood looking anxious and both Luke and Sarah only moved a few metres before stopping. "What are we going to do?" Sub Lt Mullion asked.

"Wait till we have some big strong ratings here to lift the lad off," the PO suggested.

Blake looked dismayed. "But I can't just sit here! I'm getting hot. I'm thirsty, and the tide is coming in," he cried.

It was too. Andrew looked down and noted a very obvious ripple of water as a small wave washed twenty centimetres up the beach. The water flowed around the bottom of the mine. A quick estimation against the tide line at the top of the beach showed that most of the mine would be submerged at high tide.

What are the tides today? he wondered. He thought that high tide was at about 1700hrs but could not remember how high it was. *Is it a spring tide or a king tide?* he puzzled.

That got him feeling embarrassed for not knowing the phase of the moon. "This mine obviously floated up here on a king tide," he suggested.

"Possibly," the PO replied.

It was at once obvious to Andrew that the PO was also kicking himself mentally for not knowing the state of the tide.

Blake looked even more frightened. He looked anxiously down and then licked his lips. "Can I have a drink, please?" he muttered.

Andrew nodded. He said, "Where is your water bottle Blake?"

Blake pointed behind Andrew. "In my bag over there."

"I'll get you a drink," Andrew said.

He turned and walked back five metres to where Blake's bag lay at the top of the beach. As he did, Sarah took two more photos. She and Luke moved a few more paces away along the beach but seemed reluctant to leave.

As Andrew walked back towards Blake with the water bottle, Blake changed his position to get his balance better. But in doing so he went into an awkward crouch, balancing right on top of the mine with both feet together and with only one hand to help steady him. Then, as he reached out a hand to take the water bottle, he slipped.

To Andrew's horror, Blake slid sideways and his right boot slammed down across the dry seaweed and onto one of the horns. For a second Andrew froze in fright as he stared at Blake's boot. Blake's face registered sheer terror, and even as he began to tumble he pushed and sprang sideways.

Andrew dropped the water bottle and reached out to try to catch Blake. But Blake was moving too fast and was too big. All he managed to do was grab a sleeve as Blake went past in a sideways spring like a huge frog. Both boys went crashing to the beach and rolled on the sand. As he fell flat, Andrew glanced fearfully back at the mine, half expecting it to explode.

Blake obviously had the same fear as he sprang up and bolted back along the beach in the direction they had come from. Sub Lt Mullion stood open-mouthed and the PO looked aghast.

But there was no explosion. After a few seconds during which he tensed ready for the worst, Andrew rose to his feet and dusted the sand off his hands. By then Blake was fifty paces away and still running.

"Blake, come and get your water bottle," he called.

Blake did not answer but kept on running. Sub Lt Mullion picked it up and looked sheepish, then said, "I will give it to him. Sarah, you come with me. Andrew, you and Luke go the other way and warn the others."

Sarah nodded, took another photo and turned and walked quickly up the beach. She scooped up Blake's carry bag and moved to join Sub Lt Mullion. Andrew badly wanted to get a close look at the mine, but the PO waved him away.

"Go and warn the others. Send Leading Seaman Lafferty to me."

"Aye, aye PO," Andrew replied.

He cast one last look at the mine and hurried over to join Luke. The two friends then set off at a fast walk southwards along the beach.

As they walked reaction set in. "Bloody noddy!" Andrew mumbled. "Only a rusty old one indeed!"

Luke laughed and wiped sweat from his brow. "He knows better now," he commented. Then he added, "I fair cacked meself when he slipped just then and his boot hit that horn."

"Me too!" replied Andrew with feeling.

He did not want to admit it, but he was sure he had almost wet himself. *Am I a coward?* he wondered. He did not think so, having faced some very dangerous situations over the last few years, but it was a niggling worry.

Within two minutes the pair was out of sight of the mine. It was hard walking on the sloping soft shell grit and coral sand but the boys pushed themselves. Both were soon puffing and sweat poured out of them. Andrew took out his water bottle and drained half of it.

"I must do more exercise," he muttered as he wiped stinging perspiration from his eyes.

A minute later they saw the other group. They were moving slowly and were conscientiously picking up rubbish. To Andrew's botheration, Tina and Carthew were together and well ahead of the others. As she saw the boys coming, Tina straightened up and Andrew tried to read the look which crossed her face. Hostility? Regret? Annoyance? He could not tell.

Carthew spoke first. "What are you two doing?" he asked.

"You have to go back to the patrol boat. There is an unexploded sea mine on the beach just around the corner," Andrew explained.

Carthew's eyes lit up with interest. "Oh yeah! Let's go and look. I've never seen one."

Andrew shook his head. "The PO said to go back to the patrol boat."

As he talked, he met Tina's gaze and she blushed and looked away. Nancy Blackett and Lt Ryan joined them and Andrew saw Nancy flicking curious glances from him to Tina. The thought that he might be an item of gossip made Andrew feel hurt and burn inside but he explained to the OOC and to the Leadings Seaman when he joined them.

Lt Ryan pointed back southwards and said, "Back we go. Leading Seaman Lafferty, you go and join Petty Officer Phillips."

"Aye, aye, sir," the Leading Seaman said.

As he hurried along the beach, Carthew mumbled about going to have a look but was firmly over-ruled. With bad grace he turned and started walking back the way they had come. To Andrew's chagrin Tina stayed beside him and avoided his eyes.

As they trudged back along the beach, Andrew and Luke described the mine and Blake's antics. Lt Ryan was not amused and shook his head several times.

"You people should know better," he said. Then he added, "I saw a documentary on TV last Anzac Day about divers bringing up cordite sticks from the wreck of a British battleship in the Dardanelles. It was sunk by a mine in 1915 and when they put a match to the cordite it still burned fiercely. That cordite is nearly a hundred years old. So never touch unexploded mines or bombs and never trust old explosives."

Andrew knew from his reading about the sinking of two British pre-dreadnought Battleships in the Dardanelles and the damaging of another. After searching his memory for a minute he named them.

Irresistible *and* Ocean *sank and the* Inflexible *made it back to safety,* he thought.

For a couple of minutes he mulled over that tragic battle of long ago, itself the tragic prelude to the much bloodier Gallipoli campaign in which the Anzacs experienced their baptism of fire.

He remembered reading about the laying of a small new minefield by the Turks using their converted tug the *Nusrat.*

It was certainly economy of effort, he mused. Risking one tiny tug to lay a few mines stopped a fleet of battleships and sank two. *Mines are definitely value for money and deadly things.*

Three years earlier, when in Year 8 he had been partly involved in saving an American cruiser from being mined in the Cairns shipping channel. A group of terrorists had planned the operation and his classmate and friend Graham Kirk, now an army cadet, had been the one to save the situation.

As soon as they reached the boat, Lt Ryan, Graham and Luke were ferried out to the patrol boat. By the time they boarded the patrol boat Sub Lt Mullion, Blake and Sarah had joined the others on the beach. The boat went back to ferry them out. Meanwhile, Andrew and Luke described the mine to Lt Cdr McDowall. The captain noted the details and then called LS Lafferty on the hand-held radio. This one worked but only just. The PO and leading seaman were recalled.

The cadets were sent to lunch while waiting. In the mess Blake came in for a good deal of ribbing, especially about his comment that it was only a rusty old one.

"Yeah well, it hasn't blown up has it?" Blake challenged. "And I hit it pretty hard when I jumped off."

"Fell off!" Luke countered.

A good-natured argument started. This was ended by the captain and OOCs coming to the mess. Lt Cdr McDowall said, "We have radioed COMAUSFLEET and they are putting out a NOTAM."

"A what, sir?" Blake asked.

"NOTAM. A Notice to Airmen and Mariners; a warning signal," the captain explained. He continued, "We have been ordered to proceed to Cooktown to pick up a team of E.O.D. specialists. They will come from Clearance Diving Team Two in Sydney."

"E. O. D.?" queried Sub Lt Mullion.

"Explosive Ordnance Disposal," Lt McDowall answered.

Luke put up his hand. The captain pointed to him. "Yes?"

"Sir, is it a World War Two mine?"

"It appears to be although we don't know the exact type," Lt Cdr McDowall answered. "The diving team chaps will be able to tell us that."

"Where did it come from sir?" Blake asked. "I didn't know any mines were used in this part of the world."

Lt Cdr McDowall said, "Oh yes they were! During World War Two, the RAN laid thousands of the damned things along the Great Barrier Reef. There were minefields in most of the main shipping channels. They were put there to make it hard for Japanese warships, especially submarines to get inside the reef. It took a real effort to sweep them after the war and we lost a few men and a minesweeper doing it."

"Oh! Oh, I never knew that," Blake said.

At that, Sarah snorted and said, "You should pay more attention Blake. Didn't you see the Disney movie 'Finding Nemo'? There were mines in that."

"Oh poo to you!" Blake retorted.

"That will do you two," Lt Ryan said.

Luke looked puzzled. "But sir, how did our ships get in and out if we wanted to?" he asked.

Lt Cdr McDowall looked surprised then explained. "When mines are laid their position is plotted by the minelayer. Gaps are left as clear channels for our ships to use. These usually have doglegs in them to make it difficult for any enemy ships to watch and then follow."

"Did the mines get any Japanese ships sir?" Carthew asked.

Lt Cdr McDowall shook his head. "Not that we know of. There is nothing in the Japanese records either so I'd say not.

"So the only ship sunk off the Australian coast during the war was one of our own by one of our own mines?" Carthew said in a sarcastic tone.

"Oh no, not by any means," Lt Cdr McDowall replied. "German raiders laid minefields off Sydney and Newcastle and off Cape Howe, in Bass Strait near Melbourne, and off Adelaide in Spencer Gulf. They sank three or four ships."

Andrew remembered reading about that but he had not paid particular attention. Now he resolved to do a bit more research.

Sarah now asked, "But how do they lay the mines? I thought they just floated around on the sea."

Lt Cdr McDowall shook his head. "No. Some do but they have broken adrift and they are very dangerous to all ships. Mines are laid by ships or aircraft. They have a weight, usually made of steel. This is to anchor them to the seabed. As the weight sinks the mine floats off and a steel wire cable runs out from the weight. It is also attached to the mine and is to tether the mine. The mine has a depth gauge and valve that makes it float at a predetermined depth."

He used his hands to indicate the mine floating just below the surface of the water. "They need to be out of sight or ships have a chance of seeing them and avoiding them. Usually they are set at about five metres to get below the average wave height. This way the explosive effect is much greater. An explosion under a ship does much more damage and can even break its back if the keel is cut."

Once again, he gestured with his hands to show this. Then he said, "They also lay deep mines to catch submarines. So the mines in a minefield might all be at different depths."

Andrew had read how the 'E' Class submarines had penetrated the Dardanelles in 1915. He remembered the descriptions of the crew inside hearing the mine mooring cables scraping along the sides of the hull.

And they worried that a cable might get caught in the diving planes and the mine be dragged down to strike the hull and explode, he thought.

Then he shuddered. He did not think he could go in a submarine and that again made him wonder if he was a coward. Even though he was qualified as an Advanced Open Water Diver he hated being underwater. Several terrifying experiences had added to this phobia.

Sarah frowned and said, "But sir, if most of the mines are only a few metres under the water can't small boats get over them safely?"

"They can, but it is still a risk, and that presumes they know the mines are there," the captain answered. He then added, "But most modern mines aren't like that. We dealt with some old-fashioned moored mines in Iraq a few years ago but most mines now are like torpedoes. They lie on the bottom and have propellers and computers. When they detect a ship by sound, they work out what it is and where it is and if it is a target the mine activates and heads off at forty knots to sink it."

Andrew found the whole topic of mines both repulsive and fascinating, but the captain ended the discussion by saying they must get under way. For the next half hour Andrew stood on the upper deck and watched with the other cadets while the anchor was heaved in and the patrol boat got under way. It nosed out through the gap in the fringing reef and set off northwards.

It was 1330hrs by the time they were clear of the reef. Speed was increased and the patrol boat began to thump through the waves. Andrew stood and relaxed. The navy personnel had various pieces of equipment to test but the cadets were not given any duties so he was free to study the handling of the vessel and to look at the scenery. He had a small chart in his gear and he used that to keep track of their progress and to tick off the landmarks that were visible.

The XO saw him looking and said, "You can join us on the bridge if you are that interested."

"Thank you sir," Andrew answered. He followed the XO forward and under the shelter of the bridge canopy. That was more pleasant and the XO indicated a pair of search binocular mounted on the wind baffle. "You can use those if you like," he said.

Andrew took the covers off the binoculars then seated himself on the swivel chair behind them. He bent forward and began focusing them. As he did, the XO nodded with approval and then asked, "Been along this bit of coast before?"

Andrew nodded. "Yes sir, a few times. I came up to Cooktown by ship this time last year."

As he said this his mind went back to the voyage on the old Landing Craft *Wewak* when he and his friends had been searching for World War 2 aircraft wrecks. He and his sister Carmen had been employed as deckhands by Capt Kirk for the duration of the holidays and it had been a fascinating experience.

As the patrol boat powered northwards, Andrew alternately scanned the coastline and studied his map. Weary Bay and Amos Bay were easy to detect as was the lighthouse on Archer Point. He noted two small launches in Amos Bay near the beach and then studied a small rocky island just south of Archer Point. The chart showed it as having a lighthouse on it but it took some finding. He was intrigued to note that it was not on the highest point of the island, where he had expected it to be, but was on the lower slopes on the inshore side.

What an odd place to put a light, he thought. *I wonder why they did that?*

Curiosity made him study the shore behind the island. The island was conical and looked very rocky but the shore behind was a series of grass-covered hills, starting at a low point and moving up to progressively higher hummocks until the main lighthouse on the point. A mountain stood behind this and Andrew noted that the seaward face of this was also covered in grass and almost bare of trees. He knew this to be a natural condition having seen many other similar places.

Then his eyes detected several vehicle tracks. One led down to a palm lined beach near the low southern tip. Another came over the next large grassy hill. This track went straight down the seaward face and ended at a dark mass of what he at first took to be a natural rock formation but which a moment's careful study revealed to be artificial. He squinted and stared and made out what were unmistakably posts or girders, black with age or rust.

That looks like a jetty or something, he puzzled. As it was facing the open sea and the prevailing Southeast Trades he thought it an odd place to build a pier. *That island might give a bit of shelter but it would have not been usable in any sort of bad weather,* he thought.

The XO stood near him so Andrew said, "Excuse me sir, but I can see what looks like an old wharf or jetty just inshore of that rocky island. Can you tell me what it is?"

The XO nodded and said, "Yes. It was built as a port back in the 1970s. A man named Foster had a grand vision of developing sorghum farms inland at a place called Lakeland Downs. He built the port with a conveyer belt and grain loader but it never paid and was abandoned. They sold most of it for scrap and all that is left is that old jetty but it is no longer safe to use and I've never seen a boat at it."

The thought of that pioneering effort filled Andrew with admiration and sadness. *Pity, it sounds like it was a good idea,* he thought.

He remained alternately staring at the passing coastline and studying his map. What particularly struck him was the number of small isolated coral reefs scattered close to the coast.

It must have been hard for poor old Captain Cook and all those poor buggers in sailing ships trying to navigate this area, he thought.

Most of the reefs were just visible because of the white water of breaking waves but among the normal 'white horses' they were not all that obvious. A few had posts sticking up with lights on them.

The patrol boat's course angled steadily closer to the coast as it neared Cooktown so Andrew had less trouble identifying features. He noted Walker Bay, the mouth of the Annan River, a long strip of beach, then Mt Cook. From there on steep, forested slopes ran down to the sea with a couple of tiny bays backed by forest and beaches.

Cherry Tree Bay, Andrew noted.

Luke came and stood beside him. "Where are we?" he asked.

Andrew showed him on the map. "That last hill is Grassy Hill. The Endeavour River is just around the end of it and Cooktown is on the south bank."

"Grassy Hill? It's covered with trees," Luke commented.

Andrew could only shrug and reply, "Captain Cook named it. Maybe it was grassy back in 1770?"

There was a bustle of movement around them and the captain appeared on the bridge. Andrew noted that he was now in his short tropical white uniform. He said something to the CPO who was the ships 'Buffer' and the buffer came over to them.

"If you lads want to be on deck when we enter harbour you must change into your whites. We are a bit old fashioned in *Armidale* and like to do things properly."

"Aye, aye, sir," they both chorused.

Andrew did want to be on deck, and he fully agreed with the policy of changing into a good uniform for entering port. He hurried below and quickly changed into white shorts, white short-sleeve shirt with his badges on it, long blue socks and black shoes. His work cap he replaced with his cadet PO's peaked cap. He felt a bit self-conscious about wearing that but was also very proud of it.

Hurrying back on deck he found all of the other cadets formed up there on the port side. He joined the end of the line and stood at ease. Lt Ryan gave them a quick inspection and then stood near the officers.

By then they were close in to the shore and turning to enter the river mouth. The slopes of Grassy Hill were only a hundred metres away and Andrew noted a few buildings right on the seaward face of the hill. A road that was bench cut into the slope only a few metres above the sea led around the hillside to where a bitumen car park and a number of buildings indicated the tiny port. The small wharf and floating pontoon jetties came into view. There was a trawler at the pontoons and a yacht alongside further up but the berth at the main old wharf was empty. The patrol boat slowed and eased in to that.

Standing on the wharf were a dozen civilians of all ages and both sexes. They were mostly fishing and they stared at the patrol boat with interest before pulling in their lines. But Andrew could see that there was no-one on the wharf to catch the patrol boat's lines.

How will we tie up? he wondered.

It was easy. The patrol boat was manoeuvred in so gently that Andrew was filled with admiration. At a word of command, two ratings wearing life jackets over their whites leapt onto the wharf and hurried to take the lines which were tossed to them. Quickly and efficiently they placed fore and aft mooring lines over bollards at each end of the wharf. Then they set to work securing breast ropes.

While that was being done the crowd grew in number and Andrew stood and scanned them. Idle curiosity turned to quickening interest when he noted that there were half a dozen very pretty girls among them. The crowd wore typical casual tourist or fishing clothes and most of the girls wore only short shorts or jeans and T-shirts or casual tops.

Then his gaze locked with an extremely attractive silver-blonde of about his own age. She smiled up at him and then turned to whisper to her brown-haired friend who nodded. Then the blonde smiled at him and waved. Andrew felt quite flustered.

Is she smiling at me? he wondered. He smiled back but felt very self-conscious and shy.

But she was. When the group was allowed ashore half an hour later for a couple of hours shore leave to see the town the two girls were still on the wharf. They were fishing but when Andrew and Blake came walking past they stood up and the silver-blonde smiled again. This time there could be no doubt and Andrew was almost stunned speechless.

"Hello," she said. "Why are you boys here?"

"To meet some divers off the plane," Andrew answered.

He blushed fiercely, hotly aware that Tina and Nancy were just behind him and must be able to see him.

Blondie nodded and kept smiling. "Will you be here long?"

"Only until tomorrow," Andrew answered.

Blondie pouted and her friend giggled. "Oh, that's a pity. What are you doing tonight?"

As she said this, Tina and Nancy walked past and Andrew noted their heads turn at the question. It was obvious they had heard. Andrew blushed again and could only shake his head.

"I'm not sure. I don't know if we will be given any leave."

"You could ask," Blondie said.

Andrew nodded but was too flustered and embarrassed to reply. Blake did though. "I'm Blake and this is Andrew. If we get ashore, where will we meet you?"

Blondie smiled again and pointed towards the town. "At the café on the main street."

"What are your names?" Blake asked.

Blondie pointed to herself and said, "I'm Kristen and this is Daphne."

At that moment, Luke and Carthew arrived. Andrew nodded and felt his hopes rise. He nodded and said, "Okay, we will try. See you."

"See you later!" Kristen trilled.

Daphne, who Andrew now saw was a stouter girl with freckles and quite big boobs, giggled and met his eye.

As he and Blake walked away, he thought, *Hmm! Maybe Cooktown won't be so bad after all?*

Chapter 5

HELLO SAILOR!

As Andrew walked across the wharf with his friends, he experienced a range of emotions. Chief among them was pride. He was very conscious that he was wearing his navy cadet uniform and he was proud of that. He was also vain enough to think that he looked good in it.

Those girls back there think so, he told himself, glancing back to look at them again.

The brunette, Daphne, saw this and gave a smile and a wave. That sent another little thrill through Andrew, tempered by the fact that some of the other cadets saw it and began to tease him. In response he good-naturedly boasted, "Well, some of us have it, and some haven't!" he said.

Almost at once he regretted this as he saw Sarah glance at him and roll her eyes. Worse still, Tina was just ahead with Nancy and they both appeared to shake their heads.

Surely they didn't hear me? Andrew worried.

His emotions were then given another sharp twist as Carthew appeared from the doorway of a shop and joined Tina and Nancy. He said something that got them both giggling and then stepped in between them as they walked along. To Andrew, the body language seemed to say that if they hadn't been in uniform he would have put his arm around Tina's waist, or at least held her hand. Jealousy bit sharply and he tried to tell himself he didn't care.

Plenty more fish in the sea, he thought, again glancing back at Kristen and Daphne.

For the next ten minutes he made a deliberate attempt to ignore Tina and to study the town. The basic layout he was familiar with but he had not gotten any further into town than the concrete boat ramp they were passing at that moment.

To his right was the wide expanse of the Endeavour River. At that moment, the water was glassy calm and was dotted with a dozen anchored yachts and motor launches. Further out there was a floatplane moored to a buoy. Seeing that gave Andrew several sharp flashbacks to the Catalina flying boat he had been lucky enough to have several flights in the previous Christmas holidays.

That was real adventure, he thought.

The main road curved away from the river, skirting the base of Grassy Hill. Between the main road and the river was a park. A vehicle track ran along the edge of the park beside the water, which was fringed by a narrow beach and patches of mangroves before vanishing from view behind a huge thicket of mangroves a few hundred metres away.

On the left of the main road were a line of buildings. The most noticeable was the 'Seaview' motel, built on several levels and looking very pleasant. Beyond the motel were the police station and police houses. More shops and houses and a few vacant allotments took up the remainder of that side of the street before they reached the main part of the town.

The footpath was pleasant to walk along, being lined with large mango trees which provided plenty of shade. Andrew pointed out the monument which showed exactly where Captain Cook had beached the *Endeavour* for repairs. Further along were an old cannon and a bigger monument.

The cannon at once attracted the attention of the others and the three of them walked over to look at it. To Andrew's mixed relief and regret, Tina, Nancy, and Carthew kept on walking. Having heard and read so much about Cook's exploration during the last few weeks Andrew stared at the place with interest. The park was right on the edge of the beach and in it sat the stone monument and a genuine old-fashioned muzzle-loading, ship's cannon.

Sarah was curious about it and detoured over to it. "When was this put here?" she asked.

Andrew pointed to the nearby sign. "It is a real ship's cannon, a 24-pounder made in 1803 and sent to Cooktown in the late 19th Century to help defend the port against possible Russian attack." he explained.

"Russians!" Blake cried incredulously. They discussed this and all bent to examine the old weapon.

"French more likely," Andrew replied. "They were the traditional enemies of the British and were allied to Russia at the time, and they had the bigger navy."

Sarah looked doubtful. "We are a long way from France," she said.

Andrew shook his head. "No we aren't. The French own New Caledonia and some reefs and islands in the middle of the Coral Sea. That was only two days steaming even then," he replied.

He then bent to study the gun. As Andrew looked along the barrel and through the notch sights on top, his imagination quickly built a daydream. He was a midshipman on one of Nelson's sailing ships, a frigate perhaps, and they had landed the cannon to help batter down the walls of a Spanish fort in the West Indies. His reading of C. S. Forester's novel *Lieutenant Hornblower* immediately sprang to mind with the attack by HMS *Renown* on Samana Bay in Hispaniola.

But it was hard to pretend and not have his friends notice, particularly while they were chattering away about how the gun was loaded and fired. From his reading Andrew thought he knew this in detail. He had also seen the excellent demonstration of gun drill conducted at the Museum of Tropical Queensland in Townsville. He was able to correct some of Blake's muddled ideas without hurting his feelings too much.

The friends strolled on along the footpath towards the main part of town and Andrew was instantly struck by its atmosphere and charm. His first impression was of a place where time had stood still for a hundred years or more. But a second, more critical look revealed much more. True both sides of the streets were lined with old buildings constructed in the late 19th or early 20th Centuries, but these were mostly in very good condition. Scattered among them were renovations or newer buildings which mostly added to the sense of place.

By ignoring the more modern structures like the Child Care Centre and Bowls Club on his right at the end of the park he was able to more fully appreciate the grand design of many of the buildings. In particular he was stuck by the splendid old-fashioned double-story hotel on the corner and the even grander old bank building beyond it with its Greek columns and splendid white façade. This was shining in the afternoon sun and gave a feel of the whole street being historic.

Sarah was impressed. "This is very nice, and very quaint," she said.

"Traditional tropical colonial," Andrew answered.

Blake frowned. "Colonial?" he queried.

Andrew nodded. "Yes. Queensland was a colony of the British when Cooktown was established. When the main part of the town was built in the 1880s and 1890s the British Empire was in its heyday," he explained.

"Aw, I knew that," Blake answered.

The three navy cadets wandered on along the footpath, gazing around with interest while mentally soaking up the scene. It was Blake who joked about ghost towns, and it was only then that Andrew realised that there were almost no people visible on the footpaths and that not one single vehicle was moving in the whole street. Only as he commented on this did one appear, quickly followed by another. He also noted that there was no sign of Tina and the other two and he wondered where they had gone.

The boys passed the Post Office and then the Cook Shire Council Offices. Andrew noted a pleasant grassy park at a lower level. This extended back a hundred metres to the mangroves fringing the river. In the park stood the town's war memorial and a flag pole. Next, they passed several small shops specialising in items of interest to tourists and a few other shops. The QWCA building was passed and they crossed a side street.

After crossing this they decided to remain on that side of the street as it was shaded from the afternoon sun and the air temperature and humidity had both risen to uncomfortable proportions, causing them to perspire freely.

The decision was almost immediately rewarded by the discovery of a café. Pleasure at the prospect of refreshments was instantly heightened when Andrew saw the girl behind the counter. She was about his own age and had the brightest blue eyes he had ever seen. These were set in a lovely heart-shaped face topped by nice shoulder-length, mousy fair hair.

Heavens, she is pretty! he thought. Then he noted with approval her trim but shapely figure. *Hmmm! Maybe I will enjoy coming to Cooktown for Christmas?* he thought.

The girl smiled at him and he seemed to be mesmerised by her bright blue eyes. He found he could not speak and then realised that he had been staring at her. How long for he had no idea but he hoped it wasn't long enough for others to notice.

Finally she broke the ice by saying, "Hello. What would you like?"

Oh tongue, don't say it! Andrew thought as he admired her loveliness. He swallowed and indicated a soft drink.

As she handed it to him, their eyes locked again and she said, "Where have you boys come from?"

"Off a navy patrol boat, the *Armidale*," Andrew replied. By now his heart was beating much faster than normal and he felt a strong desire to make a good impression on her.

"Oh? What brings you to town?" she asked as she took his money.

Andrew explained the mine and was even more pleased when she asked, "Are you going to be here long?"

Andrew shook his head. "No, only until tomorrow morning, I think. But I will be back a few days later. I am coming here for the holidays."

"Oh good!" she said, sending his hopes soaring.

Greatly daring he said, "My name is Andrew. Maybe I will see you then?"

To his relief, her eyes lit up and she smiled. "My name's Colleen. That would be nice."

At that, Blake interrupted. "Hey! Didn't your mother warn you about sailors?" he asked her.

Colleen turned to look at him and poked her tongue, then laughed. "Sorry. What would you like?" she said.

"My name's Blake," Blake said.

"Very nice, now what would you like?" Colleen replied.

Andrew was pleased to note that she did not favour either Blake or Luke with a winning smile. She chatted and served them with ice-creams and soft drinks but kept glancing at Andrew. Every time their eyes met it was as though an electric current surged across and he felt wonderful.

They stayed in the shop talking until it became difficult to think of a sensible reason to linger that did not betray his interest. Finally, both Luke and Blake began to make teasing and pointed comments. Andrew would have endured them a while longer but then Tina, Nancy, Kit, and Carthew came in the door, just as he and Colleen were exchanging smiles. On seeing Tina come in Andrew felt a stab of guilt. This was exacerbated when Tina glanced from him to Colleen and back then appeared to turn her nose up.

I don't know why I care what she thinks, Andrew told himself. *After all, she dumped me.*

So he gave Colleen another flashing smile and said, "I will see you later then."

Colleen smiled back and nodded. "See you later," she answered.

Andrew made his way past Tina, wishing he did not feel hurt and confused. Outside he and his two friends turned right and continued on along the street. But the sights of the town now paled compared to his memories of Colleen and he felt an urge like a strong itch to go back and see her.

However, he got no chance as the group walked to the end of the next block, then crossed the street. Here they paused and Andrew pointed back along the same street.

Blake shook his head. "Nah! We've seen that one. I want to go up to that next street and look at that big old building there."

That did not please Andrew, but he pretended not to care, knowing he would be teased if his mate suspected he was interested in Colleen.

Ah! But she is beautiful, he thought. *I will make a point of trying to come to town when we are at the 'Lions Den',* he thought.

The trio walked up a gentle slope to the next street. By then Andrew had a good grasp of the layout of the older part of the town.

A grid pattern astride this wide, sandy ridge, he noted. *The cross-streets go across the ridge and the main street and a few others run along the ridge.*

The group turned left and walked along the footpath. By then they were all perspiring freely and Andrew was glad of his Petty Officer's cap with its brim as he could see his friends blinking in the sun in their white sailor's caps. Perversely he was very proud of the naval uniform, enjoying every minute of showing it off, imagining himself to be a seasoned 'Old Salt' back from the wars.

The building they had noted turned out to be a convent which had been converted into a museum. But there wasn't time to go in and continued walking. Andrew made a mental note to visit it during the next few weeks. So they walked on for another block and then turned left to go down to the main street again.

By then all three were sweating and hot and losing interest. As they reached the main street, Andrew looked both ways but saw no sign of Tina, or of the other group. Feeling more disappointed than he had expected, he led the way to the right, back towards the wharf.

As he walked along the shady footpath towards the cannon and monument, Andrew was not sure how he felt. From time to time he glanced back to see if Tina was in sight, or if Colleen had appeared. Then he looked ahead in the hope of seeing the two girls at the wharf.

I hope they are still there, he thought.

Suddenly, his heart leapt and he felt it start to beat faster. Ahead of them, but on the other side of the road, were Kristen and Daphne. The two girls were walking towards town and were passing the police station. Kristen now wore a big, floppy straw hat and at first Andrew did not recognise her.

But she recognised him and waved. "Hello sailor!" she yelled across the street.

Andrew blushed at the ideas the call suggested. Then he blushed even more when he saw a blue-shirted policeman look out of the front door of the police station to study the girls, then turn his gaze on him. Worse still, a lady who was plainly a tourist and who was taking a photo of the monument next to a grey 4WD frowned and pursed her lips in obvious disapproval. Blake and Luke both chuckled.

To make things worse, Kristen came scampering across the road followed a few seconds later by Daphne. "Hello boys. How was the town?"

"Interesting," Andrew managed to reply. He was now both embarrassed and hopeful.

Kristen pouted. "Huh! You wouldn't think so if you lived here. There's nothing to do. It's so boring!"

Blake leered at her and said, "So what do you do to liven things up?"

Kristen giggled and Daphne went red. Kristen then said in a very suggestive and cheeky voice, "Wouldn't you like to know!"

Blake leered some more but Kristen ignored him and turned to Andrew. "What was your name again?" she asked.

"Andrew, and this is Blake and he is Luke," Andrew replied, indicating his friends.

But Kristen ignored them. "That's right. Well, will we see you later?"

Andrew shook his head. "I don't know. I mean I don't know if we are going to be allowed ashore tonight," he answered.

That was something he badly wanted, but he was torn over which girl he really wanted to meet: Kristen, Daphne, or Colleen?

Kristen pouted but Daphne smiled and said, "We have to go. Come on Krissy, or your mum will throw a wobbly. We might see you boys later."

Kristen scowled, smiled and nodded all in a few seconds. Then she said, "Bye! See ya later!" and she followed Daphne back across the street.

As they went, Andrew turned to watch, and got another shock. Tina, Nancy, and Carthew had come down the same side street as them and were only 50 metres away and could clearly see the meeting.

Oh, I hope Tina doesn't... Andrew began to worry. Then he shook his head. *No. Why should I care what Tina thinks? She has dumped me. I will talk to any girl I like,* he told himself. But which one: Kristen or Colleen?

But there was no shore leave that night. Back on the patrol boat they were informed of that fact. "We are not going to have the legal risks of you teenagers running around a strange town in the dark," Lt Ryan explained.

On hearing that, Andrew felt more disappointed than he had expected. It almost made him sulky but he managed to hide the fact. Instead, he sat and watched TV after the evening meal.

Just after 8:00pm a rating stuck his head around the door of the mess and said, "Who is Andrew? Is one of you kids named Andrew?"

Andrew put his hand up and felt slightly embarrassed at being called a kid. The other cadets lounging in other chairs all looked at him curiously.

"I am," he said.

The rating jerked his thumb outwards and said, "There are a couple of chicks on the wharf asking for you."

At that, Blake laughed and called, "Oh, hello sailor!"

Andrew blushed but stood up. Then he saw Tina looking at him and shaking her head and he felt even more embarrassed. As quickly as he could, he fled the laughter and teasing comments and made his way aft to the stern.

As he stepped out onto the open aft deck, a rating said, "You aren't allowed to go ashore."

"I know," Andrew answered.

He made his way to the rail and looked out. The first thing he saw was that the patrol boat was now lower than the wharf because of the tide so he had to look up. Then, as his eyes adjusted to the mix of bright lights and dark shadows, he saw two girls standing there. It was Kristen and Daphne. Kristen wore short white shorts and a yellow T-shirt with the word 'Babe' across the front. Daphne wore jeans and a white T-shirt.

To Andrew, both girls looked very busty and attractive and he felt an instant surge of arousal. He was also very self-conscious as there were several other crew members lounging around or fishing over the taffrail.

"Hello again," he said. "Sorry, but I can't come ashore."

"We know. That nice sailor there told us that," Kristen replied. "Can we come aboard?"

Andrew had to shake his head and say, "Sorry. I can't give permission. I'm only a cadet. She isn't my ship."

"Oh spoil sport!" Kristen teased, suggestively wiggling her hips as she said this.

To Graham's added annoyance and embarrassment, two of the ratings, both clad only in shorts and sandals, came and stood beside him and then Blake and Luke came on deck to join him.

One of the ratings, a tanned, fit looking man in his twenties, said, "I'm not a cadet, Sweetie. Maybe we could go somewhere."

"Oh dream on!" Kristen retorted. "You are too old."

At that, the man's mates laughed and jeered, and Andrew heard comments like 'Grandpa' and 'Cradle snatcher'. Another rating, older and with a beard, called across from where he was fishing, "Leave them be, Stevo. Let the poor kid try his luck with Chicky Babe."

Kristen poked her tongue and said, "My name's Kristen."

The rating, obviously peeved at her comments snapped, "It says Babe on your boobs."

There was more laughter and another sailor called, "I don't think she needs a sign to tell us that!"

Kristen poked her tongue again and called, "Don't be gross. I'm just trying to be friendly."

To Andrew's relief, the rating moved away. He stepped forward and said quietly, "Sorry about that. It is nice to see you. What are you doing?"

Kristen giggled and it was Daphne who answered. "We told our mums that were going fishing."

To Andrew's annoyance, Blake sidled over beside him and joined in the conversation. For something to say, Andrew asked if the girls really did go fishing. On being told all the time he asked about what the local fishing was like. That gave them all a nice safe topic to chat about and Andrew began to relax and enjoy himself.

Maybe I have a chance with these girls? he thought, his eyes meeting Daphne's and noting a soft friendliness and sympathy in them.

Chapter 6

THE DIVERS

But Andrew did not get more of a chance to talk to the two girls. Soon after the conversation began, Daphne looked over her shoulder at a car which was pulling up in the car park.

"Bugger! It's Mum. Come on Krissy, let's go."

To Andrew's surprise and disappointment, Kristen swore and then said, "Bugger! Sorry, Andrew. We better not be seen talking to ya. Look us up when you come up next week then."

"I will."

"Where ya staying?" Kristen asked as she stood and dusted her bum.

"At a place called Helenvale; the Lions Den hotel," Andrew replied.

"Oh bugger! That's way out of town," Kristen said as she started walking away. Then she shrugged and said, "Aw well, we'll manage something. See ya!"

Andrew nodded and bit his lip. He had vaguely known that the Lions Den was not in the town itself but had not really cared until now. He felt foolish as he usually made himself well informed about places and distances.

I had better find out a bit more about this place, he decided.

By then the two girls had moved well away and were pretending to fish. In the light of a streetlight Andrew saw a big woman in slacks and cotton blouse walk across to them and then lead them back to the car. The car then drove off towards town. For a few more minutes Andrew stood and looked out across the starlit sea and thought about life and its surprises and mysteries.

An hour later he went to bed not sure if he was happy or sad but knowing for certain that he was horny. That bothered him as he was usually very moral and prided himself on only taking girls out with honourable intent. But he did know that even a glimpse of Tina hurt. It was a sharp sort of pain that left him wondering if it was love or bruised pride.

That night he slept well, the patrol boat barely rocking at its moorings and the air inside kept at a pleasant 22 degrees by the air conditioning. It was the air temperature that really hit him in the morning when he emerged on deck in the morning after being roused out at 0600hrs.

Blake voiced it by swearing softly and muttering about how hot it was. Andrew agreed out of the corner of his mouth (As they were standing on the aft deck in two ranks for roll call) by saying, "Certainly bloody humid!"

It was even hotter when he stepped ashore with the other cadets after breakfast. On the wharf it wasn't too bad but the moment they moved into the lee of the hill the temperature seemed to shoot up and sweat prickled all over his body.

The cadets and their staff were ushered onto a school bus that had been hired to give them a bit of a tour. Lt Cdr McDowall and his coxswain joined them. The bus driver was a cheerful, middle-aged man who gave them a running commentary as they drove along the main street past the cannon and monuments and on into town.

As the bus drove along the main street, Andrew looked anxiously out, scanning from side to side but mostly concentrating on the right hand side. He was hoping to see one of the girls; Colleen for preference but Kristen or Daphne if not.

To his disappointment, there was no sign of them, and the bus continued on through to the McIvor Road and then turned right along it to go to the airport. Andrew sat and looked out at the passing scenery, noting the scatter of light industry and then outlying houses in larger allotments. The cemetery was passed and then more scattered houses. The road then passed through several areas of savannah woodland; dry bush with long grass and plenty of trees and much of it obviously swampy.

After winding through a range of small hills covered with dry savannah and dotted with a few houses, the road went through more bush and 'Five Acre' hobby farms and a new suburban development before passing through the closely settled suburb of Marton. It then crossed the Endeavour River via a long, narrow bridge with low sides. The river looked deep and murky and was lined with mangroves.

Luke grunted and pointed to it and said, "Be crocs in there I reckon."

Andrew could only agree. "Well, I won't be swimming in it, that's for sure," he replied.

A few hundred metres further on, the bus slowed and then turned right along the airport access road. A minute later it pulled up in the airport car park. Andrew was pleasantly surprised. The place was all very green, neat and park-like. Beside the car park was a small wooden building on low stumps. It had a veranda on the airstrip side and contained a waiting room and toilet. Clumps of palms and garden beds made the area between the waiting room and some houses and sheds further along very attractive and tropical.

The cadets and officers de-bussed and strolled around looking at things. There was only one other vehicle in the car park and two people obviously waiting. As Tina and Carthew went into the waiting room Andrew went the other way, towards the runway. There he found a large propeller set up as a memorial to the aviators of World War 2. A sign said it was off a 'Liberator' bomber. Andrew wasn't really 'up' on vintage aircraft but he had a vague mental image of a big, four engine aircraft.

Andrew felt bored. He strolled through the small garden area and then back towards the waiting room. As he did, he noted Tina and Carthew moving across the lawn to look at the propeller, so he went into the waiting room. After visiting the toilet he studied some aerial photos of the airport and surrounds and a map, then looked at the tourist promotional literature.

Finding a brochure about the Lions Den, he sat and read it and was dismayed to find that it was 28km out of town. *Drat! That is a too far to walk or ride a bike. I might not get into town very often,* he thought, images of the girls flitting across his mind to tantalise him.

Several more vehicles arrived, including two cars and two battered and dirty Toyota 'Landcruisers'. Out of them climbed typical 'bushie' type people in big hats and worn work clothing. Then a tourist minibus joined the growing collection of vehicles and two more cars. Out of one of them climbed a very attractive woman in her early twenties. She wore a form-fitting blue skirt and floral shirt and matching scarf and looked like a tourist guide or travel agent.

The plane from Cairns came in right on time at 10:00. Andrew heard its engines before he saw it. By then it was already on the runway and a couple of minutes later it taxied in and parked out on the tarmac. A vehicle drove out to it from the buildings further along and then a tractor towing two luggage trolleys. Steps were placed in position and then the door opened.

The passengers disembarked into the blazing sunshine and walked across the 50 metres of bitumen to the small gate in the chain wire fence that separated the airport from the car park. They were met at the gate by the woman in the nice clothes and some were directed to the bus and others to the waiting room. A few were obvious tourists and were vocal about the heat and humidity. Others were plainly locals and were met by some of the waiting people. Three children a few years younger than Andrew had the look of boarding school kids home for the holidays.

Andrew was then mildly surprised to see two Asian men. The two men wore distinctive 'Kopiah' caps and had long-sleeved, white shirts with ties, long black trousers and polished black leather shoes. They were plainly not tourists.

Businessmen? Andrew wondered, speculating on their nationality as either Malaysian or Indonesian.

Almost last to disembark were two fit looking men in civilian clothes. They had short haircuts and looked strong and confident.

They will be the divers, Andrew decided.

The two men were met by the patrol boat captain and led to the waiting room. There was a short wait until the luggage was unloaded. As soon as the navy divers had their gear they were taken to the bus. Lt Ryan called the cadets to come and Andrew and his friends filed aboard. As he made his way past the two divers Andrew looked at them and noted that they were very capable looking men. A couple of years earlier he had been lucky enough to watch some Clearance Divers at work out on the Barrier Reef. Ever since then he had held them in very high esteem. As a diver himself he could only admire their courage and skills.

But I am not going to be a diver when I join the navy, he thought, shuddering at some of the terrifying experiences he had endured. *Left to die out of sight of land twice!* he thought. The most recent time had been the previous April when he and Carmen had been lucky to survive. Then he shrugged. It had actually been their diving skills that had kept them alive. *And it wasn't really a diving problem. It was running into a gang of smugglers who were ready to commit murder,* he mused.

Once the cadets were seated and counted the bus driver started the motor and set off back towards Cooktown. The drive back was still interesting but seemed to take almost no time at all. After ten minutes' drive, the bus was in the outskirts of the town.

As the bus travelled along the main street Andrew again looked hopefully out but there was no sign of Colleen or of Kristen and Daphne. The only girl he saw looked too young.

Oh well, maybe I will see them next week, he thought.

The bus pulled up at the wharf and the cadets and officers all stepped off and were immediately sent aboard the patrol boat. The divers and captain followed, a couple of ratings helping with the diver's equipment. The patrol boat was ready to proceed so the cadets were ordered to line up on the upper deck in their two watches facing out. Andrew happily took his place between Blake and Luke. Standing in the sun he found a bit trying as the sun was reflecting off the water making him squint and sweat.

The mooring lines were cast off and the last rating jumped aboard as the stern was eased away from the wharf. It was a moment Andrew always loved, the moment of setting out on a new voyage. This time it was made more memorable by the last-minute arrival of Kristen and Daphne. The two girls came running out onto the wharf from the nearby shops, their breasts bouncing in their T-shirts as they ran. That sight quickened Andrew's interest and he felt a rush of desire that was so strong it surprised him.

The patrol boat was moving out stern first to turn in the stream. The girls were just in time. They stood on the edge of the wharf and waved.

Kristen yelled loudly, "Hello sailor! Goodbye Andrew! See ya next week!"

Andrew blushed with embarrassment and pleasure. He would have loved to wave back but had to stand still and content himself with a smile. This became an embarrassed grin when Lt Ryan, who was standing behind the rank of cadets, said loudly, "Well, young Collins, starting off in the grand naval tradition I see: a girl in every port!"

Andrew blushed some more and wanted to deny it. He half turned to answer, before remembering that he should not move. But it was enough for him to see Tina, who was in the Starboard Watch and had her back to him, turn her head and frown. Her look sent him into a fluster of regret and defiant male pride.

The patrol boat moved astern, turning as it went and the two waving girls were soon blocked from his view by the superstructure. Then they came into view again as the turn continued but he had to turn his head to look over his shoulder to see them and this drew a rebuke from Lt Ryan so he faced outboard towards the sandy north shore of the estuary.

Once well clear of the wharf and facing out to sea the patrol boat's engines were placed at ahead and it began to move seawards. Almost at once it began to meet larger waves and the first punch of spray came aboard.

At least the breeze is cooler, Andrew thought.

As the patrol boat powered out of the estuary mouth, he was able to half turn his head and get a view back to the wharf. This allowed him glimpses of the two girls, who still waved from time to time.

But by the time the cadets were fallen out to go below and change into seagoing rig the wharf was out of sight behind the slopes of Grassy Hill. Andrew stared that way, hoping for a last look but the girls were also gone from view. He turned and made his way below. As Andrew returned to the mess deck after changing into work overalls Lt Ryan again teased him.

"Well, you are a dark horse, young Andrew. Where did you meet them?"

"On the wharf when we arrived yesterday, sir," Andrew replied.

Lt Ryan nodded and stroked his beard. "Yes, well, you just be careful and remember that girls you meet on wharves may not be the right people for young sailormen to meet. Do you get my meaning?"

Andrew nodded and coloured with embarrassment. "Yes sir."

"Good, now up on deck with the focsle party. PO Wilkins is waiting for your part of watch."

Andrew collected Blake, Luke and Sarah and happily led them forward. They were met by the petty officer and two ratings and were issued lifejackets. "It will be a bit wet out there so you cadets hang on," the petty officer instructed. He then led them out onto the focsle through a watertight door. The cadets were set to work under supervision to coil and stow the mooring lines.

As they worked on the lines, the patrol boat began working up to full speed. This meant that it began punching almost directly into both wind and waves, the course being South East. Almost at once the bow threw up a sheet of spray. This drenched them all, drawing oaths from the navy men and cries of surprise from Sarah and Blake. Luke just grinned and Andrew laughed.

He found it exhilarating and refreshing and felt that he was at last doing a bit of real seamanship. The cold wind and trickling water did not bother him at all and he just chuckled when yet another sheet of spray enveloped them.

Blake looked anxious and clung to the rail beside them. "This is getting very rough," he cried.

At that, Andrew laughed out loud and could only shake his head and continue coiling the line in neat flakes. The previous Christmas holidays he had done two voyages on the Kirk's Landing Craft *Wewak* up to Thursday Island and back and during the second he had ended up at sea in a Force 5 cyclone. That he had found a truly terrifying experience but he had also plumbed the darkest depths of his own courage and found he could still act when required. His survival had been due to being in an ocean tug built for operations in the Arctic Ocean and with a crew of highly skilled and very professional seamen.

During that cyclone the captain had estimated the wave height at ten metres and the wind speeds at 120 knots. One monster wave had smashed in some of the wheelhouse windows and the pitch had been so alarming Andrew had found he could only remain standing by clinging on. Thus he now found the two metre waves they were pounding across just pleasant bumps.

"This is fun!" he cried.

Blake wiped spray from his face and looked unhappy and Luke just grinned. So did the navy crewmen. One of the ratings said, "You wait till you do a few patrols down in Bass Strait and see how you feel. At least this place has warm water and tiny waves."

The other rating jeered and called, "Oh give us a break, Jimmy. You'll be skiting about icebergs and monster rogue waves next."

"Yeah well, I was in a Southern Ocean boarding party," the aggrieved rating retorted.

The petty officer grabbed at Sarah's sleeve as she almost fell. He then called, "Never mind your Antarctic voyages, Jimmy. Get that bloody line secured."

The rating fell silent. Andrew moved to help him, noting as he did that Sarah was looking very pale and that she was going green under the eyes. He looked around and saw a pasty faced and anxious looking Sub Lt Mullion standing nearby, clinging to the forward gun mount.

"Ma'am, I think you had better take Leading Cadet Creswell below."

Sub Lt Mullion nodded and looked grateful. She took Sarah's arm and led her back through the doorway. Andrew helped her back, then closed and clipped the door. As he did, he looked up and saw that Lt Cdr McDowall and Lt Ryan were watching him and he thought they had a look of approval on their faces. But in case he was doing the wrong thing Andrew hurried back to help with the lines.

Andrew had seen TV news footage of the Southern Ocean boarding parties at work and had been mightily impressed by their skill and courage. He looked at the rating named Jimmy with new respect and would have liked a chance to talk to him about the experience. But there was no time. They both worked quickly and at the end Jimmy met his eyes and gave a grunt and a nod that Andrew took as approval. That made him glow inside as he passionately wanted to be a real seaman.

As soon as the focsle was secure for sea, the petty officer led the work party back inside. He jerked his thumb up and said, "You can either go up and join the lookouts or go and change and sit in your mess."

Andrew had no desire to sit inside on such a beautiful day and with such an experience, so he made his way up to the back of the bridge and joined the rating on lookout duty. Once there he glanced around and noted that the Starboard Watch were still working out on the stern. He saw Tina and Nancy, both wearing life jackets, working with another petty officer and two ratings. They were also coiling lines and he saw that Tina was looking cold and not very happy but that Nancy was laughing and appeared to be singing.

Rather than have Tina catch him looking at her, Andrew studiously looked forward and began scanning the sea. A study of the coast surprised him at how far they had come. Already they were approaching Archer Point. Once again, he noted the lighthouse on the point and then the ruins of the old wharf and the second lighthouse on the rocky island offshore.

The next hour was pure pleasure for Andrew. The patrol boat's engines thundered and drove the vessel quickly across the sparkling sea. The course angled slowly away from the coast and the low, grey discs that were the Hope Islands appeared on the horizon. As they got closer, the colours subtly changed to a green and then details such as individual trees emerged.

Lunch was piped and Andrew was sent below. He found that Carthew,

Tina, and Nancy were rostered for duty to serve in the galley and that gave him a small spurt of satisfaction. But food was not of any interest to him and he ate quickly and returned on deck to find that the patrol boat was nosing slowly in through the gap in the reef.

Once inside the lagoon, the patrol boat was anchored and the Rhib was craned over the side. The cadets were allowed on deck to watch this and Andrew found it all interesting. He badly wanted to go ashore again but did not dare ask. Thus it was a pleasant surprise when Lt Ryan came over to him and said, "Andrew, you and Blake come with me. We are going ashore to show the divers where the mine is. So grab your day pack, water bottle and hat and get into the boat."

This time the landing party consisted of Lt Cdr McDowall, the PO who had been in the first search party, the two divers, Lt Ryan, and the two cadets. They were ferried ashore in blazing sunlight but with clouds and showers of rain showing out to the east. It was 1345hrs by the time all were ashore and the diver's gear unloaded.

The party set off walking along the beach in the sweltering afternoon heat. Andrew found the glare off the white coral sand and the sea painful to the eyes. He was perspiring even before he started walking and within minutes he was sweating heavily. It took the group twenty minutes to trudge around the northern tip of the island.

As before it was a relief to come around onto the windward side of the island, even though the view was not as interesting. As the group began walking southwards Andrew noted that the wind had increased and that the whole eastern horizon was now a line of grey clouds with curtains of heavy rain under them.

The PO looked at the approaching weather and said, "We are going to get a wet bum soon."

"Do you good Sammy," one of the divers teased. "Be the first time you got wet in a long time."

The pair carried on their good-natured joshing for the next few minutes. The PO then said, "The mine is a just around this next bend."

Andrew recognised the place and his interest quickened. He suppressed an urge to hurry on ahead but did walk faster. The group rounded the small point and he scanned the beach and reef ahead.

I thought it was just along here? he told himself when his eyes found no large spherical object in sight.

The group walked on for another fifty paces before the PO shook his head said, "No. It was just back there. I'm sure of it."

Blake nodded and agreed. "It was. I recognise that tree just there. It is where I put my bag. See, there are my footprints. But where is the mine?"

"It appears to be gone," the PO commented.

"Gone?" Blake queried as he looked around.

Chapter 7

MINE ADRIFT

"Gone!" Blake cried. "But where?"

Andrew could only shake his head at that, but he also looked around in the hope of spotting the mine. Lt Cdr McDowall answered, "Drifted off on the tide, the same way is it got here," he said. Then he swore and said, "Damn! Are you sure we are in the right place?"

"Yes sir," they chorused.

"We will look a bit further along, just in case," Lt Cdr McDowall said.

So the group trudged on along the beach for another couple of hundred paces. But Andrew was sure they had been in the right place. Even so he kept scanning the now exposed tidal flats of reef inside the lagoon, hoping to spot the mine. There were plenty of small round objects but even without wading out to them he could tell they were only small coral heads.

The party returned to the place where they had believed the mine to be and looked again, this time scanning the outer reef and the waves beyond. Lt Cdr McDowall kept muttering "This is bad!" and shaking his head.

After another fifteen minutes they gave it up. Lt Cdr McDowall said to the PO and Lt Ryan, "You people go back the way we came and see if you can spot any sign of the thing. We will continue on and circumnavigate the island."

The party split into two groups and Andrew went with Lt Ryan, the PO and Blake. He wished he could have been in the other group, if only because they would have the physically more pleasant walk. Going back the same way had them walking towards the sun for ten minutes and then in the lee of the vegetation so that the air temperature was very oppressive. Sweat poured out of them and Andrew repeatedly wiped trickles of perspiration from his forehead. Salt stung his eyes and he knew he was getting sunburnt.

Twenty minutes later they were back at the boat and they sat in the shade of the bushes and waited for the captain and the divers to arrive. Even before they reached them it was plain from their body language that they had not seen any sign of the mine.

Lt Cdr McDowall again shook his head. "We had better get aboard so I can notify Fleet HQ and get another NOTAM issued."

One of the divers nodded. "Too right sir. Having a loose live mine drifting around in the shipping routes is no joke."

Blake piped up and said, "We don't know if it was live. It was only an old rusty one."

The diver gave him a hard look. "You treat them all as live, son, then you might stay alive yourself. Just because it was old and rusty doesn't mean it won't explode. The older they get the more dangerous they become because the explosives begin to decompose and break down into unstable elements. Then one bump can set it off."

"I broke one of the horns off and it didn't go off," Blake said defensively.

The diver shuddered and shook his head. "Then you are damned lucky. Don't ever touch one again. Just call us."

The other diver now spoke. "Did you count the horns lad? Could you draw us a sketch? It always helps to know what type of mine we are dealing with."

Blake looked doubtful but both Andrew and the PO said they could. Then another thought came to Andrew. "We can do better than that sir. Sarah Creswell took some photos of it."

"This Sarah, is she on the patrol boat?" the diver asked.

"Yes sir," Andrew replied.

"What sort of camera; digital or an old type with film?"

"Digital sir," Andrew answered.

"Good, we can download it to a computer and have a look at the thing. Come on then, let's get back aboard," Lt Cdr McDowall said.

Twenty minutes later they stood in a group around a laptop computer set up on a table of the mess deck. Sarah's digital camera was connected to it and the images had been copied and were now being studied. Most were personal photos and, to Andrew's astonishment and embarrassment, many were obviously of him.

I didn't know Sarah liked me, he thought.

He glanced around and met her eyes. She blushed and gave him a shy smile. Andrew then caught sight of Tina. She was watching and as she noted the by-play she pursed her lips slightly.

Does that mean she doesn't approve or that she is jealous? Andrew wondered.

He hastily looked away and studied the next photo. It was of Blake sitting on the mine. At once, the diver who had asked about the sketch, said, "Ah! Yes! A German Mark Six, World War Two alright."

"German?" Blake cried in astonishment. "We are a long way from Germany. How did it get here?"

Lt Cdr McDowall answered him. "Several German raiders laid mines off the Australian coast during World War Two."

"I've never heard of them," Blake replied.

Lt Cdr McDowall said, "They weren't operating in this area. I think only one or two of the German ships came anywhere near the Queensland coast. The minefields were laid down south.

The chief diver nodded and said, "That's right sir. The German commerce raider *Pinguin* laid a minefield between Sydney and Newcastle. She then went south and laid two minefields off Hobart and a Norwegian tanker she had captured and was using as an auxiliary laid more mines in Bass Strait off Wilsons Promontory and Cape Otway. They both laid more in Spencers Gulf."

"Did they sink any ships sir?" Carthew asked.

"Yes they did. I don't remember the details but that was how we learned about them," the diver answered.

The other diver agreed adding, "Another German raider, the *Orion* I think, laid a couple of hundred mines off Auckland in New Zealand in 1940. Another one, the *Komet*, along with a captured whale catcher, the *Adjutant,* laid more off Wellington in 1941."

"You seem to know a lot about them, Chief," Lt Cdr McDowall said.

"Bit of a hobby of mine sir. Besides, we get trained on these old mines during our E.O.D. Course. We still get the odd one," the chief diver replied.

Andrew was fascinated by this window into a far flung naval war of long ago. The thought of those brave men far from home, at sea for months in all weathers conjured up images that made him wish he had lived then. He was also intrigued. From his limited knowledge of the ocean currents of the South Pacific he could not imagine how a mine laid off the coasts of New South Wales or Victoria could possibly end up on a coral reef off Queensland.

He asked this and the chief diver nodded. "You would wonder but it is a bit more complicated than that. You are right in thinking that the main ocean currents in this part of the world go south and then west but they also run into New Zealand and get diverted northwards and into the Coral Sea. This mine might have come that way."

Lt Cdr McDowall agreed and said, "And don't forget that along the Queensland east coast, and particularly inside the Great Barrier Reef there is a northerly coastal current generated by the prevailing winds."

Tina now spoke for the first time. "But sir, surely this mine hasn't been drifting around in circles for seventy odd years?"

The chief diver answered. "It may not have been. It might have remained moored to its anchor until quite recently when the steel wire cable has finally broken. It may have only been floating for a few months."

Lt Cdr McDowall clicked on another photo and then enlarged it to study the broken off horn. As he did, Blake said, "I did that sir, when I climbed on it."

"Bloody hell! You are lucky boy. Don't try that trick again or you might not be around to tell anyone," Lt Cdr McDowall said. He then looked at the other photos before straightening up. "Alright, we had better get under way. I am not going to sail around looking for this bloody thing. That is better done by aircraft. I will inform COMAUSFLEET and we will take ourselves back to Cairns."

He left the mess deck and the cadets at once began excited chatter. Lt Ryan sent them back to their duties and Andrew returned to being a lookout. He was glad of that as he had no desire to be trapped below if the patrol boat should strike the mine as it moved out into the open sea. This emotion was reinforced by genuine fear when the ship's loudspeakers ordered all hands on deck and lifejackets donned.

"A precaution in case we hit this floating mine," the 'Swain explained.

That caused most of the cadets and even many of the regular naval crew to appear concerned and to turn and stare anxiously at the surrounding sea. By then the anchor was aweigh and the patrol boat was already swinging to face the narrow channel in the reef.

As the patrol boat nosed slowly out through the entrance Andrew stared at the waves on the deeper water with something akin to dismay.

Bloody hell! It will be hard to spot the mine in all this chop, he thought, noting the hundreds of 'white horses' on the wave tops.

Suddenly the whole sea looked sinister, and he felt a distinct chill grip him. He had often read accounts of ships sailing in mined waters or of them being mined but had never before really appreciated the degree of bowel-loosening fear that the knowledge that there was a real, live mine somewhere in the ocean nearby could cause.

As he scanned the rippling, slopping wave tops he had to admit to himself that the emotion that was gripping him was fear.

I must be more of a coward than I thought, he told himself.

That got him all anxious lest any of the others should see this. With a conscious effort he made himself stand still and he even forced half a smile onto a face that felt like frozen rubber.

A few sidelong glances revealed that Luke was openly scared, and so was Sarah. Even Carthew looked a bit drawn and pale.

Good! Hope he wets himself, Andrew thought as he watched Carthew turn and say something to a worried looking Tina.

Once well clear of the reef the patrol boat turned to port and began butting its way south towards Cairns. That told Andrew that the navy had not ordered them to search for the mine. This was confirmed by Lt Ryan a few minutes later.

"When the captain reminded HQ that he had cadets on board they at once ordered him to exit the area ASAP," Lt Ryan explained.

The cadets were kept on the upper deck for the next hour until they were well clear of the area that the mine might be in. Andrew enjoyed this enormously but it was obvious that some of the others did not. The patrol boat moved at 'best speed'; in the conditions but even so she thumped into every wave, sending sheets of spray up over them.

By the time the cadets were allowed below the patrol boat was off Cape Tribulation and close to the coast. The scenery was so spectacular and interesting that Andrew was reluctant to go below. Even though the jungle-covered mountain tops were frequently hidden by rain clouds they still looked most impressive, particularly the spiky rock outcrop on top of Mt Pieter Botte.

The XO of the patrol boat pointed to it and said, "It is named after a similar mountain in Mauritius, and that was named after a Dutch admiral whose fleet of sailing ships was wrecked there back in the 17th Century."

Andrew thanked him and nodded. The XO then pointed at the next mountain to the south and said, "That is Thorntons Peak. There is an aircraft wreck on the side of it."

"Yes sir, I know. I flew over it last year when we were looking for World War Two aircraft wrecks." He then described some of the searches and their results. The patrol boat captain, who was listening, added. "I have been told that Thorntons Peak is taboo to the local Aborigines, that it is inhabited by a tribe of Amazon women."

Andrew stared at the massive mountain and wondered. Then vivid memories of his one expedition up into the jungle up on Mt Graham to look for an aircraft wreck made him shake his head.

"I can't imagine living on that thing," he said.

"Yes, they can have it," the XO agreed.

They discussed aircraft wrecks until the patrol boat passed Snapper Island and the XO had to attend to other duties. Andrew went below to have a cup of cocoa but found Carthew and Tina sitting at a mess table deep in conversation. After the drink and a visit to the heads he went on deck again and watched the Low Isles slide past a few miles away.

It was 1600hrs by then and the watches changed. Andrew was allocated to a team checking firefighting equipment and spent the next hour helping to unroll and then re-roll fire hoses. He did not mind because there was little to see because the patrol boat was well out to sea as it crossed Trinity Bay. It was not until 1715hrs that he went on deck again, this time in his best uniform for entering harbour.

The patrol boat slipped into Cairns Harbour along with a dozen tourist catamarans, yachts, and motor launches. It made Andrew feel very good to be standing on deck in uniform as they passed these. But being in the Port Watch was a disadvantage as he was facing away from the city and was not particularly interested in the mangroves and mudflats on that side of the inlet. From time to time he snuck a peek to starboard and admired his home town. He was very proud of Cairns and glad he lived there.

It is a great place! he told himself.

He also noted that the rusty old freighter they had arrested was no longer at the wharf. It was now moored up the Inlet opposite the mouth of Smiths Creek. But he had no time to study it as the patrol boat turned and nosed in to the wharf at the Navy Base and he found himself looking down at the activity there.

After thanking Lt Cdr McDowall and crew for the experience, the cadets filed ashore with their kitbags and walked through the front gate and across to their own depot in the compound next door. For Andrew, leaving the patrol boat gave him both a feeling of regret and of pleasure. But he knew he had enjoyed the experience and was more determined than ever to make the navy his career.

Back at their depot there was the embarrassing problem of how to say goodbye to Tina for the Christmas holidays. Tina solved this by calmly saying, "Goodbye Andrew. Have a good holiday."

As she turned and walked off with her mother, there was more jealousy and hurt for Andrew. He saw Carthew walk over and intercept Tina and her mother and talk to them as they walked to their car. To Andrew it appeared that Tina was responding very favourably to Carthew's advances, with a lot of smiling and nodding.

Andrew found it a relief to get into his own parent's car and be away from the situation. Both his mother and Carmen wanted to know all about the trip and said that the story of the mine had been on the news the previous night. They wanted to know all the details and the telling of them kept Andrew busy until they arrived home.

Within minutes he was again absorbed into the routines and trivia of life at home: feeding pets, unpacking, washing, talking, watching TV. But despite that Andrew could not relax. He lay on his bed and fretted about what to do about Tina's Christmas present. It was a very nice white T-shirt with embroidered rainbow lorikeets on the front and he thought it was very pretty.

Do I give it to her and just pretend it is because she is Carmen's friend, or do I ignore her and just put it away to give to someone else some other time? he wondered.

Then he shrugged and said, "Do I really care?"

But the answer to that was very obvious to him. *It hurts, so I must,* he mused. Then he wondered once again if he still loved her, or whether the pain was just hurt pride. That got him all confused so he thought, *She said we should go out with other people, so maybe I will, just to see.*

The thought of meeting other girls certainly had appeal. Then he smiled. *Maybe I will have some luck with those girls in Cooktown?*

Smiling at pleasurable fantasies he went to his bookshelf and began looking for a reference book on German raiders of World War 2.

Chapter 8

THE LIONS DEN

Two days later, Andrew was in the family car with Carmen and his mother and father driving towards Cooktown. At 11:05 they passed through the small township of Mt Carbine but did not stop. Already Andrew was beginning to feel that they were 'a long way out' as the kilometres of seemingly endless and empty bush reeled past. Three hours earlier there had been an awkward twenty minutes at Tina's house for the exchange of Christmas presents. When Andrew had handed her the present she had thanked him but the smile had obviously been forced. In return she had handed him a present that felt very much like a book. All he could do was nod and mumble thanks while his heart had filled with regret.

From Cairns they had driven up the Kuranda Range and through the lush green rainforest surrounding that picturesque town. From there they had gone south west along the Kennedy Highway to Mareeba, passing out into the more open savannah woodland which was the dominant vegetation of most of northern Queensland. At Mareeba they had turned north and driven through more savannah along seemingly endless straights to the town of Mt Molloy. The road had been good and they had covered the distance in about half an hour.

From Mt Molloy they had taken a left turn and followed the Peninsula Development Road. This was also a good, double-lane bitumen road but again gave the impression of being nothing but long straights.

West of Mt Molloy this impression was reinforced as they drove on and on through flat bushland on a road with very few bends. It was then that Andrew had experienced that creeping sense of isolation that sometimes assailed him when well away from a major town. He looked out at the ranges of rugged mountains on both sides and hoped nothing would go wrong.

Part of his mind was on the scenery and on the fact that, apart from the highway, there were almost no signs of human settlement. The other part dwelt on his personal life and his love life, or lack of it.

Do I still love Tina? he wondered.

He suspected that he did but was also conscious of a tingling sense of excitement over the possibility of meeting new girls, or of being successful with the girls he had already met in Cooktown.

That got him speculating on what Helenvale might be like and how he could get from there to Cooktown.

I will find a way, he assured himself.

The steep climb up the Desaily Range was a change but the blistering summer heat and shimmering heat haze took the edge off the pleasure and made the scenery appear more rugged and forbidding. The country was all still open savannah woodland and stayed that way except now they were travelling through hilly country where there was very little grass cover and the soil was sandy and bare. The type of country was no novelty to him but the sheer quantity of barren, rugged hills with no houses or farms or even side roads he found worrying.

Only three side roads so far, Andrew thought as they passed another one.

He eyed the massive and very rugged mountain range that paralleled the highway on his right for many kilometres. It was a forbidding rock pile and he was glad he was travelling in a rapidly moving car with air conditioning and not out in the scorching sun walking.

To add to his concern, there was very little traffic. In half an hour they only passed two cars and a truck going the other way and no vehicle caught them up or overtook. When his father commented that they had no mobile phone coverage, he felt another slight stab of worry.

"What do we do if we break down?" he asked.

Mr Collins laughed and said, "What they did in the old days; sit and wait till someone comes along and can take a message. Then sit and wait till a tow truck or a mechanic arrived. And that could be the next day."

Andrew was not amused and when Carmen nudged him and said, "Lighten up Little Brother. It won't be the end of the world," he had felt irritated.

He resumed staring out the window, while brooding over Tina and life. Through his mind he replayed the events of the last two weeks. Memories of the four days on the patrol boat caused him to smile and he found them a stark contrast to the dry bush they were passing through at that time.

I wish there had been some action when we arrested that old freighter, he thought.

His imagination slipped into a pleasant daydream in which he found himself wounded but the only person standing on the bridge of the patrol boat. He pictured himself bravely taking command and winning the fight, and Tina's heart.

Maybe I do still love her? he pondered.

Then he changed the daydream to saving her from pirates on Hope Island. Memories of a very erotic holiday adventure two years earlier on Endeavour Island near Cardwell caused him to become aroused and he had to remind himself that Tina would not be like that.

At least not until we are older, or married.

To take his mind off images of naked girls, Andrew constructed another fantasy in which he saved Tina from the mine. For a few moments he wondered where it had drifted to. There had been no further mention of it in the news.

Perhaps it just sank in deep water? he thought.

Outside there had been a change in the weather. The car was now travelling north and out to the west large thunderstorms began to build. This was normal for a December afternoon and he studied the black clouds with interest as several built upwards into classic 'Thunderheads'. For a time it looked as though they would drive right into heavy rain but in the end they missed it by a kilometre or so.

Just after midday they reached the Palmer River, the fabled 'River of Gold'. Andrew knew enough history to have a vague grasp on the importance of the 1873 gold rush to the European settlement of Far North Queensland, so he looked at it with interest. He was helped in this by his father slowing the car and turning it off the highway just at the south end of the bridge. He drove it down a bumpy dirt track to the river bed a hundred metres downstream of the bridge. At a small grassy flat just above the dry, sandy bed of the creek the car was parked.

"Lunch," Mr Collins announced.

The engine was switched off and they all climbed out. As soon as the doors were opened they were engulfed by stifling heat. Andrew was expecting it but was still almost surprised by the physical presence of the temperature and humidity. As he stretched he looked at the nearest thunderstorm which was still looming not far to the south west he was very aware of the smells of the place. In particular he noted the almost pungent reek of eucalyptus oil which was weeping into the atmosphere from the surrounding bush.

To add to the Australian 'Bush Christmas' atmosphere was the shrill and continuous high-pitched whine of cicadas. Despite the heat and humidity Andrew smiled.

I like it, he thought.

He studied the 100-metre-wide bed of the river and liked it even more. The 'river' was just a tiny trickle in a sandy bed studded with large trees and small 'islands' of sand dotted with clumps of bush and flood debris. It was all very typical Australia and bush and Andrew felt quite at home.

Lunch was eaten in the shade of the paperbarks which lined the river bed to a background noise of distant thunder. It seemed to Andrew that the storm was moving closer and he was very aware of the oppressive heat. He wiped sweat from his face and opened his mouth to comment on this.

Suddenly Carmen yelped and slapped at her arm. "Ouch! Ooh, beastly thing!" she cried.

It was a march fly and Andrew immediately spotted another buzzing near his own bare legs. Between mouthfuls of sandwich he swatted at it and then others which took its place. Between the heat and the march flies and then the numerous ants it was all slightly uncomfortable and the family ate as quickly as they could. They then repacked the lunch things in the car and got in. A few minutes later they were at the roadhouse on the far bank of the river.

After refuelling and enjoying a cold soft drink and ice-cream, the journey was resumed. They were just in time to escape the approaching thunderstorm and quickly outran it. Andrew settled back to studying the map he had and looking out at the passing bush.

Ten minutes were spent at the lookout at the top pf the Byerstown Range, and once again Andrew was impressed by the relative isolation and ruggedness of the country. This was reinforced when his father pointed to the jumble of rugged hills and lines of distant, jungle-covered mountains off to the east. No road was shown on the road map going into most of that area.

"Your cousins live over there somewhere," Mr Collins said.

Andrew studied the area and then the map. As far as he could see, no road was shown on the map going into that area, except one third class track from the north. "Are we going to see them?" he asked.

"Yes, after Christmas," Mr Collins answered.

"How do we get there?" Andrew asked.

Mr Collins pointed to the third-rate track on the map. "Along this. It leads south from Cooktown to Mt Penniless."

Carmen looked and said, "Mt Penniless! I don't like the sound of that. What's it like?"

Mr Collins shook his head. "No idea. I've never been there."

"What are the cousins like?" Carmen asked.

"Nice. You've met them, Cousin Bessie and her kids," Mr Collins answered.

Spits of rain sent them back to their car and they resumed the drive. Ten minutes later they were driving past wide, open fields that were being farmed. Within a few more minutes they came to the small town of Lakeland Downs.

Mr Collins waved his hand to indicate the town and surrounding country and said, "This whole area was just bush when I was your age. It was all cleared and turned into sorghum farms by a man named Mr Forster back in the 1960s. He had a grand vision of developing the region."

Carmen frowned. "This is a long way from any market. How did he plan to sell it?"

At that, Andrew had a vivid image of the rusty old wharf at Archer Point. "I can answer that," he said.

He then explained the now derelict and rusting port facility seemingly in the middle of nowhere. As he explained that, the car was driven on past the turn-off that led to the very tip of Cape York Peninsula. Looking along it Andrew experienced a series of vivid flashbacks to seeing from the air the vast and almost trackless expanses of 'The Peninsula' the previous Christmas. They drove towards Cooktown past the town and on through kilometres of open farmland.

After turning sharply to the east, the road went down into more normal Australian savannah woodland. As it did, Andrew was granted more glimpses of seemingly endless mountain ranges in the distance.

The road remained good, mostly new double lane bitumen. Speed stayed at a constant 100kph. The homestead of 'Springvale' cattle station was passed and they drove through a range of small hills. The country flattened out and the bush became thicker, with many larger trees including lots of white-trunked eucalypts. The West Normanby River was crossed via a long concrete bridge.

A few minutes later they crossed the East Normanby River by a similar bridge and the road turned sharply north and traversed a large flat area via a long causeway before curving east again at a pass through a rugged range of hills. On the far side the direction was east and crossed more flat country with several large swampy areas just visible off to the left. 'Kings Plains,' Andrew noted from his map.

Won't be long now.

There were more long straight stretches of road and another small range of hills, then the road curved left and went north before turning east again along the base of a line of dry hills. At the eastern end of these the road curved abruptly left and went down through a small cutting and onto a long concrete causeway and bridge. As they went left Andrew noted a dirt side road and picnic area down on his right and just beyond, at the very end of the causeway, a vehicle parked on a sandy area beside a deep pool of water.

"Annan River," he said as they drove across.

He looked both ways and was impressed. The river ran through a small gorge about 200 metres wide and with a long line of steep bluffs and cliffs stretching downstream to the left as far as he could see. The whole bed of the river was a jumble of boulders and below the bridge the water ran in a deep cleft. On the far bank the road went into a cutting and curved sharply to the right.

Almost at once an amazing mountain of black stones appeared ahead. Carmen cried out in delight and said, "Oooh! The Black Mountain."

Andrew had heard of it and had seen the tourist brochures so was expecting it but was still impressed. He stared at the huge pile of black rocks and noted that it was studded in places with clumps of vegetation. Then, as they rounded a curve to the left, he saw that there were more mountains and hills made of black rocks.

"There's a whole range of them," he commented.

Carmen was just agreeing when their father suddenly stood on the brakes and slowed the vehicle. Andrew looked through the front windscreen in alarm, wondering why he had done that. He saw that it was not an emergency. Rather they were at a turn-off and there were road signs pointing off to the right saying: HELENVALE, ROSSVILLE and CAPE TRIBULATION.

"Nearly missed the turn," Mr Collins said apologetically.

He set the car moving again and swung off the main road and onto the side road. Within 50 metres this degenerated into a very bumpy and corrugated gravel road.

"Bloody hell! That is a sudden change!" he added.

There were 3km of gravel road and nearly all of it rough. After a kilometre or so they crossed a small dry creek and Andrew noted a dirt road going off on the left. A sign said: MUNGUMBY LODGE.

"What's that place like, Dad?" he asked.

"Very nice, but also up-market. It is a wonderful place for bird watchers and that sort of thing," his father replied.

By then they had come out into open country and the road ran almost due south. The open paddocks were dotted with beef cattle and after about a kilometre the road went past a station homestead and its associated outbuildings. It then dipped to the left down a cutting in a steep, grassy bank before curving sharply to the right. At that, point it crossed a narrow but deep creek with large fig trees beside it.

MUNGUMBY CREEK, read the sign.

Almost at once the road curved left through a pleasant glade of trees. Andrew saw that there were open paddocks on the left, then another steep bank with houses on top, all half-hidden among trees. Behind them rose a mountain covered with forest. On the right he got a glimpse of a river which his map told him was again the Annan.

As the road straightened out, Andrew saw a cluster of buildings ahead on the right of the road. They were nestled in under a line of mango trees. Out in front was a length of bitumen road and a parking area. On it was parked a line of cars. Andrew knew at once that this was the Lions Den hotel. But he had expected more of a town. As far as he could see, there were just the few houses on top of the slope away to the left and all the rest was open paddocks or bush.

"Not much of a town," he commented.

His mother laughed and said, "I think there was, but about a hundred and fifty years ago."

Carmen looked left and right as they approached the hotel and replied, "No, not much. I wonder if there is a shop?"

On the right they passed an open area of mowed lawn behind a closed gate. A vehicle track led across it to a glade of splendid large trees. Just visible among these were some huts on high stilts and a couple of parked vehicles.

Mr Collins swung the car in to a stop just beside that gate and near a wooden deck outside the hotel. He switched off and for a minute or so they all just sat and looked at the place. Andrew felt a sudden attack of shyness and anxiety and then a sort of dismay when he saw that the actual hotel looked very old. There was a veranda along the whole front of the building, its awning held up by old wooden posts and all half-hidden by the row of mango trees. Behind that was the front wall of the hotel and it appeared to be just corrugated iron with half a dozen doorways through it.

After a minute Mr Collins said, "Well, this is it."

He opened the door and climbed out. The others did likewise. Andrew's father led the way between the parked vehicles to what appeared to be the 'front door'. As they stepped up off the pebbles under the line of mango trees onto the low wooden veranda, a big, bearded man came out of the last door on the right. He was dressed only in a blue singlet and tattered old blue jeans and carried a carton of beer in his arms. He glanced at them and Andrew experienced the unpleasant sensation that the man's eyes were mocking and that his lips had curled into a sneer. It made him feel that the man was looking down on them, possibly despising them for being 'Southern Tourists' and 'City Folk'.

It annoyed Andrew even more to watch the man's eyes rake Carmen with an appraising look. This reaction was exacerbated when there was a sudden loud crash on the corrugated iron roof just above their heads. Andrew jumped with fright and the man let out a jeering laugh. He then all but shouldered Andrew out of the way as he stepped down off the veranda. From above came a rattling sound and off the roof fell a mango. It thudded onto the ground just behind the man. It was then that Andrew particularly noted that the man had bare feet and he wondered how he could walk on the pebbles and gravel without pain. The man went to a battered old grey Land Rover parked among the line of vehicles.

As the man opened the driver's door of the Land Rover another man, a thin weasel with a straggly 'Goatee' beard and wearing dirty jeans and T-shirt, came hurrying out.

He called, "Hey Sean, wait for me man!"

Sean scowled, muttered an obscenity, then nodded, "Yeah, okay. Hurry up then Weed."

Weed pushed his way past, leering openly at Carmen as he did. He went to the passenger door of the Land Rover and climbed in, swearing the whole time.

Andrew blushed at hearing the men swear and muttered to Carmen, "Sorry Sis."

Carmen gave a wry smile. "It's alright Andrew. It's not your fault. I've heard worse at school and from sailors on navy ships. Besides, if we are coming to a country pub it has to be par for the course doesn't it?"

"I suppose so," Andrew replied. But he wasn't happy. He rarely swore himself and was very protective of his sister.

He followed her through the doorway and found himself in a large room which was a mixture of bar, dining room and pool room. On his right was a small L-shaped public bar. The part of the bar facing the front of the building had a small 'room' about 2 metres wide and 5 metres long. In this space were a row of six bar stools with two men and a girl sitting on some of them. The other part of the bar faced the dining room. Three doors led out of the back of the dining room. The walls were corrugated iron and were totally covered with names written in permanent marker pen or with photos, plaques, badges and other souvenirs.

For a few seconds Andrew was confused by the sheer array of visual stimuli. Then he began to sort out the various items. In particular he noted the skin of an enormous python which was nailed to the wall on the left beyond a pool table. He stared at the snake skin in amazement and tried to estimate its length.

Must be at least six or seven metres, he decided.

He knew that scrub pythons grew to a huge size but had never seen such a massive skin. He was about to draw Carmen's attention to it when he was distracted by having to greet the publican and his partner. There were introductions and then they were led through one of the doors behind the bar and into a nice new modern kitchen and pantry area.

Here they were briefed on the way the hotel was run and then the publican said, "I will just show you around and you can settle in." He then paused and looked through a side window that gave a view back along the main road towards Cooktown. "Oh, sorry, we might just put that off for a few minutes if you don't mind. Here comes the bus and it could get pretty busy for a while."

Andrew's mother at once said, "We will help you. Just show us what to do."

"Thanks, but I won't need all of you or it will get too crowded in the bar. The kids can just watch from the veranda while I show you two what to do," the publican replied.

He led them through to the front again. This time Andrew's mother and father both followed him into the bar area via the storeroom at the rear. Andrew and Carmen went through the dining room to the front veranda.

As they stood there another mango fell onto the roof with a loud crash. Again Andrew jumped with fright and then he blushed and felt silly about reacting that way. He now saw that the ground beneath the trees was littered with ripe mangos that had fallen from the trees.

A large motor coach pulled up out on the bitumen area in front and the passenger door opened. A dozen people climbed off. One was obviously the coach driver as he directed the people to the bar and toilets and then moved to open one of the luggage bins under the coach. The people, mostly tourists judging by their clothing, began to walk around, talk, take photos and stretch. Several headed for the toilets. Others made for the bar.

Andrew was about to devote all his attention to a very pretty female tourist when another person stepped down off the coach. It was a young boy of about 5 or 6 years of age, and even from a distance he looked dejected. The boy stood beside the coach and looked uncertainly around. When the coach driver pulled out a battered suitcase and dumped it at his feet the young boy seemed to flinch and cringe.

"Poor little bugger. He looks a bit lost," Andrew said to Carmen.

Carmen nodded. "He certainly looks miserable," she agreed.

"He looks like he has been crying," Andrew added.

Then he muttered with disgust when the coach driver just pointed to the veranda and then walked off, leaving the little boy alone.

Andrew looked around for the adult he assumed was meeting the boy but none of the people he could see seemed to be taking any notice and most were moving away into the dining room or bar.

The little boy stood all alone for a few more seconds before picking up the suitcase and walking with it towards the hotel. It was immediately apparent to Andrew that the suitcase was too heavy for the little boy as he stumbled several times and then stopped to put it down.

"Poor little bugger!" Andrew muttered. He stepped down off the veranda and hurried between the parked vehicles towards the boy.

The little boy saw him coming and stood looking at him fearfully. That sent a pang of pain through Andrew. To reassure the boy he smiled and said, "Hi! My name's Andrew. Let me help you with that suitcase."

The little boy stared anxiously up at him but he kept a tight grip on the suitcase. Andrew hesitated and thought, *What do I do now?*

Chapter 9

POOR LITTLE BOY!

A ndrew hesitated when he saw how frightened the little boy looked. The sight of those anxious big brown eyes staring up at him made him feel quite sad.

"It's alright. I was just going to help you move your suitcase to the veranda," he said.

Still the little boy did not answer. Carmen appeared beside him and crouched down. "Hello. My name's Carmen. Are you waiting for someone?" she asked.

The little boy nodded but did not answer. Carmen paused then prompted him, "For your dad?" she hinted.

The little boy nodded again and a tear formed in the corner of one eye. Andrew distinctly saw his lips quiver and he felt a wave of sympathy. He looked around again but still no adult had appeared to claim the little boy and everyone else off the bus, including the driver, had vanished into the hotel.

Carmen reached over and gently placed her hand on the handle of the suitcase. "Let us help you move this heavy case up onto the veranda. It isn't safe being here in the car park."

Again the little boy nodded but this time he let go and Carmen lifted her hand to take hold of his. Andrew waited till they had walked past before picking the case up and following. As he did, the little boy looked anxiously over his shoulder to check that he was. Once on the veranda, the little boy was seated on a bench seat and the suitcase placed beside him. Carmen then sat on one side and Andrew on the other.

"There you are. You will be safe now," Carmen said.

Even as she said this, a mango crashed onto the roof overhead and the little boys gave a startled flinch and gave a frightened look upwards.

Andrew had jumped with fright too and now gave an embarrassed grin. "It's alright," he said. "Just a mango."

At that moment, the publican appeared at a door further along and called, "Can you two give us a hand with the food please?"

Carmen answered, saying "Yes," to the publican and then, "You just wait here and we will be back," to the little boy.

The boy looked very anxious, and Andrew wondered if they should leave him, particularly as a vehicle was reversing out past the coach.

"You stay there and don't go near the cars," Andrew said. Then he hurried after Carmen.

"Poor little mite!" Carmen said. "What sort of parent would not be here to meet the little fellow when he arrives?"

Andrew could only agree, but for the next half hour the little boy was forgotten in the rush of cooking hamburgers and toasted sandwiches and so on for the people off the coach. Both Andrew and Carmen were in the kitchen cleaning up when the coach departed and before they could go out to the front their parents arrived with the publican.

"Let's finish that tour of the place," the publican said. He led them out the back door and stood to point out various features.

At the back was a grassed area. On the other side were two toilet and shower blocks: male and female, both painted blue. To the left at the far side of the grassy area were two portacabins, rows of small rooms in portable buildings able to be loaded on the back of trucks and moved. At the end of the hotel was a concrete extension with more rooms and beyond that a large open shed containing a boat, a parked 4WD and an assortment of tools and odds and ends of timber, pipes and metal sheeting. A driveway came in from the front around the left and then curved right across the grassy area between the hotel and the ablution blocks then went off down a slope under some big trees.

Andrew looked to his right and noted that the back yard was on quite a noticeable rise. Immediately behind the kitchen and on top of the slope was a sort of cabin consisting of a timber frame and floor but with a tent permanently erected on it. Beyond that the grass of the back yard sloped down to the side yard.

He followed the others to where they could see the side yard. From the top of the slope he was able to see the front gate and a vehicle track that led in across the open side lawn. This went past a single large tree and then past where he stood to wind its way in under the stand of large trees beyond. Among these stood three more of the tent cabins but these were raised on timber stilts and half hidden in the foliage. A dark green 4WD was parked at the closest one.

The publican pointed beyond it. "The river is just down there, and a picnic area. We also get campers and they can set up their tents on the side lawn here or down near the river, whichever they choose." He named the daily rates for both the camping and the tent 'lodges'. Andrew was amazed at the difference.

The group walked around that side of the hotel and along the top of the slope to where a timber deck with railings around it stuck out from the front and side of the bar. Wooden steps led up to it. On the side deck were six wooden tables, each with timber bench seats on either side. Flowering plants and trees made it all look very attractive and Andrew could only agree when Carmen said it was a very pretty place.

After listening to the publican describing why they built the deck and what it was used for, the group made their way in under the awning over the front veranda. They were led into the bar and then around behind it. The publican's wife was there serving two men who sat on bars stools. Because both Andrew and Carmen were under 18 they would not be working in the bar area but they still listened as the serving arrangements and storeroom layout were explained.

The two men, tin miners so Andrew now learned, both left and drove away. A glance through the front door of the bar showed that there were no vehicles parked at the front, other than their own. Andrew's father went out to drive it into the side yard near the open store shed. The publican led the others through the dining room and out to the back yard. Here he showed them three 'motel' type rooms which took up the south side of the building. They had obviously been added on later and were the concrete block structures Andrew had noted earlier. Each of the rooms contained two beds with bedside tables and a wardrobe.

"This is where you people can live for the month," the publican explained. "That way my wife and I can leave our own rooms as they are without having to pack everything away. It just means that you need to cross the back yard to go to the toilet or to have a shower. I hope you don't mind."

"That will fine," Andrew's mother replied.

Andrew was allocated the room closest to the front. Carmen had the next and their parents had the third, closest to the back yard and kitchen. A few minutes were spent unloading the car and moving belongings into the rooms. While they did this Andrew took the opportunity to walk over to the fence on the south side of the yard at the end of the portacabins. Beyond it were open fields which extended for a kilometre or so. These fronted the main road on his left and extended back for several hundred metres to a line of trees that he presumed marked the course of the river. About half a kilometre away was a house, set well back near the trees and with a couple of horses grazing in its front yard. A few hundred metres beyond that house the roof of a second was just visible.

Andrew's father joined him and said, "When I was a boy, that was all thick scrub, almost rainforest."

That saddened Andrew but he could only shrug. More people inevitably meant the destruction of the natural environment. He looked to the left and saw that the wooded slopes of Helenvale Hill reached right to the road for as far as he could see, the main road being right at its base.

I might climb that, he thought.

He returned to the car and collected another kitbag and carried it into the room he had been given. Andrew then tested the bed and decided that it was a very pleasant room and that it would do nicely. Already he felt better about spending the holidays there.

And it will be even better if I can get to Cooktown to meet those girls, he thought. It had already crossed his mind that that there was a distinct shortage of girls at the Lions Den.

He was then called to come to the kitchen to help with dinner. By then twilight was setting in and the sun had gone from the building. Andrew was starting to feel a bit weary. Food was served up by his mother and the publican's wife and he carried the plates through to the dining room. When the food was on the table they seated themselves and began to eat.

Almost immediately they were interrupted. A vehicle pulled up out front and a big burly man in blue overalls came in and asked for petrol. The publican greeted him warmly and stood up, then said, "You people had better come and watch this. We provide fuel and you will need to know how to operate the pump."

Andrew had noticed a diesel pump near the far end of the mango trees when he had gone out to help the little boy but had thought no more about it. He stood up and followed the others out of the front door and across the veranda. Outside it was almost dark with only a light bulb near the bar to light up the veranda.

As he stepped onto the veranda, Andrew glanced to his right and saw a small shape half hidden in the shadows. He stopped and pointed. Carmen looked and cried out, "Oh, that poor little boy is still here!"

She walked along the veranda towards him, followed by the others. As they approached him it seemed to Andrew that the little boy shrank in size as he contracted into a huddle, his knees up against his chin and both hands at his face.

Carmen knelt down. "Here we are again. Are you alright, little man?"

The small boy nodded and his eyes grew wide with anxiety. A thumb crept into his mouth.

Andrew's mother also knelt down. "Are you waiting for someone?"

Again the little boy nodded. They waited but the little boy said nothing. Seeing the worry and unhappiness on the little boy's face caused Andrew's heart to swell with pity and feelings of helplessness.

Andrew's mother persisted. "What's your name, little man?"

No answer. Andrew saw scared eyes swivel from one to the other and the little boy seemed to hunch even tighter. Then an idea came to Andrew. He moved to the suitcase and found a label attached to the handle. He turned it to the light and read: TERRY PHILBY.

"His name is Terry Philby," Andrew said.

"Terry. That's a nice name," Carmen said. The little boy's eyes swung to look at her and he gave a tiny nod. Carmen took that as encouraging and said, "Are you hungry, Terry? Would you like something to eat?"

Little Terry nodded but still looked very anxious. Andrew's mother held out a hand and said, "You come with me Terry and we will get something nice to eat."

By this time they had been joined by the man who wanted fuel. He said, "Philby? I wonder if he is related to Dave Philby?"

The publican looked at him and nodded. "Might be, but knowing Dave it's a bit hard to imagine him not meeting the boy. I will give him a ring and find out. Sorry Jack, I will get you your diesel now."

He and the man called Jack moved out to the petrol pump. Andrew's mother said, "Bert, you and Andrew go with him and learn how to use the pump. Carmen and I will look after young Terry."

Again she reached out and this time little Terry took his thumb out of his mouth and called, "Boy!"

Andrew was just stepping off the veranda but on hearing that he stopped and looked back. "What did he say?"

"Boy," Carmen replied.

The little boy nodded and pointed at Andrew. Again he said, "Boy."

When Andrew's mother tried to take his hand he pulled away and this time he fixed Andrew with an intense stare. Andrew knelt in front of him and said, "Would you like me to help you, little man?"

Little Terry nodded and Andrew thought his heart would burst. He reached out and the little hand grabbed at his and gripped it tightly. Andrew smiled and stood up. He went to walk towards the kitchen but Terry shook his head vigorously and pointed at his suitcase. "Port," he said.

Andrew nodded. "Okay Terry, we will take your port with us. Quite right not to leave it out here where anyone could take it."

He reached out with his other hand and took hold of the suitcase. Terry nodded and encouraged by that Andrew started walking towards the dining room door. To his relief, little Terry slid off the seat and went with him, his sweaty little hand clinging tightly to Andrew's.

It had been a long time since Andrew had felt quite so emotional about anything, but he found his own throat choking up and his eyes prickling with tears as he walked slowly with little Terry. It made him glad that the veranda was mostly in shadow and that the dining room light was not very bright.

In the kitchen Andrew placed little Terry's suitcase in a corner and pointed to a chair but his mother shook her head. She said, "You need to wash your hands and face before you eat and you might like to go to the toilet too. Would you take Terry to the toilet please Andrew?"

Andrew nodded and looked at Little Terry's face, half expecting him to say no. But Little Terry nodded and again took Andrew's hand and walked with him. This time he did not make a fuss about his suitcase and Andrew was able to lead him across the back lawn to the ablution building.

It was instantly obvious that Little Terry badly needed to go and was very grateful for the chance. When he had finished and come back out of the cubicle, Andrew washed his own hands and face to set an example and was amused to note that Little Terry copied him without having to be prompted. Andrew handed the little boy a towel and then waited till he had dried himself. After hanging the towel up he led him back across the lawn. By then it was quite dark outside and Little Terry clung tightly to him, looking fearfully around. To Andrew, used as he was to the noise and bustle of living in a city, it all seemed very quiet.

Once back in the brightly lighted kitchen, Little Terry allowed Andrew's mother and Carmen to take over. They sat him at the end of the kitchen table and gave him a cup of warm Milo and then placed a plate of food in front of him; kid type food with small cuts of chicken and freshly cooked potato chips; small slices of cheese and some tiny beetroot. Another plate was placed next to Little Terry's and Andrew was told to sit there. He did so and noted that Little Terry appeared to visibly relax. He picked up the cup of Milo with both hands and sipped at it, his eyes still looking anxiously around.

As Little Terry put down the cup, Andrew smiled at him and said, "This food looks good."

To help ease the tension he started to eat, his mother nodding with approval. Little Terry watched for a few seconds then started to eat as well. Within minutes he had forgotten them and wolfed the food down.

Carmen watched and shook his head. "Starving, poor little mite," she muttered.

"Probably hasn't eaten all day," Andrew said. He turned to Little Terry and said, "Did you have any lunch little man?"

Little Terry, his mouth full of food, shook his head. Then, after swallowing, he very shyly pointed to the cup and whispered, "Can I have some more please?"

"Of course," Andrew's mother replied. She quickly prepared another cup of warm Milo and put it in front of him.

Andrew's father and the publican and his wife came into the room, and he asked, "How's he going?"

His mother answered. "Good. Have you contacted his relatives yet?"

The publican shook his head. "No. I will do it now."

He left the room and the others sat down to eat. Andrew nibbled at his food and kept glancing sideways to check that Little Terry was alright. The conversation moved to the characters that patronized bush pubs and this one in particular.

The publican's wife was in the middle of an amusing story when the sound of vehicles pulling up reached her. Doors slammed and boots sounded in the dining room. Loud voices sounded out front. The publican appeared with a written note.

"It is the boys from the mine," he said. "They want their tea. Here's the order."

The publican's wife took the list and nodded. "Okay, time to start cooking," she said.

As she stood up, Andrew's mother said to the publican, "Have you contacted little Terry's family yet?"

The publican shook his head. "No, not yet. I rang the mine but they said that Dave Philby had just gone on shift and wouldn't finish until six tomorrow. They switched me through to him and he said that Terry is his brother Barry's son. When I asked him where Barry was he said he lived in the jungle across the river near Wallaby Creek but he didn't have a phone. So we can't contact him and I don't know where he lives."

Andrew's mother frowned and said, "So what is going to happen to Little Terry?"

The publican shrugged and said, "Dave said he would collect the boy in the morning if his brother hadn't done so first. I guess we will have to keep the lad here."

During this conversation Andrew had kept glancing at Little Terry to see his reaction. He noted the anxious look on the little boy's face grow and then the lips began to tremble. Little Terry's eyes watered and he blurted out, "Isn't... sniff... isn't m... m... my sniff... d... dad come... coming to... sniff... get m.mm. me?"

"We don't know where he is, but your Uncle Dave will pick you up tomorrow morning," the publican explained.

At that, Little Terry burst into tears again, causing Andrew's heart swell with pity. Andrew's mother reached across to hold the boy and said soothingly, "It will be alright."

Little Terry sniffled and raised his tear-streaked face. B... b... but wh... where wi... will I sleep?"

Andrew's mother said, "You can sleep here. We will look after you."

Little Terry looked even more anxious and several tears trickled down his cheeks. He looked around the kitchen in a way that made Andrew think he thought that his mother had meant literally what she said.

That made him smile. He said, "You can sleep in one of the bedrooms."

Little Terry nodded but still looked anxious. The publican and Andrew's father both went out to the bar. Andrew's mother then got up to help prepare food for the miners. Carmen joined her.

As she worked, she asked the publican's wife, "This mine these men work at. Where is it?"

"About ten kilometres south of here, up a small valley that joins the Annan. It is off the road to Mt Penniless."

"Mt Penniless? We have relations that live there," Carmen commented.

"Oh yes? Who?" the publican's wife asked.

The conversation shifted to a discussion of who lived at Mt Penniless and to who Cousin Bessie might also be related to. Andrew learned that there were only a few people now living at Mt Penniless. It had once been a tin mining town but was now mostly bush and to him it sounded very much like the back end of nowhere.

"Certainly the end of the road," the publican's wife agreed.

Andrew's mother suggested that he take Little Terry out to watch TV now that he had finished eating. Andrew led the boy through to the dining room where there was a TV mounted on the wall. The TV was obviously satellite as there were no local ads but Andrew didn't mind. He saw that there were four men in overalls with bright yellow vests and shiny reflector strips on them; the miners in their safety clothes. He now discovered that eight miners lived at the hotel, being accommodated in the portacabins.

The miners were rough looking men but seemed friendly enough and did a lot of laughing and joking as they drank beer and then settled at one of the dining tables. There was then an amusing and (to Andrew) an irritating little scene when Carmen brought out two plates of food. The miner's eyes lit up and they very obviously gave her the once over, with evident approval.

A miner who looked to be in his twenties smiled and said, "Why hello, Sweetie! My name's Tim. What's yours?"

"Carmen," Carmen answered, returning the miner's smile.

"What brings you to this part of the world?"

"Working here for the holidays," Carmen answered.

"Oh good! We could do with a pretty face around here," he said.

Carmen sniffed and said, "Don't get fresh. Now, who wants desert?"

She took their orders and they kept flirting and teasing her. That irritated Andrew, but Carmen seemed amused and chattered cheerfully back. That she did not at once freeze them out annoyed Andrew and got him worried.

She shouldn't flirt, he thought, *and especially with older men.*

During the conversation Andrew learned that the mine was for tin and that about twenty men worked at the site. Some lived in Cooktown and others at a place called Rossville which was along the road that went south to Cairns.

Other vehicles arrived and the bar filled with people. Most were real 'Bushies' in old shirts and long trousers and with felt hats and riding boots. There were a couple of older women but they appeared to be fairly coarse and unattractive to Andrew and he could understand the miner's interest in Carmen.

Just after, some of the people began playing pool at the nearby table and the noise became loud enough to make it difficult to listen to the TV. Andrew's mother appeared at his elbow and gestured towards Little Terry. Andrew turned and saw that the little boy was yawning and that his head was nodding.

"Time he was in bed," she said.

"Which room will we put him in?" Andrew asked as he stood up.

Little Terry climbed down off his chair and looked very anxious. He said softly, "Boy."

"What did you say?" Andrew asked.

Little Terry pointed at him and said, "Boy."

"Yes I am," Andrew replied, puzzled by what he meant.

His mother laughed. "He wants to be in the same room as you."

Andrew could only gape and feel foolish. His initial reaction was annoyance as he did not want to share but then he saw the gleam of pathetic eagerness in the little boy's eyes and he at once felt guilty.

"Of course. You show him the way. I'll get his suitcase," he said.

A few minutes later, Andrew led Little Terry across the back lawn to the bathroom and made sure he cleaned his teeth by doing so himself. The little boy was then led back to the room where Andrew found that his mother had turned back the sheets and placed Little Terry's pyjamas on the bedspread.

There were a few embarrassing minutes while he changed into his own pyjamas, feeling very self-conscious that the little boy could see his bare bottom. To help the little boy from feeling shy he stood with his back to him until he had also changed. He then helped him into the bed.

Both Carmen and Andrew's mother slipped in to say goodnight and to cheer Little Terry up. The little boy pulled the sheet right up so that only his nose and eyes were visible, but he looked anxious.

Andrew then bent over him and said, "Goodnight little man. I'll be just there if you need me."

Little Terry gave a tiny nod and his eyes followed Andrew as he walked to his own bed and climbed in. Then Andrew reached out and clicked the light off. There was a stifled gasp from Little Terry and then Andrew heard stifled sobs. The idea of the lost little boy crying made Andrew feel unhappy as well so he slid out of bed and padded over to the other bed.

"It's alright Terry. I am here," he said. "We will find your dad tomorrow."

As he said this, he gently patted Little Terry on the head. A small hand slid up out of the bedclothes and clamped on to his. Andrew let him hold it for a few minutes but then tried to free himself so that he could go to his own bed. He had it in mind to go back to the TV but as soon as he tried the tiny fingers tightened their grip and Andrew saw, in the dim light coming through the window, the little boy's wide open, anxious eyes.

With a sigh of exasperation, Andrew sat on the edge of Little Terry's bed and allowed him to hold his hand. Minutes slowly ticked by. Andrew could dimly hear the voices at the other end of the hotel and several vehicles came and went. From time to time another ripe mango thudded onto the iron roof. From the screeching and squabbling sounds overhead Andrew deduced that fruit bats, 'flying foxes' as North Queenslanders call them, were busy eating the fruit. Andrew explained this to Little Terry and urged him to close his eyes and go to sleep. But Little Terry's eyes stayed open for what seemed like a very long time.

As soon as they slid shut, Andrew moved to withdraw his hand, only to have the grip instantly tighten. The eyes did not open but Andrew sighed and sat on the bed to wait until the little boy was really asleep.

The door opened and his mother peeked in. When she saw him sitting on the bed she tiptoed across and looked down.

"Poor little mite!" she whispered. Then she kissed Andrew on the forehead and said, "It is very good of you to look after him. Thank you. Goodnight."

She left and Andrew stayed sitting until he became stiff. To ease his back and knees he eased himself onto the bed and stretched out.

He woke up some time later to find that he had been asleep on the little boy's bed and that Little Terry had at last let go. Very slowly Andrew eased himself into a sideways position and slid off the bed onto his knees. Little Terry moved restlessly when he did so Andrew froze until the movement had stopped, then moved again. At last he was able to stand up and relax. He saw that Little Terry was now curled up and was sucking his left thumb.

Poor little man! Andrew thought sadly.

Pondering on what sort of person could place a child in such a situation he made his way to his own bed and climbed in. The night was hot and still so he did not even pull the sheet over himself. For a while he lay awake thinking. He was very conscious of the stillness outside. From the lack of noise he deduced that the bar had closed and that the people had gone. He became very conscious of the silence. Then he jumped as a mango fell with a bang. This time he smiled and then relaxed and lay thinking.

I wonder what tomorrow will bring? he wondered as he slid into the depths of sleep.

Chapter 10

CHARACTERS

Andrew woke to find that the temperature had dropped just enough for him to feel a slight chill. He tugged the sheet up over him, his sleepy brain noting that the light through the window was a dim grey. Then he slid back into a restless sleep.

Some time later he was woken by the sound of his bedroom door opening. He opened an eye and saw that it was his mother. She smiled at him and raised a finger to her lips and said, "Shh!"

Andrew followed her gaze and saw that Little Terry was sound asleep but on his bed. The little boy was curled up between him and the wall and had snuggled in against him. He still had his thumb in his mouth and he looked so young and helpless that Andrew felt an instant pang of pity.

Without waking Little Terry he managed to slip out of bed and his mother then gently covered the little boy with the bedspread. As she did, he stirred and murmured but then snuggled in and settled again. Andrew smiled at his mother then collected his clothes, towel and toilet bag and made his way out to the toilet.

As he crossed the back lawn, Andrew noted that the lawn was soaked with either dew or rain. A glance upward showed only a few scattered clouds so he decided it was from dew. Certainly the air felt wonderfully fresh and cool. His watch told him it was only 06:30. He breathed in deeply and felt quite happy.

I think I am going to like this place, he thought.

He showered, shaved and dressed in shorts and short-sleeved shirt. He then stood and combed his hair. While he did this two of the miners appeared, both bleary eyed and with towels over their shoulders. They said cheery hellos and went into the toilet and showers.

Andrew went back to his room, passing Carmen as he did. She wore her dressing gown and slippers and as she crossed the lawn the young miner named Tim came out of a portacabin on his way to the ablutions.

He saw Carmen and called out, "Hello Cinderella! Where did you leave your glass slipper?"

"The same place that I left the mice that were turned into horses to pull my coach," Carmen replied.

She continued a cheerful and teasing conversation with the man until she went into the ladies ablution block. Andrew did not approve of this by-play at all and wondered how he could warn Carmen about the men.

She is much too young to be flirting with those men, he thought.

Back in his room Andrew found Little Terry just waking up. This was helped by the loud crash of another mango on the roof directly above their heads. Little Terry cringed and looked scared for a second, then put his hands to his face and giggled.

Andrew grinned back. "Just a mango," he said.

"What are mangos?" Little Terry asked.

Andrew was astonished. "Fruit. They grow on the trees outside. They are very nice."

"I've never seen them," Little Terry replied.

"Where do you come from?" Andrew asked.

"Sydney," Little Terry answered.

That confirmed Andrew's suspicions and he nodded. "They don't grow there. Mangos are tropical fruit."

"What's tropical?"

Andrew opened his mouth and then shut it. *Oh boy, this could be a long day!* he thought. He said, "I'll show you a mango after you have washed and changed. Come on, get up."

He took Little Terry to the ablutions with his towel and a change of clothes. As they came out he passed three of the miners who were heading for the dining room. From the voices Andrew deduced that his mother and Carmen were already at work there. He waited outside until Little Terry had changed and then took him back to the room to place the pyjamas in his suitcase.

After helping Little Terry to pull on his shoes, Andrew said, "Come on, I'll show you a mango and we will get a nice one to have with our breakfast."

Andrew went to leave the room but Little Terry cried out and held up a foot. For a second Andrew wondered what was wrong and then he twigged.

"Can't you do up your shoelaces?" he asked.

Little Terry shook his head and looked sad. Andrew controlled his frustration and went over to him. He knelt and tied both shoelaces. While he was doing this Carmen knocked and stuck her head around the door.

"Breakfast time boys," she called. When she saw what Andrew was doing she smiled and nodded with approval.

Little Terry stood up and said, "Has my dad come yet?"

Carmen shook her head. "No, not yet."

Little Terry's mouth turned down. Andrew did not wait. He took his hand and led him through to the front of the building. As they stepped onto the veranda, Andrew opened his mouth in surprise. Lying on a bench near the door was a sleeping man. The man had a luxuriant black beard and wore only filthy dark blue shorts and a torn dark blue singlet. He was lying on his back and was snoring loudly.

Andrew looked askance at the sleeping man and quickly led Little Terry past and out under the mango trees. As he did, the sleeping man grunted and did a loud fart. That really embarrassed Andrew but Little Terry chortled mischievously.

"Fffrrrt!" Little Terry said and then giggled again.

Andrew made no reply but started looking for a good mango. As he did, one suddenly fell from the tree above and landed right beside him with a loud thud. He jumped and Little Terry laughed again. Andrew wasn't amused. He picked that one up but it was half green and the flying foxes had chewed a large hole in one side.

A few minutes searching rewarded him with four nice, ripe mangos. He showed these to Little Terry who sniffed them with approval. Andrew then led the way in under the trees towards the dining room. At that moment, the publican stepped out through the door carrying a broom. He gave them a cheerful good morning.

Andrew pointed back along the veranda to the sleeping man. "I think he might have been drunk," he said.

The publican laughed loudly and said, "He certainly was. That is 'Irish'. He often gets drunk and he has the good sense not to try to drive after he's had a skinful." He pointed to a battered old grey Land Rover parked further along.

"Irish?" Andrew asked.

"Not his real name but he's a dinki-di Irishman. We reckon he is hiding out in the jungle from either the IRA or the British," the publican explained.

At that moment, the sound of a vehicle came to them and a blue station wagon appeared from the south. The publican groaned and said, "Oh blast! Here comes Billy and he will want a drink."

Andrew was astonished. He vaguely knew that there were laws regulating when hotels could open to serve alcoholic drinks. But he shrugged, thinking it was no concern of his. He led Little Terry inside as the vehicle pulled up. Sure enough Billy wanted a drink but he also wanted fuel. The dining room had four miners seated in it, but they were all eating fast and barely said hello as he passed.

One miner did say, "Hello little man," to Little Terry.

Andrew's parents, the publican's wife and Carmen all greeted them as they entered the kitchen. They were seated at the table and given breakfast: Weetbix with warm milk and brown sugar; then hot buttered toast with honey or jam. Andrew explained mangos to his mother and she quickly peeled two and then sliced them into smaller pieces and placed them in a bowl. Little Terry looked at them very suspiciously but Andrew did not mind demonstrating this time. He quickly ate three slices and Carmen took one as well. With that encouragement Little Terry carefully tried a piece. His face told the story. He liked it. Another piece went in and soon he was eating the mango as fast as he could.

The publican's wife took cut lunches through to the miners who trooped out to the back yard where their vehicle was parked. They drove off, heading south.

A few minutes later another vehicle came from the south and pulled up outside. Andrew glanced at the clock.

"Not even eight o'clock and they are arriving," he commented.

The publican's wife laughed and said, "They will arrive at all hours of the day or night and still demand service!"

"Do you serve them?" Andrew asked.

"Depends who they are and what time it is," the publican's wife answered.

Footsteps sounded and the publican arrived with another man, a miner by his safety vest and overalls. He was a big, ruddy faced man with thinning sandy hair and twinkling brown eyes.

The publican said, "Here's Dave. Well Dave, do you know this little nipper?"

Dave stooped and looked at Little Terry and Andrew saw a series of expressions cross his face, recognition, pleasure and anger, the latter swiftly mastered and masked. He nodded and strode over to Little Terry.

"G'day Terry, old mate! It's your Uncle Dave. How are you?"

Little Terry's face lit up and he slid off his chair and dashed across to him. "Uncle Dave!" he cried.

Uncle Dave scooped him up in his arms and hugged him. Andrew fleetingly glimpsed pity and even the start of a tear on the big miner's face before he hid his emotions with a grin.

"Great to see you little mate. Did your mum bring you? Is she here?"

Little Terry shook his head, his face beaming with pleasure as he rested secure in Uncle Dave's arms.

"No. She just put me on the plane," he said.

"Plane? I thought you came on the bus from Cairns?" Uncle Dave said.

"On the plane in Sydney. A man put me on the bus yesterday," Little Terry answered.

Andrew saw Uncle Dave's face redden, though whether it was from anger or embarrassment he could not tell. Uncle Dave's mouth set for a moment in a thin line and he gave a slight shake of his head. Then he changed his expression with an obvious effort and smiled.

He turned to the group and said, "Thanks for looking after him. I will pay for his accommodation and meals and take him to his dad."

The publican shook his head. "No need. We were glad to help."

"I insist," Uncle Dave replied. He lowered Little Terry to the floor and held his hand. "We will get his gear and get going if that is alright."

Andrew stood up. "I'll get his suitcase," he said. He hurried through to his room feeling very relieved that the little boy was now safe. He liked Uncle Dave and felt sure he would look after Little Terry.

On his return to the veranda with Little Terry's suitcase Andrew was embarrassed by Little Terry pointing to him and saying, "Big boy looked after me. I slept in his room and he made sure the big bats didn't get me."

"Big bats?" Uncle Dave said, cocking an eyebrow.

"Flying foxes. They…" Andrew began to say. At that moment, another mango crashed loudly onto the roof just above them. He laughed and said, "They made that happen a lot."

Uncle Dave laughed. "They do. Well thanks, son. What's your name?"

He held out his hand and shook Andrew's. Andrew told him and then introduced the other members of his family.

Uncle Dave said, "You here long?"

Andrew answered, "For a month. We are running the pub while the publican and his wife have a holiday."

"They need one. Well, we will be seeing you then. Thanks again. Come on Terry mate," Uncle Dave replied. He led Little Terry out to a white Toyota Landcruiser with amber safety lights on top and an orange flag on a long whip aerial. As he loaded the suitcase and the boy in, Little Terry looked a bit anxious and gave Andrew a special wave.

The Landcruiser drove off, leaving them grouped on the veranda watching. Carmen was the first to speak. "Poor little boy," she said. "It sounds like his mum doesn't want him and has just shipped him out."

"It does," agreed the publican. He then called out along the veranda. "Good morning, Irish! Rise and shine and come and get some breakfast while you can."

A bleary eyed Irish was introduced and he looked genuinely embarrassed to be found in the state he was in by the women. He mumbled apologies and hurried off out the back to wash and spruce up.

Andrew was further introduced to the business of running a bush pub. He cleared the miner's breakfast things from the dining room table and helped wash them up. Then he went out to learn how the fuel pump worked and refuelled Billy's 'jalopy'. After that he was set to work picking up the mangos scattered along the front of the building. In the process he was hit by one that fell and struck his shoulder. It did not really hurt but made him more careful.

He had just wheeled a wheelbarrow full of mangos to the bar end of the car park when a dark green 4WD appeared from the direction of Cooktown. It came to a screeching halt under the trees near Andrew and a tall, fair-haired man with a half-grown sandy coloured beard climbed out. The man looked tired and unkempt and had bloodshot eyes. He ignored Andrew and strode towards the bar. The publican met him in the doorway.

"G'day Barry. You just missed your brother. He's taken the boy to your place."

"Boy? What boy?" Barry asked grumpily. "I just stopped for a drink."

The publican frowned. "Your boy I think, a kid named Terry. Little fella about six or seven years old. Said his mum put him on the plane in Sydney."

Barry swore crudely, making Andrew blush because his mother and Carmen had appeared behind the publican. Then Barry said, "So Dave picked him up?"

"That's right. I think he was taking him to your place," the publican answered.

Barry swore again. "Bugger! Well I ain't there. I've been in town. Stuff that selfish cow! I don't need the kid here. This ain't the place for him, especially at this time. Anyway, can I have a drink?"

"Bar's not open yet," the publican answered stony-faced.

Barry swore again then muttered about 'needing the hair of the dog' before turning and walking angrily back to his vehicle. Once again he ignored Andrew and just climbed in, started up and drove on southwards.

Andrew joined his mother and Carmen on the veranda. "That was Little Terry's dad I think," he said.

"I heard," his mother answered.

"Talk about the pot calling the kettle black," Carmen cried. "Selfish indeed!"

Andrew could only agree and feel even more sorry for the little boy. When Little Terry had gone off with Uncle Dave Andrew had been really cheered up but meeting the boy's father quite depressed him. He resumed collecting mangos and then wheeled the whole lot well away from the hotel and dumped them.

As he walked back, he looked around, sniffing the fresh morning air and enjoying the tranquillity and greenness of the scenery. But by the time he returned the wheelbarrow to the open shed the sun had begun peeking over Helenvale Hill and he was perspiring.

Andrew made his way inside to ask what else needed to be done. Sweeping, he was told so he spent the next hour with a broom. Then he was shown how to operate the water pump and where various oils and lubricants were kept in the shed. By the time this was done it was morning tea. By then the bar was open and doing a busy trade with five vehicles parked outside.

Andrew went to the kitchen and enjoyed a glass of cordial with Carmen. Their mother came and went and they could hear their father in the bar. He had now taken over from the publican and his wife. They were busy packing and dropped in for a cup of tea and a biscuit. After morning tea the publican and his wife packed their car and then came in to say goodbye.

"Hope you enjoy the experience, and we wish you a merry Christmas," the publican said.

His wife echoed these sentiments and there were handshakes all round. Then the publican and his wife went out to their car and got in. With much waving and cheerful calling of 'Merry Christmas' they drove away.

Their departure left Andrew feeling both relieved and also a bit anxious. Now his family had the responsibility for running a bush pub at one of the most important times of the year. Andrew knew enough from what he had overheard to understand that the hotel was an extremely important focus for the social life of the locals.

No sooner had they returned to the kitchen and settled on the stools than a tall, reddish haired youth in his late teens strode in.

"Hi!" he called loudly, thrusting out his hand as he did. "I'm your cousin Sandy."

There were more handshakes. Carmen raised an eyebrow and said, "Sandy?"

"Alexander," Cousin Sandy replied, favouring Carmen with a dazzling smile.

Andrew took an instant dislike to Cousin Sandy. He was a good looking youth but seemed to be very full of himself. But Andrew hid his feelings and managed to smile. Luckily Carmen did most of the talking.

"What do you do Sandy?" she asked.

"Drive trucks mostly," Sandy replied.

"What sort of trucks," Carmen asked.

"Cattle trucks mostly but anything really," Cousin Sandy replied.

He began describing all the makes and brands of truck that he had driven and to Andrew it seemed as though he was just 'big-noting' himself in an attempt to impress Carmen.

Andrew was saved from this by his father coming in and asking him to help move stock in the storeroom. Lifting and shifting crates of beer and spirits appealed to Andrew more than listening to Cousin Sandy so he quickly made his excuses and fled, leaving Carmen to listen to him.

She took him to task over this at lunch time, after Cousin Sandy had gone. "You toad, Andrew," she said. "Leaving me to put up with Cousin Sandy's descriptions of what a marvellous fellow he is!"

Andrew could only laugh. "Serves you right," he replied. "You shouldn't flirt with older men."

"I was not flirting!" Carmen cried indignantly. "I didn't encourage him at all."

"What about those miners this morning?" Andrew retorted.

This time a distinct blush mottled Carmen's neck and cheeks and she snorted and denied she had done any such thing.

Their mother ended this by saying, "That will do children. That's enough of that sort of talk. Now, what are you going to do after lunch?"

Andrew had thought about that and he at once said, "I thought we might explore the river."

"Yes, alright, but don't go far and don't get lost and keep an eye out for crocodiles," his mother replied.

Andrew shook his head. "There aren't any crocs in this part of the river."

"How do you know?" his mother queried.

"Someone told me," Andrew answered lamely. "They said they can't climb up the falls down below the highway bridge."

"Someone eh? I hope they are right. Crocs are just big lizards remember. They can walk cross-country," his mother retorted.

"But the river up here is fresh water isn't it. The only crocs that are dangerous are saltwater crocs," Andrew answered.

As he said this, his father came into the room and heard him. He at once shook his head and said, "Don't you believe it son. They are called *crocodilius porosus* or 'estuarine crocodiles' but they live quite happily in brackish or fresh water. They are like all those crocs that live in other freshwater streams: Nile crocodiles, alligators, caimans of South America and so on. You be very careful near any waterhole. Don't you children swim in any of the coastal creeks or rivers, even if they are freshwater. Saltwater crocodiles quite happily live in them and if one gets hold of you, you are done for. It will do a death roll to break your joints and bones and will then drag you under to drown you. So you be careful."

"Yes Dad," Andrew replied.

He knew that from hard experience and mentally quailed at images of torn and rotting flesh. Two years before he and Carmen and some friends from Townsville had witnessed a murder in the mangrove swamps south of that city and during their desperate flight to escape the murderers they had witnessed a man being caught and killed by a monster croc. They had then spent a terrifying night up a tree while the creature rose with the incoming tide and attempted to get them.[3] For a few seconds the crocodile's larder filled his thoughts and he shuddered as horrible images of a dismembered body being stashed under the roots of a mangrove tree or under a snag in a deep hole.

He had also seen other crocodiles in the wild and had no desire to be caught by one. To change the subject he said, "Who is Cousin Sandy related to?"

His father rolled his eyes. "My side of the family. He is one of my brother Brian's sons. I have a whole swarm of brothers and sisters who have broods of kids. This part of the world is swarming with cousins of yours."

Andrew glanced at Carmen and smirked, then said, "Kissing cousins?"

Carmen scowled, then laughed. "We will see little brother. The laugh will be on you if one of them turns out to be a very pretty female cousin!"

"Fat chance of that!" Andrew said as he walked out to go to his room.

After cleaning his teeth he lay down to read for a few minutes while he waited for Carmen. Ten minutes later there was a knock on the door. Thinking it was Carmen Andrew called out, "Come in!"

The door was flung and a teenage girl strode in; a big, strapping, buxom teenage girl with ginger hair. She stopped and studied him, her hands on her hips.

Then she smiled and said, "Hi! I'm your cousin Jean."

---

[3] Read *Bowling Green Bay* by C. R. Cummings

Chapter 11

ANNAN RIVER

Andrew stared and knew he was staring and then blushed. Flustered and slightly embarrassed, he struggled to his feet. Through the door behind Cousin Jean appeared a smiling Carmen and his mother.

Cousin Jean looked Andrew up and down and then grinned. "Gee, you are good looking. Give me a kiss."

Before Andrew could react she stepped forward, slid her arms around his neck and pulled him hard against her. Then she kissed him firmly on the lips. Andrew was too surprised to resist and he was also very aware of her curves against him. Out of the corner of his eye he saw Carmen's smile change to a grin and he flamed with embarrassment.

To his relief, Cousin Jean released him and said, "Nice to meet ya, cousin. I hope we see lots more of each other."

Andrew could only nod and mumble, hotly conscious of his sister and mother and wondering if Cousin Jean was implying something else. For something to say he said, "Do you live here?"

Cousin Jean shook her head. "Nah! I live in Mossman. We are just up here for the Christmas holidays."

Andrew's mother now saved him from further embarrassment by asking them to join the other relatives on the veranda. As they made their way out, Carmen met Andrew's eye and winked, then giggled.

"No chance of meeting any good looking female cousins, eh?" she whispered.

Andrew blushed again and pretended he did not hear. But he could not stop his gaze travelling over Cousin Jean. He saw that she was slightly taller than him, had a nice waist and hips but a bum that looked just a bit too big. Her legs were shapely but covered in freckles. She wore tight white shorts and a cotton shirt that was tied to expose part of her waist.

When she turned to face him again he noted that her face was plain and freckled but that her blue eyes were very alive. She grinned at him as he was introduced to her father, mother and little brother and sister. Andrew shook hands with Uncle Brian and wondered how he could possibly be the father of strapping big Cousin Jean, as he was a weedy little man with thin face and body.

He also learned that Cousin Jean's mother, Aunty Ethel, was his father's big sister. The other two cousins, 12 year old Charmaine and 10 year old Simon, said hello but seemed very shy.

Carmen and her mother did most of the talking while Andrew cast frequent shy and curious glances at Cousin Jean.

Carmen asked, "Where are you staying?"

"At 'Home Rule'. It is a holiday camp about twelve kilometres south of here in the rainforest," Aunty Ethel replied. "It's a lovely place. You must come and visit us."

"We will," Andrew's mother assured her.

It transpired that Uncle Brian was a road worker for the Mossman Shire Council and that they went to Home Rule for holidays every year. There was a lot of gossip between the adults, which bored Andrew but in which Carmen joined.

Andrew found himself beside Cousin Jean. She said, "Are you still at school?"

"Yes. I start Year 12 next year," he answered.

Cousin Jean nodded and said quietly, "I start Year 11. But I'm sixteen. That makes me legal."

Andrew was quite unsure what to make of this. *Does she mean she is over the 'age of consent for sex'?* he wondered. *And if it does, what is she implying?* He found he could only nod and blush. *Surely she can't be that brazen and forward?* he wondered.

But then his mind exploded into a riot of fantasies, and he found he could not tear his eyes away from the deliciously large curves of her body.

To his annoyance, Carmen noticed this and gave him several teasing smirks. As soon as she and Andrew were alone for a moment, she smirked and said, "What was that about pretty female cousins and kissing?"

Andrew blushed, knew he was blushing and got grumpy. "Humpff!" he snorted, making Carmen trill with laughter and scuttle out of his reach.

But there was no doubt Andrew was fascinated by Cousin Jean. He found he had difficulty taking his eyes of her and he began to fantasise and speculate. It was with regret that he waved her goodbye when the family drove off just before lunch.

At lunch time Carmen twisted the knife more by asking their mother about the relations and then saying, "We should go to visit them at this Home Rule place."

Her mother looked at her and gave a wry smile before answering, "We shall. Now, what are you children doing this afternoon?"

"Oh Mum! We aren't children!" Carmen cried.

"You are, so don't play games and get out of your depth, either of you," her mother replied.

She then gave Andrew a 'meaningful' look as well and he experienced an extraordinary surge of guilt. Her eyes seemed to say, *I can read your mind!* and he blushed at the thoughts that had been squirming in it.

"No Mum," was all he could croak. To change the subject he said, "I thought we would explore the river."

"Upstream or down?"

"Upstream," Andrew answered.

His mother nodded. "Alright. Just remember what your father said about crocodiles. And watch out for snakes."

"Yes Mum."

So half an hour later, dressed in shorts and shirts over bathers and wearing boots on their feet brother and sister made their way down the grassy slope behind the hotel. They strolled through the glade of large trees and past the camping 'lodges'. A dirt vehicle track led them down to the bank of the river.

As soon as he saw it, Andrew decided he liked the Annan River. At that, point a rocky bar separated a long, deep pool upstream from a delightful set of shallow rapids downstream. A large flat rock protruded into the bottom end of the pool and gave a good view in all directions. Just upstream of it was a small sandy beach. For a couple of minutes Andrew scanned the water carefully, fear of crocodiles very strong in him. But the water was mostly shallow and very clear and he decided it was safe.

Downstream was a large area of clean white sand in small ridges topped by water bent trees. The sand was nice to walk on and provided shady and pleasant places for picnics and sunbathing. The rapids ran on the far side of this, the water only knee deep at most and crystal clear. It was also refreshingly cold. Beaches of sand and pebbles edged the rapids and another shallow stretch of the river below them. Trees lined both banks but the vegetation on the steep far bank was mostly savannah woodland rather than the rain forest Andrew had expected.

Brother and sister made their way upstream along the bank. This had bushes and shrubs growing so thickly amidst the trees lining the bank that they had trouble picking a path. But Andrew persevered because when standing on the rock he had espied a wide sandy area further upstream. After a hundred paces of pushing through what was almost rainforest he reached this. It turned out to be the sandy beach and shallows on the inside of a sharp bend in the river.

He made his way out onto this and looked around. Directly opposite was the top end of the long, deep pool. Another rocky outcrop over looked this on the far bank. The other bank was now higher and steeper and covered in quite dense undergrowth including lantana. This was growing amid savannah woodland that was almost a proper forest. That bank rose fairly steeply for about ten metres before levelling out but there was a hint of higher ground beyond.

To Andrew's left, upstream, the river shallowed into a series of knee deep rapids but these were over pebbles and coarse sand rather than rocks. The river meandered gently from one side of its bed to the other and there were several small, low islands with small bushes growing on them. Both banks were overhung by dense masses of dark green foliage.

But the river was wide enough for there to be a good 50 metres of open bed and the sun shone down brightly to light it up and make it a very attractive place. After a careful look for crocodiles, Andrew knelt at the water's edge and washed his face and felt both happy and refreshed. Carmen joined him and looked around with cries of delight.

"What a lovely place!" she said.

They lingered there for quite a few minutes watching the birds and a magnificent blue butterfly before continuing on. At the top end of the sandy beach was a pipeline and pump. Andrew assumed that it was for the hotel but when he followed it up under the trees past a pump he found a vehicle track that led up into the dry rainforest at an angle that indicated that it actually went to one of the houses south of the hotel.

He and Carmen only went about fifty paces up the vehicle track before stopping at a line of marker pegs.

"Be the property boundary," Carmen suggested. "We had better not trespass."

Andrew agreed. For a few minutes he just stood and studied the dry rain forest they now found themselves in. It was quiet dark and gloomy with plenty of trees but very little undergrowth. Instead, there was a lot of deadfall, mostly dry leaves that crackled underfoot. A couple of scrub turkeys scuttled away, causing his heart to flutter with anxiety until he identified what they were. He had not forgotten for one minute his mother's warnings about snakes or wild pigs.

Finding what appeared to be an old road which ran parallel to the river, he set off along it. When this trended up inside the boundary markers he left the track and walked through the open forest and then down onto the sandy bed of a small flood overflow channel. This led them out to the open river bed again after about a hundred metres

They walked along the river bed on the sand and pebbles beside the water for the next hundred metres until the river changed direction and the main stream of the river changed over to their side. This forced them up onto the higher bank. At first they could walk along another flood channel under a line of shady trees but then the channel ended and they had to follow the top of a bank that was sharply eroded on their right with a three metre drop to the water. They crossed another vehicle track and water pipe going up the bank and Andrew noted that it led to where the roof of a house was just visible.

The second house, he decided.

They pressed on, hoping to come back to the road as his map indicated they should. The 'going' became quite difficult and painful and the animal pad they were now following wound through head high guinea grass or blady grass which was thickly matted with lantana and very prickly bushes.

After a hundred metres of this they passed under a power line which crossed the river. A vehicle track led up the bank and across a weed-covered field to the base of Helenvale Hill. Andrew knew that the main road was somewhere there at the base of the hill, but he also decided that the vehicle track led up through someone's paddock and he did not want any trouble over trespassing, so he suggested that they continue on.

The river curved back to the right and brother and sister entered a belt of rainforest growing on the bank. It was quite dense and more nearly the wet tropical rainforest than the dry forest behind the hotel. There were even a few clumps of the viciously barbed 'Wait-a-while' plant.

Both Andrew and Carmen had some experience of this from a weekend expedition to try to find a World War 2 aircraft wreck in the Graham Range the previous year so they managed to safely negotiate the area.

As they pushed through the jungle beside the river, Andrew heard two vehicles go past only a short distance away and that cheered him up too as it told him that the main road was close. He was about to suggest they turn left and make their way through the narrow belt of jungle to the road when his eye detected a clearing of some sort ahead.

As that looked closer, he made his way on along the riverbank for another 25 paces and found himself on a gentle slope in under large trees. In a shallow cutting, with its sides long collapsed, he saw another vehicle track which went down to the river bed and across it at yet another shallow ford. This vehicle track, unlike the others, had signs of frequent and recent use.

Andrew walked down the steep, leaf mould-covered slope to the bed of the river and stood between the muddy wheel ruts. He saw that the river bed here was made of white and grey pebbles and that upstream to his left was another long, deep pool. The pool was lined on both banks by dense jungle which overhung the water on both sides. But the main stream was still 50 metres wide and Andrew saw that the vehicle track went up the other bank through a very distinct tunnel in the rainforest.

After looking around for a minute or so, Carmen rinsed the sweat off her face in the river and then suggested it was time they headed home. So they turned and walked in under the trees and up the shallow cutting through another tunnel of rainforest. Sunlight ahead indicated that the vehicle track came out into a clearing so they followed it. Sure enough they emerged on the main gravel road a minute later.

Brother and sister stood on the road and looked both ways. It was better than the average country gravel road but only just. On both sides was a wall of forest, thicker along the river than on the slopes of the hill.

Carmen pointed south. "This is the road to Cairns isn't it?"

"Yes, after passing through half a dozen other places along the way," Andrew agreed. He checked his map. "There is a place called Rossville about another ten kilometres down the road."

As he said this his eye noted other places on the map: a side road and a clearing in the jungle and the name 'Home Rule'. Through his mind surged a vivid memory of Cousin Jean and of how she felt and smelt. To his consternation, he experienced a surge of arousal that quite concerned him. Then he blushed at his lustful thoughts, even though his rational mind told him that his sister could not possibly read his mind.

But then he wondered if she could when she said, "It goes past Cape Tribulation and on down to Mossman, doesn't it?"

"Yes," Andrew agreed and he remembered that Cousin Jean came from Mossman. Thinking about her made him blush some more.

To hide this he turned and began walking north in the direction of the hotel. Carmen walked with him and chattered on about the butterflies and birds she could see or hear. In this way they reached the next bend, where the road curved to the left.

As they reached the bend, Andrew heard the sound of a vehicle approaching from the north. He and Carmen moved to the grassy verge as the sound indicated the vehicle was being driven at speed.

Locals who know the road, Andrew surmised.

Around the corner came a dark green 4WD, all spattered in mud and being driven far too fast for safety. At the last minute, the driver seemed to notice them as the vehicle slewed and skidded, then raced past. As it went by Andrew got a glimpse of the people in it. The driver was Barry and in the passenger seat, staring towards him wide-eyed was Little Terry.

Andrew turned to watch and raised a hand to wave, even though the incident had given him a scare.

"Little Terry, with his dad," he called to Carmen.

She nodded and went to reply then frowned as the vehicle suddenly slowed, its engine noise rising sharply as the driver used his gears to slow down. For a moment Andrew thought the driver was going to stop and then come back to talk to them, but then he saw he was wrong. After barely slowing to a safe speed, the green 4WD turned abruptly off the main road and vanished into the jungle down the same track he and Carmen had just walked up.

"That must be where they live?" Andrew suggested.

Carmen nodded. "Maybe. I hope that little boy is alright. He didn't look very happy just then."

"Probably scared stiff at the speed his dad was driving," Andrew suggested.

The pair resumed their march. This brought them into a section of road along which the afternoon sun was shining and both quickly began to sweat. The road then curved back to the right and patches of open grass showed between the road and the jungle lining the riverbank. A couple of minutes later they rounded yet another curve on a gentle rise, and Andrew saw they were at the end of the long straight that led past the hotel. It was about half a kilometre long and the second of the houses was in an open field off to the left.

Along the way, Andrew kept alternately glancing towards the two houses set back in the open fields to the left and into the open forest growing on the steep slopes of Helenvale Hill on his right. He noted several horses in a paddock near the second house and also a dog but saw no people.

The walk back to the hotel only took ten minutes but by the time they arrived Andrew was hot and dusty and felt he had walked enough. It was a relief to step up into the shade of the front veranda. He and Carmen went through into the lounge-dining room and saw their mother serving in the bar. They went to the side bar to tell her what they had seen and accepted from her a bottle of cold soft drink each.

As he took his, Andrew eyed the characters in the bar and noted several real 'bushies' with stockman's hats and shirts and also a couple of obvious tourists, one wearing shorts and sandals with long socks.

Brother and sister settled on a padded bench seat on the veranda and began to sip their cold drinks. As they did, the clip-clop of a horse's hooves sounded and into sight rode a stockman. A blue heeler cattle dog trotted at the horse's heels.

At the sight of the stockman, Andrew nudged Carmen and muttered, "This bloke is the genuine article."

"Like stepping back in time a hundred years," she agreed.

The man was about fifty with a sun-browned and lined face. He wore a battered grey felt hat, a light blue work shirt and faded blue long trousers. On his feet he wore the ubiquitous elastic-sided riding boots and spurs. But what really caught Andrew's eye was that he had a 'six-shooter' revolver in a holster strapped to his hip. A rifle hung in a saddle bucket and a coiled stockwhip hung from the pommel.

The stockman dismounted and tied the horse to a fence post across the road where there was grass for it to crop and then he walked across towards them, the dog trotting at his heels. As the stockman stepped up onto the veranda he gave a half-smile at Andrew, doffed his hat in a courteous old-fashioned way to Carmen and muttered, "G'day." He then said, "Stay Bluey," as he strode through into the bar.

'Bluey', the cattle dog, did obediently 'stay'. He flopped onto the veranda, tongue lolling out and tail half-wagging as he eyed brother and sister. Andrew looked at the dog with concern, worried that it might bite but then saw that it was a working dog and well-trained and that it was also quite friendly. He knew enough not to try to pet the creature and resumed sipping his drink.

A few minutes later another vehicle arrived, a battered green truck with a covered tray back. It had an ex-army look about it. It parked under the trees almost in front of Andrew and two men got out, two of the most villainous looking men that Andrew had ever seen. One was a big bear of a man in dirty blue singlet and grubby dark blue shorts and the other was a tall, lean, hatchet faced man dressed in well washed blue shorts and shirt. The big bear had bare feet but the other wore work boots. The men barely glanced at Andrew and Carmen as they went into the bar.

The only things Andrew overheard was the big bear saying, "What will you have, Jan?" and Jan, the lean, mean looking one, replying, "Whisky, thanks Wes."

Carman shook her head and whispered, "They look a fairly rough pair."

Andrew nodded. "I agree, and they've got a gun in their truck." He nodded towards the vehicle where he had just noted the gun, a rifle of some sort, hung up in clips across the back of the cab.

But further conversation was ended by their mother appearing and telling them to have their showers and get changed ready for tea.

"But it's early yet, Mum," Andrew protested.

"Maybe, but the miners will come off shift soon and they will all want a shower so get in while you can," she replied.

Chapter 12

SUNDAY PICNIC

Andrew slept well that night. Even the flying foxes squabbling and the mangos hitting the roof did not disturb him much. Nor did the still humidity of the air. When he woke in the morning he felt fresh and rested. Just walking across the cool dewy grass to the ablutions made him feel alive.

I like this place, he decided.

As on the previous day the miners were up early but they were not going to work. A couple said they were going fishing and two more said they were going to town. As on the previous morning Carmen flirted with them as she served their breakfast and that bothered Andrew.

Also, as on the previous morning, after breakfast Andrew was set to work sweeping and picking up mangos. This was interrupted twice by vehicles coming from the south that needed refuelling. Andrew learned how to do this and it made him feel a bit more useful. He even chatted to the people in the vehicles when they asked him who he was and how long he would be there.

There was then a lull for an hour or so during which he lay on the front sofa on the veranda and read a book. During this time three more vehicles went past going north and two going south. Only one of them looked local and the driver, a bearded man Andrew had never seen, waved as he went by.

Then just before 10 o'clock things began to liven up. First a Toyota ute arrived with two stockmen. They went into the bar. Then another vehicle came from the south and Andrew recognised 'Irish'. They chatted for a few minutes before Irish also went into the bar. Then three cars arrived and stopped at the side gate. One of the drivers came and asked Andrew's dad if they could go through for a picnic on the riverbank.

Andrew's dad nodded and called, "Andrew, open the gate for these people please."

Andrew made his way along under the mango trees to the gate. He was not really interested and had not looked carefully at the cars but as he came close to the first one he saw a mop of silver-blonde hair above a cheeky grin at a rear window and his spirits leapt.

"Hi Andrew!" the girl called.

"Hi! (*What the devil is her name?*) er... Kristen," Andrew replied.

He now noted that her busty brunette mate Daphne was beside her in the back along with another younger girl. In the front was a tubby blonde woman with huge boobs bulging out of her top who could only be Kristen's mother, and the man who gave him a sharp glance as he got into the driver's seat Andrew decided was her dad.

Andrew blushed but in his mind instantly reorganised his somewhat hazy plans for the day so as to try to get to meet the girls. As the cars drove in along the side track across the lawn, he watched and just knew he had to try. Just knowing they were there set him all a tingle.

This became something more akin to an urgent itch when he strolled casually down to the river a few minutes later and saw the girls in their bathing costumes. Kristen wore a bikini and Daphne wore a plum coloured one-piece. To Andrew's eyes there seemed to be tantalising glimpses of quivering female curves wherever he looked. Even Kristen's mother was half exposed with a low-cut top to her bathing costume that revealed a staggering quantity of trembling cleavage.

But first there were the parents and other adults to get by. Kristen's father and another middle-aged man were busy setting up a portable barbeque while other adults were unfolding what seemed to be dozens of chairs and tables. Luckily the adults had decided to set up their cooking and eating arrangements at the end of the vehicle track up from the river so Andrew was able to saunter through and down the foot track to where the children were busy playing and splashing in the shallows.

When Andrew came out into the open through a gap in the trees, he was confronted by the sight of Daphne bending over facing him. The sheer size and splendour of her bosom made him gape and his itch became the distinct stirrings of arousal.

Daphne looked up and saw him but remained bending over. "Hello Andrew. Are you coming for a swim too?" she asked.

"If I'm invited," Andrew replied, trying not to appear to be looking while at the same time enjoying the view. He hoped he sounded suitably cool and gallant.

Daphne beamed and crouched down, her knees pushing her bosom up so that it bulged noticeably. Andrew could hardly tear his eyes from the spectacle, and he knew his hands were twitching and just yearning to touch.

"I'd love to," he replied.

Kristen was nearby with two younger girls of about ten or twelve and she looked up and said, "Oh, please do!"

Andrew noted that her bikini top was so small that it appeared that her breasts would pop out at any moment. He goggled at them for a few seconds before remembering not to stare.

"I will go and get my bathers," he said, flushing with arousal and guilt.

"Be quick," Daphne called as he hurried away up through the trees and across the sand to the track.

By this time Andrew knew that he was not thinking straight but he could not seem to help himself. More than anything he wanted to be swimming with those girls. But he also foresaw that his mother and Carmen might not be amused and might immediately see how he was affected. There were also the girl's parents, now seated on the folding chairs in the shade and drinking beer from cans in stubby coolers.

Andrew sauntered past them, pretending not to be interested but actually blushing with guilt at his lustful thoughts. He found it a relief to be up among the lodges and out of their gaze. Then he slowed his walk and considered his next move. He did not want either his mother or his sister seeing him with the girls.

That led him to walk up the vehicle track behind the ablutions and then to skirt around behind them to near the portacabins before strolling in an apparently casual way across the back lawn to his room. In reality his heart was hammering and he was awash with guilt and anxiety.

As quickly as he could, he changed into his bathers, uncomfortably aware that they were a bit too tight and that he was already getting aroused. To hide his intentions, he then pulled on shorts and shirt again. After a quick check that no-one was watching from the kitchen, he made his way back down to the riverbank via the same route. The only variation was to veer to the right, avoiding the adults at their barbeque. Another foot track that led down to the river from the camping ground gave him covered access to the river bed.

He found the girls still playing in the shallows at the top end of the rapids. They were working to build a dam by piling stones in the gaps between the rocky outcrops. As Andrew peeled off his shorts and shirt, Daphne looked up and gave him a big smile. That encouraged him, so he walked over to join them, noting as he did that Kristen had a very lovely shape from behind.

Andrew waded in and began picking up rocks and adding them to the loose piles that composed the dam. He worked so that he faced Daphne and she began chattering happily to him while she continually bent over to work on the dam. The whole time Andrew enjoyed seeing her in her swimsuit. To his consternation, his mouth went dry with lust and he quickly became aroused.

She must be aware that I can see a lot? he thought, noting Kristen giving him grins as she also bent forward. Only the little girls and one little boy did not seem to notice, but they also kept casting odd glances at him.

Andrew quickly became so aroused that he had to be careful that he did not stand up, lest they see it. But he was quickly put to the test when one of the little girls dragged an inflatable mattress into the water and went floating off down the rapids on it. When she came wading back up dragging the air mattress behind her, the other little girls insisted on having a go. Then the small boy wanted a ride. Kristen walked with him to make sure he was alright. She then had a go. As she waded back upstream, pulling the air mattress Andrew could not help admiring her curvy shape.

"You have a go, Andrew," she said, offering him the air mattress.

"Oh, Daphne can have her go first," he insisted.

With his heart pounding with lust and anxiety, he remained crouched in the shallows. So Daphne had a go and then she came back, breasts wobbling, every line of her body keeping him aroused as she offered the mattress to him.

Rather than make a fuss, Andrew quickly took the air mattress and moved across to the deeper channel. In doing so he had to stand up and take several steps and he flamed with embarrassment. As quickly as he could, he lay face down on the air mattress and went sliding off down the rapids.

But the rapids only went for 50 metres and within a minute he came to the top end of the next long pool and he had to face walking back.

Rather than drag the air mattress, he tried to pick it up and carry it in front of him. In this he was mostly successful except that he was sure the girls could tell he was aroused and that their smiles were actually knowing smirks.

As he reached the girls again, Kristen said, "Let's all go for a ride on the mattress." She took hold of the mattress and said, "You hop on behind me, Andrew."

Andrew saw no choice as he remained bent over holding the mattress against the current. He then slid on behind Kristen. As he did, the mattress buckled in the middle and she slid back hard against him and he found himself pressing against her. To add to his pleasure and discomfiture, Daphne moved and swung her leg across the air mattress and sat behind him. Andrew found her legs against his and her breasts pressing firmly against his back. The two little girls and the little boy then climbed on behind her.

Then they were off down the rapids. But the water was so shallow and the air mattress so overloaded that it dragged along the bottom most of the way and they had to keep using their feet and hands to push or had to lift their feet to get over rocks. In the process Andrew found himself with girls pressing and rubbing on him from both directions. He was sure that Kristen could feel his maleness and he was in a lather of anxiety lest she be offended.

But then she showed him that she wasn't, that in fact the opposite was the case. When they got to deeper water, the air mattress capsized and everyone ended up in thigh deep water on a sandy bottom. As they stood up and went to get back aboard, Kristen very obviously looked at it and smiled, then bumped against him as they resumed their seats.

Andrew found that air mattress ride one of the most erotic and arousing experiences of his young life. And it got better. They drifted on down the next reach, a long, shallow curve with sandy bottom and a few gentle rapids and rolled over again. This time one of the little girls, obviously Kristen's little sister, got water up her nose and began to cry so Kirsten comforted her and moved to sit behind Andrew with the little sister holding her.

Daphne moved to the front and as she sat down she bumped against Andrew. He tried to move back but couldn't. She then leaned back against him so that her thighs were touching his.

The raft drifted on, with people using their hands to paddle when it slowed too much in the deeper stretches. By then the air mattress was at the curve below the hotel and here the banks changed so that there was a steep bank lined with grass and trees on the right and a fairly deep channel directly below it. On the other side of the river the water gradually shallowed to a long sandy beach on the inside of the wide curve.

As they slid around this curve, Daphne surprised Andrew even more by grabbing hold of his hands and bringing them around to her front. She held them clasped against her stomach. That was enough to send him into a palpitation of worry in case Kristen or the little girls behind could see.

By then they had drifted around to where Mungumby Creek flowed into the Annan. Andrew saw that right at the mouth of the creek the river widened to form a deep and murky looking pool of dark blue-green water. Several large tree trunks were caught on the outside of the bend as snags.

Then something else in the shadows under the bank caught his eye and his heart skipped a beat. But then he relaxed. *Not a crocodile,* he thought with relief, seeing that it was only a half-submerged log. But even so it got his brain working again and anxiety about crocs crept in.

"I think we had better start back," he suggested.

The girls did not argue but it proved harder to do than suggest. The current was just strong enough to make it very slow and hard work paddling back upstream. So they angled over to the shallows on the far bank and climbed off the rubber mattress. Andrew did not really want to stand up and walk but he had no choice, so he took hold of the thing and tried to keep it between him and the little girls.

But that meant that both Daphne and Kristen were able to see his arousal, to Andrew's embarrassment. Almost gasping with anxiety he noted that their eyes were continually glancing with evident interest. The obvious fact that they were not offended emboldened him and he stayed aroused for most of the 200 metre walk back upstream. To hide his state for much of the way, he hurried ahead and skittered along in the shallows, splashing up water and making a game of things.

In this way they arrived back at the top end of the rapids. As they neared the place, Andrew's mind feverishly turned over plans to try to get one or both of the girls away on their own. But he had failed to think of one and was all tongue tied. He was saved by the arrival through the trees of a boy of about 8 or 9 who called to Kristen to bring Cecilia.

Kristen gave Andrew an annoyed look but obediently took her little sister and made her way up towards the barbeque area. To Andrew's relief, the other little girl and boy and the young messenger went as well. To Andrew's surprise, he found himself standing beside the river with Daphne.

"What will we do now?" he managed to say.

She giggled and gave him a knowing look before answering, "What would you like to do?"

That got Andrew's mind and body going again but also paralysed him with anxiety. He knew what he wanted to say but did not dare. Instead, he stammered, "How about a swim?"

"Alright," Daphne purred back.

She led the way to the deeper water above the rapids and slid in. Andrew followed her, relieved to be able to hide his aroused condition. The water was surprisingly cold but it had no effect on his heated state.

They did not swim far before she stopped and waited for him. Andrew found himself standing in neck deep water facing her and wondering what to do next.

She looked at him and then said, "Would you like a kiss?"

Andrew could not believe his luck. He nodded eagerly and moved closer. The next minute they were in each other's arms and kissing. It was instantly obvious to Andrew that Daphne had been kissed before, probably many times. But it was nice and she was willing. He put his arms around her waist and pulled her close, not caring that she might feel his hardness. She obviously could as she writhed and pressed her body against his and his senses went reeling into overheated overdrive.

He found he was pressing hard against her and some part of his heated brain warned him to slow down and be careful. But she seemed warm and willing and the urge to do more grew until he did not care.

But then voices on the bank above them induced a sudden dose of reason and caution. Annoyed and at the same time fearful, Andrew drew away from Daphne and looked up. He could not see anyone but could tell that the voices were just up through the screen of trees and bushes.

Afraid that they be caught, and that he might get into trouble from the parents, he knew were just up at the barbeque area he whispered, "Let's move upstream a bit further."

To his pleasure and relief, Daphne nodded eagerly and smiled at him. They released each other and began swimming silently up the river, keeping close in under the trees as far as they could.

After about 50 metres they began to run into shallow water. To stay in the deeper flow meant moving across to the other side of the river.

That will make us very visible to anyone looking up the river from the barbeque area, Andrew reasoned.

So he stood up and walked up onto the sand under the overhanging trees. Daphne followed him, smiling, her eyes alight with excitement. Now no longer concerned what she could see, Andrew took her hand and walked with her further upstream and around the bend on the nice sandy beach. When he was sure they were out of sight of anyone down at the rapids, Andrew stopped and faced her. By this time his heart was hammering with aroused passion and anxiety but he really wanted to kiss Daphne, and maybe to go a bit further.

She seemed very willing and came to him in a tight embrace that got them pressed hard against each other. To Andrew it was wonderful. He revelled in the feel of her smooth skin, the coolness of the water drops drying on his skin in the breeze, of the taste and scent of her. He was also fearfully aroused by the sensation and appearance of her arousal and mounting desire. The way her eyes widened and her breath came in rapid pants added to his interest.

After a couple of minutes of heated kissing they released each other. For another minute or so they just stood and looked into each other's eyes and Andrew marvelled at how wonderful nature was and of his own good fortune. He also understood that he was breathing fast because he was also scared.

I wonder if she will let me? he wondered.

Andrew had never had sex but had seen it several times, and he was at that age where he was deeply interested and was torn by the moral dilemma and also the challenge to his manhood of not knowing whether he could do it or not. This uncertainty had built over recent times into a gnawing anxiety.

Another 25 metres along was a narrow channel in under the trees. The water was crystal clear and flowing in the shade over a smooth sandy bottom. It looked to be about waist deep. Thinking how hot it was out in the sun, Andrew led Daphne in under the trees and waded in. The water turned out to be chest deep in its deepest part and was deliciously cool.

Without any words spoken they came together again in a passionate embrace. For several minutes they kissed and Andrew thought it was the most enjoyable experience he had ever had. But he could feel those large breasts of hers pressing against him and every time they leaned apart they bulged up just in the bottom of his field of vision. The urge to touch them mounted with every minute.

Very tentatively he began to move his hands around her back and waist and then up to her shoulders and neck. She obviously liked that so next time they kissed he slid a hand down over her buttocks and thigh and right up her side. Feeling very daring, he moved his hand to her shoulders and throat and gently stroked.

After more kissing and her not rebuffing his explorations, he became even more daring and gently slipped her shoulder strap off. Andrew started breathing in hot gasps. To him she looked beautiful and absolutely desirable, and all he could do was stare and admire. They came together and kissed fiercely again. He thought he was in heaven.

Bang!

The gunshot was very close and sent a spasm of pure terror through him. In a near panic Andrew let Daphne go and looked around.

Sprung! his frightened mind cried.

Chapter 13

MIXED EMOTIONS

Andrew whipped his hands away from Daphne as though she had suddenly become red hot. As he flustered in alarm, he was confused by the noises around him. From under the trees nearby came men's voices calling loudly. From behind him came a terrible series of shrieks and howls. Uncertain what to do, Andrew sank down into the water so that only his head was sticking out. Daphne did the likewise, at the same time struggling to pull her top back up.

The next moment, two men burst out of the cover of the trees and splashed across the narrow channel only ten metres upstream of Andrew. He goggled at them in alarm, noting that both had rifles and both looked very excited. Then his eyes focused and he realised that the men did not appear to have noticed either him or Daphne. Certainly they did not even glance in their direction but instead dashed on across the small sandy island and plunged into the waist deep water of the main channel.

Only then did Andrew look back over his shoulder to see what was making the hellish noise that was making the hairs on the back of his neck stand up. He saw that it was a dog, an orange-coloured dog, and it was writhing and twitching in violent convulsions. As it did, the dog emitted terrible howls of agony.

Dingo, Andrew told himself.

The unfortunate animal was unable to stand because its left hind leg was broken. By the blood and general mess, it was obvious that the bullet had done the job. Watching the stricken animal struggling frantically for its life appalled Andrew. The dingo was in such obvious fear and pain that its frantic attempts to scrabble up the steep bank caused Andrew to feel a sort of ghastly pity.

The animal's plight obviously had no such effect on the two men when they stopped on the other bank, as both were crying out with pleasurable excitement. One wore dark blue shorts and dark blue shirt and had a sharp face with a hooked nose. Only when he turned side on did it occur to Andrew that he had seen both men before.

The identification was helped by the second man calling loudly, "Shoot the bloody thing again, Jan! Don't let him get away!"

The evident blood lust in the second man's voice quite disgusted Andrew, who was still crouching in shock. But then his own survival instincts kicked in and he reached across and grabbed Daphne's hand and started walking towards the cover of the trees.

She started to protest to slow down but Andrew put his finger to his lips and hissed, "Shh! I don't think they saw us and we don't want them to."

Fear showed plainly in Daphne's eyes and she nodded and stumbled after him. As they waded ashore, Andrew kept glancing back, hoping that the sound of the wounded dingo and the men's own shouting would drown any noises they might make.

As Andrew looked back, he saw the man named Jan raise his rifle to aim. But the dingo was jumping and twitching so much that he had to keep adjusting his point of aim. That at least kept the men's attention focused that way and Andrew and Daphne were able to push up through the bushes and in under the big trees along the bank.

Just as they reached cover, the rifle fired again. Even though he was expecting it, Andrew flinched and he glanced back in time to see the dingo hurled flat by the force of the bullet that hit it in the chest. This time it lay on the bank just clear of the water. To Andrew's dismay, he saw that its eyes were still open and that it appeared to still be alive and struggling feebly.

Revulsion was added to disgust when the second man, a thin man with a straggly beard who Andrew had seen before, raced across and stamped his boot on the dying animal's neck. But that was only the beginning, and Andrew's disgust shot right up when the man laughed and stamped on the dingo, grinding his boot heel into its neck. Then he pulled out a wicked looking sheath knife and bent to grab the still struggling dingo.

The hatchet faced man, Jan, shook his head and said, "Geez, you is an animal Weed."

Andrew could only agree as he watched the thin man, Weed, begin slicing into the still living skin of the dingo. *Weed,* he thought, remembering the man who had leered at Carmen the day they arrived. Then he thought, *Judging by his accent, that Jan is a South African or something like that.*

Gagging noises behind Andrew made him glance behind him. It was Daphne. She was wide-eyed with horror and was retching. Andrew realised that the two men were still not aware that they were there, so he motioned to keep moving and led her on into the dry rainforest, leading her by the hand. As they made their way up into the undergrowth, Andrew had one last horrific glimpse of Weed peeling the dingo's scalp, exposing pink flesh and white bone and tendons and a gush of blood. The sight made him nauseous and he knew he was revolted by the entire incident.

When they were about fifty paces into the forest, Daphne looked back and whispered, "What was he doing? Why was he cutting at that dingo?"

"He was scalping it," Andrew replied.

"Why would he do that? It was revolting and very cruel," Daphne said. She looked very pale and obviously all thought of love had passed.

The incident had had the same effect on Andrew and he just felt sad and sick. He said, "The government pay a bounty for dingo scalps I think." It was something he had heard in the bar but had not paid much attention to the details.

But then Andrew was jerked back to his plight and the possibility of discovery by hearing voices. They were ahead of them to the left, somewhere along the riverbank.

Quite clearly Andrew heard Kristen's voice call, "Daphne! Daph, hey Daph. Where are you?"

Then a man's voice asked why she was down at the river when everyone else was up at the barbeque. *Oh no!* Andrew thought. *That might be her dad looking for her!* He felt his stomach contract.

Andrew's first instinct was to go the other way and to try to avoid the man, but then his pride kicked in and he swallowed with anxiety.

Better not, he told himself. *It will look even more suspicious if we get caught.*

So he led Daphne over towards the voices. It was easy going as there was very little undergrowth but he disliked walking on the thick carpet of dry dead leaves. Fear of snakes or scorpions caused him to tread warily.

Within twenty paces Andrew came out on the vehicle track that he and Carmen had found. He followed this and within another twenty paces came to where a fence blocked their path. Luckily it was partly broken down and the wire crushed low enough to step over. He climbed over and turned to help Daphne.

As he did, Kristen came pushing up through the thick growth of bushes along the riverbank, followed closely by a middle-aged man dressed in T-shirt, shorts and thongs. Kristen still wore her bikini.

She stopped on the foot track beyond and said, "Oh there you are. I wondered where you two had got to."

The man joined them and Andrew felt a surge of guilt. He could feel himself blushing and that made him even more anxious. The man frowned and said, "There you are, girl. Where the devil have you been, eh?"

"For a walk, Dad," Daphne answered.

"Walk? I thought you said a swim?" her father snapped. He cast suspicious glances at Andrew as he spoke, making Andrew feel queasy with worry.

Daphne answered, "Yer... er... yes we did, but the water got so shallow we had to walk."

Her father fixed Andrew with a hostile glare and snapped, "And who are you?"

Before Andrew could answer, Daphne said, "This is Andrew, Dad. He is a navy cadet."

"Oh yeah?" her father replied, his eyes alight with suspicion. "And what are you doing here, boy?"

Andrew wasn't sure if the man meant in the jungle or at the Lions Den, so he said, "I am staying at the hotel. I was just showing Daphne the river."

As he said this, Andrew saw Kristen cover a snicker and that caused him to blush even more. Daphne's father was obviously not impressed.

He snapped, "Well you can bloody well ask before you go sneaking off with my daughter." He glared at Andrew, who felt sick with worry and guilt. Then the man turned to Daphne and said, "You get back to your mother, girl! And put some clothes on and make yourself decent. Now what was that shooting? Have you got a gun, boy?"

"No sir. It is two men. They shot a dingo," Andrew replied. He was flaming with embarrassment but managed to stand his ground and kept the quaver out of his voice.

Daphne's father grunted and then turned and walked off after her. She hurried on along the foot track in the rain forest. Andrew followed more slowly, Kristen walking behind him.

To add to his discomfiture, Kirsten whispered, "Showing her the river were you?"

She said it in such a suggestive way and with such a knowing smirk that he blushed again. Then annoyance took over and he gave a surly grunt and turned off down a side track to the beach at the top end of the deep pool.

Kristen did not follow him, for which Andrew was glad. He now felt thoroughly ashamed and just wanted to creep away without further incident. So he walked through the trees in the river bed to retrieve his clothes, only to meet Carmen coming the other way.

Carmen stopped and looked him up and down, then said, "I didn't know you were down here swimming. Where are your clothes?"

"Just along here," Andrew replied, blushing again as his guilty conscience smote him.

"You alright? You look a funny colour," Carmen commented as she turned to walk with him.

More guilt! Andrew shook his head and said, "We just saw a dingo shot. It was awful." He described the two men and the shooting and brutal scalping of the dingo.

Carmen nodded and said, "We heard the shooting. Mum and Dad were worried, particularly when they could not find you. Who were you with?"

Andrew shrugged and did not want to answer. By then they had reached his clothes and he began to pull them on. But Carmen wouldn't let the subject drop.

"Were you with those girls from town?"

Andrew nodded and Carmen gave a told-you-so look and shook her head. As quickly as he could, Andrew dressed and set off back up the hotel. To avoid the girls' parents he took a track that detoured away from the barbeque area. Carmen followed, giving him another quizzical glance as she did. And there was more embarrassment. As he crossed the campground, Andrew saw that he and Carmen were visible to the people in the barbeque area and he burned with shame. It seemed that every step was an embarrassment and he still felt distinctly uneasy even after he had passed on out of their sight.

It didn't help that he had to make explanations to his mother. In doing so he glossed over the details of the swimming (And did not mention at all the kissing and petting, for which his conscience made him burn again). But he went into detail about the two men with guns who had shot and scalped the dingo.

His mother nodded and said, "Yes, that was what we were worried about. We heard the gunshots and wondered if you had taken one of the guns."

"Mum! Fair go! You know I wouldn't do anything like that. Besides, I didn't even know there were guns here," Andrew replied hotly.

To his relief, his mother accepted that and he was able to slip away to his room. Once there he lay down and pretended to read. But his mind would not focus on printed words on paper. Instead, it was fixed on heated and vivid images of scantily clad female forms and of the fantasies that rose from those images. He became very confused because he wasn't sure he liked Daphne at all.

Andrew was set to work shifting stock in the storeroom by his father, so he did not even see Daphne and the others leave later in the afternoon when they drove back to town. For that he was actually thankful, as he had no desire to have another confrontation with Daphne's father.

I will manage to see her again, he told himself, and that was his hope and fantasy for the evening and far into the night.

That evening there was heavy rain and that kept the drinkers away and cooled the oppressive humidity. The rain continued for most of the night, solid tropical downpours that thundered on the iron roof so loudly it made conversation difficult.

For Andrew it was a tiring night of fevered imaginings and heated memories. He had trouble sleeping and tossed and turned for hours, glad of the rain as it made it cooler and also covered the sound of his fidgeting.

It was pleasantly cool to begin with on Monday morning. Rain showers drifted across every half hour or so but rarely lasted more than ten or fifteen minutes. This time it was mostly fine misty rain and Andrew noted that it all seemed to come from the southeast, across Helenvale Hill.

From the sea, he mused, surprised at how much he felt like wanting a glimpse of the ocean. *I don't think I could live in inland Australia,* he decided. Even a week without seeing the sea seemed like a very long time.

After the morning rush of sweeping and helping with breakfast for the miners before they hurried off to work, Andrew joined Carmen and his parents at the breakfast table. His mother had cooked him a full meal of bacon and eggs and toast and he found he needed it.

As he ate, and after the rain had been discussed at length, he asked, "Is there anything happening today, Mum?"

His mother nodded and said, "Yes, we are going to Rossville to have lunch with Aunty Beryl and Uncle Jack. Then we are going on to have a look at this Home Rule place to say hello to Aunty Ethel and Uncle Brian."

At the mention of Rossville, Andrew had met Carmen's eyes and the image of Cousin Sandy flitted across his mind. But even before he could frame the thought that he might get a bit of his own back when Cousin Sandy flirted with Carmen (If he was there), his mind was filled with images of Cousin Jean. These got him both interested and anxious but he tried to hide both emotions and pretended only mild interest in the expedition.

"So who minds the hotel?" he asked.

"Your father. Now eat up and then help us clean up the campground and barbeque area. Those people yesterday left a bit of rubbish," his mother said.

At the mention of 'those people', Andrew had vivid images of Daphne and particularly of them pashing in the water and he experienced a surge of guilt. This was exacerbated when Carmen gave him a sardonic smile, her eyes glinting with mischief. To cover his confusion and to hide the fact that he was blushing, Andrew stood up and moved to do the washing up.

There were more mixed emotions as he helped Carmen and his mother pick up the litter and empty beer bottles down near the river. While he worked, Andrew puzzled over whether he liked Daphne and what he perceived to be his own weak character. Never before had he been so consumed by lust as to just want to have sex regardless. Always in the past any physical love had been the natural and pleasant result of emotional caring and love.

What really bothered him was that he knew he urgently wanted to get Daphne in his arms again, and his mind fantasised about what they might do. Even his shame and guilty conscience could not override the arousal and urgings of his body. He found it worrying.

The worry was exacerbated by the knowledge that in a couple of hours he might meet with the very physical Cousin Jean. She had seemed so experienced and forward that he felt stirrings the moment he thought of her.

So it was a fairly anxious boy that climbed into the family 4WD at 10:45. He sat in the back. Carmen and his mother sat in the front. They waved Mr Collins goodbye and left him to cope with four tourists who had just arrived in two 'campervans'.

The family drove south along the road, with the wooded slopes of Helenvale Hill on the left and the open fields and two houses on the right. Just after passing the second house, Andrew noted the powerline heading off across the river. He also observed how the line of trees along the riverbank converged on the road.

To his mother he said, "That is where we walked the other day."

As the 4WD rounded the first bend and he saw the side road going off on the right into the tunnel of jungle Andrew added, "And that is where we came up from the river."

As he said this Andrew noted a sign nailed to a tree on the edge of the jungle beside the road. It read:

PRIVATE PROPERTY
KEEP OUT, OR ELSE

"I didn't see that sign the other day," Andrew commented.

"No," Carmen agreed. "Just as well we were out on the main road before that horrible Barry fellow arrived."

The road wound on for several kilometres with the high ground on the left and a dense wall of jungle on the right. At times the jungle was so thick it overhung the road to form natural archways. Andrew followed their progress on his map and knew they were approaching a bridge over Wallaby Creek before they reached it. As the 4WD rounded the curve and it came into view he was able to tell his mother and sister.

Carman laughed. "We can see it is Wallaby Creek by the sign, Mr Smarty Pants. Oooh! Isn't it nice?"

Andrew had to agree that it was. It was about 25 metres wide and looked to be about waist deep, crystal clear water on a smooth sandy bottom.

Immediately across the creek on the left was a house and on the right of the road were open fields. Beyond the house was a patch of dense bush but Andrew noted it was not rain forest but eucalyptus scrub with a lot of undergrowth. After a kilometre they came to a road junction. The signs said that the road on the right went to Shiptons Flat, Mt Poverty, Mt Penniless and several tin mines.

"That must be where Simon and Tim and the other miners work," Carmen suggested.

Andrew agreed but was a bit worried that she used the young miner's name in such a familiar way. He said, "We are going to Mt Penniless aren't we Mum?"

"Yes, after Christmas, to see your cousin Bessie and her kids," his mother answered.

She turned the 4WD left and continued on along the main road. There was a short section where the road was deeply rutted and quite boggy. Next, they came to a better stretch. Several roads went off into the bush on either side and Andrew noted that the vegetation was much more open and was now savannah woodland with almost no undergrowth. As the road began skirting the base of a mountain on the right, the ground cover became so spares that he could see bare sand in many places. Grass trees, spindly tufts of dry grass and leaf litter became the predominant ground cover.

The road went up and down over several low ridges and Andrew saw that Wallaby Creek was close beside the road. It was now quite different, its bed a jumble of huge granite boulders and the water flowing much faster.

The road went east along a valley and Andrew could clearly see the jungle clad mass of a mountain called The Big Tableland away across the other side. Ahead of them grey clouds and a curtain of rain indicated bad weather.

After another two kilometres they began to pass houses set up against the base of the mountain along dirt side roads. Then suddenly the road changed to bitumen and the houses thickened up.

"Rossville," Andrew said.

"That's what the road sign said," Carmen agreed with a chuckle.

Rossville struck Andrew as an odd sort of town. It had no main street and no shop and the houses were a real mixture of nice modern ones and old shacks. As the family drove along the winding road, Andrew's mother said, "When I first came here as a teenage girl this was just a collection of tiny huts and the only people were tin scratchers, dole bludgers or feral hippies."

"Which one were you, Mum?" Carmen asked.

"Humpf! Don't you get cheeky, Young Miss!"

Andrew looked out and saw several expensive looking houses and expensive 4WDs or cars. "Things have changed since then," he observed.

They turned off up a short side street and stopped on the grassy footpath outside what looked like a normal high-set Queenslander. It stood in a yard fenced off from the dry savannah forest and could have been almost anywhere in North Queensland. In the driveway and out front were parked three battered looking utility trucks.

"Uncle Jack's," Mrs Collins announced.

And there were the relations: Cousin Sandy wearing only a pair of tattered jeans, his little brother Cousin Bart (Clad in T-shirt and shorts), Aunty Beryl and finally Uncle Jack, clad in blue singlet and blue work shorts. In among them, with much tail-wagging and aimless barking, came three dogs: a ginger-white mutt, a mangy looking Kelpie cattle dog cross breed with half an ear missing, and a grey and white bull terrier cross with a scarred face and bent tail.

There was a lot of handshaking and patting of dogs and then they were bidden upstairs. During this Andrew was both peeved and amused to watch Cousin Sandy making an obvious attempt to impress Carmen by strutting, flexing his muscles and generally acting tough. Knowing how much Carmen disliked such people allowed Andrew to relax about having to watch out for his sister.

Lunch was a pleasant enough affair in a very ordinary kitchen-dining room at the side of the house. It was very obvious that Aunty Beryl was making a big effort to make them feel welcome and Andrew decided he really liked her. She was a genuinely nice person. Uncle Jack just sat silent most of the time, as did Cousin Bart, who was a nice enough lad. Cousin Sandy made up for all of them by talking, boasting and telling tall tales about the country to try to impress them.

To that extent it was a relief when Andrew's mother insisted that they must get on to 'Home Rule'. The families made their way slowly down the steps in dribs and drabs with delays to admire the pet cockatoo, watch the dogs chase sticks and to study the crab pots and fishing rods under the house. The final amusement for Andrew was to see how Cousin Sandy had Carmen cornered so he could make a final attempt to talk to her.

When Carmen slid into the seat beside him, she gave Cousin Sandy a 'That would be interesting,' answer.

"What was that about?" Andrew asked as his mother started the engine.

"Cousin Sandy wants to take me fishing," Carmen replied, giving Cousin Sandy a smile and wave.

Andrew could tell by the way her smile did not reach her eyes that she was less than impressed. He laughed and waved, and said to her as they backed out, "Fishing eh? He's been fishing for your attention the whole time."

"I know, flexing his muscles and telling me how good he is. Yuk!" Carmen replied. But she kept a nice smile for the others as Mrs Collins turned the vehicle onto the road and drove away. Then she gave Andrew a sideways look and a grin and said, "Now it's your turn. I wonder if Cousin Jean will be there?"

Cousin Jean! Andrew thought, and his mind flooded with erotic fantasies and hope.

Chapter 14

A NASTY SHOCK

Andrew found the drive to Home Rule both interesting and testing. The scenery provided the interest but heated thoughts and worries about Cousin Jean provided a test of his emotions and body. The road turned off the main road between houses and went down through a belt of trees to a narrow bridge over Wallaby Creek. At that, point Wallaby Creek was almost a gorge among huge grey granite boulders on the left and a long, deep pool under overhanging jungle on the right.

On the other side of the creek, the road went up a short steep slope onto level ground and from bright sunlight into a tunnel of jungle that was pleasantly cool. From then on it was in jungle almost all the way, a mostly single lane gravel road that was very pretty to drive along. Apart from a couple of turnoffs to houses set back in clearings in the jungle, there were no other signs of human settlement for over two kilometres.

After about a kilometre and a half, the road came into a short clearing with Wallaby Creek close on the right. The creek had changed its nature once again and was now even more beautiful, flowing over sand and small rocks in a sunlit glade amid dense tropical rainforest.

Carmen was delighted. "This is really pretty!" she cried. "This is real tropical jungle. Oh! Look at the butterflies!"

Several large butterflies with brilliant blue wings flitted about in the sunlight and Andrew had to agree; it was pretty. The road then plunged back into even denser rainforest. The vehicle track itself was only one lane and quite muddy. Drops of water were dripping from the leaves.

"It's been raining here," Andrew commented.

He looked into the jungle and experienced a variety of emotions. He thought it both interesting and beautiful, but he had also had some experience of walking through tropical rain forest on various expeditions and adventures and he did not really like it at all.

Too hard and too claustrophobic, he thought.

The road came to a junction with a side track and turned abruptly left, still in thick jungle. But within a hundred metres it came to a large clearing and bright sunlight, or at least it was for a minute or so because a wall of heavy rain swept over them from the far end of the valley. Before it was all obscured Andrew was able to get a fair idea of the layout of the place. He saw that Home Rule was in a valley with mountains on three sides, the highest on their left. The clearing appeared to be at least a kilometre long and was lined on both sides by a wall of dense jungle. A few hundred metres ahead, the track forked and the left branch led to a house and sheds enclosed in a hedge of vegetation and trees. On the right were a couple of new sheds and a parked tractor.

Andrew's mother turned them onto the right fork, and she said, "That is the original homestead of the Home Rule property."

"Home rule?" Carmen queried. "For who?"

"The Irish," Andrew's mother replied. "It is from the 19th Century when England ruled all of Ireland and the Irish wished to govern themselves. Obviously some Irish settler was keeping the idea alive even on the other side of the world."

"I thought it might have been some move for a separate state for North Queensland," Andrew said. "I'd be all for that."

They drove on past the homestead and Andrew stared hard into the drizzle to check if what he was looking at was what he thought. "This looks like an airstrip," he said.

"It does," Carmen agreed.

It wasn't a very big airstrip, just a grass landing ground a few hundred metres long and barely wide enough for a plane to safely get down. By the time the vehicle had reached the far end the ground had changed to undulating pastures dotted with large trees and cattle. It also opened out to reveal a large park-like area with a dozen buildings nestled among the edge of the jungle down to their right.

This was the Home Rule Lodge and campground. They parked at the gate just as the rain shower passed. As soon as the worst of the drizzle had eased, they all climbed out and squelched their way across the soggy lawn to the office. Here they were given a very friendly welcome and the manager offered to take them to find the relations.

These were clustered under an awning outside one of the cabins. As soon as he saw them, Andrew's interest shot up as he noted girls in bikini tops and shorts. One of these was Cousin Jean, and as soon as she recognised him her face lit up with a smile of welcome. It was so obvious that Andrew blushed and hoped that his sister and mother would not notice.

They did though. Carmen grinned and Andrew saw his mother give him a worried frown, then glance at Cousin Jean and then back at him. This caused him to blush again. He was thankful that the flurry of introductions took place, taking their focus off him. But it also made Andrew aware of Cousin Jean's mother and father, and he became anxious lest they be able to guess his thoughts.

Cousin Jean looked very desirable. Her bikini top only covered half her breasts and cupped them so that they bulged upwards in a very provocative way. Andrew found he could hardly stop himself from glancing repeatedly at the rounded swelling of her bosom and he began to feel aroused. He also noticed that the exposed flesh that he could see had a liberal sprinkling of freckles.

She must wear that sort of top a lot, he thought.

Then the even more wicked thought came to him that perhaps she often went topless. The image that conjured up caused him to become even more aroused. It also gave him the urge to try to get her away on her own. Memories of her first kiss got him very keen to experience that again. But he had to pretend he was a nice polite boy, so he sat and joined in the social chit-chat with a sense of growing frustration and a horniness that made him squirm.

For an hour they all sat and talked. Partly this was because of the social situation but also because of another heavy shower of rain. As the rain stopped Cousin Jean said to him, "Let me show you around."

Andrew nodded and glanced at his mother and sister, hoping that they would not notice. But it was plainly obvious that they had. As he stood up his mother looked at him and said, "Don't you children go too far. It might rain again."

"No, Mum," Andrew replied, blushing strongly as he did.

Did what she said have a double meaning? he worried, that 'too far' biting at his conscience.

Feeling very self-conscious he walked off along a concrete path with Cousin Jean. The thought that his sister and her parents might be guessing what he had in mind made Andrew prickle with guilt and awareness. But he urgently wanted another kiss from Cousin Jean so he made himself keep walking.

She led him past several other cabins where other families were camped. There were also a number of camping groups under the trees along the edge of the grassy clearing. Beyond them was Wallaby Creek. Several foot tracks led down to the water. Once down beside the water, Andrew was struck by how pretty it was. Along that part of its length it was a gentle flow of clear water with a bluish tinge. Trees overhung both banks but did not meet overhead and left a gap for the sunlight.

Cousin Jean turned to face him and gestured to the scene. "It's pretty isn't it?"

"Yes, it is," Andrew agreed.

Then he found himself tongue tied as he stood looking at her. She faced him, a smile on her lips and what he thought was an invitation in her eyes. To his hopeful but anxious mind, her eyes seemed to grow in size and to draw him in until he had the impression of being mesmerised by them. 'Like a bird hypnotised by a snake,' was how he put it to himself later.

"I like you," she said. "Kiss me."

At that, Andrew was almost paralysed. Never in his life had he met a girl like her. But it was what he had been hoping for and he was brave enough to act so he stepped forward and took her in his arms and did so. Within seconds he felt as though his brain was melting and his body was on fire as he felt her female curves pressed hard against him.

For what seemed like hours, but must have only been minutes, they kissed. As he became more aroused, Andrew became more daring. His hands began to explore the safer regions of her body. That she did not mind was obvious from the way she responded and from the look in her eyes.

I might be in luck here, he thought.

But he wasn't. It began to rain. Andrew heard the downpour coming but held on kissing as long as he could. Only when the cold, heavy drops began splatting on the leaves overhead and then dripping down on them did Cousin Jean finally let out a squeal and release him.

"Oh drat!" she gasped. "I was just starting to enjoy that."

"I was enjoying it right from the start," Andrew replied.

"Oh you are sweet!" Cousin Jean replied.

She grabbed him again and gave him another kiss, then took his hand and hurried up the bank to find shelter. As they came out into the open lawn, the rain really hit them. At the same moment, Andrew spotted his mother under the veranda roof outside a building. With a guilty start he shook his hand free and bolted across the already squelching lawn.

As he and Cousin Jean arrived gasping, giggling and soaked at the cabin, Andrew's mother said, "You two left that a bit late. Didn't you hear it coming?"

Andrew and Carmen answered at the same time. "Yes, but we were off along the riverbank there," Andrew said. Cousin Jean said, "No, we were looking at scrub turkeys."

The contradiction caused Carmen to chortle and Andrew to blush with guilt. His mother looked at him with a wry smile on her face and said, "Well, I did warn you not to go too far."

Andrew could only give what felt like a sickly grin and settle in a chair. For the next hour he sat listening to family gossip, occasionally speaking but mostly just hoping that there would be another opportunity to get away with Cousin Jean. She seemed to be of like mind as she kept meeting his eyes and giving little shrugs and looks. These kept his hopes high, but the rain kept falling and no plausible reason presented itself, so all he could do was sit in increasing frustration.

Nor did he get a chance to speak to Cousin Jean privately to try to arrange another meeting. To his frustrated annoyance, his mother, her mother, or Carmen was always there. It was a grumpy boy that finally walked out to the vehicle during a break in the rain. As he was driven away, all he could do was wave and give Cousin Jean 'meaningful' looks.

During the return trip, Andrew barely noticed the scenery and only answered in monosyllables or short sentences. All he seemed to be able to do was fantasise about Cousin Jean, becoming very aroused again in the process. In what seemed like no time at all, they were back at Rossville and turning right onto the main road. Then it was a short strip of winding bitumen and then the corrugated gravel road. The only factor that did make an impression on Andrew's heated mind was Carmen's noting that the rain had not been falling along that part of the valley.

It was dry and dusty, even though more heavy rain could be seen falling behind them. Nor was the road wet at the junction of the Mt Poverty Road. Only after they had crossed Wallaby Creek did they pass through a short stretch of dripping jungle and along a wet, greasy road.

Andrew stared out at the passing rain forest without interest. His mind was on girls, and he wondered if he was immoral because of his current lust for them.

Or am I just normal? he thought.

Suddenly, the vehicle braked hard and slewed on the wet clay. Andrew came out of his day dream with a start and looked around. His attention was immediately focused on a little boy standing in the middle of the road facing them. It was Little Terry.

"Terry! What's he doing here?" Andrew cried.

His mother switched off the motor and put on the handbrake as she said, "I don't know, but I am going to find out."

All three climbed out. Little Terry looked scared until he recognised them and then he let out a whoop of delight and ran to Andrew.

"Big boy, hello! You look after me," he said.

Andrew was surprised, pleased and worried. He patted Little Terry's head as the boy clung to his waist.

"What are you doing here, little man? Where are you going?" he asked.

Little Terry raised his face to answer. It was only then that Andrew saw that the little boy's face was streaked with tears. Little Terry said, "I... I'm (sniff) looking for (sob) m... m... my d... d... daddy."

"Your daddy? Why, where has he gone?" Andrew asked. Concern and anger both welled up and he gave his mother and Carmen an anxious frown.

"I d... d... don't (sniffle) kn... kn... know," Little Terry sobbed. "He went... went (sob) off this... mor... morning (sniff) in his car."

Carmen knelt and said, "Did you leave home to find him?"

"N... N... no. He left me at the (sniff) the house up the road there," Little Terry answered. He pointed back towards Wallaby Creek Bridge.

"Do the people there know you have walked away?" Andrew's mother asked.

Little Terry shook his head. "No. They... they got drunk and started arguing, so I left."

Andrew was appalled and could tell that his mother and sister were as well. His mother said, "Where did your daddy go?"

Again Little Terry shook his head and a big tear trickled down his left cheek. The sight of that really tugged at Andrew's heart strings and he felt his anger and sympathy both rise.

He said, "Which way did your daddy go?"

Little Terry shook his head. "I don't know," he sobbed.

Andrew's mother bit her lip. "Where were you going, little boy?"

"To Daddy's shed," Little Terry answered.

"Where is that?"

Little Terry pointed on along the road the way they were going. Andrew said, "We know where the turn-off is, Mum. It is a couple of kilometres further along."

Andrew's mother nodded and said, "We will take this little fellow there. That is if he wants. Do you want a lift home little boy?"

Little Terry looked very anxious and was silent for a minute. Then he said, "If I can sit next to Big Boy."

"Of course you can," Andrew's mother replied.

So Little Terry was helped into the back seat and buckled in beside Andrew. Andrew's mother and Carmen then got in and the motor was started. As they began to move a sprinkle of rain began to fall. The thought of the poor little boy walking alone in the rain along the jungle track made Andrew feel quite angry.

A couple of minutes' drive had them at the turn-off where Andrew and Carmen had seen Little Terry's father drive in. By then the rain had stopped but the road was damp, showing that it had rained recently. Carmen directed her mother to turn off. She slowed the vehicle and turned left off the main road, only to stop at the sign nailed to the edge of the jungle.

"That isn't very friendly," she said.

Then she put the vehicle into low gear and drove into the tunnel of rainforest and down through the gloomy cutting to the riverbank. Here she stopped and looked anxiously at the water.

"I wonder how deep that is?" she said aloud.

"I will check, Mum," Andrew replied.

He undid his seat belt and climbed out, then pulled off his sneakers and socks and tossed them into the back seat. Cautiously he waded into the water. He was surprised at how cold the water was but was relieved to find that the water was only knee deep on a bed of pebbles and small rocks. It was only fifty paces to the far side and he had no difficulty.

As soon as Andrew was across, his mother drove carefully across to join him. The vehicle had no trouble but Andrew did wonder what the crossing might be like after a lot of heavy rain upstream. His mother stopped the vehicle and he climbed back in. She then drove it up into another cutting in the black mulch of leaf litter and soil in another tunnel of gloomy rainforest.

On top of the bank was more rainforest, the vehicle track winding off into it. But Andrew's mother had to stop almost at once. The road was blocked by a shiny new steel gate. A new, four-strand barbed wire fence extended off on both sides parallel to the riverbank. On the gate was another sign which said:

PRIVATE PROPERTY
KEEP OUT OR ELSE
TRESPASSERS WILL BE SHOT
WE AIN'T JOKING

Carmen read the sign aloud and then muttered in annoyance and said, "What do we do now?"

Andrew's mother turned to Little Terry and asked, "How far is it to your daddy's house little man?"

"He hasn't got a house," Little Terry replied. "He lives in a shed. It is just along there a bit." He pointed ahead.

Andrew's mother frowned and said, "Well, the gate isn't locked so we will take this little fellow home. Open the gate please Andrew."

Andrew climbed out and did so. The gate was held by a short chain looped around the post. There was a padlock hanging on it, of the combination lock type, but it was undone. The chain was easy to undo and the gate swung open easily. Andrew opened it and then stood and waited till his mother had driven through. He then shut the gate and climbed back into the vehicle. By then he was feeling a bit anxious in case they got into trouble from Little Terry's dad, but he reasoned that the man should be grateful they had brought the little boy home safely.

They drove on along a winding single lane dirt vehicle track for perhaps a hundred metres. Out to the right Andrew saw an overgrown tangle of mounds of earth and scooped out hollows that plainly were not natural.

"It was an alluvial tin mine years ago," his mother explained. "The miners bulldozed away the trees and topsoil and then sluiced the dirt into troughs to separate the tin. It was very destructive to the rain forest and even after fifty years you can see that the jungle hasn't gown back in places."

Into view came two corrugated iron sheds. The first was half open and smaller and the second was large and newer and had a large padlocked door. Parked just beyond the second shed was a large truck which looked to be ex-army: dark green and with a canvas canopy over the back. Andrew's mother parked the vehicle and they all climbed out.

"Hello!" she called. "Is anybody there?"

There was no answer so she started walking towards the open door of the smaller shed.

Crack! Bang!

Andrew flinched as a bullet cracked past quite close.

Chapter 15

NASTY CUSTOMERS

Andrew felt fear surge through him and he looked anxiously in the direction the shot had come from. As he did, there was a second one. *Bang!*

Again he flinched but this time he saw a man standing just beyond the second shed. It was Jan the South African and he was dressed in very short blue shorts, dark blue short sleeved shirt and ankle boots. In his hands was a rifle with a telescopic sight fixed above the barrel. Even as Andrew's gaze focused on the weapon the man cocked it again.

The man, Jan, yelled angrily, "Get out of here! This is private property. Clear off, or else!"

Andrew's instinct was to go, even though he was quickly becoming furiously angry at the threatened violence. Then he saw that his mother already was.

She stood, hands on hips, and shouted back, "Don't you threaten me, mister! You put that gun away!"

Jan curled his lip in a nasty sneer and kept the rifle pointing at them. "And you do what you are told and get off this land. It is private property and you got no right to be here."

"And you have no right to threaten us with violence!" Andrew's mother snapped back.

"You are trespassing," Jan retorted. He walked slowly towards them, his black eyes glaring dislike.

"So take us to court! Now stop pointing that gun at us or I will call the police," Andrew's mother replied coldly.

Jan sneered but did move the rifle to point to one side. He stopped ten paces from them and said, "How did you get in?"

Andrew answered that. "The padlock was unlocked," he said.

Jan swore and then said, "So what you come here for, eh?"

Andrew's mother gestured to where Carmen was helping a very scared Little Terry out of the vehicle. "We found this little boy wandering along the road and we brought him here. He said his father lived here."

Jan glanced at Little Terry, then swore again. That really annoyed Andrew's mother. She snapped, "You can mind your language in the presence of my daughter, thank you."

Jan's reaction was to sneer but he said, "Yeah, the kid's father lives here. But he ain't here now."

Carmen lifted Little Terry down and said, "Where do you live, Terry?"

Little Terry pointed to the small shed. "In there," he whispered.

To Andrew he looked frightened. This was confirmed when Carmen said, "Well you go in there."

"Not without my daddy," Little Terry wailed and he turned and clung to her, his eyes wide with evident fear.

Andrew's mother looked troubled and she said to Jan. "Who are you? Do you live here?"

"Yes," Jan replied, ignoring her request for his name. "Come on, kid, get inside."

Little Terry clung even tighter to Carmen and shook his head. "Not go with bad men," he said. Tears began to well into his eyes and trickle down his cheeks.

Jan looked angry but now lowered his rifle. "You the people looking after the pub, eh?"

Andrew's mother said yes. Jan scowled and said, "Well then, if the kid won't stay with me, then you take him with you. When Barry gets back I'll send him to get the boy."

Andrew's mother looked unhappy but Little Terry nodded and looked at Andrew with big eyes that made him feel awful. At that moment, Andrew heard the roar of an approaching vehicle and from further along the track appeared a battered grey Land Rover. But it wasn't Barry. As it squealed to a halt near the big shed he saw that it was being driven by the big, burly man named Wes. To add to his alarm Andrew also noted what looked like an automatic rifle clipped to the back of the cab behind the driver.

Wes climbed out and said, "What's goin' on here? What was that shootin', Jan?"

Jan gestured with his rifle. "These people came here with Barry's little boy."

Wes scowled and said, "Well you people can just take him with you and get off this property."

"Why can't he stay with you if he lives here?" his mother asked.

"Because we are working and using machinery and we ain't got time to look out for him. So clear off, and take the kid with you. His dad can look after him when he gets back," Wes replied.

"That's not fair," Carmen said.

Wes leered at her, to Andrew's intense annoyance, then said, "Tough girlie! You can be his baby sitter. Now clear off!"

Andrew's mother tried to reason with the men but they were adamant and very unfriendly. So she finally shrugged and said, "Andrew, put Little Terry back in the vehicle."

Andrew did so and then climbed in himself. As his mother started the engine, he heard Wes say, "Follow them, Jan, and make sure that bloody gate is locked."

Andrew's mother waited till Carmen was aboard and then reversed in a semi-circle and then turned the vehicle around.

As she started driving back along the jungle track, she said, "Well! What a pair of ugly customers!"

"Certainly very unfriendly," Carmen agreed.

"Bad men," Little Terry said.

"Why is that, little man?" Andrew asked.

"Always shooting guns and saying horrible words," Little Terry replied.

Andrew nodded. "They were the ones shooting dingos the other day. I wonder, should we report them to the police?"

By then they were back at the gate. This time Andrew stayed in to look after Little Terry and to keep watch on gun-toting Jan who had come loping along the track behind him. Carmen got out and swung the gate open but seeing Jan coming climbed back in and told her mother to drive on. Andrew's last glimpse of Jan was his scowling red face as he closed the gate again.

They drove down to the river and slowly across. To Andrew's concern, he saw that the water was noticeably higher.

Probably because of all that rain upstream, he surmised.

It was now deep enough and the current strong enough to cause the 4WD to shudder and even slip sideways a bit. The water foamed half way up the doors and Little Terry looked quite scared until they powered out the other side.

Then it was up the steep cutting and through the tunnel of gloomy jungle and back to the main road. Here they turned left and accelerated. Andrew found it a distinct relief to be away from the place, but he did not want to admit that he had been scared.

Five minutes later they parked in the back yard of the hotel. At his mother's suggestion, Andrew took Little Terry to the toilet and then to the kitchen for a snack. As the sad little boy drank a glass of coke, Andrew's mother and father and Carmen drew him aside to discuss the situation.

When the incident at the shed in the jungle had been explained, Andrew's father was deeply angry. "What a nerve! I should call the cops," he growled.

Andrew agreed. "They are certainly a bad lot. That Wes fellow had an automatic rifle in his truck, an SLR or FN. I am sure they are illegal."

"You sure?" his father asked.

"About the type of rifle? Yes. I have even learned how to do drill with an SLR. They are old 7.62mm semi-automatics that were used in the 1960s and 70s. The Navy Cadets have a few still and the Federation Guard uses them for ceremonial drill," Andrew answered.

"Hmm. I wonder what those fellows are up to," Andrew's father said, rubbing his chin and looking thoughtful.

Carmen spoke next, her voice hot with indignation. "They are either criminals on the run who are hiding there or they are growing drugs in the jungle," she suggested.

"Possibly. Is it a farm?" her father asked.

"No, just jungle and an overgrown tin mine," Andrew answered.

"It seems very unfair for us to have this poor little boy foisted on us," his father said.

Andrew's mother nodded. "It is, but we couldn't just leave the poor mite beside the road."

"We will play with him," Andrew said. "Come on Car."

He put down his empty glass and went to get Little Terry. Carmen followed and for the next hour the three of them played hide-and-seek and hopscotch and a bouncing ball game. Little Terry wasn't very good at any of them but was pathetically grateful for the attention.

Carmen watched his little face light up with laughter at Andrew's silly faces and she shook her head. "Poor little mite! I don't think he gets much love," she said.

That idea really saddened Andrew, who found it hard to understand. He had grown up enfolded by love from parents and big sister and could not really understand what it might be like not to have that.

The games took them out onto the veranda. For twenty minutes they played happily skipping and looking for mangos but it began to be hard work keeping Little Terry interested.

For something else to do, Carmen brought out paper, pens, and coloured pencils and began teaching Little Terry how to draw. The three sat on chairs at a small table near the far end of the veranda away from the bar. Andrew drew a patrol boat and Little Terry was so pleased that he wanted one too. Andrew's attention became so focused on drawing that he paid scant attention to the frequent comings and goings of vehicles.

Suddenly, a movement on the floor over against the wall caught Andrew's eye. Without really thinking what it might be, he glanced down, and froze with shock!

There, only half a metre from Little Terry's dangling feet, was a metre and a half of snake!

The olive-brown reptile had been sliding along the veranda next to the wall. But now it had stopped and was looking at them. Andrew's heart leapt in alarm, and he felt a sudden surge of rising panic.

Do I call out to warn people, or will they jump up and startle it so that it strikes? he wondered.

Then Carmen said, "What's wrong Andrew?"

That forced a decision. "Don't move, snake!" he whispered, his eyes fixed anxiously on Little Terry.

Carmen glanced down and let out a gasp. Her eyes widened with horror, and she also shifted her gaze to Little Terry.

"Terry, sit still and don't move your feet please," she whispered.

"Why not?" Little Terry asked, glancing down at his feet.

Then Andrew saw his eyes go wide and he yelped and pulled his feet upwards with a convulsive twitch. Seeing that sent Andrew cold with shock and he tensed ready to run. To his horror, he saw the snake swing back into the 'S' shape that he knew was a prelude to striking. Its forked tongue began to flicker in and out, a sight that sent Andrew's blood running chill. The reptile began to sway its now raised head slowly from side to side.

"Oh Terry, stay still!" Andrew croaked.

He felt the grip of terror himself, knowing that his own legs and feet were probably well within the striking range of the snake. It was a type he could not identify but was sure it was poisonous.

A 'Brown' or a 'Taipan', he thought. Knowledge of how deadly such snakes were reputed to be added to his apprehension.

To his slight relief, Little Terry sat hunched on his chair, his eyes saucers of fear. His whole body started to tremble.

"Get it away from me!" he sobbed.

This kid is going to panic and have a fit of hysterics, Andrew thought. *And that will cause the snake to bite.*

But what to do? Andrew could see beads of sweat breaking out on Carmen's face and he noted that she had gone a deathly pale. She was closer to the snake than him, on the outside of the table, but he could not think what to do next. The sound of voices and laughter from the direction of the bar did not help.

How can I get help without alarming the snake? Andrew wondered.

Then he heard heavy footsteps and experienced another bout of fright as the snake turned to face the noise.

To warn the person, Andrew held up one hand and pointed with the other. To his relief, the person stopped and he heard a voice mutter, "Bloody snake, bejaysus!" Then the man began to edge away.

Irish, Andrew surmised. But at least someone else knew and they might be able to do something.

Then Little Terry wobbled on his chair. Andrew had palpitations as he saw the snake turn to look up at the boy.

"Sit still Terry. Don't move!" Andrew hissed.

There were voices at the far end of the veranda now and then boots crunching on gravel out to the vehicles and others moving along the veranda towards them.

Stay away you fools! Andrew thought.

But he was also relieved. The adults were now aware of the situation and hopefully they would know what to do. Meanwhile, all he could do was try to keep his muscles from trembling or twitching. He felt an almost overwhelming desire to pull his feet upwards or to bolt and had to use all his will power to force himself to remain seated.

The seconds dragged into minutes and Andrew heard his mother's gasp and his father calling, telling them not to move. There were more footsteps out among the vehicles and the snake turned to face that way. It was obvious to Andrew that the snake was becoming more agitated and his nerves seemed to strain even tighter. Fear made the bile rise up into his throat and he felt dry mouthed and sick in the stomach.

This can't go on much longer, he thought desperately, very aware that Little Terry was starting to fidget and edge away on his chair.

"Sit still, little man. Let the adults deal with it," he croaked.

Bang! Crack! Whang! Whee!

Andrew flinched as a bullet snapped past him, struck the snake, then the concrete floor and wall before ricocheting up past his head and through the iron roof. Even as shock and a spasm of terror coursed through him, his mind noted that the snake was now writhing around at fantastic speed in a squirming tangle. It was obvious that it had been hit by the bullet and almost torn in two but it was now lashing out, hissing and biting at the legs of the chairs.

Despite his fear, Andrew reached across and grabbed Little Terry's arm and hauled with all his might, dragging the boy up onto the table and across it. As he did, he rose and tried to step back but the chair caught under his legs and he stumbled and tripped. But before he fell, strong hands grabbed him. He glimpsed Little Terry being whisked from his grasp by another pair of hairy arms. Carmen sprang back, knocking her chair over and scuttled past.

Andrew found it was Irish who had him in his grip. The man grinned and set him on his feet.

"Well saved, boyo!" he cried.

Another glance convinced Andrew that the snake was no longer a threat. His mother pushed past with a long-handled broom and began sweeping the still writhing reptile along the veranda.

As she did, she turned and spat sideways, "You stupid fool! You could have killed one of the kids."

Andrew now saw that the person who had fired the gun was Jan. He stood just next to the nearest mango tree and was holding his rifle ready to fire again. He grinned but also went red at Andrew's mother's words. Andrew suffered a rapid series of intense emotions. When he recollected just how close the ricocheting bullet had gone to him he felt alternate waves of chill and heat and his fear turned to snapping anger.

"You bloody nearly hit me!" he cried angrily.

Jan scowled at him and retorted heatedly, "Well that's fine thanks for saving you!"

"Shooting at concrete was a dumb thing to do," Andrew snapped.

"Oh, and you'd know would you boy!" Jan jeered. By now he was angry in return and glared at them.

Before Andrew could answer his father said, "Thank you for acting. Now please put the gun away."

Jan sneered again and for a second his rifle angled towards him. "That's gratitude!" he said. "And I just came to have a quiet drink."

Andrew mother returned from sweeping the dying snake off the far end of the veranda. She stood in front of Jan and said, "Well we won't serve you, not after the way you treated us this afternoon."

"Are you saying I can't buy a drink here?" Jan asked in apparent astonishment.

"That's right," Andrew's mother replied. "Now please leave."

For just a second Andrew thought he saw murderous hate in Jan's eyes and he sucked in his breath out of fear for his mother, who now stood facing the man armed only with her broom.

Jan scowled and ground his teeth and then spat and said, "You can stick yer hotel then, you ungrateful people."

With that he spun on his heel and stormed over to his vehicle, placed the rifle inside, climbed in and started the engine, then backed out and drove away. As the Land Rover accelerated towards Cooktown, Andrew let out a sigh of relief.

He wasn't the only one. Irish breathed out audibly and said, "I wasn't enjoyin' that at all, at all. He is a nasty bit of work that one."

"South African is he?" Andrew's father asked.

Irish nodded. "To be sure, and not the best of the species. I heard he was one o' them mercenaries who fought in places like the Congo and so on. I wouldn't like to cross him myself."

"Well, he isn't welcome here," Andrew's mother said. "That bullet must have missed Andrew by a whisker. Are you children alright?"

There was an amount of fussing and Little Terry began to cry. So they took him inside and gave him a small chocolate to eat. When he had calmed down Andrew and Carmen took him out to see the now dead snake. Andrew found the dead reptile both fascinating and repellent. Just thinking about the whole horrible incident made him shudder and feel ill.

While they were doing this another vehicle pulled up and Andrew saw it was Little Terry's Uncle Dave. He strode in with a big smile on his face and hailing cheerful greetings. Then his gaze fell on Little Terry.

"Hello Terry, my boy. Is your dad here?"

Little Terry shook his head and Uncle Dave looked along the veranda at the other vehicles his face crinkling into a puzzled frown.

"Er, so did he leave you here then?"

Again Little Terry shook his head. Carmen answered, "No, we found him walking along the road."

"Walking along the road!" Uncle Dave cried. "Where? When? Where is Barry?"

"We don't know," Carmen answered. "Little Terry said he left him at some house near Wallaby Creek and drove off. The men at his shed couldn't tell us either."

"You went there? What did they say?"

Carmen replied, "They fired guns and were very rude and told us to clear off. They said they wouldn't look after Little Terry because they had to work."

"Work! That bunch! That will be the day!" snorted Uncle Dave. "Anyway, how on earth did you get in? I couldn't."

Andrew's mother explained the whole incident. As she did, Andrew could see that Uncle Dave was becoming more and more angry. From time to time he breathed out in evident disgust or disbelief, shaking his head at the same time.

They were interrupted by the sound of another vehicle approaching from the Rossville direction and into view came Barry's Land Rover. It pulled in and was parked and Barry climbed out. As Barry walked towards them he gave a grin which quickly changed to a puzzled frown as Uncle Dave strode forward to meet him.

Andrew did not hear much of what was then said but he could tell that Uncle Dave was angry just by his body language and by the way he pointed towards Little Terry. The exchange was then cut short by Little Terry running forward calling, "Daddy! Daddy!"

Barry bent and took the boy in his arms and lifted him up. As he did, he made a last comment to Uncle Dave, who snorted in evident disgust and turned away. Barry shrugged and turned to Little Terry, asking how he was and how he got to the hotel.

When Little Terry pointed towards Andrew and his mother, Barry looked surprised. Andrew said, "We found him walking along the road near Wallaby Creek."

"Yeah, well, thanks. I had to attend to some urgent business," Barry explained.

It sounded very lame to Andrew and he thought that Barry looked guilty, but he was then angered by Barry carrying Little Terry into the bar and asking for a beer.

Andrew was called away from there by his mother who sent him to help prepare dinner for the miners. While he worked at peeling potatoes Andrew discussed the snake incident with his mother and Carmen. This led them to talking about Little Terry and how unhappy he was.

"It is no way to bring up a little boy," Andrew said. "I feel so sorry for him. I wish we had some toys for him to play with."

"There might be some here somewhere," his mother suggested.

At that, an idea that was half-formed seemed to crystallise in Andrew's mind. "Perhaps we could go to town tomorrow and buy some, just in case?"

At that, Carmen smirked and said, "To town, eh? Are you sure it is to buy toys that you want to go to town?"

Andrew scowled and blushed, his mind filled with images of Daphne and Kristen. "Yes, of course," he snapped back.

Carmen trilled with laughter and said, "You should see the colour of your face!"

At that, their mother said, "Stop teasing you children. Anyway, we are going there tomorrow. We are taking Grandma Cynthia to town; and we need to buy food and also some more Christmas decorations. I can only find a few here and they are in very poor condition.

"Who is Grandma Cynthia?" Andrew asked. He was puzzled by all these relations and about who was who.

His mother answered. "She is Aunty Beryl's mum. She and Grandpa Herbert live near Black Mountain."

Andrew nodded but then he thought of Daphne and Colleen and could not help getting excited hopes.

But how will I get away to see them without Mum and Carmen knowing? he wondered.

Chapter 16

TO TOWN

How to get away to meet the girls became the focus of Andrew's thoughts for the evening. Even while he was eating tea or helping serve the miners in the dining room, or even washing up afterwards half his mind was on the problem.

After the chores were done, Andrew made his way out to the front veranda. By then it was getting dark and he was astonished and annoyed to find that Little Terry was still there. He was sitting on a bench while his father drank and talked to a man Andrew had never seen before. Of Uncle Dave there was no sign, and a quick check of the parked vehicles revealed that his was no longer there.

That poor little kid hasn't had anything to eat for hours, Andrew thought.

He wondered if he should offer the boy something. But Barry looked so angry and drunk that he hesitated to approach him to ask.

Then Barry disgusted him more by getting up and ordering Little Terry to get into the Land Rover. Barry followed, his unsteady walk indicating that he was more than half drunk. Andrew shook his head and wondered if he should intervene.

He shouldn't be driving in that state, he thought. It made him both angry and anxious.

But before he could find his father or mother to try to get them to intervene, Barry had climbed into his vehicle, started it up and backed out. As the Land Rover set off with a roar of its motor and a crunching of gears, Andrew could only shake his head and feel sad.

Poor little kid! he thought.

He went inside and described the incident to his mother and Carmen. His mother looked very unhappy and muttered about it not being right. She was interrupted by the screech of flying foxes fighting and the crash of a mango on the roof. Then another miner called for service and Andrew was sent to take his order.

After that, Andrew sat and watched TV. Then he went to his room and read for a while before preparing for bed. This time as he lay awake in the moist tropical darkness, he had plenty to think about, and to fantasise over. Images of Daphne and Cousin Jean melded to heated images and fantasies that got him very aroused, and also quite anxious and confused.

There was heavy rain during the night but in the morning the sky was clear and the air moist and fresh. By this time Andrew had settled into a routine and was able to quickly get his chores done and have breakfast. After helping serve the miners their breakfast, he went to have a shower and shave. The shave he took considerable care over, all the while his mind speculating about the girls in Cooktown. He even added some aftershave lotion and the aroma of this earned him another bout of mild teasing from Carmen.

She made a big deal of sniffing, then saying, "You are only going to Cooktown, Little Brother. You don't want people to get the wrong idea."

Andrew scowled and blushed and said, "I've been to Cooktown before, so don't tell me about it."

Carmen smiled and he blushed again. He found it a relief to be called to help refuel a miner's 4WD. Then he worried that he had gotten oil or diesel on his hands. But by then his mother had the family 4WD backed out and ready. Mr Collins gave them a cheery goodbye and Andrew, Carmen, and their mother set off for town.

For the first few kilometres Andrew looked out without too much interest. He did note that the Annan River was flowing well from the night's rain but it was not in flood. They crossed Mungumby Creek and drove up past the cattle station homestead and along the straight. Carmen asked their mother to stop the car at that point as she wanted to take a photo of Black Mountain. Andrew had to admit that it looked most impressive from that angle, with the morning sun on it.

The route took them back out to the bitumen road a few kilometres on. At the T-junction they turned north. About two kilometres further along the highway, when the second major 'black' mountain of the Black Trevethan Range was close ahead and the main feature on their right, Mrs Collins slowed the 4WD and turned off to the left along a dirt road.

The dirt road curved along the side of a low ridge to a farmhouse set on the crest. Down on the creek flat to their left were fruit trees and vines. On the right, along the ridgetop, were a water tank, a shed and a garden. Behind the small house were a fowl run and then another creek line. Beyond that was the dramatic jumble of black boulders and stones that made up the second 'Black' Mountain.

Nearly an hour was spent at the farmhouse while Mrs Collins chatted to old Grandma Cynthia, a lovely old lady who lived there with her retired sea captain husband. As most of the conversation was about relations and babies and who was married to whom, and family scandals and the like, Andrew was not very interested and amused himself by playing outside with the dogs.

While he was doing this, Carmen came out and said, "Grandma has asked us to collect the eggs; and she said to watch out for snakes while we do. Apparently these rocky hills are thick with death adders."

Into Andrew's mind flashed images of the snake the previous evening and he looked anxiously around. Up to now he had been depending on the dogs to warn him of any reptiles, but he saw that there were many rocks, logs, and piles of old iron where a snake could hide. Having seen death adders at the zoo and in displays at school, he felt a shudder of revulsion and fear at the thought of the fat, deadly creatures.

Collecting eggs from the hen's nests was another new and not entirely enjoyable experience, although Carmen seemed to think it was good fun. The smell and the general dirt and unpleasantness of the scattered feathers and excrement made Andrew wrinkle his nose with distaste and he was very careful where he stepped.

Grandma Cynthia was then helped into the 4WD with her shopping basket and they set off again. By then it was 10:30 and Andrew was starting to fret that the day would be over and he would not have time to get to meet any of the girls. But the country the road was passing through was new so he studied his map and looked around with interest.

First to really grip his interest was the lookout at the saddle between the two Black Mountains. Only then did Andrew really appreciate just how rugged the mountains were and how big many of the rocks were. He saw that neither mountain was very big as mountains go, only 465 metres and 359 metres respectively, but they were so rough they were most impressive. The black stones were very jagged and irregular and were stacked up in huge heaps. Both mountains were almost devoid of topsoil and vegetation, with just the odd clump of bushes growing amid the litter of black stones.

After a short stop for photos the drive was resumed. The road went down onto a flat plain of open dry savannah woodland. Two kilometres along they passed a gravel road which went off on the left to a water supply pump station. Another kilometre on and they crossed Trevethan Creek on a concrete bridge. The creek had a good flow of water in it.

The road ran on, curving gently, wide and smooth with a good bitumen surface. It skirted the end of a range of hills which Andrew's map told him ran all the way to the sea at a place called Walsh Bay. The road then went up over a low saddle and then down into slightly thicker savannah woodland, curving back to the left in a wide sweeping curve.

The junction to another gravel road was passed. This one was on the right and the sign said: ARCHER POINT. Into Andrew's mind came the images of the lighthouse on the big grassy hill, of the conical island with the small lighthouse and of the ruined port facilities.

I must go there one day, he thought.

For something to say he related what he had been told on the patrol boat about the attempt to develop a port.

The road went north through quite dense paperbark country for another 7 kilometres before crossing the Annan River again. Here the river was quite different. It was sluggish and tidal and both banks were lined with mangroves. The map told Andrew that the sea was only 5 kilometres to the east and that the river was starting to form an estuary. Signs on both banks gave grim warning to the fishermen that the river was the habitat of estuarine or saltwater crocodiles.

Grandma Cynthia shook her head and said, "Don't you children go for a swim in any of the coastal creeks or rivers, even if they are freshwater. Saltwater crocodiles quite happily live in them and if one gets hold of you, you are done for. So you be careful."

Once again Andrew mentally quailed at the traumatic images such thoughts brought up and he nodded in agreement.

The road now ran across the Meldrum Creek Wetlands on a causeway and Andrew studied the huge paperbark trees standing in a reedy swamp. Several more turn-offs were passed, including a good bitumen road that led to new housing developments at the north end of Walker Bay. By then they were in quite dense forest with long grass and weeds lining the road and numerous houses on either side.

The road skirted the west side of Mt Cook, a conical mountain covered with quite dense vegetation. It then swung to the right and they were in the newer part of Cooktown. As they drove along the street past the houses Andrew felt his excitement rise and he began to fret about how to make contact with the girls.

With luck they will be in the main street, he thought hopefully. But how to get away from Carmen and his mother?

Not easily was the answer. For the next hour Andrew walked around from shop to shop with his mother and Carmen. Grandma Cynthia took herself to a church hall to meet her friends. As the shopping proceeded, Andrew kept looking hopefully around for a sign of the girls. But it wasn't until lunch time came and his mother suggested they find a cafe, and Andrew had led them along the main street towards the one he wanted to visit, that he finally saw a couple.

Daphne and Kristen were sitting at a table on the footpath outside the cafe. With them were three scruffy looking youths. The sight of the youths bothered Andrew as he didn't want trouble with the local lads. Nor did he have a plan to get the girls away on their own. To add to his irritation, one of the youths, who had been sitting with his back to them, turned to look at them and Andrew saw it was Cousin Sandy.

Cousin Sandy at once stood up and greeted them, beaming a big cheesy grin at Carmen. Carmen was very cool in her answer but Cousin Sandy seemed not to notice. Both Daphne and Kristen looked hard at her and at Andrew's mother and he hoped that they wouldn't embarrass him. But they did.

Both said, in very friendly tones, "Hi Andrew!"

Andrew's mother gave them both a surprised look as she went into the cafe. Andrew blushed and gave a casual response which hid his real feelings. The sight of Daphne in tight shorts and a T-shirt that strained over her ample bosom sent his heart rate and hopes soaring.

Torn between pretending not to know the girls very well and good manners, he stopped to chat. Carmen had to stop as well, her progress blocked by an enthusiastic Cousin Sandy who was giving her the full blast of his charm.

Carmen was introduced to the girls and was polite but distant. Andrew found he was very hopeful about Daphne and he itched to try to arrange to meet her again. But with the others there he was not brave enough to start such a conversation. Having his mother just inside the cafe and giving him frequent glances did not help.

Then Andrew looked into the shop and his heart leapt and his interest soared. Colleen of the beautiful face and dreamy blue eyes was there. She was looking his way and appeared a bit anxious. But as their eyes met she gave him a dazzling smile and he felt he just had to go to her. It was as though a magnetic force dragged him into the shop. Muttering hasty 'See you laters' to Daphne and Kristen he went.

Colleen was standing behind the counter with a woman who could only be her mother. The two mothers stood talking, allowing Andrew a time to just stand and admire Colleen. Both stared into each other's eyes and Andrew felt sure that this was one of those mystical events that were supposed to happen in life.

Is she the one? he wondered, his heart pounding but his mind seemingly in suspended animation.

Colleen broke the ice by speaking first. "It's nice to see you again," she said.

"I told you I would be back," he answered, hotly conscious that both mothers were listening and that Carmen had at last torn herself away from Cousin Sandy and was now beside him on the other side.

Colleen's mother looked from her to Andrew and said, "Have you two children met?"

Andrew nodded and tore his eyes from Colleens to meet her gaze. "Yes. I came here on a navy patrol boat a week or so ago."

"Are you in the navy? You look too young," Colleen's mother replied.

Andrew's mind and emotions raced. *Is she trying to warn me off with all this talk of children and age?* he wondered.

In reply he said, "No. I am a navy cadet. I am still at school."

Colleen spoke next. "What grade are you in?" she asked.

Andrew knew at once that she was trying to work out his age. *She is interested,* he thought happily.

He said, "I have just finished Year Eleven. I will be in Year Twelve next year."

Colleen smiled and nodded and said, "That's good. I will be in Year Ten."

She must be about 14 or 15, Andrew deduced. She was two years younger than him but still within the acceptable age range so that he would not be accused of 'cradle snatching' by his peers.

Colleen's mother now interrupted to ask what they wanted to purchase and she sent Colleen off to the back room to help prepare the food. She then indicated a table inside and Andrew's mother and Carmen made their way to it. Andrew seated himself where he could get glimpses of Colleen as she worked and was rewarded by several smiles. To Andrew's embarrassment, Carmen noted several of these and gave a wry smirk that made him go red. But Colleen was so beautiful he was willing to persevere. Daphne's charms seemed to melt into insignificance beside Colleen's looks and personality.

To Andrew's delight, it was Colleen who set the table and brought out the food. Each time she seemed to have eyes only for him and he responded, while trying to pretend he wasn't especially interested. That he wasn't entirely successful was born out by Carmen meeting his gaze as they started to eat and the knowing look on her face made him blush.

Andrew would have happily stayed there all afternoon and he anxiously tried to find a way to get a few private words with Colleen, but to no avail. There was always someone else. Worse still, as they stood up to go and the two mothers said goodbye and Andrew gave a casual 'see you later' to Colleen, along with a deep and meaningful glance, he noticed both his mother and her mother looking at them and frowning.

Feeling both elated and guilty, Andrew walked out, straight into another situation. Not only were Kristen and Daphne still outside with Cousin Sandy, but Cousin Jean had arrived. She wore tight shorts and a tight shirt and looked bigger and bustier than ever. When she saw him her eyes lit up and she scuttled over and threw her arms around him.

"Hi Andrew!" she cried. Then she kissed him full on the lips.

Andrew was in a turmoil of pleasure and anxiety. He really enjoyed the feel of her and would have happily responded, except that Kristen was looking surprised and grinning, Daphne was looking annoyed and hurt and he was hoping that Colleen could not see what was going on.

Cousin Jean only released him when his mother spoke to her, saying, "Hello Jeanie. Is your mother in town too?"

"Yes Aunty, she is at that shop over the road there," Cousin Jean replied.

She still held Andrew and pressed against him and he became even more anxious as he began to get aroused.

He looked at Daphne and met her obviously jealous stare. "She is my cousin," he muttered lamely.

"Oh yeah!" Daphne snorted, giving Cousin Jean a hostile glare. Carmen giggled and Kristen made a wry face.

Andrew went red and knew it. He glanced into the cafe, hoping that Colleen was not watching. To his relief, she was not in sight. As casually as he could, he disengaged from Cousin Jean, his mind racing as he tried to come up with a strategy that would not offend the girls. But he had a suspicion he had done his dash with Daphne.

She doesn't look amused, he thought.

After a bit of chatter, Cousin Jean went into the cafe and Andrew reluctantly followed Carmen and his mother across the street. As they hurried across to get out of the blazing sun as quickly as they could, Carmen looked hard at Andrew and whispered, "You are sly dog, aren't you Andrew?"

All Andrew could do was grunt. That caused Carmen to chuckle with laughter and she said, "You had better make up your mind boy, or you will end up with none."

Andrew badly wanted to say it wasn't like that, but he knew it was and all he could do was go red. When Carmen wasn't looking, he cast a wistful glance back towards the cafe. This revealed Daphne and Kristen walking off along the footpath with the youths and no sign of Colleen.

Oh well, maybe? he hoped.

Along the street was a shop that sold all manner of things. Aunty Ethel was there and Andrew's mother joined her and began talking. Andrew thought that might be a good time to slip away but Carmen called to him from the next aisle. Mildly irritated but interested, Andrew went to look.

He was pleased to find that the aisle was mostly toys and craft items. Carmen pointed to the toys and said, "This is what we want, just in case we have to look after Little Terry again."

Andrew nodded. "Yes, and anyway, we can give him a Christmas present. I doubt if he will get much from that horrible father of his."

So brother and sister walked slowly along and studied the range. Andrew was pleased to find some small plastic farm animals. They were in a packet and he counted two cows, two sheep, a goat, a horse and some geese. It was quite cheap so he picked it up. Then he noted packets of plastic 1:35 scale people, one of cowboys and another of Indians. There appeared to be about a dozen in each packet. These were added to the shopping.

Carmen found a coloured bounce ball and a packet of coloured felt pens. Then Andrew found packets of 1:35 scale plastic soldiers. They came 25 to a packet and were Napoleonic War miniatures, both British and French. They were very cheap but they were unpainted. Andrew turned a box of French cavalry over in his hands and was sorely tempted. Carmen joined him and looked and he explained the problem.

"They are just grey plastic. To look any good they need to be painted in bright colours."

"We could do that," Carmen said.

Andrew bit his lip and thought hard. "These need the sort of oil-based paints you use on plastic kit models. They are fairly expensive. And we'd need brushes and thinner."

Carmen pointed to a nearby rack. "Is that them there?"

"Yes," Andrew agreed, still worried by the possible expense.

"Then we will buy what we need," Carmen said firmly. "And what we don't use you can take back to Cairns and use on your models or give them to Graham Kirk to use on his ship models."

That settled it, so Andrew made a careful selection of all the colours he thought they would need: three of red and three of blue, brown, black, white, dark green, gold, silver and grey. Then he bought four small brushes, each of a different fineness; plus a bottle of thinner to wash them.

Feeling very pleased the pair took their purchases to the counter and paid for them, then waited till their mother joined them. When she was shown what they had bought and had explained why she was very pleased and approving. "That is a lovely thought children. For being so nice I will give you each another twenty dollars."

That made Andrew feel even better, and he found he wanted to get back to the Lions Den, girls notwithstanding, to start painting the tiny people. But there were two more shops for him to endure, one of them full of dresses and ladies' underwear and frilly things that made him feel quite embarrassed.

Then it was time to go. There was no sign of any of the girls so Andrew had to be content with hoping and fantasies. So it was into the vehicle and then back to the church hall to pick up Grandma Cynthia. After that it was a twenty minute drive back to Black Mountain.

Mrs Collins declined Grandma Cynthia's invitation to come in for a cup of tea, much to Andrew's relief. She was a lovely old lady, but he just wanted to get back to the Lions Den. So they said goodbye and turned the car around and drove off.

As they turned onto the highway, Andrew's mother said, "She is lonely, poor old dear, and she would love us to stay and talk, but we are leaving your father too much on his own. So we need to get back. There may have been some problem he needed help with."

And there was. When they crossed the Mungumby Creek bridge and turned into the straight ten minutes later it was at once apparent that something unusual was happening in the roadway in front of the hotel. But only as they got closer did the true nature of it become apparent.

"Oh my God! What is happening here?" Mrs Collins cried as she slowed the car.

Andrew looked through the front and what he saw made his chest tighten with anxiety. Standing in the middle of the road were three men and two horses. Two of the men had guns which they were pointing at each other, and the third man was his father.

And he was standing between the two!

Chapter 17

STAND-OFF

A ndrew stared at the drama with a rapidly growing sense of horror when he saw that the man standing between the two men with guns was his father. On the side closest, beside a saddled horse, was the stockman he had seen a few days earlier. On the other side was Jan the Mercenary. Both the stockman and Jan had rifles and were pointing them at each other. Mr Collins was obviously trying to calm the situation. Anxious faces were peering out of the doorway along the veranda.

Andrew's mother braked the vehicle to a halt near the side gate, switched off and went running towards the men. Carmen got out but stayed near the car. Andrew got out, feeling a sick sense of helpless dread. He walked slowly towards the group, his hands opening and closing and his heart hammering with apprehension.

As Andrew's mother approached the group, his father tried to wave her away. To Andrew's dismay, she ignored this and rushed over to them, demanding to know what was going on. Andrew's father turned to hold her away, looking harassed as he did.

"It's alright, dear, stay out of it please," he pleaded.

"What is going on?" she demanded to know.

Andrew's father gestured behind him and at the same time tried to wave Andrew and Carmen away.

"You kids keep away," he ordered. Then he said, "This man (he nodded towards Jan with distaste evident in both his voice and in his mouth) pulled up near the diesel pump to get fuel. But Jacky Kulburra was already there with his truck. He swore at Jacky, called him a damned kaffir and other insulting names and told him to get out of the way. Jacky objected to being spoken to that way and answered him back so this fellow punched him and knocked him down. Normy saw this and took exception to it and said so. Then Jan threatened to shoot him if he didn't mind his own business, so Normy went to his horse and got his rifle. By then this Jan character had climbed into his truck and also pulled out a gun."

Andrew's mother turned to Jan, her hands on her hips. "You can put that gun down and get out of here."

"That bluidy kaffir called me names. He must apologise," Jan snarled back, his rifle still pointed at the stockman.

"You insulted him first so maybe you should apologise to him!" Andrew's mother snapped. "Now stop pointing that gun and go."

"No! Not till he apologises."

"If you don't leave I will call the police," Andrew's mother replied.

"Huh! The police! They will not get here in time," Jan retorted.

Andrew's mother turned and said, "Carmen, go and phone the police please. Andrew, get inside the hotel."

Both Carmen and Andrew were close to the veranda by then so they moved to obey. Andrew did not want to. He was so anxious about his parents being out there in such a potentially deadly situation that he wanted to stay but could not see how he could help.

But as they reached the mango trees Jan turned and pointed his rifle at them. "Don't you bluidy kids call the coppers. You go in there and I shoot."

At that, they both froze. A look of horror fixed itself on their parent's faces and for a few seconds there was no movement. Then the stockman said quietly, "You stop pointing that gun at them kids or I will drop you right now!"

Jan turned his head and saw that the stockman had raised his rifle and was aiming it at his head from five paces away. He swore and stepped sideways so that Andrew's mother was between them and moved his own rifle to aim at the stockman again. From the way he staggered, Andrew wondered if the man was drunk. It was a potentially deadly stand-off and Andrew felt quite at a loss as to what he could do. He found he was gulping for breath and his heart was now hammering hard.

There were a few more tense seconds before a movement near Andrew drew his attention. He saw that Irish had come out of the hotel and was now close beside him behind the trunk of a mango tree. In his hand he held an old .303 army rifle.

World War 2 vintage, Andrew thought.

Irish whispered, "You kids get ready to get out of the way."

Andrew shook his head. "Give me the rifle," he insisted.

Irish shook his head. "No. I know how to use this."

"So do I. I'm a Quartermaster Gunner in the Navy Cadets; and they are my parents. I will use it." He was surprised at his own certainty and determination.

Irish met his eyes, then nodded. "I hope ye don't have to, Boyo. It will be a terrible thing to have on your conscience."

"Not as bad as having stood by and done nothing when I could have," Andrew answered grimly.

"Aye, there is that. And besides the courts will be more lenient on you if you shoot that bastard than if I do with my background I be thinking," Irish replied.

With that he handed the rifle to Andrew. Andrew took it and at once checked the safety catch and then opened the bolt to check the load. As he snapped the bolt closed, chambering a round, Jan turned his head and saw what he was doing. Once again his rifle swung towards them. But then he hesitated.

Andrew took the chance and stepped behind the mango tree. Irish scuttled across behind the next tree, using some parked vehicles for cover. Carmen stood frozen with anxiety. Andrew went into a kneeling position and aimed the rifle around the right-hand side of the tree.

As he did, he said, "Carmen, phone the police."

Then he knelt in cover and brought the rifle sights to bear on Jan. As Andrew tried to steady his aim he realised that his heart was hammering fast and his hands were sweaty but he calmed himself with grim resolve. A feeling of dread filled him as he carefully pushed off the safety catch and placed his right forefinger on the trigger.

Now ready to shoot, he shouted, "Jan, lower your gun and walk away. If you shoot anyone I will shoot you, and believe me I can use this."

Jan stared at him, his head swinging from one threat to the other. Andrew saw him lick his lips and shake his head and thought that he was realising he could not win, no matter what he did.

I hope he doesn't do anything really stupid, he thought. But he was sure he would pull the trigger if he had to.

Then, to his relief, Jan lowered his rifle and held up one hand. "Okay, I hear you, boy. Keep your cool, eh. Don't pull that trigger by accident."

Then he sneered and swaggered off back towards his vehicle. Andrew kept his sights on him until a vehicle blocked his line of fire. Then he stood up and kept aiming until Jan climbed into his truck. The memory of that insulting 'boy' made his trigger finger seem to itch but he now relaxed.

Jan started up his truck and then drove off, swinging the truck round to head back south. As he did, he yelled, "You will regret you pointed a gun at me boy! You'll pay for that!"

Then he was gone. Andrew slipped on the safety catch and stood leaning on the tree, sweating and trembling. Irish came over and patted his back and then took the rifle back.

"Well done, boyo! That was brave. Good lad!"

Andrew's mother walked over and hugged him, then scolded him angrily for taking such a risk. As she did, Andrew met his father's eyes and understood that his mother was just releasing tension. After his mother stepped back his father shook his hand.

"Well done son. I am proud of you."

Andrew glowed at the praise. The stockman added his share and so did a shy Jacky Kulburra. Feeling somewhat embarrassed Andrew took the opportunity to ask Jacky if he had his fuel. When Jacky said no, Andrew went with him to the fuel pump and busied himself with the refuelling. As he did, he tried to act cool and unaffected but inside he was boiling with emotion and found his hands were shaking.

Hoping that nobody was noticing Andrew took Jacky's money and went in to the hotel. By then his mother had been on the phone to the police, adding to Carmen's account.

After putting down the phone, his mother said, "The police are on their way."

That statement caused some difficulties. Normy the Stockman suddenly became less than anxious to have the law involved and Irish mumbled he had better be getting along. Both quickly left. Other witnesses also seemed to vanish on various excuses. By the time three police arrived half an hour later there were only two people left in the bar.

The police looked worried and two had rifles in addition to their normal hand guns. The police parked their vehicle and came over to where the small group waited outside the bar. A big, leathery-skinned sergeant led the group.

"Sergeant Bull," he said.

Andrew's father introduced them and Andrew self-consciously shook Sgt Bull's hand. Andrew's parents then related what had happened.

As he did, Sgt Bull gave him a quizzical look and said, "I've seen you before. Where might that be?"

Andrew felt an unreasoning rush of guilt and blushed. He said, "We were in town this morning. It might have been then."

Sgt Bull shook his head. "Nope. I was at 'Hopevale' until just before we got this call."

Then he shrugged and smiled. To Andrew's relief, he ended the enquiry and went on with the questioning. A senior constable took notes and the third policeman stood looking around with his rifle held at the 'port arms'. Andrew's parents related what had happened.

When the story reached the point where Andrew was mentioned as having taken the rifle from Irish and having aimed it, Sgt Bull frowned and said, "And how does a young bloke like you get to be familiar with rifles?"

"I am a Navy Cadet. They trained me as a Quartermaster Gunner," Andrew explained.

Sgt Bull nodded and then said, "Were you in town a week or so ago when that navy patrol boat came in about the floating mine?"

"Yes I was," Andrew answered.

Once again, he felt guilty but wasn't sure why. Then into his mind came the image of a policeman looking at him from the door of the police station.

This image was confirmed when Sgt Bull said, "Ah yes, I remember. You are the young sailor those girls were talking to over near the old cannon. Kristen and Daphne."

At that, Andrew blushed and tried to avoid giving his mother a guilty glance. Heated images of being in the river with a near naked Daphne added to his sense of guilt and unease.

"Yes," he mumbled.

He noted his mother give him a sharp look and his father smiling. Carmen added to his discomfiture by saying, "Well, hello sailor!"

"That's what they said," Sgt Bull confirmed. "Now, tell me about this gun business."

An embarrassed and anxious Andrew related his part, adding defiantly, "And I would have shot him if he had done anything to my mum and dad."

Sgt Bull grunted and gave him a hard look. "It is just as well you didn't shoot anyone, young fella. That could have ruined your whole life."

The questioning went on. It became quickly obvious that both Normy the Stockman and Irish were well known to Sgt Bull and the other policemen.

"We know where they both live. We will call on them in due course," Sgt Bull said. "Now, this Jan fellow, where does he live?"

"In a shed a few kilometres up the river," Andrew said.

One of the other men interrupted to say, "No he don't. He might work there but he lives just near me in Rossville." He gave the address and the senior constable wrote it down.

The questioning done the policemen accepted a soft drink each and then climbed back into their vehicle and drove off towards Rossville. Andrew retreated to his bedroom, ostensibly to read but actually to think things over. The incident had shaken him up much more than he had realised. What particularly bothered him was the knowledge that he was sure he would have pulled the trigger.

Am I killer? he wondered unhappily.

The police returned later on their way back to Cooktown. Sgt Bull reported that they had found Jan at his home in Rossville and that he had given quite a different story. The police said they had confiscated his rifle until a decision on charges was decided. Sgt Bull said they would speak to Jacky Kulburra when they next saw him.

Andrew's mother was not happy with that. "That man should have been locked up!" she snapped.

"It seems that Normy Watkins may have threatened him first and he only pulled out his rifle in self-defence," Sgt Bull replied.

Accepting this went against the grain, but Andrew had to concede that it was a possibility. In the end they had to be content with knowing that the police had Jan's rifle.

"But I'll bet he has more or can get another one," Carmen suggested.

"Possibly, but we searched his house and he has been cautioned, so no more trouble please," Sgt Bull said. He then drove off to interview Normy the Stockman.

By then it was dusk and the miners were returning. Work overtook the family and Andrew was kept busy helping serve and wash up. During this there was another annoying incident.

Tim the Miner called across the room to Carmen, "And what are you doing later this evening beautiful?"

Carmen smiled and replied loudly, "I will be with my boyfriend, so bad luck to you."

Tim's mates all laughed and teased him but Andrew wasn't happy. *Is she just saying that or does she really have a boyfriend?* The thought that his big sister might be having a secret affair with someone (One of the miners?) really bothered him. *She is too young,* he thought.

But he knew he was being a hypocrite and that annoyed him as much.

* * *

That evening, Andrew and Carmen started painting the 1:35 scale model people. First they laid old newspaper on a table in Andrew's room. Next, they selected which people to paint first.

"We have a lot," Andrew said. "And we've only got two days to do this."

All the packets of model people were placed on the table and brother and sister studied them. Andrew was particularly taken by the pictures of bright uniforms on the boxes of Napoleonic soldiers.

"These will look really good," he suggested.

Carmen shook her head. "They will, but look at all the fiddly little details that need to be painted if we are going to do them properly. No, I don't think we have the time." She picked up a packet of the much cheaper cowboys and Indians. "These will be easier and we can easily make a toy farm to go with it. I think they will be better for Young Terry."

Reluctantly Andrew had to agree. Each packet of yellow plastic people also included two horses, one for a cowboy and one for an Indian. He could tell which ones because the tiny people were made with bow legs with tiny studs on the inside of their ankles. The studs obviously clipped into holes on the flanks of the horses. All the other plastic people were moulded onto a flat base so they would stand up.

Andrew opted to paint the cowboys. "Graham said to always do the base colours first and then the small details on the outside later," he advised Carmen.

"And try to do the light colours first so the dark ones don't show through if you accidentally paint too much," Carmen replied.

For the next two hours the pair happily painted. By 9:30pm all of the little people and the horses had the base colours done. Carmen cleaned her brush in thinner and said, "That's enough. We have to wait till the paint dries before we do any more. I am going to the kitchen."

"What for? To see your boyfriend?" Andrew said, half teasing and half testing.

Carmen laughed and then poked her tongue at him. "Poo to you, Little Brother! That was only to put that silly Tim in his place. If I want to sneak away to meet a man you won't know."

That comment bothered Andrew even more but he had to concede that Carmen would soon be 18.

She is nearly an adult, and I hope she finds true love, he thought.

But the thought of his sister being intimate with men bothered him deep down. He had always seen her as pure and noble and the thought that she was actually a flesh and blood young woman was a bit disturbing.

He followed her through to the kitchen and they had a supper of cake and Milo. The conversation turned to the afternoon stand-off and that got Andrew concerned.

What if that Jan comes back to get me? he worried.

That fear was still strong after Andrew went to bed. As usual his rational mind told him not to be silly but the lurking terrors of the darkness crept out to bother him. For several hours he slept fitfully, starting awake at every strange sound or mango crashing onto the roof. A shower of rain and some gusts of wind did not help, adding creepy, dripping and moaning sounds to feed his imagination. That Jan was a killer and might try to get some revenge he had no doubt.

In the morning Andrew woke feeling tired and slightly depressed. With consciousness came anxiety about Jan's possible revenge.

I wonder what the day will bring? Andrew thought as he slipped out of bed.

Chapter 18

THE CHRISTMAS TREE

Wednesday morning was taken up with work around the hotel, starting with the breakfast for the miners, then with painting the model people. While Andrew helped serve breakfast and then clear the tables afterwards he watched the by-play between Carmen and the miners.

Is she really having a secret affair? he wondered. But there was no particular clue to indicate which of the young men Carmen might fancy.

While Andrew was sweeping the front veranda after his own breakfast Irish arrived in his old jalopy. He was well dressed by his own standards, even to long sleeved shirt and shoes.

He gave an anxious grin and said in his best Irish accent, "And the top o' the mornin' to yer, me boy. And it's a foin day to be sure."

"Hello Irish. The police were looking for you," Andrew replied.

"I know, and they found me, worse luck!" Irish replied.

"You going to town?" Andrew asked.

Irish nodded and looked rueful. "Yes. The dratted coppers reminded me that I have a fine to pay or it will be the worse for me; the clink they hinted."

Andrew wondered what Irish had done wrong but he resisted the temptation to ask. Instead, he said, "Do you think that Jan will give us more trouble?"

"Yes I do," Irish replied. "He is a mean one that. You be on your guard me boy."

"He won't hurt me will he?" Andrew asked, feeling a wave of cold that he knew as fear. The idea shocked him and he felt his stomach turn over.

"Not so you'll know who it is I wouldn't think. When he's sober he's a cunning rat. He will try to make it look like an accident and he will make sure he has an alibi," Irish warned.

That thought made Andrew feel even sicker. "What about my family?" he asked, anxiety about Carmen's safety rising to the top of his thoughts.

"Maybe, but it was you who really hurt his pride," Irish said.

"Do you know where he is now?" Andrew asked.

Irish nodded. "I saw him and that Barry character having an argument back along the road near Wallaby Creek bridge," he said. Then he shrugged and said, "Anyway, can I have some diesel? I better get to town to pay this fine or I will be in more trouble."

Andrew refuelled Irish's car and he drove off towards Cooktown. As he did, his car ran over several mangos and Andrew thought he had better pick them up as the squashed ones were quite messy. He collected the wheelbarrow and a rake and set to work. As he did, he heard a vehicle coming from the south and looked anxiously that way. But it was a large cream coloured truck with half a dozen Aborigines aboard. He thought it was Jacky Kulburra driving but wasn't sure. He waved as it went past, then resumed raking.

As the truck vanished around the bend at Mungumby Creek, Andrew heard a second vehicle coming from the south. It was traveling much faster and even as he looked he saw a green truck burst out of the cloud of red dust left by the first truck. As soon as he saw it Andrew felt his stomach and chest tighten with anxiety.

Is that Jan's truck? he wondered.

It was. As the truck roared past Andrew saw Jan in the cab. The man glared at him and shook his fist. But he didn't stop. To Andrew's relief, Jan drove on towards Cooktown. As the sound of the truck died away, Andrew realised he was trembling. He found he was sweating profusely and his heart rate was right up.

Not wanting to admit to being scared, Andrew put it down to the heat as the tropical sun was now blazing down from a clear blue sky. Thinking a cold drink would be a good idea he went inside. There he told his parents what Irish had said and about Jan driving past. He then made a point of getting Carmen alone and warning her.

She nodded and said, "I will be careful. Now, let's do some more painting or we will run out of time."

For the next hour they sat and added details to the cowboys and Indians and to the two horses. By then Andrew was feeling very satisfied with the results.

"They are starting to look really good," he said, holding up a cowboy for closer inspection.

"Better than just being yellow plastic," Carmen agreed.

Lunch followed. During it their mother said, "Your father is visiting Mungumby Lodge this afternoon. Would you like to go with him?"

Andrew did want to, but he said, "But that will leave you here on your own."

His mother shook her head. "That Jan fellow won't do anything to me. You just go with your father."

Seeing that his mother was determined Andrew put an idea that had been simmering at the back of his mind.

"Could we walk up to look at the Mungumby Falls?" he asked.

"Where are they?" his mother asked.

"Up a road a couple of kilometres past the lodge," Andrew answered.

His mother looked doubtful. "You had better ask when you get there."

But just in case they were allowed, Andrew made sure that both he and Carmen were dressed for bushwalking in long trousers and long sleeved shirts and with strong boots. Andrew took a small backpack with his map, camera, a raincoat and binoculars and water bottle.

The drive to Mungumby Lodge only took 15 minutes. The side road was an ordinary country gravel road most of the way and then a bush track which wound through fairly ordinary dry bushland. Only towards the end did the vegetation show signs of thickening up into rainforest. After passing a house on the left and dipping down through a fair-sized gully, they reached a small turn-around outside the fence to the lodge. Mr. Collins parked the car beside two others on grass under the trees.

As they got out, Andrew noted a vehicle track leading off uphill and pointed to it. Carmen nodded and indicated a sign which said that it was a 3-kilometre round trip to the falls. But first they had to visit the lodge. Andrew's first impression was of an imitation South Sea village: a cluster of little wooden huts surrounded by lawn and in among trees. After passing through a gate and down a path between two huts, the main building came into sight. To Andrew's surprise, it was a timber building of bungalow style with wide verandas.

The owners were expecting them and were very friendly. They led them out to a very pleasant open room at the rear. This was more of a covered deck with rainforest beside it than a veranda and was the dining room and entertainment area. After being seated and given a soft drink, Andrew learned that most of the clientele for the lodge were interested in nature, especially birds and butterflies.

Even as he was told this, Andrew noted several butterflies fluttering around the sloping back lawn. Most had yellow wings but one was the large 'Ulysses' butterfly with its brilliant blue wings.

The conversation was mostly business oriented and that did not interest him. So after finishing his drink Andrew said, "Excuse me, Dad, may Carmen and I walk up to the Mungumby Falls?"

Mr Collins raised an eyebrow to the owner and he nodded. "It is easy to find. Just follow the track, but please don't get lost. We don't want to spend Christmas searching for you in the jungle."

"We won't. I've got a map and a compass," Andrew replied.

"Don't be long; an hour at most please," Mr Collins added.

Andrew and Carmen hurried out to the car and then set off up the walking track. The track was obviously an old road and was clear and easy to follow except for a carpet of deadfall and sticks. As they puffed up the ever-steeper slope, Andrew took out his map and studied it.

Carmen said, "I wonder why they built this road. It is getting very steep."

"I read that it went to a mine. Later they extended it right up to the top of the mountain. That is a place called the Big Tableland. The map says there was a saw mill there and I read that there were tin mines as well," Andrew answered.

He had been hoping for good views out over the surrounding country as they got higher up the mountain but found that the rain forest restricted this to a few glimpses. All he could recognise were the Black Mountains and the course of the Annan River and the homestead of the cattle station. Just once he got a glimpse of the hotel and that was only with the aid of his binoculars as it was so hidden by the mango trees.

It took them more than thirty minutes of sweaty puffing to reach the falls. They were a bit of a disappointment to Andrew as he had seen many similar waterfalls on the Atherton Tablelands or around Cairns. But he was still glad he had made the effort.

I need the exercise, he thought as he regained his breath and wiped perspiration from his face.

The afternoon sun was blazing down through gaps in the tree canopy and there was almost no breeze. The still, humid air felt stifling and he had a big drink. Then he passed the water bottle to Carmen.

"Drink up. I don't want you getting heat exhaustion," he commented.

"Oh piffle, Little Brother! I can look after myself better than that," Carmen replied. But she had a drink and then passed the bottle back. Then she checked her watch. "Dad said an hour. We had better start back."

Only when Carmen mentioned looking after herself did thoughts of Jan cross Andrew's mind. He glanced anxiously at the dense jungle hemming the track in.

We are very isolated here, he thought.

A spasm of quite unreasonable fear gripped him, and he started back down the mountain at a fast walk.

After a couple of minutes Carmen called out from behind him, "Slow down, Little Brother! It isn't a race."

Andrew did slow down but still kept looking anxiously ahead and behind. He did not want to alarm Carmen so he said, "We need to get back and go looking for our Christmas Tree."

"Yes you... Oh, lookout! Snake!" Carmen cried.

Just in time Andrew heard the hissing sound and saw the movement near his feet. He sprang back even before his eyes had focused. It was a snake, an olive-brown one about 75 centimetres long and from the way it had curled into a striking 'S' shape he had no doubt it was a poisonous type. He quickly took several more steps backwards, his mouth dry with fear and his heart hammering rapidly.

The snake raised its head and kept watching them, hissing as it did. Andrew noted its forked tongue flicking in and out and he shuddered at how close he had come to being bitten. So he moved even further back. Carmen moved with him. Only when they were a good six or seven metres from it did the snake suddenly lower its head and start to slide away. When it moved it went so fast Andrew had difficulty seeing it go.

"Where did the bloody thing go?" he asked, unable to detect any part of the snake in the deadfall and leaves beside the track.

"Into the jungle. Come on," Carmen said. She led the way forward, edging across to the right hand side of the track to be as far as possible from where the snake had vanished from sight.

Andrew followed, his eyes anxiously scanning the scrub and his heart in his mouth. "Well, that's bushwalking for the day. Give me the sea anytime," he said.

Carmen laughed but it was a brittle sound and Andrew knew she had received a fright as well. They hurried on down the track, their eyes now directed more at the ground than at the scenery. Thus they only glimpsed the scrub turkeys and the kingfisher that flitted past, the blue of its wings bright in a bar of sunlight.

Only when they were nearing the lodge again did Andrew remember to be on his guard for Jan. But they reached the lodge car park with no problems and Andrew relaxed. There was no sign of their father at the car so Andrew led the way to the gate into the lodge.

As he and Carmen walked between two wooden huts he was surprised to see the two Malaysian businessmen whom he had seen at the airport a week or so earlier come out of one of the huts. The two men again wore their distinctive 'Kopiah' caps and had long-sleeved, white shirts with ties, long black trousers and polished black leather shoes. They were sweating in the heat and looked quite out of place in that environment.

As he passed the two men, Andrew said hello, just to be friendly, but neither man replied. Both wore dark glasses so he could not see their eyes. Their faces remained set and they went on towards the car park. As there was now only one other car there apart from their own, a white Range Rover, Andrew assumed it was theirs.

"Odd characters to find here," Andrew commented to Carmen as he turned right and walked across the lawn to the main building.

"Why? They might be in the tourist industry," Carmen suggested.

Andrew did not think so. "They would be more friendly in that case," he suggested. Then he added, "They don't look very interested in the wonders of nature. They are probably here to arrange for some wildlife smuggling or something."

"That's ridiculous. You are just being prejudiced," Carmen replied.

Andrew blushed and shrugged, then pushed the Malaysian businessmen out of his mind as a flight of brilliantly coloured parrots squawked past. Without thinking he said, "Tina would love this place."

Then he remembered she had dumped him and he felt a little stab of hurt pride. A flush of shame warmed his neck and cheeks. Tina was a real bird lover and bird watcher. For a few seconds he had vivid flashbacks to when he had rescued her from a gang of bird smugglers at Lake Tinaroo a year and a half earlier. That was when their relationship had really begun.

And I think I still love her, he thought unhappily.

Carmen appeared not to notice his embarrassment. "Yes she would," she replied.

Their father was waiting for them and offered them another soft drink. They had to describe the waterfall. Carmen then described the snake incident. The two owners of the lodge both looked serious and nodded.

"Yes, we get snakes here a lot," he said.

Soon after that they said their farewells and walked back to the car. Fifteen minutes later they were back at the Lions Den. They then related the story of the walk to their mother and she got all anxious about the near miss with the snake.

After a snack and a cold drink, Andrew suggested that they do some more painting but Carmen shook her head.

"Later. Let's go for a walk along the river and see if we can find a suitable tree to make into a Christmas Tree."

Andrew had to agree to that and because it was so hot he suggested a swim as well. Both changed into bathers and sandshoes and then set off. The dogs came with them, running happily in all directions. As they walked along, Andrew noted that there wasn't a cloud in the sky. The air was scented with eucalyptus oil and abuzz with the sound of cicadas.

There were also march flies, as Andrew discovered when one bit him right between the shoulder blades. He slapped and squirmed but couldn't quite reach so Carmen whacked it for him. She laughed, then cried in pain when one bit her on the left leg. After that they kept an eye on each other.

It was only when they were down in the dry rainforest beside the river that Andrew wondered if it was wise for them to be there. *That Jan fellow and his ugly mate were both here with guns the other day,* he remembered. He also had hot memories of being in a passionate clinch with Daphne as he and Carmen waded upstream past the spot where it had happened. *I wonder if I still have a chance with Daphne?* he mused, thinking about the look on her face after Cousin Jean had kissed him.

That got him thinking about girls again and his mind roved over the possibilities and relative merits of Daphne, Colleen, and Kristen. Those thoughts got him mildly aroused and he did experience twinges of anxiety and regret (or was it guilt?) as he passed the shallows where he had kissed Daphne.

But the more frightening memory of Jan shooting the dingo overrode such fantasies and he looked anxiously at the dense undergrowth on both banks. For that reason he suggested to Carmen that they not go too far upstream. After another hundred metres he suggested they try their luck in the other direction. To Andrew's relief, Carmen agreed.

Going back downstream they both slid into the shallow water and paddled or dragged themselves along by their hands. This saved them from the worst of the March fly attacks. It was also very refreshing and easier and the only fly in Andrew's mental ointment then was the niggling thought that maybe crocodiles could get up past the falls.

Down below the big pool they went back to walking, staying on the sandy bank closest to the hotel. Here they located several of the trees Andrew was looking for, she-oaks.

"They look the most 'Christmassy' of the local trees," he said. He did not think there was much chance of finding a pine tree in the jungle.

Having selected a suitable small tree they swam and relaxed in the rapids for half an hour before strolling back up to the hotel. On the way they passed more groups of campers who had arrived and were setting up tents just up on the bank. There were also vehicles parked at two of the lodges and people carrying gear up the steps.

"Looks like this is going to be a popular spot over Christmas," Andrew suggested.

"I think it might be. I suppose it is the social centre of the area," Carmen replied.

Back at the hotel, they completed painting the cowboys and Indians and Andrew insisted they make a start on the Napoleonic figures. In the next hour they painted all the hands and faces on over a hundred small plastic people and white trousers were added to nearly all. Andrew enjoyed it very much and it relaxed him.

But by then the hotel was filling up and the miners were arriving home. Kitchen and dining room work took over. Andrew was again annoyed by Carmen flirting with the miners and also saw Irish in the bar. Irish gave him a grin and a thumbs-up but did not come to speak to him. Andrew took that as good news and pushed the anxiety about Jan further into the back of his consciousness.

That night there was more TV watching and painting of the little people. It also began to rain quite heavily. That cooled everything down and helped Andrew sleep. He slept very soundly, even the flying foxes and the odd mango crashing on the roof having no effect on his slumbers.

Andrew woke on the Thursday morning to the sound of another

heavy shower of rain. But this soon stopped and by the time breakfast was over there was a clear blue sky with the tropical sun shining down to make the air steamy and oppressive. That made for hot, sweaty work while Andrew did his chores. When he finished these at about 9:30, he suggested to Carmen that they do some more painting.

She shook her head and said, "No, not till we have the Christmas tree up and decorated."

So brother and sister collected hats and hand tools and set off down to the river. Along the way they passed the campers and also another group who had stayed the night in a 'lodge' but were now packing their 4WD. After saying cheery good mornings the pair made their way down to the river bed.

For fifteen minutes they walked up and down, studying the trees. Andrew finally decided that the best was a She-oak on the other bank but the river looked to be higher from the recent rain, so he hesitated.

"We will get wet," he said. "I will go back and put my bathers on."

Carmen laughed, "Those shorts need a good wash," she said, "So it doesn't matter."

It was so hot that Andrew agreed. The water felt cool and refreshing and he decided that it wasn't too deep. So they waded in at the top of the rapids. Within five steps Andrew knew he was taking a bit of a risk.

This current is a lot stronger than it looks, he thought as the water swirled up to his thighs and tugged at his legs. *If I slip I could get hurt as I wash down the rapids.*

He said, "It's too dangerous. You go back Carmen."

"No. Just help me across," Carmen replied.

Taking her hand, Andrew edged across. The water reached up to his shorts and he was thoroughly soaked by the time they crossed and so was Carmen. But he didn't care. It had felt refreshing and exciting. And they had reached their tree. It was only about four metres tall and was quickly cut down with the hand saw that Andrew carried. Then they had to negotiate the rapids again.

This time they were less careful and Andrew slipped. At once the current swirled him away. As he went down, Andrew clung grimly to the saw with one hand and the butt of the tree with the other. But that didn't work. The strong current swung him hard against a rock and he was bruised and half stunned.

Carmen still had a firm footing and was holding the other end of the tree. She shouted, "Let go of the tree and swim. I will take the tree across."

By then Andrew had little choice as his grip was slipping on the wet bark anyway. He tried to shout back but got a mouth full of water. The next moment he had let go and was bouncing down the rapids. He opted for feet first and on his back to try to control the movement but a couple of painful whacks on his tailbone quickly indicated that this might not have been the best policy.

For a few seconds he was genuinely scared but then he was down past the rocks and into the deeper water where the bottom was sand. He relaxed and even laughed at the thrill. His only problem was keeping hold of the saw. A few strokes with his free hand took him to the shore, and he waded back up to the sand bar at the bottom end of the rapids. A laughing Carmen met him there. She was soaked and dripping water as well but still had the tree.

"I fell in too," she explained. Then she swatted at a march fly and laughed again.

Laughing and happy the pair carried the dripping tree up to the hotel. The tree was stood against a shed. Then they tried to sneak into their rooms to change but their mother saw them and told them to put the wet clothes into the wash. She wasn't angry and thought their little adventure funny. After drying themselves and changing Andrew and Carmen went to the kitchen for morning tea. Then they set to work erecting the tree in the far corner of the dining room.

The tree was too tall and they had to lop the bottom metre off. Then the butt was placed into a bucket. Carmen then held it upright while Andrew placed stones in the bucket to hold it and to keep it vertical. Christmas paper was then wrapped around the bucket to hide it. This was sticky taped on. Next, the pair set to work adding stars, silver and gold balls, plastic angels and other baubles.

As they worked, Andrew studied the tinsel coming out of the box and said, "This isn't very good. It is too old and has lost half its colours. We need better decorations than this."

"Well, there aren't any," his mother replied, "So make the best you can of them."

"We could go to town to buy some," Andrew suggested.

At that, Carmen burst out laughing. "To town, eh? I wonder what else might be there in the shops?"

Andrew blushed and scowled at her but his mother smiled and said, "Yes we could. But not today. You will have to wait until tomorrow to see your little floosies."

"Mum!" Andrew wailed, blushing again. But he knew she was right.

Tomorrow then, he thought happily, his mind racing with hopes and fantasies.

Despite the poor quality of many of the decorations, they did the best they could to decorate the tree. While they worked Andrew was pleasantly excited with the usual Christmas atmosphere and anticipation of presents and with thoughts of the girls he might kiss. Once the tree was ready, they went to their rooms and collected presents that were already wrapped and brought them out to place under the tree. Then they went back to their rooms to wrap more presents.

By the time they had finished it was lunch time. After lunch Andrew and Carmen settled to more painting. This time red, blue or green coats were painted on the little soldiers. Andrew found it immensely satisfying work.

At every brush stroke they look better, he thought.

His father came to the door of his room and called, "Andrew, there is a truck wanting fuel. I'm busy in the bar. Could you refuel it please?"

"Yes Dad," Andrew replied.

He carefully cleaned his brush in thinner and then wiped it dry before placing it down. Then he walked through to the front and out past the mango trees to where a large brown truck waited. As Andrew approached it, a man stepped out from near the cab.

It was Wes, Jan's mate. Andrew stopped in his tracks.

Chapter 19

CHRISTMAS EVE

Andrew stared at Wes and wondered what to do. To his own annoyance he knew he was scared. Wes stood looking at him, hands on hips and resembling a hostile gorilla.

Do I refuse him fuel and send him away? Andrew wondered. His mind raced and he thought, *His friend Jan is banned, but he isn't. So do I or not?*

He decided that he should, unless his parents said no. Swallowing to moisten his suddenly dry throat he asked, "Do you want fuel?"

Wes grunted and nodded. "Yes. Fill it up."

Andrew felt his stomach moving from fear and that helped steady him. Trying to act cool and relaxed he unscrewed the filler cap and placed the nozzle of the pump into it. Then he began to fill the tank.

It was a big tank and took 100 litres. That took several minutes to fill and during that time Wes stood beside him watching. No words were spoken and Andrew felt very anxious. The stress added to the humidity caused him to break into a sweat.

Wes added to the tension by walking to the back of the truck and returning with a jerry can. "Yer can fill that up too," he said, placing the can down beside Andrew.

The jerry can might be to get fuel for his mate Jan, Andrew suspected.

But he did not ask. Instead, he filled the can. In his nervousness he overfilled it and spilled diesel flowed down the outside of the can.

Wes grunted and said, "Ye'll have ter wash that boy."

"Yes. Sorry," Andrew mumbled.

Blushing at his clumsiness and annoyed because he knew he was afraid of the big man. As quickly as he could, he carried the jerry can to the hose and washed it down. He then lugged it back and Wes placed it in the back of the truck.

"I'll pay in the bar," Wes said.

He then climbed into the cab and started the engine, leaving Andrew wondering if he was going to drive off without paying. He knew it was a foolish thought and that annoyed him too. Wes didn't. He just parked the truck across the road and walked into the bar. Andrew went there as well to tell his father the amount. Then he gratefully retreated to his painting, leaving his father to talk to Wes, who was now drinking beer.

Andrew spent the remainder of the afternoon painting and reading. In the evening he helped with dinner for the miners, ate his own meal, watched TV and did some more painting. During all of this he daydreamed about girls. Several times he constructed erotic fantasies in his imagination. To his own mild annoyance, he found that when he tried to picture the girl he wanted to be with in a particular scene it was Tina who came to mind.

That night he dreamed about her. In the cold light of dawn he could not remember the details of the dream, only that he had been with Tina. For some reason they had been swimming in the sea at night and were miles from land and hoping to reach a small flat island. As usual there were 'things' in the water but he had no idea how he got there or if they got out.

"Hate that dream! Why do I keep having it?" he muttered as he rubbed sleep out of his eyes.

But he knew why, the terrifying memories of being in the grip of the current at Longbow Reef the previous year when he and Carmen had been lucky to survive; and those 18 hours in the ocean after the floatplane crash and then the terrifying experience of being deliberately left in the water by the dive boat at Echo Reef when they had been diving on the wreck of the *Merinda.*

"I hope I never end up in the sea again," he told himself as he made his way to the ablutions.

Once outside Andrew cheered up. It was a bright, sunny morning and felt quite fresh. *Christmas Eve,* he remembered. *And we are going to town. I might see Colleen, or Daphne, or Cousin Jean.*

But first there was work to be done. As Andrew worked at his raking and cleaning chores out the front four vehicles went past towards town. The first was a car full of Aborigines from Wujal Wujal. The second he decided were tourists from the look of their overloaded 4WD. The next was a local woman from one of the houses across the road. Last was Barry. He had Little Terry with him and Little Terry gave him a big smile and a wave.

Andrew waved back and thought, *We must get those cowboys and Indians packed and wrapped before we go.*

That was what he and Carmen did next. As he placed the box of cowboys under the Christmas Tree with Little Terry's name on the card another thought came to him. "I hope that Little Terry's dad doesn't object to us giving the little boy a present," he said.

"He won't want to or I will give him a piece of my mind," Carmen said fiercely.

After morning tea they set off for town. Andrew's mother drove with Carmen beside her. Andrew sat in the back, which suited him as he could daydream in relative privacy. Along the way they pulled in at Black Mountain to get a shopping list from Grandma Cynthia and to collect her mail for posting. They then drove to Cooktown.

The town was noticeably busier than on their previous visit and their mother joked about traffic jams and parking problems in the main street. But Andrew didn't care about traffic. He was focused on meeting girls.

Colleen for preference, he thought, looking up and down the street.

There seemed to be plenty of girls walking around, but none that he knew. So he trailed along with his mother and sister to the shop to buy more decorations for the Christmas Tree. This was an enjoyable ten minutes and he found a silver star that lit up which he insisted they buy. Strings of silver and gold tinsel streamers were also purchased, along with some plastic Santas and angels.

Andrew wanted to go to the cafe to see Colleen but could not think of an excuse to do so; or at least not one that wouldn't draw teasing smirks and comments from Carmen. So he walked along the footpath behind his mother and sister feeling sulky, sweaty and rebellious. There was no breeze and the air had a sweltering dryness to it.

Along the way they passed a hotel. Sitting on the gutter outside was Little Terry. He was playing with an old bottle top and looked quite sad. Andrew felt instantly sorry for the little boy.

"Hello, Little Terry. How are you?" he said.

Little Terry turned his head and his sad expression fled, to be replaced by a dazzling smile. "Hello boy!" he cried. He scrambled up and rushed over to hug Andrew.

That made Andrew feel simultaneously pleased and sad. "Where's your dad?" he asked.

Little Terry pointed into the hotel. "In the pub," he replied. "He said wait here for him."

Andrew glanced through the door into the public bar and saw Barry sitting on a bar stool. Barry was chatting to the barmaid and did not once glance in their direction. But he did take several sips of his beer.

Poor little kid! Andrew thought resentfully.

Carmen thought so too and said it after they had walked on. Their mother agreed. "What hope do poor little blighters like that have in life?" she said angrily.

Andrew could only agree, but soon after that he forgot about Little Terry as he saw Colleen. She walked across the street and went into the cafe. Immediately he began wracking his brains for an excuse to go there. But rather than be teased by Carmen, he said nothing and strolled on in his mother's wake to the next shop. Then they went to another shop, then to the Post Office.

It was nearly another hour before his mother at last said, "It is time for lunch. I wonder where we could buy some?"

"There is the cafe on this side of the street in the next block," Andrew suggested, trying to sound casual.

His mother smiled. "The one where the pretty little girl with the big blue eyes serves behind the counter?" she replied.

"Mum!" Andrew cried, blushing furiously. "Anyway, her name is Colleen."

"I know. I'm just teasing you," his mother replied. "I spoke to her mother the other day. She thinks you are very handsome."

Andrew blushed even more at that while Carmen giggled. He did not know if his mother meant that Colleen thought he was handsome or whether it was her mother. But the thought of mothers discussing him he found a cause for worry. He was also anxious lest his mother suspect the sort of thoughts he had been having about girls recently.

Colleen was there and she gave him a big smile and a cheery 'Hello'. That made him blush even more. When her mother came out from the back of the cafe and smiled at him Andrew went even redder. He found he was tongue tied and flustered. And he got no chance to talk to Colleen on her own. The best they could manage was after the meal when she whispered, "When are you coming to town again?"

"Tomorrow I think, for church," Andrew answered.

A frown creased her brow and she looked quite concerned. "What church is that?" she asked. By the tone of her voice Andrew could tell that the question was important to her.

"Anglican," he replied.

At that, she bit her lip and a stab of worry pierced his heart. "Oh!" she muttered. "I may not see you then."

"Why not?"

"We are Catholics," she answered.

Andrew was quite astonished and also felt right out of his depth. But he could see it was a sensitive topic, so he shied away from it. By then his mother had paid and was saying her farewells.

All Andrew could do was say, "I hope you have a merry Christmas. See you again."

"Merry Christmas and see you again," Colleen echoed, but to Andrew it seemed as though a light had gone out in her eyes.

Still trying to keep up a bold front, Andrew followed his mother and sister out onto the street. Almost at once his emotions were assaulted again. As they crossed the street he saw Little Terry still sitting outside the hotel. The little boy was playing in the dust of the driveway beside the hotel and looked thoroughly tired and down.

"Hello, Little Terry. Is you dad still in there?" Andrew asked as he reached him.

Little Terry looked up and again his face lit up. "Hello Big Boy and Carmen. Yes he is. I wish he would stop drinking. I'm very hungry."

"Oh you poor little tyke!" Andrew's mother said. But there was nothing they could do so they left him playing and walked on.

"Some parents shouldn't have children," Carmen said as they made their way to another shop.

Andrew could only agree. Seeing Little Terry like that made him both sad and angry.

There were more shops to visit and they drove to several, either because of the distance or because of the quantity of food and other things they purchased. They went to a baker and a butcher and a supermarket and loaded bag after bag into the vehicle.

"This is a lot of food, Mum," Andrew said as he stood in the blazing sun at the back holding several shopping bags and wishing he had a hat on.

His mother took one of the bags and stowed it securely and said, "We will have up to twenty people to feed for dinner tomorrow," she explained.

"Twenty!"

"Yes. There are four of us, plus the six miners; that's ten. And we were warned to expect a few from town and some of the locals and relations have booked for lunch."

"Which relations?" Andrew asked, images of Cousin Jean springing to mind.

To his embarrassment his mother smiled before answering. "Aunty Ethel is bringing her family over," she said.

Cousin Jean! Andrew thought hopefully.

Then he blushed, fearing his mother could read his mind which had flooded with erotic images. He tried to pretend he wasn't really interested and handed his mother the other bag of groceries.

Once the vehicle was loaded Andrew said, "Can we just drive down to the wharf before we go home Mum?"

"Why, I thought you had seen your little girlfriend," she replied.

Carmen laughed and spoke over his blushing protests. "He's got more than one Mum. There must be at least three."

"There are not!" Andrew retorted angrily, guilt making him both angry and embarrassed. "I just want to see the sea," he added. This was partly true. Some need deep inside him made him hunger to see the ocean and ships.

"Alright," his mother agreed.

Carmen said nothing but smirked as they climbed in. Their mother started the vehicle and drove back to Charlotte Street. As the vehicle's air conditioner cooled the interior, she sighed and said, "Oh, that's better! It is getting really hot."

"Christmas in Australia," Carmen commented.

As they drove along the main street, Andrew looked hopefully out. But he did not see any girls at all. What he did notice was poor Little Terry still sitting outside the hotel.

Poor little kid! he thought.

He now hoped that either Daphne or Kristen might be fishing at the wharf but the only females visible appeared to be middle-aged tourists. Andrew was disappointed but he still enjoyed spending a few minutes looking at the waves and the boats. Then they drove back along the main street.

Once again Andrew saw a lonely and unhappy Little Terry sitting outside the hotel. All he could do was shake his head.

The drive back to Helenvale was uneventful. By this time Andrew knew the road well enough to not be very interested in looking out. Instead, he fantasised about girls. But even that wasn't an entirely satisfactory experience as he could not make his mind up about which girl he really wanted to be with. Images of Daphne mixed with those of Cousin Jean and Colleen. Even Tina made intrusions into his images and he had to make a real effort to concentrate.

Back at the hotel everything was normal. A line of vehicles was parked at the front and clusters of drinkers sat on the veranda or in the bar. A couple of young men were playing pool. The vehicle was parked at the back and Andrew helped carry the shopping in. He and Carmen then had a drink and biscuit before redecorating the Christmas tree. They also hung up a few more decorations. During this several of the drinkers made passes at Carmen. She laughed and flirted and did not seem to mind.

Andrew did, eyeing the men distastefully. *Dirty old men!* he thought.

He and Carmen then went to their rooms and wrapped some more presents and then sat and painted more of the little soldiers. This time Andrew added white cross belts and brown to their packs and muskets. Carmen did the details on the cavalry horses: saddles, bridles, and saddle cloths which had badges and embroidered edges.

The afternoon passed quickly. Andrew was happy enough except for the heat. He found the perspiration dripping off him, even sitting in the shade. The scent of eucalyptus pervaded the area and the shrill whine of cicadas drowned out most other sounds.

Then Andrew was given the chance to get a bit of his own back when Cousin Sandy arrived and sought out Carmen. As Cousin Sandy talked to her, he kept one hand behind his back. When he at last moved it into view it had a gift wrapped in Christmas paper in it.

"For you," he said. Carmen blushed but managed to smile and say thank you but Andrew could tell she was secretly not impressed.

"I'll leave you to it," Andrew said, standing up and grinning.

Carmen gave him a 'Just-you-wait' look but then pointedly ignored him. Andrew chuckled and went off to the kitchen. Carmen joined him a few minutes later, with Cousin Sandy trailing hopefully behind. As she came in, she gave Andrew a quick glare and then rolled her eyes. Cousin Sandy seemed oblivious to the atmosphere and kept prattling on about fishing and how good his new ute was. Andrew sipped a cold soft drink and gave Carmen teasing smirks when Cousin Sandy wasn't looking.

It was their mother who saved them when she came in and said, "I'm sorry Sandy, but I must ask you to leave the kitchen. It is time we started cooking tea for the miners."

Cousin Sandy looked irritated but nodded and left, saying, "I'd best be getting home anyway."

No sooner had he left than another problem arrived. Barry parked his Land Rover and got out. Little Terry followed. Carmen saw him and gasped, "Oh Andrew, you keep Little Terry here while I make sure none of those model soldiers are out where he can see them."

Andrew did so. Little Terry ran over to him as his father went into the bar. Andrew asked him if he wanted a drink but he said he needed to go to the toilet. As they walked through the dining room Little Terry saw the Christmas tree in the corner. His eyes lit up and he gasped and hurried over to it.

"Oooh! A Christmas tree!"

Little Terry saw the presents under the tree and knelt to look at them. He picked one up and read the name on the card.

Looking up hopefully, he said, "Is there a present here for me?"

Andrew and Carmen looked at each other and then glanced over to where Barry was just visible drinking beer in the bar. Feeling somewhat anxious lest Barry object, Andrew nodded.

"Yes, but you can't have it until tomorrow."

Little Terry's eyes gleamed and he looked eagerly at the parcels clustered under the tree. There were now more than Andrew could easily count, the others having been added by their parents.

There must be twenty at least, he estimated. It certainly looked good.

After picking up several presents and not finding his name Little Terry said, "Which one is mine?"

Carmen pointed and said, "That is one, the one with the Santas on it." Little Terry picked it up and eagerly studied it and then shook it. It was obvious he had no idea what it was. He asked but Carmen laughed and said, "You will have to wait."

Little Terry looked frustrated and for a moment Andrew feared he might start to cry. But Little Terry put the present down and ran eagerly across to the bar calling, "Daddy! Daddy! Big Boy and girl give me a present."

Andrew and Carmen followed, both anxious that Barry not abuse them for doing so. "I hope he doesn't say he can't have it," Carmen muttered. When they reached the door of the bar, Barry scowled at them, so she said, "I hope you don't mind."

Barry just grunted and shrugged, then turned back to his drink. Little Terry turned back to Andrew and Carmen, and said, "Santa is coming tonight. Daddy said so."

"He is," Andrew agreed, forcing a smile. Not wanting to stay anywhere near the surly Barry and the couple of drunks in the bar he said, "Now come and have that drink."

They took Little Terry out the back and after a toilet visit and a drink of cordial sat him on the front veranda and began to play toy cars with him. It was dusk by then and the miners were arriving back. That meant work in the dining room. They left Little Terry playing and went to work.

The miners were in a party mood and most carried drinks from the bar to the dining tables. Simon and Tim did a lot of good-natured flirting with Carmen. Their rivalry was very obvious and a source of some entertainment to the other miners. Annoyed by this, Andrew could not help saying, as he placed a plate of food in front of Simon, "You need to watch out. Her cousin Sandy is taking her fishing next week."

Simon looked annoyed and embarrassed but did not respond. Carmen pursed her lips and gave Andrew a sharp look.

"What about Cousin Jean?" she asked him.

Andrew blushed at the amused laughter of the miners and quickly made his way back to the kitchen. Dinner proceeded with brother and sister looking for opportunities to score points off each other. Then, while Andrew was doing the washing up, his mother came back from the dining room with more dirty plates and made a statement that moved him so much he felt his eyes go moist.

"The miners have asked if they can put their presents under our tree," his mother said. "Do you mind?"

Andrew shook his head. "No, Mum. I think that is a really nice idea."

Carmen agreed and went to tell the miners. From the cheer that went up Andrew gathered that it was a very popular decision and he felt glad. He knew that most of the miners would be away from their homes over Christmas and he found that sad.

After dinner the miners began to sing and tell jokes. There was a lot of drinking and the story telling. Unable to hear the TV above the hubbub, and not liking the beery atmosphere Andrew went out to the front veranda. He had been going to walk out into the cool evening air to check the sky but found Little Terry still sitting there looking miserable. That annoyed Andrew even more. A glance showed Little Terry's father still drinking beer in the bar.

"Have you had anything to eat Little Terry?"

Little Terry looked hopeful but anxious. "Not yet," he said. "Daddy said he take me home soon."

"I hope so," Andrew said.

No sooner had he said this than there were loud and angry voices at the bar. Barry's father stormed out, shouting back through the door, "Unfriendly bastards! Won't even give a man another drink!"

Andrew's father appeared at the door. "You have had too much to drink already."

"What's it to you!" Barry retorted, clutching at the post for support.

"Because the law says it is my business," Andrew's father answered. "I have signed a contract to administer the lease and that makes me and my family legally liable and involved. If you get injured because of drink that we sold you then we could be taken to court."

"Ah! Bloody lawyers!" Barry spat. "Mob of mongrels they are! Took all me money and gave it to that sneaky, cheating bitch! Or kept it for themselves more like. Anyway, let go of me. I don't have far to drive."

"No."

"Don't you tell me what to do!" Barry shouted.

At that, Andrew tensed ready for a fight but Barry just muttered and swore and stumbled out to his vehicle. Andrew's father followed.

"Don't you try to drive that thing. You are over the limit."

"Get stuffed!" Barry shouted, angrily pulling the door open and climbing in. As he slammed the door, Andrew's father tried to wrench it open but failed. The Land Rover's starter began to whirr.

Little Terry jumped off his chair and ran along the veranda calling, "Daddy! Daddy! Don't leave me!"

Andrew ran after him, followed by Carmen. As he did, he saw his mother's anxious face show through the door to the bar, along with half a dozen of the miners'. But Barry did not wait. He started the engine and revved it until it roared. Then, with a grinding of gears and a spray of dirt and gravel he accelerated the Land Rover backwards out of the line of parked vehicles. Sand and stones showered over Andrew and Little Terry and stopped them for a moment. Barry skidded the Land Rover to a stop out on the road and crunched the gears into forward. The engine roared and the Land Rover leapt forward, almost striking Andrew's father who was still calling on Barry to stop. Only as the Land Rover accelerated away did its lights come on.

Little Terry ran out onto the road and stared after the rapidly dwindling lights. Andrew joined him, then Carmen and their father.

Andrew's father was breathing heavily. "Mad bugger!" he said.

"Daddy!" wailed Little Terry.

Then he turned to look up at Andrew, tears streaming down his cheeks. He said, "It will be alright Little Terry. We will look after you."

"But... but... Daddy promised," Little Terry sobbed.

Carmen crouched to face him. "It's alright, little man. You are safe here. He will come back when he realises you are still here," she said.

But Little Terry would not be consoled. His chest and shoulders heaved and the blubbing became almost hysterical. Seeing the little boy in such intense distress brought tears to Andrew's eyes as well and he bit his lip, wondering how he could calm him.

He said, "It will be alright Little Terry. Remember, it is Christmas. Santa will bring presents tonight."

At that, Little Terry turned huge tear-filled eyes to him and wailed, "B... but... he... w... w... won't (sob) kn... kn... (sniffle) know... whe... whe... where I am to b... b... (blub) b... bring m... me... m... my... pres... (sniff) present!"

Chapter 20

SANTA

A ndrew was shocked and it took him a few moments to fully comprehend what Little Terry was saying. Then he saw Carmen's horrified face and the enormity of the situation dawned on him.

Poor little bugger! He thinks he won't get any presents for Christmas because he won't be where Santa Claus thinks he lives.

The sight of that tears-streaked face and quivering lips made his own emotions churn and his eyes go moist.

"Don't worry Little Man. We will make sure Santa knows where you are," he said.

Little Terry looked up with a look that was a mixture of hope and despair. "B... b... but... (sniff) how?"

Carmen now took control. "We will telephone him and let him know right now. Come with us," she said.

She reached out and took his hand. Little Terry's face lit up and he walked quickly with her in to the dining room. Andrew followed and as they reached the telephone he raised a quizzical eyebrow to her. He could see the outline of her plan but not how she was going to implement it.

After picking up the telephone, Carmen said to Little Terry, "You just wait till we get through to Santa's. Now, this might take a while, and we may not get Santa straight off. He must be very busy tonight getting all the toys and presents ready for all those children. We might get one of his helpers to begin with. Will that be alright?"

Little Terry nodded eagerly, his face now alight with hope. That worried Andrew and he gave a slight frown to Carmen.

How is she going to do this? he wondered.

Carmen smiled at him and said, "Trust me." Then she began pushing the buttons. Andrew stood smiling down at Little Terry and straining his ears to overhear. The dial tone sounded clearly and then a female voice answered. "Hello!" it said.

Tina! Andrew thought, instantly recognising her voice. It was enough to send a sharp pang of regret through him.

Carmen said, "Hello, this is Carmen. Is that Santa Clauses'?"

Tina's voice came back faintly to Andrew. She sounded puzzled but happy. "Carmen, is that you?"

"Yes, it is. Are you one of Santa's helpers? This is very important please."

Something in her voice must have transmitted itself to Tina as she replied, "Yes, this is Santa's Workshop. How can I help you?"

"You are one of Santa's helpers? That is great! I have a little boy here who is very worried that Santa won't know where he is sleeping tonight. If I tell you his name and where he lives can you please make sure Santa is told?"

"Of course. Is this boy's name Andrew?" Tina asked.

Carmen laughed and said, "No. His name is Terry and he is five years old. He is staying with us at the Lions Den Hotel. He will be sleeping in Andrew's room."

"Lucky boy!" Tina replied.

Carmen darted Andrew a glance and he blushed at the implication. *Does she still like me? Does she want to spend the night with me?* he wondered.

Then Tina said, "Do you think the little boy would like to tell Santa himself, just to make sure?"

"I'll ask," Carmen said. She looked down at Little Terry, who appeared to be hanging on every word. "Would you like to talk to Santa, Little Terry?" Little Terry nodded, apparently speechless with joy. Carmen said, "He'd love that, if Santa isn't too busy."

Tina replied. "No, he isn't. I will get him. Just wait a minute."

The line went quiet and Andrew grinned at Little Terry who smiled excitedly back. Andrew met Carmen's eyes and she looked very happy. It all made Andrew feel very proud of her and he felt quite emotional again.

The phone came alive again and a booming "Ho! Ho! Ho!" voice sounded. Andrew at once recognised it as Tina's father's and again he felt humbled and pleased.

Trust her to think of that, he thought.

Little Terry so was so excited and overawed that he could hardly speak but bit by bit 'Santa' drew out of him where he was and what he wanted for Christmas. The conversation went on for a good five minutes before 'Santa' handed back to Tina.

Little Terry handed the phone back to Carmen and she said, "Thank you Santa. You are wonderful. Now, Santa's Helper, would you like to say hello to the other boy here, the one Little Terry calls 'Big Boy'?"

"Big Boy, eh?" Tina chirped and Andrew blushed at the innuendo. Then she said, "Just tell him Merry Christmas from me; and Merry Christmas to you too Carmen."

"Merry Christmas and thanks for that. Bye!" Carmen replied. She then said, "Okay, that is fixed. Now, let's get this little man some tea and get organised for bed."

The next hour was taken up with getting Little Terry something to eat and then bathed and ready for bed. As they did, this, Andrew puzzled over how to do a bit of 'Santa-ing' himself. When Little Terry was busy talking to their mother he put the problem to Carmen.

"We need a stocking to put on his bed."

"That's easy. A pillow case is all Mum and Dad usually use," Carmen replied.

"Mum and Dad? I thought Santa brought them," Andrew answered with a grin.

Carmen laughed and gave him a light punch on the upper arm. "Goose! Next, you will tell me that you still believe in the Tooth Fairy."

"I do! But what are we going to put in this stocking?" Andrew asked.

"Some little toys and some lollies and a chocolate, and maybe a small book. Let me have a look while you read him a story and get him settled," Carmen said.

Andrew led Little Terry to his room, sure that the little boy would not sleep anywhere else and not wanting to possibly upset him by even suggesting it. There he read him a short story and got him to lie down. The noise of the miner's party died down and silence settled except for a few murmuring voices and the occasional clink of a bottle or glass. Several vehicles started up and drove off.

While Andrew and Little Terry talked, the flying foxes began a squabbling commotion in the mango trees and several mangos crashed onto the roof.

Little Terry looked up anxiously and said, "Do you think we will hear Santa's reindeer?"

Andrew shook his head. "Probably not. I think they stay just above the roof so they don't wake anyone."

"Will the flying foxes bother them?"

"I don't think so. Santa has been coming to North Queensland for many years without any problems. It will be okay. Now you had better get to sleep because he doesn't come while you are awake," Andrew said. He went and switched off the light.

But Little Terry was too emotional to want to sleep. He lay awake, from time to time asking questions about Santa. Andrew lay on his own bed in the darkness, happy but sad. To his own surprise he found his own thoughts continually turning to Tina.

It must have been the sound of her voice, he reflected. The frequency and intensity of the memories disturbed him. *Maybe I do still love her?* he decided.

Which got him all confused over how he felt about the other girls. Daphne, that was just lust. He could recognise that. And Cousin Jean even more so. He wanted to have a physical experience with her but actually found her forthright personality quite intimidating.

And what about Colleen?

She bothered him most. She was so pretty and so 'peaches and cream' and romantic that he felt sure he could fall passionately in love with her.

At last Little Terry dropped into a restless sleep. Andrew got up and went to find Carmen and she showed him a packet of plastic animals, a small chocolate, a colouring book and some pencils and a bag of lollies from the bar, plus a dozen coins and some small packets of chips.

"Not much, but it will have to do," she said.

Andrew agreed and then said goodnight to his mother and father. His mother said, "You should have been asleep hours ago. Santa only comes to good little boys."

"Mum!" Andrew replied.

But he was now happy. Thankful that had such good parents he kissed them both and hurried back to his room. He found Little Terry sitting on his bed crying and very distressed.

"It's alright Little Terry," Andrew said, upset that he had been away when the boy had woken up. "I just went to say goodnight to my mum and dad. Now, you hop back into your own bed."

In reply Little Terry shook his head. Andrew didn't have the heart to insist. "It will be hot and sweaty," he warned.

On an impulse he hugged the little boy and then got him to lie down against the wall. Then he lay down beside him and tried to compose himself to sleep. Little Terry did not help by reaching across and taking a firm grip on his right hand.

Then sleep would not come for Andrew. Little Terry slipped off into a snuffling doze but he lay there wide awake, his mind full of memories, fantasies and hopes. There was also some anxiety.

Tina is joining us with her friend Adele in a few days. Will that just be all embarrassing and tense? he wondered.

Then he fanned himself as there was no breeze and perspiration trickled out of him. Even at midnight it was still so hot that he could not bear even a cotton sheet over him.

"I must get up and put Little Terry's stocking on his bed," Andrew told himself. He wondered if he could lift the little boy back onto his own bed without waking him.

It was the last thought he remembered before he woke on Christmas Day.

* * *

It was the sound of delighted chuckling that brought Andrew back to consciousness. He opened his eyes and look across the room to see that Little Terry was sitting up on his own bed, his face alight with pleasure as he dug into a pillow case. Already out on the bed were a toy car and some packets. Little Terry had obviously already found his chocolate because Andrew could see a smear of it around his mouth.

 Little Terry saw him move and looked, then cried out, "Look! Look! Santa did find me!"

"That's great Little Terry. Merry Christmas!" Andrew replied as he sat up.

Little Terry pointed and said, "Merry Chwistmas too. And look, Santa brought you some presents too."

Andrew looked and realised that what his feet had been pushing against was a pillow case with presents in it. He experienced a moment of intense pleasure and then felt slightly foolish. But it was nice.

Mum and Dad must have played Santa Claus again, he thought happily.

Into his mind came those previous Christmases as he got older when he had doubted the existence of Santa Claus and had discussed this with Carmen and then lain awake to try to see if it really was Santa, or whether it was his parents as his older friends suggested. Never once had he caught his parents being Santa but he knew it was them.

Feeling very happy he dug into the pillow case and quickly dug out the presents. They were all small ones but still gave a spurt of pleasure at each little discovery. There were lollies and his favourite, a Cadburys Caramello chocolate, a toy car (Bright red), a small plastic kit model of a British Destroyer of World War 2 (HMS Cossack), a *Phantom* comic, a small pocketbook of Australian fish and a small plastic submarine.

Carmen arrived next and a few seconds later their parents. Andrew smiled and said, "Thanks Mum and Dad."

His father grinned back and said, "Don't thank us. Thank Santa."

Little Terry now burst in excitedly, calling for them to see what Santa had given him. "There's a red car too, just like Big Boy's," he added, holding the Matchbox toy up for them to see.

Santa's presents were a big hit and started the day off on just the right note. Andrew left Little Terry to play while he showered and shaved and then, with some difficulty, got him out to the kitchen table, still with the red car clutched firmly in one chocolate smeared hand.

After they had eaten breakfast, Little Terry jumped down and ran into the dining room where the miners were starting to gather for their breakfast. They were not working that day so breakfast was half an hour later, at 7 instead of 6:30. Andrew and Carmen followed him with their parents bring up the rear. As they did, the miners that were there gave a rousing 'Merry Christmas!'

This was returned. Carmen then said, "Which is it to be: presents first or food?"

Andrew saw Little Terry kneeling hopefully at the base of the Christmas Tree. "Presents, at least for some," he said.

His mother agreed. "Yes, but we must be quick. We are going to church and that starts at nine thirty."

Mr Collins waved them all to move into a semi-circle. "You chaps all sit here and the kids can bring the presents one at a time."

Andrew disliked that 'kids' comment but did as he was told. He moved to crouch beside Little Terry. Little Terry said eagerly, "Which one is mine?"

Andrew picked up the packet of painted cowboys and gave it to him. "This one is for you, from me."

"Thank you, Big Boy," Little Terry said, taking the present and at once starting to rip the wrapping paper off.

One of the miners laughed and said to his friend, "Big Boy? I thought that was what young Miss Carmen here called you Simon?"

Simon scowled and blushed and Andrew darted him a glance of dislike. It gave him some malicious pleasure to note that Simon looked unshaven and hung over.

His mother snapped at the first miner, "That will be enough of that, thank you!"

There was a moment of embarrassed silence, broken by Carmen picking up a present and reading, "From Rob to Johno. Here you are, Johno."

She walked over and gave it to a middle-aged miner who grunted gruff thanks to his mate. Andrew took the hint from Carmen and picked up another. It was to Simon from Johno. He took it over and handed it to Simon, pretending to be happy. Simon thanked him and the tension eased.

Carmen handed one to their father so Andrew gave one to his mother. Then he handed another to one of the miners. As they did, another bleary-eyed miner arrived in a soiled T-shirt and scruffy jeans: Tim. He muttered about needing a drink and was told by Andrew's mother that the bar wouldn't be open till ten and he could have tea or coffee and while it was being prepared he could go and have a wash and tidy up. An embarrassed Tim withdrew.

By then Little Terry had opened his present and was holding one of the tiny cowboys. A look of wonder grew on his face. "These little men are weally gweat," he cried, his voice squeaking with excitement. It seemed hat he had never seen such toys before.

Carmen then handed him her present of Indians and he eagerly attacked the paper. While he opened it Andrew took a present to his mother. It was from him and was an embroidery kit with sew-to-instructions that became a picture of a bunch of flowers. She was suitably pleased and gave him a hug and a kiss, making him feel even happier and more loved.

Then Carmen handed him a present. It was from her and when he opened it he found a box containing a computer game called, *Carriers at War IV*. It included the British aircraft carriers of the Second World War in their many operations in the Mediterranean and Atlantic. He was pleased but as he had no computer it would have to wait until they went back to Cairns.

He and Carmen then handed more presents to miners. As they did, Irish drove up and came in to join them, to general greetings. He stopped and admired the set-up and cried, "Well, this is a foine arrangement. Now all that we need to make it a real Christmas is some snow."

They all laughed but Andrew, who being Australian had only ever known Christmas in the blazing heat of summer, thought, *No, this is how Christmas is to me.*

He happily noted the rising temperature and humidity and the rising crescendo of whining from the cicadas, and it felt good and normal to him. Even the scent of eucalyptus seemed to be part of it.

Irish handed a present to Andrew's mother saying, "With the permission of Mr Collins I would like to give his lovely lady a small token of my esteem."

Andrew saw his mother give a maidenly blush and he could tell she was pleased. His father just grinned and waved his hand. The present was only a CD of music but it was the sort of Irish music that Andrew knew his mother really enjoyed listening to. As there was a CD player in the corner it had to be put on at once. This led to a short break for tea, coffee or soft drink before more presents.

Andrew received a DVD movie from his mother titled 'The Battle of the River Plate' about a battle in World War 2 between three British cruisers, the HMS *Ajax*, HMNZS *Achilles* and HMS *Exeter* against the German pocket Battleship *Graf von Spee*. He had seen it before but was still pleased to have his own copy.

His father gave him a radio-controlled model of a Coast Guard launch, complete with control and batteries.

"I will try her out on the river," he said, his mind instantly flitting to previous scenes on the river. Heated images of Daphne flooded his mind.

These caused him to squirm mentally with guilt and doubt as Carmen handed him his next present. It was from Tina. A very mixed swirl of emotions went through him: fond memories; hurt, guilt; pleasure at getting a present. In that instant he knew that he still cared for her very much and he wondered if they might rekindle their relationship.

She will be here in a couple of days, he thought hopefully.

The present was a book. It was about aircraft carrier design and looked to be very interesting. It was crammed with photos, cut-away drawings, tables and lists. "This will be interesting," he said as he placed it with his other presents. As he did, he noted Carmen looking at him thoughtfully and he blushed.

Then his emotions were stirred some more when his mother said, "Well, time for us to go to church. Thank you all. Now, you children get ready."

At the mention of church, Andrew had a sharp mental image of Colleen. Then he thought of Tina and he felt very confused. He despised himself for being disloyal and weak but could not shake his hopes of romance with Colleen.

There was a bit of tension when Little Terry realised he was being left behind. As the tears began to form in his eyes, Carmen knelt and said, "We won't be long, Little Terry. Besides, your dad might come to get you and you need to be here."

"That's right," Andrew added. "Your dad might have more presents for you."

Little Terry perked up at that and Irish helped by stepping forward and saying to Little Terry, "Why don't you and I go and play a game with these nice new toys of yours eh?"

Little Terry accepted that and Andrew, Carmen, and their mother were able to get away without further drama. They drove off at 8:30. Along the way they went in to visit Grandma Cynthia at 'Black Mountain'. Andrew did not really want to do this but resigned himself to being good mannered. His mother gave both Grandma Cynthia and her husband Christmas presents. One looked suspiciously like a 'six pack 'of beer to Andrew and the other was some sort of knitting or embroidering. The old lady was gratifyingly touched and grateful. That made it all seem worthwhile but Andrew still fidgeted impatiently as he stood at the door.

Luckily, they did not go inside as all he now wanted to do was get to town in the hope of seeing Colleen. So he waited patiently, sweating heavily and fanning himself with his hand. In the low ground behind the mountains the summer air was stifling and the heat seemed to reflect off the rugged black rocks on two sides. March flies began to buzz and attack, and the cicada's whine was so loud they made it hard to hear.

It was a relief to get back into the vehicle at 9:00 o'clock. They drove on quickly towards Cooktown. Twenty five minutes later they arrived in town.

As they drove in, Andrew's mother glanced at the clock on the dashboard and muttered, "We will be late for church if we don't hurry."

It seemed that they were as when they pulled up outside the church there were plenty of parked cars but very few people outside. As he climbed out of the vehicle, Andrew looked hopefully in both directions along the street but there was no sign of any of the girls. He had really been hoping to see Colleen and was quite cast down. However, he hid this and followed his mother and sister into the church.

The service had not yet started, but many of the pews were occupied. Andrew self-consciously took a seat, feeling very much the outsider and stranger. But the service, when it began, was the normal routine he was familiar with and he was able to relax and join in. Normally Andrew paid no attention to organised religion, only attending for the minimum major two festivals: Easter and Christmas.

But he had absorbed enough of old-fashioned doctrine to have a healthy regard for his conscience and for the possible consequences of being a sinner. So when the priest called on them to renounce evil and to confess their sins he was smitten by heated images of himself with Daphne and with Cousin Jean and he felt quite guilty. He was also conscious of being a hypocrite, as he was sure that if the chances to be with them arose again he would succumb to the temptation.

In spite of that, he enjoyed the church service. It was so much a part of what he believed Christmas to be that it made the day seem complete and also settled his anxious conscience. So it was a happy lad who walked out at the end of the hour. He shook hands with the minister and mumbled a greeting before walking back out into the blazing sunshine.

The sun was so hot and bright that he was forced to squint and for a few seconds he just stood and allowed his eyes to adjust. Then his focus returned and he looked around in hope of seeing one of the girls.

And there was one! Colleen was walking towards him and smiling!

Chapter 21

CHRISTMAS DAY

Colleen! Andrew's heart leapt. *God, she is lovely!* he thought, marvelling at her grace and beauty.

Only now did he realise just how shapely she was. She had a real womanly curve to her waist and hips that set his pulses racing and her hair sparkled in the sunlight in a way that made his heart turn over.

Then anxiety and a vague sense of guilt made Andrew look hastily around to check whether his mother or sister was watching. To his relief, Carmen was nowhere to be seen and his mother was busy talking to the minister and another lady at the church door. Hoping that the twenty or so people already outside would provide sufficient cover, he walked quickly towards Colleen.

As he reached her he gave a hesitant smile, worried lest he be mistaken. To his relief, she beamed a smile back at him and said, "Hello Andrew. I was hoping I would catch you here."

Andrew was pleased and he replied, "I wanted to see you too."

Then it dawned on him that Colleen had not arrived by chance, and he felt even better. *If she has bothered to find out what time my church finishes, she must be interested in me,* he thought.

To confirm this he said, "Did you go to church?"

Colleen nodded. "Yes, at nine o'clock. We just finished."

At that moment, Andrew noted two more teenage girls come around the next corner and headed in their direction and again he felt his heart rate shoot up, but this time with anxiety. It was Daphne and Kristen. Daphne wore the shortest and tightest of white shorts and her pink 'Babe' T-shirt. Kristen wore hip-hugging jeans and tight yellow T-shirt. The effect, to Andrew's adolescent male brain, was pure sexiness and he felt a spasm of arousal. This was tinged with worry.

I hope they don't see me with Colleen, he thought. But that hope was dashed almost instantly as they both looked and Kristen pointed. The girls changed direction and came walking towards them. *I hope they don't know Colleen,* he thought.

But they did. They called 'Merry Christmas' and waved. They did this so noisily that the old ladies near Andrew looked and then frowned with obvious disapproval when they saw how the two girls were dressed.

Daphne arrived first. "Hi Andrew, Merry Christmas. Hi Collie Baby!"

Before Andrew could react, Daphne gave him a kiss and said, "What did Santa bring you?"

"Some books and computer games," Andrew mumbled. Blushing with confusion as he noted his mother looking in his direction he said, "Do you two know each other?"

Daphne laughed and nodded. "Yep. We all go to the same boarding school."

That was bad news for Andrew as he saw his chances of playing the field rapidly diminishing. "Which one is that?" he asked.

"Mount St Bernard Convent in Herberton," Daphne answered.

Andrew nodded and said, "I know where that is."

He remembered seeing it on the cadet exercise the previous year when he had been torn with jealousy over Tina kissing Graham Kirk. That was when he had realised he really had strong feelings for Tina. He found that thinking about her while looking at Colleen caused him some uncomfortable emotions.

By way of explanation he said, "We stayed over the road at Woodleigh College at the end of a cadet exercise last year."

His hopes of seeing more of Colleen went up slightly as Herberton was only 120 kilometres from Cairns and he often went to the Atherton Tablelands. But the mystique of it being a convent got him doubting if being closer would be any use.

Daphne then lowered his hopes even more by saying to Colleen, "You want to watch this guy, Collie. He is a real 'smoothie' with the ladies. A big girl gave him a kiss just outside your shop the other day."

Andrew had been expecting her to mention them being down the river so was relieved but embarrassed. Blushing and anxious he hastily said, "Fair go! She is my cousin. She was just saying hello."

Kristen chortled with laughter and said, "Just saying hello eh? Oh well, it must all be 'Kissin' Cousins' out there in the woods where the 'Hillbillies' live."

"Nothing much else to do," Daphne added. This time her voice had a sharper edge and there was a malicious glint in her eye.

Andrew wanted to deny he or his relations were 'Hillbillies' but images of Cousin Sandy and the road to Home Rule gave him pause. Instead, he just said, "I come from Cairns and Cousin Jean comes from Mossman."

Andrew's discomfiture was added to by Carmen appearing beside him and by the sight of his mother working her way across as she exchanged greetings with people. Colleen increased the pressure by saying, "Anyway, I came to tell you that I might see you tomorrow. We are coming out to Helenvale for a picnic."

At that, Andrew's eyes met Daphne's and this time he was sure there was malice and possibly jealousy there. He half expected either Daphne or Kristen to make a comment that would ruin his chances, but Daphne just said, "That's a nice place for a picnic. We might come too."

The thought of her being there as well sent Andrew into a tail spin of fluster and anxiety. At that moment, his mother arrived and said, "Hello girls. Merry Christmas."

"Merry Christmas!" they chorused back.

Andrew's mother then said, "I hate to break up your social life Andrew, but we must get back to the hotel for lunch."

Colleen smiled and said, "We have to go too. I have to help mum get ready for Christmas dinner. See you tomorrow, Andrew."

With that the girls turned and walked off. All three kept glancing back, sending Andrew into a sweat on top of that induced by the blazing tropical sun.

I don't think I have any chance with Daphne anymore, he told himself. But that did not really bother him and he was now sure she wasn't at all his type. Nor was Kristen. But Colleen? He sighed. *She is just so beautiful!*

He admired the graceful curve of her back and waist and the shimmer of the sun on her golden hair and his chest seemed to form a tight ball of what he knew with certainty was a crush.

He was sure he was now in love and had high hopes of the relationship developing. All the way back to Helenvale he daydreamed and indulged in romantic fantasies where he and Colleen were in some desperate adventure from which he could save her.

By 11:15 they were back at the Lions Den. The first person Andrew looked for was Little Terry. He had been hoping his father might have collected him but even before he had climbed out of the car Little Terry appeared. He was clutching a couple of the plastic animals. Despite being needed to help in the storeroom and the kitchen Andrew was told by his mother to play with Little Terry.

"We will manage. That poor little kid needs a playmate more than we need your muscles," she said.

So Andrew sat on the concrete veranda to play with Little Terry. Very quickly he discovered that the little boy had no real idea of how to play with either model animals or toy people. To help him Andrew began to invent a game with one of the cowboys and his horse, saying he was the farmer. He then showed Little Terry how to imagine the story and to make movements and sound effects. Soon he had Little Terry pretending to round up the sheep, with a couple always breaking free and having to be brought back by the sheepdog. Then the cow and the bull provided much entertainment. Andrew quite forgot the passage of time and his age as he played.

Then he looked up to see his mother watching silently from the nearby doorway. "Oh! Hi Mum. Is lunch ready?" he asked, embarrassed to be caught making moo cow noises.

His mother nodded and smiled. Then she said very seriously, "That is just so nice to see. You have made this little boy's Christmas for him. That is wonderful. Thank you, Andrew."

Andrew blushed both with embarrassment and pleasure. He shrugged and said, "Come and have lunch Little Terry."

His mother helped them tidy up and then led them through to the dining room. All the miners were there, along with a group of locals. Andrew was amazed. He hadn't realised what an important social event Christmas dinner at the pub was.

As he seated Little Terry, one of the miners, Old Seth (Who wasn't really old, only middle aged) said, "Good on yer son! You are doing that little fella a power of good."

"Thanks," Andrew mumbled.

"He will make a great father," another miner commented.

That caused general agreement, except Tim the Miner said, "Fair go! Don't marry the poor bugger off too soon. He hasn't even got a wife yet."

There was good natured laughter and then Simon said, "He'll soon be a dad if he keeps wheeling the girls off down the river the way he does."

Andrew blushed at the roar of laughter that resulted. He met his mother's eye and blushed even more. She wasn't amused.

"That's enough of that talk thank you! Now, who wants the roast chicken?"

The dinner began. Andrew was roped in to help serve and was soon sweating profusely as he hurried back and forth carrying plates of steaming roast meats and vegetables. It was a very 'traditional' Christmas dinner with all the trimmings and no concessions to the fact that it was not snow-covered England outside but sweltering tropical Australia. Not that Andrew minded. To his mind this was how Christmas should be.

When everyone else was served he carried out his own plate and sat next to Little Terry, encouraging him to try new foods. It was painfully obvious that the little boy had very limited experience of foods and it gave Andrew great pleasure to introduce him to new things. He also made sure the little boy's glass was topped up with soft drink: bright red 'Cherry Cheer'.

After lunch Andrew helped with the washing up and clearing away. Little Terry wanted to help too but dropped several gravy-covered knives and forks on the floor and got all upset. Just in time Carmen grabbed two plates that Little Terry was carrying. "We can cope with wiping the floor but broken crockery will spoil the little boy's day," she said.

Andrew agreed. Seeing a movie about Santa on the TV he suggested that Little Terry sit and watch. To his relief, the little boy agreed and Andrew was able to leave him and get on with the work. As he lugged a dozen dirty plates into the kitchen, the perspiration trickled into his eyes, the salt stinging them.

He grumbled and wiped his face. "Strewth it's hot!"

"Thirty six degrees," his mother said. She was hot and sweaty too. She took the plates and then said, "After this is done, why don't you children take the little boy down to the river. It will be cooler there and he could even have a swim."

"I don't think he has any bathers," Andrew said.

"He can swim in his shorts or in his undies for that matter. Or even with nothing on if there are no tourists down there," his mother replied.

Andrew felt a bit embarrassed by the idea of his sister seeing a naked boy, even a little one. But Carmen just agreed matter-of-factly. So after the work was done both she and Andrew changed into bathers, collected hats and towels and the bag of toys and sat with Little Terry till the movie finished. They then sent him to the toilet before leading him down across the lawn towards the river. As they went down the grassy slope towards the lodges, Little Terry squealed with delight and ran happily ahead. Seeing him so happy made Andrew feel good. But it also angered him that the little boy's father was not there.

What a way to treat your son on Christmas Day! he thought.

There were some tourists down at the river but Andrew led the way down through the trees to a sandy hollow beside the water just below the rapids. There was plenty of shade and a breeze blew along the river so that it felt reasonably cool.

"Nice," Carmen agreed. "And... Ow! The only fly in the ointment are these dratted march flies!"

She slapped at one and then chased another away that had been about to land on Little Terry. Andrew laughed until he was bitten on the back through his shirt. Towels and toys were dropped and shirts and shorts removed. Little Terry was a bit anxious about that but Carmen encouraged him.

Andrew went to test the water and found it refreshingly cool. He turned and said, "This is great. Come on!"

But Little Terry stood on the bank in his undies and looked scared. His face crumpled and his lip began to quiver. Carmen held out her hand, but he wouldn't take it.

She said, "It will be alright, Little Terry. The water isn't cold."

Little Terry let out a quivering sob and cried, "But mine can't swim."

Once again Andrew was surprised and saddened by the little boy's lack of experience. He waded in a few steps and said, "It isn't deep, Little Terry. I will make sure you are safe."

Very gingerly Little Terry put a toe in, then a foot. After a few hesitant seconds he stepped forward so that both feet were in. Andrew lowered himself to kneel in the shallow water. His attention was distracted at that point by two female tourists in their twenties. Both wore skimpy bikinis and had quite shapely bodies and he tried to ogle them without making it obvious that he was in any way interested.

Little Terry learned fast. In a few minutes he was sitting and then lying in the shallows. Soon he was splashing, running and falling over. Both Andrew and Carmen warned him about snags and showed him how to detect underwater rocks and how the change of colour indicated the deeper water. The three of them began to have a lot of fun playing in the water. Andrew even gave Little Terry rides on his back out to the edge of the deeper water.

The fun ended when Andrew thoughtlessly pretended to be a crocodile and crawled towards Little Terry. Little Terry became very scared and ran out of the water. Carmen realised what had happened and quickly told Andrew to stop it. Annoyed with himself Andrew stood up and waded out. He helped calm the frightened little boy down but no amount of coaxing would get him to go back in.

Andrew said, "It's alright, Little Terry. There are no crocodiles in this part of the river above the falls."

But Little Terry shook his head firmly and said, "Mine daddy said big crocodiles will eat me up if I go in the river."

"Do you know what crocodiles are?" Carmen asked.

Little Terry nodded. "Daddy showed me pictures and I saw them on TV."

Andrew gave up. Instead, he moved to the toys. He and Carmen then set about making a play farm for the animals and the cowboy and his horse. Little Terry joined in enthusiastically. The cattle had to be rounded up and then the sheep. The dog was sent to get the trays and the pigs herded in.

"We need some yards or fences to keep them from wandering off," Andrew said.

He began picking up twigs from among the deadfall. After breaking them into short lengths of about 7 centimetres he shoved them upright into the sand, each twig about 10 centimetres from its neighbour. These were placed in a straight line across the open sand.

"These are the fence posts," he explained. "We will just pretend that there are wires between them." Next, he put two uprights with two longer sticks placed diagonally in an 'X' between them. "And this is a gate."

Little Terry was obviously thrilled to see the fence grow to form a paddock. Carmen joined in to make another side and then Little Terry went scampering about collecting twigs. Soon there was a model paddock measuring half a metre each way.

Andrew dusted sand off his hands and stood up to admire it. "Now we need another paddock for the sheep. This one is for the cows."

Soon they had two paddocks and then a third small one. "For the pigs," Andrew said.

The animals were all then taken out and the game of rounding them up and herding was played again. As they finished Carmen said, "We need a house for the farmer." She set to work to build one using four small forked sticks as uprights. Two cross-beams were placed between the forks of each pair and then rafters of sticks added. Finally thin sheets of paperbark were placed on top to form the roof. The cowboy was then placed inside lying down.

Little Terry was delighted. He clapped his hands and then said, "What about cowboy's dog?"

"He can sleep in there with him," Andrew said. He placed the toy dog on its side beside the cowboy.

"And his horse?" Little Terry asked.

So they built a shelter for the horse. Then they built a sty adjoining the pig pen. Next, Andrew added a long row of fence posts to make a roadway with two more paddocks. While he did, he slapped at more march flies which bit him but by then they were so engrossed and so used to them they barely noticed. Only when he thought about it did Andrew notice the heat, the smell of eucalyptus and the shrill whine of the cicadas.

He stood up and watched the little boy playing happily and felt very pleased. Then he studied the two bikini girls who were visible through a gap in the trees and felt even happier.

Colleen will be here tomorrow, he thought. Images of Daphne and of Cousin Jean swirled in to blur the prefect image of Colleen but he was happy, until he got a vivid mental picture of Tina. *She will be here in a few days. I wonder?*

His daydreaming was ended by the sudden appearance of Little Terry's father on top of the bank. For a few moments Andrew felt both anxious and vaguely guilty, fearing the little boy's father might resent them paying with him or giving him presents. To add to this feeling of unease, Andrew noted that Barry looked very unkempt. He had not shaved for several days and the thick stubble was very obvious. His eyes were bloodshot and had dark rings under them and his clothes looked as though he had slept in them. Then Barry swayed and slurred his speech and Andrew had the horrible suspicion that he was drunk.

But Little Terry was overjoyed. His face lit up and he ran up to him, arms spread. "Daddy! Daddy! It's Chwistmas!" he cried happily.

Barry gave him what looked to Andrew like a crooked grin and knelt to hug him with one arm. To Andrew's distress, he saw Little Terry's nose wrinkle at his father's body odour and then he tried to move his face away from the rough stubble.

His father seemed oblivious to this. "I got you a present. Here it is."

Barry brought his other hand from behind his back and gave Little Terry the present. Little Terry's face lit up and he eagerly began to tear open the Christmas paper wrapping. His father let him go and he sat on the sandy slope and tore off the last of the paper. The present was a radio-controlled car. When Little Terry saw the picture of it on the outside of the box his eyes gleamed and he cried with delight.

The box was opened and the car and its radio control unit were taken out. The car was red and gold and had wide rubber tyres and gleaming silver headlights, and fenders. Two wire aerials added to its appearance. Little Terry held it up for them to see, his face a picture of pleasure.

Andrew knelt to examine it and smiled. "It's a real beauty, Little Terry!" he said as he admired it.

When Little Terry put it down on the sand and began to push it Carmen said, "You shouldn't have to push it, Little Terry. It has got an electric motor."

This was pointed out and Carmen picked up the instruction booklet that had fallen out and quickly read it. During all of this Barry stood looking down and grinning but not really looking happy. Little Terry became impatient.

"Make car go, please!" he said.

Carmen bit her lip and asked to see the car. Reluctantly Little Terry surrendered it to her. She opened a panel and looked.

"It needs batteries," she said, and handed it back.

Andrew looked at the box and saw the words BATTERIES NOT INCLUDED. Carmen showed this to Barry. He looked sheepish and then swore under his breath.

"I didn't think of that," he said, flushing with embarrassment.

Little Terry now became insistent that they make the car go. His happiness dissolved into frustration and then distress.

"Make go!" he shouted as his disappointment grew. Tears began.

Andrew shook his head and looked at Barry with contempt. *What a pill!* he thought. But he was upset at Little Terry's disappointment.

He said, "We have some batteries up at the hotel."

Carmen gave him a grateful smile. So they packed up the toy animals and cowboy and then walked back to the hotel. Little Terry was still upset but the promise of making his car work eased his tears to a few sobs.

Andrew took the batteries out of his new radio controlled boat. Luckily these were the same type as they needed for the car. Then he discovered that the radio control unit also needed batteries so he went and got them from his unit. Little Terry got teary again and Andrew grew angry about Barry's inefficiency.

"Useless father he is!" he muttered to Carmen.

Carmen nodded. Andrew hid his annoyance and dislike while he and Carmen inserted the batteries. Then he clicked the switch, half fearful that the car would not work and that Little Terry would be very upset.

Luckily the car did go. It went really well. Andrew drove it for a bit, just to test it, but Little Terry quickly got impatient. His little fingers twitched and reached or the control unit.

"Give!" he cried.

Before Andrew could comply, Barry grunted, "Give the kid his toy."

That rankled Andrew but he swallowed back an angry retort and handed the control unit to Little Terry. Rather than make a scene he stalked off to the kitchen. Carmen followed, leaving father and son to play out on the bitumen in front of the hotel.

"Selfish, ignorant!" Andrew said as he sat down in the kitchen.

His mother wanted to know what was wrong, so he and Carmen described the incident. Their mother agreed but said, "At least he has turned up. I was afraid he might not."

She then shooed them away as she had to prepare the evening meal. Andrew went to his room and lay down. He tried to read but thoughts of Little Terry, and then of girls, kept intruding. Cars came and went and quite a party developed on the hotel veranda. From time to time he heard the buzz of the radio controlled car and a happy shout from Little Terry.

At least that sad apology for a father did turn up, he thought.

So he was quite surprised when Little Terry appeared at his door half an hour later hugging his new car and tears streaming down his face.

"Daddy gone!" he sobbed.

Chapter 22

PICNICS AND PRESSURE

Andrew sat up, appalled. Little Terry ran to him and flung himself into his arms. For a minute or so Andrew just hugged the sobbing little boy. Carmen's head appeared at the door. When told what had happened she came in and helped sooth Little Terry. But it took twenty minutes to calm him down and by then Andrew was feeling quite upset and angry himself.

He and Carmen took Little Terry to the kitchen and explained what had happened to their mother. She shook her head a tut-tutted, then said, "He was drunk. Your father said he could not have any more to drink and told him to lie down on the veranda couch."

But Barry had only done that for a few minutes. When Irish was asked if he had seen Barry he said that he got into an argument with two of the miners and then stormed over to his Land Rover and drove off.

"Which way?" Andrew's mother asked.

"Towards Cooktown," Irish replied.

"Oh dear! I hope he hasn't gone back to get more to alcohol," Mrs Collins said.

Andrew's father had joined them and he said, "I hope he is going to come back for this poor little boy!"

As there was nothing else to do, Andrew suggested to Little Terry that they go back down to the river for another swim and to finish making the farm. It was late afternoon by then, but their mother agreed.

"Anything to take the poor little tyke's mind off things," she said.

So until dusk set in Andrew, Carmen, and Little Terry played at making farms. Little Terry calmed down and became happy again and Andrew's temper cooled enough for him to appreciate the two female tourists who were still wandering about the campsite in their brief bikinis.

The evening meal followed. Little Terry was fed with the others and Andrew sat next to him. By then most of the guests and miners were tired and several were the worse for drink so meal time was not as happy as lunch.

While they ate the rumble of thunder began to sound in the distance. This grew steadily closer and louder while Andrew and Carmen were clearing the tables and washing up. The sounds caused Little Terry to become anxious and agitated. He would not sit and watch the TV and kept walking to the kitchen for reassurance.

Then a particularly loud crack of thunder sounded and for the first time the flicker of lightning lit up the scene. Little Terry looked scared and began to whimper.

"I think we might be in for a storm," Andrew's mother said.

No sooner were the words out of her mouth than there was an even louder bang and the lights went out. Andrew jumped with fright and thought he might have screamed along with everyone else but wasn't sure. From the bar came loud yells of laughter and a call for lights. From nearby came the terrified wails of Little Terry. Andrew moved quickly to find him. Another flash of lightning lit up the scene and he was able to reach the frightened little boy.

"It's alright Little Terry. As long as you are in a building you are quite safe," he said.

But he was scared himself and knew it. His rational mind battled with his own animal instincts. A trembling Little Terry clung to him.

Andrew's mother quickly struck a match and then lit the two old-fashioned oil lamps that stood on the sideboard. These at least dispelled the gloom. Then another noise attracted Andrew's attention and he hastened to reassure Little Terry, who was already looking fearfully in the direction from which the sound was coming.

"That's the rain falling on the top of the jungle Little Terry," he explained.

Carmen said, "Let's go out the front and watch it."

Andrew took Little Terry's hand and followed Carmen through the dining room to the front veranda. A dozen people were standing there, all watching the sound and light display. The bar was lit by the feeble glow of another oil lamp and Andrew saw his father lighting an old kerosene 'hurricane' lantern.

From the front they could see out across the open fields to Mungumby Creek. Every few seconds the scene was lit up by a flash of lightning. Then a vivid bolt went searing down to strike the trees over near the mountains.

"That will have given that mob at Mungumby Lodge a wakeup call!" chortled one of the locals.

Then the wind and rain arrived. It came from the west so the veranda was sheltered from the worst of it. Only a bit of spray blew in. Little Terry huddled in against Andrew, who could feel him flinch every time there was a lightning strike. The rain drummed so loudly on the iron roof and mango leaves that people had to shout to make themselves heard.

CAAARACK!

A bolt of lightning struck a tree up on Helenvale Hill. It was so close that the sound came simultaneous with the brilliant flash. Everything was lit up stark white for a second and everyone cried out in fright and jumped, even the adults. The sound was so loud it seemed to envelope them. For a few seconds the image of the bolt was retained on Andrew's retina, even after it had gone dark again.

While blinking and crying out with excitement, he realised that Little Terry was clinging to his leg like a limpet. Then he felt him quivering and bent down to speak.

"That was a good one!" he cried.

Another flash of lightning, luckily much further away, lit up Little Terry's face and Andrew realised he was sobbing with fear. He knelt and hugged the little boy and tried to soothe him.

"It's alright, Little Man. We are safe here," he said.

But Little Terry stayed scared even when Carmen also held him. Luckily the worst of the thunder and lightning moved quickly away down the valley towards Black Mountain and the rain and wind eased from savage gusts to a steady downpour.

"Typical tropical thunderstorm," Irish commented. "All sound and fury for a few minutes and all over in an hour."

It was. By 8pm the rain had stopped and the wind dropped to an eerie stillness. The only natural sounds then were the dripping of the run-off and the whine of insects. Little Terry slowly relaxed and was taken back inside for ice-cream. Andrew and Carmen had some too, enlivened by the novelty of eating by lantern light which seemed to attract more insects than the electric lights.

To Andrew's disgust and Carmen's amusement, a large moth fluttered in, flapped around the hot glass of the lamp and then crashed into his half-melted ice-cream.

"Oh bloody hell!" Andrew cried.

He fished it out and then grinned at the way Little Terry was chortling with mirth at his discomfiture.

Andrew's father went out to the shed and started a diesel generator and the lights came back on. Life quickly returned to normal. Andrew and Carmen watched TV with Little Terry and then moved him to bath and bed. There Andrew sat beside him and told him one of the stories his own father had been fond of relating; a tale about a British Navy lieutenant named Archibald who served in the 1920s and 30s and who was a diver and the pilot of a float plane. Andrew easily made up a story set in the West Indies, which included a bad thunderstorm.

"We know what storms are like, don't we Little Terry?" he said.

Little Terry hugged his sheet up under his chin and nodded happily. Andrew smiled and patted him, then went on to relate how, while flying over the coral reefs of the Bahamas Archibald had spotted a wrecked ship on the bottom of the sea and how he had landed and dived down to find a treasure chest.

Having dived on several real wrecks and even helped find a treasure Andrew had no trouble making this up. He started to introduce a shark into the story but then changed his mind.

Might give the little chap nightmares like I get, he mused. So he ended the tale on a happy note.

Little Terry drifted off to sleep holding his hand. Andrew was then able to move to his own bed and lie down. But he did not find sleep easily. Through his mind ran memories of diving and adventures with float planes, especially the one the previous year when he had saved Tina from the bird smugglers.

Tina! He found he could not get her out of his mind, even when he tried to introduce images of Colleen. But they were too sweet so he added others: nude Letitia on Endeavour Island, Daphne down at the river, Cousin Jean. The knowledge that Tina and her friend Adele would join them in a few days made him quite anxious and confused. This was not helped by the knowledge that Colleen was coming the next day for a picnic.

He was woken many hours later by the sound of Little Terry whimpering. Feeling hot and sweaty in the still night Andrew sat up and blinked away the sleep.

"What is it Little Man?" he asked.

"S... s... sn... snake," Little Terry managed to cry.

Bloody hell! Andrew thought.

A sudden shaft of pure terror froze him for a few seconds, and he broke into a cold sweat. He stilled his breathing to allow his ears to work but no stealthy slithering sound came to him so he strained his eyes to see if he could spot the reptile.

"Where is it Little Terry?" he asked, groping for his torch.

Little Terry did not answer so Andrew aimed his torch and clicked it on. In the beam he saw a frightened little boy sitting up in his bed – but no sign of any snake. Again he asked where it was. Little Terry shook his head then scrambled out of bed.

Andrew was aghast and cried out, "No! Stay where you are!"

But it was too late. The little boy was so frightened that he ignored the warning and dashed across and leapt onto Andrew's bed. When he was safe Andrew let him cling on tightly while he kept looking. But he could see no sign of any tail or scaly coil behind any of the cupboards or chairs. It took him an effort of courage to lean over and direct the torch beam under his bed. That was scary because he feared being bitten in the face.

Under his bed was his suitcase and he could not see behind it. *Oh bugger!* he thought.

Reluctantly, but knowing he would not be able to sleep with the thought of the possibility of a slithering horror lurking under his bed he eased Little Terry's arms from him and then gingerly stepped out of bed. By then he was sweating and quite scared. He checked again that the door was closed and that there was no snake on the floor nearby. Then he bent down and gripped the handle of his suitcase.

With a sudden tug he pulled it clear. Nothing.

After checking under Little Terry's pillow and sheets Andrew climbed back into his own bed. Only then did Little Terry confess that he wasn't sure.

"Mine might have dweamed it," he confessed.

"Oh you poor little blighter!" Andrew said, hugging the trembling child to him and feeling a great upwelling of relief and pity.

After that it took nearly an hour for Andrew to drop off to sleep again because his imagination kept picturing a snake in the room.

But the door is closed so how could it get in? he wondered.

The answer was: during the day when the door was left open. Once again he climbed out of bed and this time turned on the light and again searched the room. Still nothing.

By then Little Terry was sleeping soundly so Andrew turned off the light and lay down again. This time he did drift off into a restless sleep.

* * *

When Andrew woke next morning, he felt tired, anxious, and excited.

I might see Colleen today, he thought.

Little Terry was still asleep so he quietly went out to have a shower and dressed, then went to the kitchen. His mother was there cooking and she said good morning then, "You had better bring Little Terry here."

"Yes Mum."

Andrew went back to his room, only to find a weeping Little Terry sitting up on his bed. "What's the matter, Little Man?" Andrew asked.

"Big B... bb... boy (sniffle) l... l... leave (sob) me!" Little Terry cried.

At that, Andrew felt both saddened and annoyed. "Sorry. I just went to the toilet. Come on, out of bed. Mum said time to get up. Toilet and shower for you."

Little Terry calmed down and allowed himself to be led to the shower and toilet and then to the kitchen. He was fed while Andrew and Carmen served the miners. It was back to work for most of them, even though it was Boxing Day.

Tim the Miner called to Carmen, "And what are you doing today, Beautiful?"

"Going to see relations," Carmen answered.

Seeing a chance to get his own back Andrew added slyly, "To see Cousin Sandy."

Carmen scowled and blushed and poked her tongue at him. "And Cousin Jean," she retorted.

It was Andrew's turn to blush and he retired to the kitchen. The morning settled into its routine. Chores soon had Andrew out front of the hotel picking up mangos. By then it was 7:30 and the miners were leaving for work. Even at that hour of the day sweat was soon trickling off him as there was still no breeze. The sky was a dark blue and completely clear of clouds. Andrew could only shake his head and marvel how dry everything looked, considering the drenching of the night before.

After the jobs were done, he and Carmen sat on the veranda and played with Little Terry. As they did, Andrew commented, "At least now there are plenty of toys and games to keep us entertained."

Little Terry said, "Mine want to go to wiver to pway cowboys and moo cows."

"We will later," Andrew answered.

He did not want to go down to the river until Colleen arrived. *If she does,* he worried. He then felt guilty and hoped that Carmen would not guess his thoughts. To add to his worries was the knowledge that they were going visiting after lunch.

I hope Colleen comes this morning. If she comes after lunch, I won't see her.

She did. A few minutes after he had thought this, a car pulled up at the gate leading to the river. It was Colleen and her family. Andrew's father called him to open the gate and show them the way.

Andrew stood up and said, "You bring Little Terry and the cowboys down to the river, Car."

Then he walked along the veranda to where the cars waited. As he did, he felt very self-conscious as he could see people watching him. He saw Colleen and wanted to smile but managed only a nod and a faint grin. Next, to her was her little brother and in the front of the car were her mother and man whom he presumed to be her father. To have her father looking at him made him feel unreasonably guilty. He told himself that was unfair because he had no devious designs on the man's daughter.

This is true love! he told himself as he opened the gate.

In his mind he was sure his motives were true and pure. "I'll show you where to park," he said to her father.

Walking quickly he led the way across the side lawn and down under the trees. The cars were directed into a space away from the lodges and the tourist's tents.

After the cars were parked, Andrew pointed and said, "You can use that barbeque and the swimming hole is just down that track."

Colleen's father nodded and obviously had no idea that Andrew knew his daughter. Her mother smiled and said, "Hello, Andrew. It's a nice day."

"It will be hot later," Andrew said. "We had a big thunderstorm last night."

The storm was discussed. It had not reached Cooktown where they had endured a sweltering night. Only now did Andrew allow himself to look at Colleen. As he did, his heart seemed to seize up and stand still. Then it began to beat rapidly.

God, she is beautiful! he marvelled. Drinking in the perfection of her heart-shaped face and brilliant blue eyes. *I'm in love!* he told himself. But how to tell her? And how to get her alone to do so?

The arrival of Carmen and Little Terry changed the dynamics and the conversation shifted to other topics. Andrew stayed out of it, exchanging meaningful glances with Colleen. He was sure, from the way she was meeting his gaze, that she felt the same way. His heart seemed to swell and fill his whole chest and he felt sure he was on the edge of the most wonderful romance, of one of life's great joys and mysteries.

But how to get Colleen alone? Andrew was unable to solve that one and he knew that Carmen was starting to flick glances from him to her. Feeling happy but frustrated, Andrew reluctantly said, "See you later," and went off down to the river with Carmen and Little Terry.

Little Terry ran straight to the 'farm' and started to play. Some animal had knocked over some of the little twigs marking the fence lines but these were quickly repaired and Andrew set to work to make a couple more paddocks with lanes between them. Carmen made another shed for the cow to live in and fixed the pig pen. While they did Andrew kept his ears attuned to the tinkle of Colleen's lovely, musical voice and had the frustrating experience of seeing her flit across between the trees as she made her way to the river just upstream of the rapids. He itched to join her but could think if no excuse. Instead, he kept playing, feeling increasingly frustrated.

Then suddenly she was standing in front of him in her one-piece swimsuit. His eyes drank in her lovely smooth legs and curvy female shape, enough to take his breath away. To his eyes she was perfection itself. He realised she had been watching for a few minutes.

She said, "That looks like a nice game. May my little brother, Danny, join in?"

Danny was about ten but looked very shy and lonely. Seeing an opportunity to get to be near Colleen, Andrew quickly said yes. There were a few tense moments while Little Terry made up his mind to share but then he nodded. Very quickly he took over and proceeded to teach Danny how the game was played. Carmen sat back and smiled at Andrew. He felt very happy and started to chat with Colleen, explaining who Little Terry was and why he was there.

"It's very good of you to play with him," Colleen said, smiling sweetly and placing her hand on his arm.

The touch sent Andrew's hopes and heart rate soaring. Then she leaned forward to join the play and Andrew was granted tantalising glimpses down the front of her swimsuit. Her breasts were nicely shaped and the sight of them was enough to make his mouth go dry. Aware of his hammering heart and twitching fingers, Andrew tried to look without anyone noticing. Colleen's parents came to look and nodded with approval and went back up to their car to talk to their friends.

Half an hour later, as interest in the game began to flag, Little Terry provided another opportunity to be with Colleen when he said, "Mine want to swim."

Andrew thought that a good idea. "You can swim in your shorts, Little Terry, and I will swim in mine."

Carmen stood up. "I will go and change into my bathers."

She left and suddenly there was only Andrew, Colleen, and the two boys. He and she exchanged glances which sent Andrew's hopes even higher. He led the way downstream to the lower end of the shallow rapids.

"The pool at the top of the rapids is too deep," he explained.

But his real motive was that the pool at the top of the rapids was almost visible from where her parents were while the lower end was fifty paces away. He had vague hopes he might get her alone to be able to speak to her.

Once there, he self-consciously peeled off his shirt. Colleen watched and he saw her eyes widen with approval. She smiled and moved to run her hand over his shoulder and upper left arm.

"Gee, you have nice big muscles," she said.

Her voice and touch sent his body into instant arousal but somehow he didn't care if she noticed.

A glance showed the two younger boys splashing in the shallow water twenty paces away. Andrew and Colleen stood in a gap in the trees among the last vegetation. His eyes met hers and he felt a surge of desire.

Swallowing, he heard himself say, "I would like to kiss you."

He had meant to say he really liked her but it just came out. But before he could correct the slip, she smiled and snuggled in against him.

"That would be nice," she murmured.

The next thing Andrew knew she was in his arms, pressing hard against him, their mouths together. And she was nice to kiss. She tasted and smelt good and the feel of her smooth, warm skin set his emotions surging. He began to wonder how he could get Colleen away to somewhere more private. Lust and desire warred with his knowledge that they had a duty to supervise the two young boys while they were in the water. With a groan of pure frustration, he gripped Colleen firmly and kissed her passionately again.

Voices!

Not her parents. Carmen and some other females. Then Andrew recognised them.

Daphne and Kristen!

Chapter 23

BEER AND BBQ

Daphne said, "You shouldn't have left them alone together." Then she giggled.

Andrew cursed mentally and reluctantly released Colleen. She sighed and muttered with annoyance, "I was just starting to enjoy that."

That comment really put Andrew on top of the clouds but he was also very aware that he was now fearfully aroused. *Daphne and Carmen will notice,* he thought.

To save himself the embarrassment he said, "Into the water, quick!"

Without waiting for agreement, he spun round and hurried across the sand and into the shallows. As soon as it was knee deep, he flopped down beside Little Terry. The coldness of the water came as a shock and quite took his breath away, but he felt relieved. Colleen waded into the water ten metres upstream and began gently splashing with her hands.

They were only just in time as Carmen, Daphne, and Kristen appeared through the trees at that moment.

"There they are," Kristen called.

Luckily, Little Terry had decided that Andrew made a good 'island' and started climbing on his back. Andrew hoped it would look like that was the game they had been playing all along.

Andrew said hello and tried to act cool and relaxed but was now in a fever of anxiety lest Daphne say something that let Colleen know she had been down the river with him before. To his relief, she didn't but she gave him a few sour glances.

The girls all wore bathers and looked very attractive and desirable to Andrew, but anxiety caused his arousal to die away so he was able to stand up and join in the 'chasey' games and water fights. But he found it hard to look at Daphne's voluptuous curves and not have vivid and arousing flashbacks to their earlier meeting. But she did not compare with Colleen. She was his ideal.

As they played and swam, Andrew kept looking at her and marvelling at her beauty and attractiveness. He was also still shocked at his own very ardent desire to have a physical relationship with her. Somehow it mocked his good intentions but also added a sharp dash of spice to the situation.

And she obviously feels the same, he thought.

Little Terry began to complain of being cold so they moved back to the sand and resumed playing with the toy animals and cowboys. More people arrived and Andrew looked up and saw that it was Little Terry's uncle Dave.

Uncle Dave said, "Hello kids. Hi Terry. Where's your dad?"

Little Terry's mouth turned down and he said, "Daddy sayed he not want me and that he was going to town."

"To town, eh? Well, in that case you had better come with me and we will take you home," Uncle Dave answered.

"Can mine bwing my Chwistmas presents?" Little Terry asked.

"Christmas presents? Sure."

Carmen said, "We gave him these toys and a few other things. We didn't... well, we didn't like to see him have Christmas with no presents."

Uncle Dave frowned. "Why wouldn't he get any presents?"

Andrew and Carmen exchanged glances. Andrew knew Carmen did not want to speak ill of anyone or get involved in another family's business, so he said, "Barry left Little Terry with us over Christmas. We made sure Santa came for him."

Uncle Dave was thoughtful, then nodded. "You did, eh? Well, that's very good of you. Thanks. Do you know where Barry might be?"

Andrew shook his head. "No. We haven't seen him since Christmas Eve."

Uncle Dave muttered, "Bloody Hell!" Then he shook his head and said, "Okay, bring all your presents if you want to Terry and let's go."

The toys were packed up and Carmen went with them to collect the presents up at the hotel. Andrew wanted to go but his desire to stay with Colleen was stronger so he stayed and they all went swimming again.

Time seemed to fly, and it was to Andrew's great regret that Carmen returned and said, "We have to go, Andrew. We are going to Home Rule after lunch, remember."

Daphne smirked and added, "To see Cousin Jean, your kissing cousin!"

Andrew thought of kissing Cousin Jean and of how forward she was and blushed. Then he noted a slightly puzzled and anxious look on Colleen's face, and he became quite concerned lest she misunderstand.

To his dismay, Colleen asked, "Who is Cousin Jean?"

Daphne darted Andrew a lynx-like smile, and said, "The big girl who kissed Andrew outside your shop the other day."

Colleen looked even more puzzled and worried. "Oh. I didn't see that," she said.

Andrew was secretly furious with Daphne but also knew he deserved her dislike. He forced a smile and said to Colleen, "She is my cousin. They are just teasing me."

Colleen still looked anxious but nodded. They moved out of the water and made their way up to the BBQ area. Here Colleen stopped and gave Andrew a wry smile and what he took to be a meaningful look. He could only sigh with frustration and smile back; then pretend that there was nothing between them.

With a heart that was full of hope and regret, he turned and followed Carmen back up to the hotel.

* * *

At the hotel, they pulled clothes over their bathers. Presents were collected and placed in the car. Then, as Andrew went to get in, he saw Colleen at the end of the front veranda. She wore a T-shirt over her bathers and gave him a wistful smile.

Noting that his mother was busy packing the car and that Carmen was nowhere to be seen Andrew hurried over to Colleen. As he got closer she moved back around the corner. Andrew followed her. A quick glance both ways along the veranda assured him that they were alone. He stopped and looked at her and was sure that her eyes were telling him the story. He reached out and took her hands and she stepped closer and turned her face up. Her lips parted slightly and he took this as his cue. With out a word exchanged, he held her to him and kissed her.

She responded and then sighed as they leaned back. For a few seconds Andrew could only gaze into the misty liquid blue pools of her eyes. A feeling of wonder and then of rapture engulfed him. So did a spurt of mounting arousal. He kissed her again, more fiercely this time.

A noise made him look past her. It was Carmen. She had come out of the front door and was looking at them.

"Sprung!" she cried. But she smiled and said, "Come on, little brother. Mum is waiting."

Blushing but still feeling euphoric Andrew gave Colleen another kiss. Then he whispered, "Phone me so we can arrange to meet again."

Colleen nodded and gave a regretful sigh. Andrew did not want to leave her but turned and followed Carmen to where his mother was waiting in the car. He and Carmen climbed into the car and their mother started the engine. As she backed out, Andrew looked back for a sight of Colleen but she was nowhere to be seen. But he was ecstatic.

I'm in love! he thought.

His mother drove them south along the main road. As they rounded the bend and passed the turn-off to Barry's 'farm' Andrew looked down the vehicle track and shook his head, wondering what life must be like there for Little Terry.

And I wonder what Barry does for a living? he mused.

Growing drugs was the unkind thought that followed. It seemed logical and the climate and soil were right. But his thoughts soon left Barry and his cronies and shifted to the possible delights ahead.

Cousin Jean. I wonder if I will get another kiss? And maybe a bit more? he thought hopefully. A flood of erotic images swirled in his mind and lust and arousal mixed with guilt as he thought about Colleen. *But I haven't promised her anything,* he rationalised. *We barely know each other.* But the guilty niggling persisted, as did the conflicting images. He sighed and told himself he was a weakling and a rat and that he really did love Colleen. *Or at least I want to,* he told himself.

But first he had to endure a visit to the relations at Rossville: and more of Cousin Sandy trying to impress Carmen with his smooth charm. Even his little brother, Bart, tried to get in on the act. Andrew found this both amusing and irritating. The only thing he learned for sure was that a fishing expedition was planned for three days' time. Normally Andrew had no interest in fishing and would have said no, but the mention of Archer Point as the location made him say yes.

I'd like to see the place, he thought, remembering how unusual it had looked from the sea.

Then it was on to Home Rule. Once again Andrew really enjoyed the drive through the dense jungle, especially when it was flavoured with heated anticipation of Cousin Jean. When they arrived at the holiday camp, Cousin Jean was the first to greet them. She wore a floral shirt that strained at its buttons and some sort of cloth wrap around her waist. Just the sight of her was enough to get Andrew excited so the warm touch of her skin when she kissed him caused him to become instantly aroused. That was embarrassing and he struggled to hide his condition, especially as her parents had come out of the hut and were watching.

But they did not seem to notice anything amiss and Andrew was relieved to note a sort of amused grin on her father's face. Burning with lust and embarrassment, Andrew managed to extricate himself from Cousin Jean's embrace and went back to the car to collect the small present that he had bought her. It was a music CD and some handkerchiefs, which she seemed to like and gave him another gushing kiss.

Cousin Jean's father picked up another beer and laughed, then said, "Give the poor bugger some air, Jeanie!"

That made Andrew blush even more. He noted smirks on the faces of Cousin Charmaine and Cousin Simon and that annyoed him. To have her little sister watching and knowing made it worse. It was with relief that Andrew was able to sit on a chair near the barbeque.

Barbequed steak and sausages were the main course for lunch. Andrew was able to stand and stood next to Cousin Jean while he buttered his bread roll and then collected his steak. Cousin Charmaine came and stood on his other side and Andrew became uncomfortably aware that she was beaming hopeful smiles at him and also hanging on every word and gesture between him and Cousin Jean.

Then Andrew's frustration and irritation was increased by the arrival of another family. A large, cheerful man with stubby shorts and a huge bare chest and beer gut offered him a beer and then sat down next to Cousin Jean's father. Two teenage youths, both clad only in bathers and with 'stubbies' of beer, came and began chatting to Cousin Jean. They ignored Andrew and began making crude hints to Cousin Jean. She giggled and responded, adding jealousy to Andrew's emotions.

Feeling a bit defeated and out of his depth, Andrew retreated to a chair over to one side and sat to eat his steak. As he chewed on the meat, he saw the two youths both toss their empty beer bottles on the lawn and then go to an Eski to get another bottle each. As they did, Cousin Jean turned and walked over to Andrew. She stood right in front of him so that his vision was filled with her bare legs and lower body.

She leaned forward so that he was granted an eyeful of straining buttons and bobbling cleavage. She said, "You look a bit annoyed."

"I am," he replied. "I want to get you away on your own."

"Oooh! You do, do you?" she giggled. She glanced around and then said, "And why do you want to do that for? What do you want to do?"

"Whatever you will let me," Andrew answered boldly.

He found himself quite breathless at his own daring and cast anxious glances at the adults to see if he had been overheard. But his mother was busy talking and the beer drinkers were all laughing and telling jokes.

Cousin Jean said, "Sounds like fun. Okay, I will sneak away and you follow in a couple of minutes. Go to the toilet block and then across to the creek bank. I will meet you there."

With that she turned and walked off across the lawn and around the back of a hut, leaving Andrew wondering if he had heard her aright. For the next few minutes he sat with his emotions and body in a turmoil of growing desire and fear.

What I she says I can do it? he worried.

He knew that would present him with a moral dilemma that he would find very difficult to choose. But he wanted to be with her. The urgency of his lust got him so aroused his entire body seemed to squirm and itch.

And he did not want either his mother or Carmen to notice that he was not there. But how to leave without attracting attention?

This problem kept him seated for a few more minutes until finally he broke into a sweat. He knew his arousal would be obvious to anyone who looked the moment he stood up and that added to the stress. Finally he made a decision. After gulping air to calm his now rapid breathing, he glanced to check that neither Carmen nor his mother were looking and then stood up and quickly walked off towards the toilet block.

Every step seemed hard as his muscles felt all tense from self-consciousness. With an effort of will power he made himself saunter across the ten metres of lawn and around the corner of the next building. Not once did he look back. The sense of relief he got from being out of sight was only temporary. It was almost instantly replaced by deep anxiety about the coming meeting.

Cousin Jean was waiting down beside the creek. When he came into view she gave a big smile and hurried over to hug him. After a really physical kiss she leaned back and said, "I'm glad you came."

Andrew managed a grin in return but in fact he was now half regretting it and his rapid heart rate was as much from fear as from desire. But the urge was there and very obvious. Cousin Jean pressed against him, then stepped back.

"Hmm, you feel good and ready," she commented.

That statement sent Andrew into an even greater state of confusion. He blushed with embarrassment even as his desire increased. He was shocked to discover that he now felt a real urge of lust.

But that was what she seemed to want. She said, "Let's go a bit further along the creek, in case somebody comes."

That told Andrew volumes about her previous experience and that both saddened and heartened him. *I might be in luck,* he thought.

With his hopes rising and heart hammering in anticipation he followed her along a sandy foot trail beside the creek. After about a hundred metres they came to a lovely little pool about ten metres across. The sun reached down to light it up and the whole place looked beautiful to Andrew. Just above the pool were some shallow rapids and at that point an old vehicle track came down out of the jungle.

"This will do," Cousin Jean announced.

Without more ado she grabbed Andrew and began kissing. Andrew thought it was wonderful, except for a little niggling hurt inside when he found he was comparing Cousin Jean's kissing style to Colleen's.

Then suddenly there was more hurt, sharp, stinging pain in his left calf. march fly! "Ow! Bloody thing!" he cried, breaking the embrace and slapping at it.

Cousin Jean laughed, until one landed on her. Andrew then noticed several others circling, waiting their chance. Cousin Jean swatted at one as it tried to bit her arm. Then she said, "Let's get in the water where they can't bite us."

"Have you got your bathers on?" Andrew asked.

Cousin Jean's face dimpled into a mischievous grin. "Yes, but I could take them off."

The idea had enormous appeal to Andrew but also scared him. His throat constricted and his mouth went dry. He croaked, "We'd better not."

Cousin Jean nodded and smiled. "Okay, if you like."

With that she began to undo the buttons on her blouse. Within seconds she was wearing only her bikini. As Andrew undid his own shirt buttons, his fingers trembled. His eyes were drawn to admire Jean's curvy body and he knew what he wanted to try to do but was very scared. But rather than rush things, he waded into the creek and lay back, enjoying the cooling relief of the water.

As more march flies arrived, Cousin Jean quickly waded into the pool, giggling and crying out at how cold it was. With a sigh of pleasure, she subsided into the water so that only her head was showing. Without a word they came together in a passionate embrace and he kissed her fiercely.

Andrew's desire surged to become heart-pounding lust and he wondered if he dare go further. But just as he plucked up the courage to try, Cousin Jean stopped kissing and looked past his head.

"Oh bugger! Piss off Charmaine!" she called.

Chapter 24

THE BACK END OF NOWHERE

Andrew looked around in alarm and saw Charmaine standing on the bank at the end of the old road.

She smirked and called, "I knew this was what you would be doing. You'd better hurry up. Those horrible Coulson boys are coming along the creek bank looking for you."

Cousin Jean swore and Andrew experienced another spasm of alarm. He already felt embarrassed and the fear of such a public humiliation did not appeal. It obviously didn't appeal to Cousin Jean either as she let him go and splashed ashore.

"Quick Andrew! I don't want those yobs to catch us. They will tease me something chronic if they do."

Charmaine nodded, and added, "Or they will blackmail you, saying they will tell Mum and Dad if you don't let them do things to you."

By then Cousin Jean was on the bank near their clothes. She looked hard at her little sister and said, "Do they try to get you to do things?"

Charmaine curled her lip and said, "Of course they do! They are gross males. But I don't let them. I want a good man."

As she said that, she glanced at Andrew with a suggestive glance and his mind raced. *She must like me!* he thought with astonishment.

It had never crossed his mind that the little sister might find him attractive. He waded ashore, glancing downstream, as he did. As he reached the beach, he heard voices down the creek. Then he glimpsed movement through the trees. He snatched up his shorts and pulled them on and hastily zipped them up. Then he slipped his feet into his sandals.

As he did them up, Cousin Jean slipped on her thongs and said, "Andrew, grab your shirt. Charmaine, get going! Let's get away from here before they arrive."

She turned and set off up the old road in the jungle, her blouse still undone and the cloth wrap in her hand. Andrew snatched up his shirt and followed them. As he went up the slope, he struggled to get his arms through the sleeves.

They were just in time. As he reached the top of the bank, he heard loud voices and laughter down near the creek and glimpsed the youths crossing a gap in the jungle. One held a beer bottle in his hand.

"I'll bet they are just along here somewhere," he called to the youth behind him.

Spurred by a desire to avoid the youths Andrew hurried along the jungle track behind Cousin Jean and Charmaine. To his annoyance, both the girls thought it a great joke and kept giggling.

"Sssh!" he hissed. "They will hear us."

"Doesn't matter," Cousin Jean answered.

By then they had reached the end of the track and came out onto a wide expanse of mowed grass. The buildings of the holiday camp were about a hundred metres away. The grass was short but the ground wet and squishy underfoot. Andrew found walking on it unpleasant as the mush wet his feet and sandals and left them covered in mud. Luckily, it was a sort of wet sand rather than clay and it easily washed off.

To do this, they stopped at a tap at the end of one of the buildings. While they were busy washing their feet a cry from across the lawn made Andrew look. It was the youths, three of them.

One pointed and said, "Told you it was their tracks."

The youths hurried across the lawn towards them. Cousin Jean did not wait but walked off around the corner of the building. Andrew decided that the best plan was to act innocent and relaxed so he resumed rinsing the mud off his sandals. Charmaine stayed with him. The plan seemed to work as the youths said very little when they reached them. There was certainly no teasing and they looked slightly baffled.

Andrew did not stay to talk but also walked off to rejoin the barbeque. As he rounded the corner of the building he saw that little had changed. People still stood or sat and were drinking or talking. His mother was talking to Aunty Ethel. She did notice his return but only raised one eyebrow. Carmen was more interested and kept glancing his way. Luckily, Charmaine and the youths all followed him around the corner so it did not appear that he had been anywhere on his own, or with one other person.

But after that the barbeque became a very frustrating session for Andrew. There was, he felt, too much beer and too much pointless chatter and too many jokes in bad taste. He kept watching Cousin Jean and that did not help, making him both aroused and jealous as the youths kept hanging around her and making suggestive comments and what they thought were witty jokes but which Andrew thought were just crude and gross. Cousin Jean seemed to laugh at them all, and that annoyed him more. In two hours he got no other chance to get her alone to talk to her.

He found it a relief when it was time to go. By then some of the youths and a couple of the men had drunk so much beer they were becoming objectionable, and Andrew could see that neither his mother, nor his sister, were impressed. Farewells were said and Cousin Jean came and gave Andrew a goodbye kiss. It was on the mouth but he was surprised and shocked to find that she tasted of beer.

I didn't notice her drinking, he thought.

He then realised she was more than half-drunk, and she slobbered all over him and hugged him tight, setting his fires alight again.

It was a confused boy that travelled back to the Lions Den in the back of the 4WD. He was glad they did not stop in Rossville on the way past. Back at the hotel he took himself to his room and lay down, ostensibly to read but in reality to allow his emotions to sort themselves a bit and to avoid embarrassing situations as his body kept becoming aroused.

* * *

That evening, Andrew felt very confused. He found himself torn about which girl he wanted to be with. There was also a degree of self-loathing at what he perceived to be his own weakness. On top of all that was the knowledge that Tina was coming in two days' time, and he was quite unsure how he felt about her.

Watching Carmen flirting and then actually dancing with several half-drunk miners did nothing to ease his mind. In disgust at life in general and himself in particular, he took himself to his room. For a while he read. But then his thoughts turned to Little Terry and the games they had been playing.

A farmhouse would be nice to have, he thought.

When he had been in Year 3 his teacher had got the class to make cardboard houses on 1:35 scale. It had actually been an exercise in use of the ruler but Andrew vividly remembered the pleasure he had derived from such a simple thing.

I could make a little house like that. I'm sure Little Terry would like it, he told himself.

With that in mind he went in search of cardboard. There was none of the nice white card he had used for models so he had to make do with used cereal packets. These were opened out and he then measured the rectangles of grey card and did some planning. Then he set to work with ruler and pencil and quickly drew the front and side walls of the house. These measured 10cm by 14cm and he added a window in the end wall and two in the front, plus a doorway 2cm wide by 4 high.

The walls were cut out and then used as a template to make the other two walls. A roof was marked out, measuring 14cm by 16cm. This was ruled to represent corrugated iron and then he cut this out. Paint was then added to the roof and doors. When Carmen came to say goodnight she smelt the fresh paint and looked in to see what he was doing.

"This is really good, Andrew. What a great idea!" she cried. She studied his work and then added, "We can make some other buildings too."

Andrew liked that idea and agreed to help do that the next day. Carmen then said goodnight and left. Andrew turned his light off and lay back to think. This was mostly fantasising, and he slipped into a restless sleep full of erotic 'almost' situations.

The first three hours of the next morning were taken up with morning routine and chores. It was a very hot, very dry day. The cicadas seemed louder than usual, and the march flies were very active, some even venturing into the building.

After morning tea, the whole family climbed into the 4WD, Irish having been employed to act as barman for the day. Andrew made sure he had his maps and camera but had trouble getting enthusiastic about the trip. What he wanted to do was go back to Home Rule to try to get Cousin Jean away on her own. But there was no way he even dared hint at this, so he resigned himself to a day of touring and visiting relations.

"Now, just how am I related to these people at Mt Penniless?" he asked his mother as the vehicle set off south along the main road.

"Your Cousin Bessie is the daughter of Uncle Jack and Aunty Beryl. She is Sandy's big sister," his mother explained.

"And she has kids?" Andrew queried. He knew they had loaded what looked like children's Christmas presents aboard before setting out.

His mother nodded. "She is 25 and has two children, a boy named Marvin, who is seven, and a girl named Selena, who is five."

Carmen asked, "Her husband is Des, isn't he?"

"Yes. He is a plant operator at the mine," their mother replied.

"Isn't he a lot older than Bessie?" Carmen queried.

"Yes. He is about forty I think," their mother replied.

Andrew wasn't sure if he approved of that but after a few minutes thought decided it was none of his business. He was just starting to realise that human relationships and love had very little to do with age. That got him thinking about girls again. The quandary over which one to like and which one to concentrate his attention on resurfaced to keep him in a state of indecision as they drove along.

Should I just try to win with Colleen? Or should I make another attempt to win back Tina? he wondered.

He knew that flirting with Cousin Jean and girls like Daphne and Kristen was just physical desire, even if it was a very strong physical desire that he knew was clouding his judgement.

To take his mind off such problems, he tried to focus on map reading and on studying the country. He already knew that Mt Penniless was the 'end of the road', quite literally. Now he saw that his previous perfunctory scanning of the map had not revealed just how isolated the place was. He noted that there was only one dirt road marked on the map and that it was in the middle of hundreds of square kilometres of mountains covered with rainforest or thick bush. The next road to the west was the main highway and it was over twenty kilometres and two mountain ranges away. To the south was an equally vast tract of jungle covered mountains.

"Mt Misery," he read, placing his finger on the map.

That did not sound good, and he realised that he was feeling just a tiny bit scared of going to such an out-of-the-way place. He now noted that the road to Rossville, Daintree and Cairns went off to the south east.

It is only one mountain range away, but a big one, he noted.

By then they were at the junction of that road and the Shiptons Flat, Mt Poverty Road. As this was all new territory, Andrew paid close attention and traced their progress on the map. He was pleasantly surprised to see that the Annan River flowed along beside the road for several kilometres under a very pleasant grove of trees. On the left was a low ridge covered with quite dry, open savannah.

The road was quite good until the entrance to the mine. After that it deteriorated quite dramatically and speed had to be reduced to cope comfortably with the potholes and washouts. On the left they got glimpses of the tin min and Andrew was surprised to note that it was an open cut. He had imagined that it was an underground mine.

The road then wound up and down around hills covered with trees but almost bare of grass. Several small, dry creeks were crossed and then the road jumped up over several very steep hills and became even rougher and narrowed in width to one lane. It became so steep that they were reduced to first gear and all-wheel drive.

Andrew's father stopped the vehicle at the top of a steep ridge in open bush and said he needed a toilet break. Andrew took the opportunity to get out and do the same, walking into the trees to where he had a good view back down the valley.

This is certainly wild country, he noted, very conscious that they were now a long way from anywhere.

Back in the vehicle the trip was resumed. A few kilometres on they entered rainforest. Soon after that they came to the junction that led to Shiptons Flat. There was no sign, but because of his map reading Andrew was able with certainty to direct his father to take the right road. They drove on through rain forest along a wide, flat ridge. Glimpses of cleared land out on the left indicated some sort of farm or grazing property but no buildings were seen.

The road became even narrower until leaves were brushing the sides at times. It then plunged dramatically down. Andrew became quite anxious in case of accident or meeting a vehicle coming the other way. When he looked out all he could see through the gaps in the jungle were big, jungle-covered mountains looming up on all sides. It gave the impression that they were being hemmed in and that they were entering a part of the country cut off from normal civilisation.

At the bottom of the ridge they came to the Annan River again at the point where a large creek joined on the left. "That is Parrot Creek," Andrew said. "And this place is called 'The Forks'."

There were two bridges, both narrow and made of steel set in concrete. The whole river bed appeared to be stones, most about the size of a cricket ball. Large boulders studded the actual stream. At this point the river was no bigger than a large creek. The water was crystal clear and with the lush vegetation it all looked very pretty. On the other sides the bridge approaches and road were just wheel rust in the masses of large pebbles.

Carmen studied the scene and said, "This must all go under water when it rains heavily."

Andrew looked out and saw flood debris lodged up in the trees and agreed with her. "The cousins must get cut off during the wet season," he suggested.

"I think they do," his mother replied.

"But what if they have an accident and need an ambulance or the doctor?" Carmen asked.

"They phone for a helicopter I suppose," their father answered.

As he said this, he slowed the vehicle and swung it off the 'road' into a side track. "I was told this is a very pretty place. We will stop for a few minutes to stretch our legs and see the sights."

There were several side tracks in under the trees in the river bed and the vehicle was parked in one of them. Thankfully Andrew climbed out and stretched. Then he walked unsteadily across the pebbles towards the river. Carmen followed while their parents busied themselves with cups and a thermos flask for tea.

Twenty paces along, Andrew looked to his right along yet another side track and noted another vehicle parked there. It was an old green Land Rover. Seeing the vehicle did not surprise him but the men standing beside it did. With a spasm of anxiety he noted Jan and Wes. And they were talking to the two Malaysian gentlemen, who incongruously even here in the jungle wore long-sleeved white shirts and ties and their distinctive 'kopiahs'.

Even as Andrew recognised them the men all turned to look. Hostile scowls appeared on their faces and Andrew experienced a peculiar sensation of unease.

I have trespassed into something here, he thought. It took him an effort to keep on walking and to pretend that nothing was wrong. As he walked on towards the now visible river, his mind raced. *Should I stop Carmen and warn her?* he wondered.

He found that his heart rate had shot up and that his hands were suddenly sweaty. But he was too late. Carmen had walked into sight of the men. She glanced at them and then quickly looked away and kept on walking. Andrew stopped at the edge of the river, barely aware of the beauty of the place; of the green tinged water and masses of ferns and vines hanging down the steep slope of the other bank.

Carmen joined him and said, "Those men back there. Two of them are those horrible men who fired guns at us."

"Yes, Jan and Wes," Andrew answered. He glanced anxiously over his shoulder and whispered, "I don't like this. I think we have blundered into something illegal. I think we should get out of here as quickly as we can."

Carmen nodded. "I agree. Come on, this way."

She turned left and followed the bank downstream towards the bridge. As brother and sister made their way along the bank, pretending to be innocent tourists, Andrew glanced to his left and got glimpses of the men through gaps in the trees. They were still standing at the front of the Land Rover and were watching them. Andrew now noted a white 4WD parked beyond the Land Rover.

"I'll bet they are organising a drug shipment," Andrew suggested.

Carmen nodded again and said, "Something like that. It certainly looks suspicious."

Andrew admitted to himself that he was scared. *They could kill us and easily hide our bodies in all this wilderness,* he thought.

He tried to tell himself he was being silly and that they had every right to be here. But he was also realistic and knew that in the real world people could just be in the wrong place at the wrong time.

It was a real relief to get back to their vehicle. As they arrived Andrew said, "Dad, Mum. We should leave here quickly. Those horrible men who had the guns are here. I think they are up to no good."

His father took a sip of tea and frowned. "You think we might be in some sort of danger?"

"Yes Dad."

"Okay, we will get going." Mr Collins gulped the rest of his tea and handed the empty cup to their mother.

She did not argue but quickly packed the thermos and cups in the basket and placed it in the vehicle. Andrew and Carmen climbed in and did up their seat belts. Within a minute both parents were aboard and the engine was going. The vehicle was reversed out and turned to continue the journey. While this was going on Andrew kept looking anxiously along the side track. All the while he feared that Jan or Wes would appear. His mind conjured up horrifying images of the men having guns and of shooting them. The idea of being murdered on a lonely bush track caused him to break into a sweat and to shiver.

As the vehicle ground its way up a steep, rough section of road away from the river, Andrew let out his breath and sighed with relief. "Sorry," he said. "I may have been foolish, but I just felt very uneasy back there."

He then explained how he and Carmen were sure the men were up to no good. Drug growing in the jungle was agreed on as the most likely illegal activity in that part of the country.

His father agreed, then added, "Better to be safe than sorry. This is a very isolated place and we are a long way from any police station."

What the men might be up to was discussed for a few more minutes. Andrew worried that the men might follow them, and he experienced a spurt of fear when he realised that the road was a dead-end.

We are trapped, he thought anxiously. Then he shook his head. *I am being paranoid. The men wouldn't do anything because we haven't actually seen them doing anything wrong.*

To help himself relax, he tried to concentrate on the map reading. The road deteriorated further after they passed another turnoff to the left. "That track goes to Grasstree Pocket and Stuckeys Gap," he said.

The road got worse and worse until they could only proceed in first gear and 4 wheel drive. The vehicle lurched and bounced over rocky outcrops, potholes and washouts. These were made worse because the track wound its way up a steep ridge and then across six creek crossings. Five of these were across the same creek. This had a small flow of water, but Andrew could tell by the V-shaped cross-section of the valley that it would be a raging spate after rain. That got him looking anxiously up but he saw that the sky remained clear of clouds.

They came to another un-signposted track junction. Andrew's father pointed and said, "That one goes to Mt Poverty. This one goes to Mt Penniless."

He swung the vehicle onto the Mt Penniless track and Andrew shook his head in dismay as the track was so narrow the leaves on each side brushed against the vehicle. The road went down a steep slope and across a small creek then up an even steeper grade on the other side. Then it wound its way along the bottom of a narrow, steep-sided valley before climbing up onto a steep ridge covered in savannah woodland. Then it dipped into jungle again.

The further they went up the valley the more rugged the country became. The jungle gave way to sheoak country and masses of rocky outcrops. Andrew began to experience a claustrophobic sensation. Then the road turned off a ridge and wound its way across the side of the steep slopes on a narrow bench cut. Travelling along this was scary too and the only relief were occasional glimpses right back down the valley so that Helenvale Hill and the Black Mountains could be made out in the far distance.

We are really isolated now, Andrew thought. *This really is the back end of nowhere!*

Chapter 25

ANXIETY

Ahead of the vehicle a skyline appeared through the trees, indicating that they had arrived at a saddle between two peaks. A glance at the map confirmed this and a minute later they crossed the watershed onto fairly level ground. This was heavily timbered with tall, straight trees and the word 'woods' flitted through Andrew's mind. He noted that they were now near the headwaters of the East Normanby River and he noted the words 'Normanby Tin Workings' on the map near several building symbols. Just east of them was a smallish mountain named Mt Penniless.

"We are nearly there," he commented as the 4WD dipped down through a small creek.

A hundred metres on they came to a track junction. The 'road' on the right went off towards the north and up a low hill. A steel shed was just visible. The vegetation changed to open savannah. On the left it became dense tropical rainforest again. They took the left fork and drove on towards some buildings that were just visible among the trees.

This was the home of Cousin Bessie and her husband Des. They met them at the front gate, along with several tail-wagging dogs. Andrew took an instant liking to Cousin Bessie. *She is a beautiful woman,* he thought. Later he added to this by deciding she was a lovely person. Des was friendly and likeable and there was shaking of hands all round. They were then led into the house.

This was quite an ordinary house considering its location, and Andrew was surprised to find the two children sitting in a very cool and comfortable lounge room: Selena watching TV and Marvin playing a computer game. Andrew had somehow expected to find a backwoods log cabin and felt a bit foolish. This was on account of a couple of joking comments he had made earlier to Carmen about hillbillies and banjos.

After a short tour of the property, which Andrew now learned was a tourist destination for bird watchers, lunch was served on the back porch. This was cool enough in the shade and slight breeze but was accompanied by occasional attacks by march flies. The constant backdrop was the shrill whine of cicadas which at times seemed so loud they threatened to drown out the conversation. But after a while they just became a background noise that Andrew barely noticed.

The young cousins were so shy that it was hard to get any conversation out of them, and after a while Andrew gave up and just sat and pretended to be interested. Most of the adult conversation was family 'stuff', about relatives that Andrew barely knew or had never even heard of. Carmen seemed to soak it all up and kept joining in but he found it all a bit wearing.

So he was glad when at 2pm they stood up to make their farewells. But even then they did not immediately leave. There was a long discussion about the water supply and about how to safely dismantle an old water tower and what options there were for solar power and a small hydro plant in the river. Then birds and dogs had to be admired.

It was half past two before the family were all back in the vehicle and then another few minutes before the last goodbyes were said. Andrew waved cheerfully enough, secretly glad to be going. Not that he disliked the relatives at all.

They are very nice people, he thought. But they certainly lived in an isolated place. *At the end of the worst road in the whole world!* he told himself.

And then there was nearly three quarters of an hour of first gear grinding and bumping down that awful track over rocks, runnels and potholes before they reached the Annan River Bridge at The Forks. Only when he recognised the place did Andrew experience a few minutes of anxiety, wondering if Jan and Wes were still there. He had to tell himself to stop being silly when he worried about them ambushing the vehicle.

Why should they? We don't know anything about them, even if they are up to no good, he reasoned.

But reason was a poor tool against emotion and he knew with irrational certainty that he was scared of the men. He certainly hoped they would not meet them.

They didn't. There was no sign of any vehicles at the bridges and they saw no other vehicle on the drive back down the valley to Shiptons Flat. But only when they reached the good gravel road at the mine entrance did Andrew really start to relax.

Twenty minutes later they were back at the hotel, and he thankfully climbed out and stretched. He felt quite worn out and the constant bumping and jolting had left him with some bruises and sore muscles.

And then another source of anxiety began to assail him. No sooner were they home than Carmen reminded their parents that they had to drive to Cooktown the next day to pick up Tina and her friend Adele.

Tina! Andrew thought with something of a shock. *How will I treat her? What will I say? Do I still love her? And what does she feel for me?* It all left him confused and worried, especially when he thought about their break-up and about the girls he had met since. *Is Colleen the girl for me?* he wondered.

The tension was added to when Carmen said to him, "And don't you be horrible to Tina. Just because she has dumped you is no reason not to be nice to her."

That hurt. Andrew bristled. "I'm not like that! Anyway, I like her too much to ever hurt her."

At that, Carmen softened. "Do you still love her?" she asked.

Andrew shrugged and felt his eyes go moist. "I'm not sure. But I like her a lot and I care about her, so I won't do anything to upset her."

Carmen nodded and said, "Good," then went to the kitchen.

Andrew was left to worry alone. To try to take his mind off things, he went to his room and set to work making the cardboard buildings for the farm. As he worked he became absorbed in the task. Then his imagination suggested that they could make a whole 'Western' town. *We could make a saloon, a sheriff's office, a livery stable, shops and houses,* he thought. After more reflection he decided they could also make a fort for the soldiers.

At supper time he suggested these things to Carmen and she was enthusiastic. "That is a great idea Andrew," she enthused.

"We need to buy some cardboard when we go to town tomorrow," he said. Then he had a sobering thought and added, "But we will look a bit silly if we make all these things and we don't get a chance to play with Little Terry again.

"We will," Carmen said with conviction. "We will ask if we have to. After all we've got a couple of weeks here yet."

Andrew went to bed with his head full of plans. But then sleep would not come and he lay there perspiring in the night with his mind full of anxieties about what the next day would bring. Chief among his worries was how his meeting with Tina would work out and what, if anything, they might have in the way of a future relationship. It came to him that he still really cared about her and that he had a strong desire for them to get back together.

But will she want that? he wondered. And how to go about it so that he did not turn her off?

* * *

Andrew woke several hours later to the crack of thunder and the drumming of rain on the roof. It was another thunderstorm and he got up and went out to watch for a while. It was not as violent as the storm a few days earlier and he quickly lost interest.

At least it is cooler, he thought.

Then he jumped as a mango crashed onto the veranda roof just above him. Grinning at his own reaction he went back to his room.

But then sleep would not come. Instead, he lay awake worrying about what the day would bring.

Tina arrives today, he kept telling himself.

When daylight finally arrived Andrew felt that he had hardly slept. He got up and went out to the front veranda. The air felt quite cool and very fresh but already most of the puddles were drying up and the dripping from the trees had stopped. The sky was clear and there was little sign that there had been a thunderstorm in the night.

As no-one else was awake, he went back to his room and lay down, to fall at once into a deep sleep. He was woken from this by his mother shaking him. "Wake up sleepy head. It is time for breakfast," she said.

Andrew saw that it was nearly 7 o'clock. Rubbing his eyes he gathered his towel, clothes and toilet bag and headed for the shower. Twenty minutes later, shaved and feeling much better he sat down for breakfast. Carmen had obviously been up since six and had already eaten and served the miners who were now setting off for work.

Their mother said, "You children get a wriggle on. We have to be at the airport to pick up the girls at ten."

Being reminded of this sent another spasm of anxiety through Andrew. He finished his breakfast and went to do his chores. The sweeping, cleaning and collecting of mangos got him all sweaty as the sun was out with tropical force. That got him anxious that he might smell and he wondered if he should have another shower before they went.

He didn't but he did make sure he combed his hair and brushed his teeth and looked as presentable as he could while trying not to make it obvious he was making a special effort. Then he found he was feeling very nervous and that got him perspiring.

They set off at 9 o'clock. This time only Mrs Collins, Carmen and Andrew went as they needed the two seats for the girls. Mr Collins stayed to run the pub. "I'll be fine. Irish and I will keep the place running like a well-oiled machine," Mr Collins said.

That caused Mrs Collins to snort and mutter about them drinking the liquid assets and ending up with a debt instead of a profit. "Men!" she said to Carmen in exasperation.

Andrew barely noticed the drive to town. The whole way he was feeling anxious. He found he was biting his nails and continually running the fingers of his left hand through his hair. The closer they got to the airport the more worried he became until the nervousness upset his stomach.

This is ridiculous! I don't get seasick, not even in a cyclone, Andrew thought. But he felt distinctly queasy from worry about Tina.

They did not go into the main part of Cooktown but turned off along the McIvor Road at the edge of town. The drive north to the airport seemed to increase the tension and Andrew began to wonder if he should ask his mother to stop so that he could be sick. But pride held his tongue and he managed to keep control until they parked at the terminal.

Andrew at once got out and took several deep breaths, then hurried to the small wooden terminal building, intending to go to the toilet. But as he stepped inside he forgot about being sick. Seated there, still in white shirts with ties and wearing their kopiahs, were the two Malaysians. As Andrew came in, they looked at him and he felt a curious sensation that made his skin go cold and prickly. He could not see either man's eyes because of the dark glasses that they wore but he was sure they recognised him.

To avoid their eyes he fled to the toilet and then washed his face. *Are they meeting someone or leaving?* he wondered.

After a few deep breaths he strolled out, acting cool and unconcerned. For the next few minutes he pretended to be interested in the posters and pictures around the walls. As he did, he cast a few casual glances and surmised, from the suitcases beside the men, that they were leaving.

I wonder if their luggage is full of drugs? he thought.

Then he felt guilty as he really had no proof at all that the men were not innocent businessmen or tourists.

Having reached that conclusion Andrew went back outside and wandered over to the fence beside the apron. Carmen and his mother were there, standing in the shade of a tree, and he took the opportunity to whisper to Carmen about the men.

She nodded and said, "I hope they are leaving. They give me the creeps."

At that moment, the aircraft landed and came rolling into view, its engines roaring as the propellers were placed in reverse pitch. Andrew knew that it would land from over the estuary but was still surprised at the speed at which it arrived. He saw that it was a twin engine Metroliner. As it slowed and turned off the runway he found that he was breathing rapidly and that his heart rate had shot up. He wiped sweaty palms on his shorts and swallowed nervously.

A few minutes later the door was opened and steps placed against the fuselage. People began stepping down. Among the first was Tina. She wore white shorts and a tropical shirt that was predominantly blue, patterned with flowers. Her mousy fair hair had been bobbed and her freckled face crinkled into a smile as soon as she saw them. As his mother and sister were beside him, Andrew did not place much store on this.

It wasn't until she came through the gate and had exchanged hugs with both Andrew's mother and Carmen and they met face to face that Andrew was really tested. He found that he really wanted to hug her, to say he wanted her, to tell her that he loved her. But his tongue felt tied and he kept swallowing and telling himself not to rush it.

Don't put her off and don't embarrass her, he thought.

She gave him a grave but non-committal smile and then nodded before turning to introduce Adele. Andrew had met Adele before. She was a nice person but very plain in her looks and wore thick rimmed glasses. She had almost black hair and dark brown eyes that seemed very friendly. Her manner was shy but she did join in the conversation, which started with 'How was the flight?' and then moved on to the weather and what had been going on in Cairns during the previous week.

There was a delay while the luggage was unloaded. During this Andrew stood quietly to one side while casting anxious glances at Tina and trying to summon the nerve to hint that he still liked her. But she seemed very stand-offish and kept talking to Carmen and his mother. That dampened his ardour, and he became even more worried.

Maybe she really doesn't like me and doesn't want to have anything to do with me? he thought.

The only other thing he remembered at the airport was seeing the airline staff usher the two Malaysians out to the plane and have their suitcases loaded aboard.

I wonder where they are off to? he thought. He vaguely knew that the aircraft was flying on north to other places in Cape York Peninsula.

The next minor drama was who was to sit where in the vehicle. Andrew really wanted to sit beside Tina but was too anxious to push forward. His mother seemed to sense the situation.

She said, "Andrew, you sit in the front and then the girls can sit together in the back and talk."

"Yes Mum."

It wasn't what he wanted but he did as he was told. As he buckled up, he realised he was very nervous and that he really did care about what Tina thought.

This anxiety was pushed up several more notches when they drove into town and Mrs Collins said, "We will go to town and have morning tea and then do a bit of a drive around."

I hope she doesn't plan to have lunch at the cafe, Andrew thought. He did not want Tina and Colleen to meet.

But they did. After driving to town they pulled up right outside the cafe. To make matters worse Colleen was standing on the footpath talking to several other teenagers who sat at the tables.

I will just have to play it cool, Andrew thought as he climbed out.

Chapter 26

TOUR OF THE TOWN

As he stepped out of the blazing sunlight into the relative cool of the shaded footpath, Andrew was sweating; and he knew it was from anxiety as much as from the heat.

What can I do? How will I stop Tina from finding out I like Colleen and that I kissed her? he wondered.

This became acute when Colleen saw him and smiled and moved to say hello. She then looked at the girls with quite natural curiosity.

Andrew shrugged. "They are friends of my sisters who are going to stay with us for a week," he explained, glancing back to check that none of the girls was close enough to hear what he said.

Carmen, Tina, and Adele joined him on the footpath. To Andrew's dismay, Carmen said to Colleen, "Oh hi! You were the girl who was down at the river with Andrew on Christmas Day weren't you? What's your name again?"

"Colleen. You are Carmen aren't you?" Colleen answered.

She was relaxed and happy and did not mind her name being linked with Andrew's. But Andrew did and he squirmed emotionally as he noted Tina dart a swift look at him and then at her.

Tina was introduced and was friendly but again glanced from Andrew to Colleen and back. Then she walked past her and into the cafe. Adele was introduced next and quite happily began chatting. She seemed to Andrew to be one of those people who quite naturally liked people and could talk easily to strangers.

His mother said hello to Colleen as she went into the cafe. Colleen said, "I'd better go in and help Mum. What would you like, Andrew?"

She asked this with such an obvious double meaning that the other teenagers began to tease and make comments and Andrew blushed. Tina overheard this and gave them both a hard look and then turned her back. That put Andrew into a fluster and he broke into another sweat of anxiety. Partly this was because he now had both girls he thought he loved side by side and found himself torn over which one to choose.

It did not help when he got a good look at the pair of them standing side by side from both front and rear. When viewed from behind, Colleen had a very womanly shape, whereas Tina just looked to have a big bum. But from the front Tina's much bigger bosom was very obvious.

There is no doubt Colleen is much prettier, he mused. But was she the girl for him?

For the next twenty minutes he was kept in a state of mental anxiety lest Colleen or Tina should say something that gave the situation away. He tried to be natural and friendly with Colleen without letting on to Tina that she was anything more than a casual acquaintance. This he found hard to do and the effort had him perspiring with anxiety.

He found it a relief when they finished and climbed back into the vehicle. As he did, Colleen came to the door and gave him meaningful looks and he really wanted to speak to her but did not dare. But she did wave as they backed out and drove on along the main street.

After driving slowly along to allow time to look at the heritage buildings, they stopped at the cannon in the park. Adele liked the location and enthusiastically set to work with her camera. She insisted they all pose at the cannon. Andrew was happy to visit the cannon and, as he always did when he was there, he daydreamed he was part of a real gun crew fighting bravely to defend the port from the French (or Spanish, or pirates). And, as always, he regretted that the gun was pointed inland instead of being in a gun emplacement facing the sea.

To allow Adele to be in some of the photos, Andrew's mother took the camera. After taking several shots she said, "We will have a look at the harbour next. You've seen it haven't you, Tina?"

"Yes, Mrs Collins. I came here on the patrol boat a couple of weeks ago. But Adele hasn't been here before."

Andrew didn't mind a visit to the sea but when they got there and climbed out he realised that he had stumbled into another potential social disaster. Daphne and Kristen were there fishing. Both wore short shorts and bikini tops, sandals and big hats. To make things worse, Carmen led Tina and Adele over onto the wharf right near the two girls. Andrew followed, not knowing whether to acknowledge them or to pretend not to see them and ignore them.

Kristen solved this by calling out and waving. "Hi Andrew! Long time no see."

That left Andrew with no option but to stop and talk to them. While he did, he was hotly aware of Tina glancing at them with a frozen mask of disapproval on her face.

Oh bugger! he thought. *Tina remembers them from when we were here on the patrol boat.*

Kristen gestured towards the three girls. "Who are they?"

"That is my big sister, Carmen, and her two friends. They just flew in to spend a week with us," he answered. As he did, he was hotly aware of Daphne's sunburnt cleavage bobbling on the periphery of his vision.

Kristen looked and nodded. "I remember your sister. For a minute I thought you'd given us up for some new talent."

"I wouldn't give you up, not while you are fishing using that sort of bait" Andrew joked.

Kristen wiggled her body and giggled, "Oooh, you naughty boy!"

Tina obviously heard this. As she glanced at them, a look of disapproval crossed her face. That made Andrew feel both anxious and defiant. *She can't just dump me and then have any say in who I meet,* he mused.

But his mother was another matter. She called, "Come on, Andrew. We are going."

Andrew blushed and said, "Be careful you don't get sunburnt. See you again."

Daphne smiled and swung her bosom from side to side. "We will try not to."

As Andrew walked away, Kristen called, "See ya, sailor! See ya at the New Year party."

That brought a look and a frown from Tina, Carmen, and Adele. Andrew defiantly tried to act cool and just walked back to the vehicle without a word. As he got in his mother gave him a sharp look which he pretended not to notice. But he did find it a relief when they drove away, the two girls waving as they did. He managed to summon the courage to give a small wave in return.

I must have cooked my goose with Tina by now, he thought unhappily. The feeling of intense regret that he then experienced told him that it mattered and that he wished he hadn't. *Maybe I can make it up?* he pondered.

But the next location they visited didn't help much either. This was

Grassy Hill. Andrew had never been there so found it interesting. They drove back to the main street and then turned left for two blocks and then left again. They then drove up the steep, narrow road to the top of the hill. At the top, Mrs Collins parked the car beside the road and they walked up a flight of steps to a lookout behind a small lighthouse.

As they did, Adele said, "For a place called grassy it isn't very, is it?"

Andrew had noted that as well, the entire hill being covered with a dense covering of trees. "Maybe it was when Captain Cook named it?" he suggested.

At the lookout they stood in a group and studied the estuary and town. Andrew was able to point out the clearing of the airport some kilometres inland. They studied the view for some minutes and Adele took some photos. Then they turned to look south along the coast and out to sea.

Andrew was immediately struck by how rugged the coast looked and by the number of small, isolated coral reefs he could see, quite apart from the larger masses of reefs on the far horizon.

Bloody hell! What a trap for poor old mariners in the old days, he thought, trying to imagine navigating a sailing ship through such a maze at night.

Over the past year or so he had several times been on vessels that had navigated those waters, even at night, and he was intellectually familiar with the layout from studying the charts. But seeing the pale blobs among the darker blue of deep water, all blotched with scraps of white made him very aware of what a dangerous piece of ocean it was.

"Captain Cook was lucky to get here at all," he said. He tried to imagine those far off days as he stood enjoying the view and the salt wind in his face.

Carmen pointed and said, "Are those islands I can see, those two dark discs on the horizon?"

Andrew looked and saw them small, grey shapes. "Yes they are. Those are the Hope Islands. They are near where the *Endeavour* ran on the reef back in 1770."

"They are where we found the mine," Tina added.

"Oh yes. What happened to it, do you know?" Carmen asked.

Andrew and Tina could only shrug. Andrew said, "No idea. I suppose it is still floating around or maybe it has got snagged on one of those reefs."

He had a vivid flashback to Blake sitting on the rusty old mine and of the netting and ropes snagged on it.

"It might have washed up on the beach somewhere," Tina suggested. "The wind and current are both blowing in this direction."

Andrew was strongly tempted to say that currents don't blow but Adele did. Tina's response was to poke out her tongue and say, "Oh poo to you!" and then laugh.

They turned to look out to sea to the east and north. Here the rugged coastline of Mt Saunders, Mt Millman, Cone Hill and Indian Head caught their attention.

"Now that is really impressive," Adele said. She set to work taking photos the view and then asked them all to stand in various spots to be included, along with the lighthouse.

While they were doing this, Andrew was tested again. A small Kombi van pulled up at the bottom of the steps and three people got out, a young man and two women in their early twenties. Both women wore very skimpy clothing and it was instantly apparent from the way the front of their blouses moved that neither wore a bra. From their speech it was obvious they were European tourists, Germans or Scandinavians. Andrew found the way their breasts bobbled inside the loose cloth fascinating to watch but did not dare stare. Instead, he tried to take surreptitious peeks without anyone else noticing.

In this he was only partly successful as he had a quick, apparently casual look, then looked away, only to find himself looking into Tina's eyes. There was no doubt in his mind that she had seen him do it. A flush of shame swept through him, then a spurt of anger at the way she made him feel bad.

Why shouldn't I look? he told himself. *She gave me the flick so she can't say anything.*

But he was ashamed and did care what Tina thought so he made a point of not looking anymore. But he wanted to and that got him confused. Frustrated he turned away and studied the coast and sea to the south again. For a few moments he speculated on what might have happened to the old mine.

Probably just floating and some poor ship will hit it, he mused.

Back in the vehicle once more they drove back down the hill. On the way they passed several tourist cars. Once at the bottom Mrs Collins drove them two blocks and turned left into Walker Street. Carmen asked where they were going now and Mrs Collins answered, "To the Botanical Gardens and the sea."

Andrew had not known there were Botanical Gardens and was not particularly interested until he arrived there. But as they got out and strolled in through the front gate the germ of an idea came to him. The place was only a few hundred metres from the centre of town yet it was very pleasant, and quite deserted. He found it quite a nice location with well-kept gardens and lawns.

This might be a good spot to secretly meet Colleen, he thought, peeved that Tina seemed to be ignoring him.

After twenty minutes of strolling, reading the names of various plants, studying the water system installed in the 19th Century and reading various informative signs, they returned to the vehicle.

The next place they visited was Finch Bay. This was only another couple of hundred metres further along. The road ended at a dirt car park behind a wall of trees. Beyond these was the bay. Andrew took an instant liking to the place. A deep mangrove creek came in from the right at the end of a narrow but nice beach. Steep, wooded hills rose across the creek and behind the beach and in the distance, beyond the sparkling waves, rose the magnificent and rugged mountains extending from the mouth of the Endeavour River to Cape Bedford.

Andrew hurried down to the beach and walked along it, then studied the mouth of the creek. It was certain to be the habitat of saltwater crocodiles so he was wary of going too close but his imagination could not help conjuring up scenes of the sailing ships days. He pictured the pirates using the bay as a place to careen their damaged ship.

Or for a landing party from a Royal Navy frigate coming in at dead of night to take the town's defences from the rear, he thought, his mind filled with images of red coated marines leaping ashore from boats rowed by seamen armed with pistols and cutlasses, all led by a handsome and dashing navy lieutenant, sword in hand (himself of course!).

Tina looked around and clapped her hand with happiness. "Oh, this is a pretty place!" she cried.

"It is," Andrew's mother agreed, "But we don't have time to stay today. We will go and have lunch."

The mention of lunch got Andrew both hoping they would go back to the cafe, yet fearful they might! But they didn't. This time his mother turned left when they got back to the main street, but they drove straight past the cafe and went to a bakery several blocks further along. That was both a relief and a disappointment for Andrew.

Lunch was a pie and a bun washed down by fruit juice. Afterwards, they climbed back into the vehicle and drove back up to the next street, Helen Street, and went left to visit the museum in the old Catholic convent. Andrew thought it was a magnificent old building but thinking about convents reminded him that Colleen went to a convent boarding school and again he felt torn about which girl he wanted to be his girlfriend.

After paying at the front office they began to tour. Many of the displays did not interest Andrew but he made a point of looking at them all. In particular he liked the rooms that had artifacts and pictures from the gold rushes of the 1870s; the pictures and models of the early shipping and the port, and the section devoted to Captain Cook and the recovery of the cannon he jettisoned to lighten the *Endeavour*.

After a while, Andrew became separated from the others as he browsed at his own pace. Thus he ended up in a room with displays about the Sister of the Sacred Heart who had set the convent up in the late 19th Century. As he read the caption to a photo of some nuns someone came into the room. It was Tina. For a moment their eyes met and Andrew experienced a feeling of intense regret that they had broken up. Her face seemed to go blank but he thought there was just a hint of regret in her expression as well. But before he could speak to her, she turned and walked back along the corridor.

That left him feeling even more confused. A mix of emotions boiled in him: wishing for her love; desire; anger at the situation; regret and a vague resentment that she could still so strongly influence his feelings.

From the museum they visited several shops to buy groceries. During these visits, Tina seemed to make a point of avoiding Andrew, always having someone else between her and him (Or so it seemed to him).

Once the shopping was done they set off for Helenvale. Andrew sat in the front beside his mother, hotly aware that Tina was behind him and could watch his every move. He pretended he was relaxed and studying the countryside but actually he was in a ferment of doubt and anxiety.

Which girl should I focus my efforts on: Tina or Colleen? he wondered. Both his heart and his head told him it should be Tina. *Not only do I love her but she lives in Cairns. Colleen might be beautiful but she lives here and goes to school in Herberton. I will never see her.*

But would Tina have him back? And how to go about finding out without making the situation worse?

It was all very stressful and left him feeling grumpy and dissatisfied. But then, on reaching the Lions Den, he was given some comic relief, and more cause for anxiety. The vehicle was parked and the girls moved their bags to Carmen's room. Despite the crowding a third bed had been shifted in and the three girls were to share. As this was right next to Andrew's room it was a potential source of frustration and anxiety but the lodges were all booked and they could not afford to give up rental accommodation.

The amusement came while he and Carmen were showing the girls around. As they walked along the front veranda, they encountered Cousin Sandy. As soon as he saw the girls his eyes lit up and he immediately took the opportunity to remind them that they were going fishing at Archer Point the next day.

Carmen nodded and said, "Only if my friends can come."

Cousin Sandy beamed a big smile at Tina and Adele and after he was introduced turned his full charm on them. To Andrew's amusement and concern, he seemed to focus most of his efforts on Tina.

She won't be impressed by a yob like Cousin Sandy, he told himself confidently; only to have his composure disrupted almost at once when Tina responded to Cousin Sandy in a very friendly way.

What made it worse was that Cousin Sandy seemed to spend a lot of time ogling Tina's bosom. That got Andrew jealous and he thought, *She won't stand for that very long.*

But she appeared not to mind and Andrew got even more jealous and confused. To make things worse he was effectively excluded from the conversation. After a few minutes of this, he went off to his room feeling even more confused and anxious.

Surely, she doesn't like him? he thought.

His doubts about his chances with Tina grew at dinner time. One of the miners, Simon, at once began to flirt with Tina. When she appeared in the dining room he whistled and called loudly, "Well, hello beautiful! Where have you sprung from?"

Andrew, who was serving at another table, expected Tina to snub him or cut him down to size with her tongue, but to his dismay she smiled and answered. Within minutes she was standing at Simon's table introducing herself and Adele and telling him all about herself.

She is way too young for him, Andrew thought in an attempt to bolster his sagging confidence. *Once he learns how young she is he will soon lose interest.* But watching her flirting and talking caused him severe doubts about his own ability to win her back.

What can I do? he wondered unhappily.

Chapter 27

ARCHER POINT

Andrew did not sleep very well that night. For hours he lay awake, perspiring in the humid heat. To begin with he could hear the murmur of the girl's voices from the next room, with an occasional trill of girlish laughter. Then he was tormented by memories and by rising desire as he thought about Tina. On top of his physical longing to be with her he was torn between which girl he really loved and which one he should devote his efforts and attentions to.

Wednesday the 29th dawned cloudy and humid and he wondered if they were in for rain. But by the time he had completed his shower and shave and gone to breakfast the clouds seemed to have cleared away. When a blazing sun rose from behind Helenvale Hill the air became stifling and sweat started to trickle from every pore.

His doubts about what to do and about his own worth were increased at breakfast time when Tina gave him a cool 'good morning' and then sat with her back to him. She even indulged in some banter with Simon the Miner, adding to Andrew's jealous concern.

Feeling quite depressed and defeated Andrew hurriedly ate his breakfast and carried out his chores. By 9 o'clock he was sweaty and in a thoroughly bad mood.

I have lost with Tina, he thought. *So I may as well try to win with Colleen.*

One result of this decision was that he relaxed and became more civil to all the girls. That seemed to ease some tension and he went to his room to pack for the day. He did not want to go fishing, it was not an activity he enjoyed, but he did want to go the coast and explore the Archer Point area.

He dressed in a pair of old khaki long trousers (the ones he called his 'sailing pants') and a long-sleeved dark blue work shirt and joggers. On his head he wore a battered old grey felt hat. But nothing so mundane for the girls! Carmen wore jeans and a long-sleeved shirt and straw hat and so did Adele but Tina wore baggy light green shorts and a tight-fitting cotton blouse on which the buttons appeared to be straining to stay done up. She applied lots of sun cream and placed a baseball cap on her head which had the logo *Captain* embroidered on it. Sunglasses and sandshoes completed the ensemble.

To Andrew she looked very attractive and desirable, and he had to swallow and tell himself not to be disappointed.

Colleen is prettier, he told himself.

But it still hurt!

Then Cousin Sandy and his father and little brother Bart arrived and it hurt even more, watching them all ogle and flirt with the girls simpering and giggling and flirting back. The only good things that Andrew found in the situation were noting that Cousin Sandy seemed to have given up on Carmen (to her evident relief) and that his little brother, Bart, also seemed attracted to Tina and had started flirting with her (to Cousin Sandy's obvious annoyance!).

This time it was Andrew's father who was driving. His mother had a strong dislike of fishing and had opted to remain and run at the hotel. Cousin Sandy strongly hinted that Tina should travel in his car, but she declined with a polite smile and instead went in the back of the Collins' 4WD, sitting between Adele and Carmen. Andrew sat in the front beside his father.

Uncle Jack led the way in his battered utility. They drove out to the highway and turned right, went through the Black Mountains and on northwards. By this time, Andrew felt he had done the trip so many times that he was bored and barely looked at the passing scenery. Only when they reached the turn-off did he take out his map and make an effort to be interested.

The first place of interest he saw was the old homestead of 'Green Hills' station. This was clearly abandoned and all overgrown and falling down. Seeing the ruin caused Andrew a feeling of sadness.

To think of all that effort and work come to this, he thought.

They drove east for 2 kilometres along the gravel road. At first the country was fairly open, but after crossing Armbrust Creek it closed in to a forest of low paperbarks. The forest was quite thick and looked to Andrew to be an unpleasant environment.

Be full of green ants and wasps and hard to navigate through, he thought, remembering encounters with similar country the previous year.

The paperbarks went on for the next 2km until the road crossed the Esk River, really just a creek with a narrow bridge over it. After that the vegetation became more ordinary savannah woodland. This persisted for the next 4km as the road wound through some low scrubby hills. For the whole of the way there were no houses or fields and only an occasional dirt side track.

They crossed a dry creek in a fairly deep gully and then came out in ironbark savannah. Ahead on the left front the hills got bigger and the large mass of Archer Hill became visible. A rough dirt road went off on the left over a low, rough little hill. Archer Hill was then clearly in view and Andrew noted that its seaward end was all open, windswept grass with a few clumps of some sort of scrubby bush. The crown of the hill and top edges of the grassed area was covered by a thicket of small, gnarled trees and bushes while the western end was more ordinary savannah woodland.

The road dipped steeply into the bed of another dry creek. At the bottom, it turned sharply to the right as the crossing was at a sharp bend in the gully. As they came up out of this the vegetation changed again to a much closer scrub and then to mangroves on the right. Lantana and other scrubby bushes clustered close beside the road on the left and part way up the lower slopes of Archer Hill, which was now right beside the road on the left.

Ahead through the trees and bushes, Andrew began getting glimpses of the sea. Then the road forked right at the back of a tree-lined beach.

"Walsh Bay," Andrew read from his map.

His first impression was that it was very pretty. The water had a greenish hue which melded into yellows close in and dark blue in the distance. Flecks of white added to the beauty. On the right, several kilometres away, the coastline became a line of mountains that slid straight down to the sea with no beaches. The mountains went on as far as he could see. The seaward slopes of the mountains were rocks and open grass but the tops were crowned in dense forest and jungle.

Bobbing on the sparkling blue waters of the bay were two motor launches. These were anchored a hundred metres out. Another two boats were drawn up on the beach. Under the trees along the back of the beach to the right were five or six vehicles and several tents. It was obviously a popular camping spot.

They did not go there. Cousin Sandy drove on towards a low, rocky point and stopped at a road junction on top of the low rise. Andrew looked around, enjoying the view. To his right was Walsh Bay. To his right front was the low rocky point running out a hundred meters into the sea. To his front was a small beach with a few straggly She Oaks at its back. Out from the beach a kilometre away was a rugged conical island. It was the one Andrew had seen from out at sea and it had the small lighthouse on its southern end.

"Rocky Island," he said, pointing.

To his left, the road went up over a grassy hill. Beyond that he could see an even higher grassy hill and this was the one with the main lighthouse on it. On the seaward end of the closer grassy hill was a dark line of rocks sticking out a hundred metres into the sea.

The old wharf, he thought, remembering the story of the failed port.

Cousin Sandy got out of his vehicle and came back to say, "The best fishing is on the old wharf over there but you can try these rocks here if you want."

Andrew pointed. "Can we go up to the lighthouse and have a look around first?"

"Okay. We will set up on the wharf before other people arrive," Cousin Sandy said, and gestured to where two vehicles and a tent were visible under the trees at the beach just in front of them.

Both vehicles drove up the grassy hill. There was a turn-off on the right at the top but Cousin Sandy ignored this and drove on down the other side and turned right among some large clumps of lantana. Andrew noted that two main spurs led down from the top of Archer Hill. The first went to the grassy hill where the wharf was and the other, much higher and steeper, to the hill where the lighthouse was. This was the actual place named Archer Point. Both spurs were covered with grass. Between them was a wide grassy bowl with a few clumps of scrubby bushes. The seaward end was a pretty little beach and a bay studded with several outcrops of black rocks.

It all looked very pretty and Carmen said so. Adele agreed and was keen to take photos. The road up to the lighthouse wound up to the left and then to the right. It was steep and Andrew's father engaged 4 wheel drive and first gear before attempting it. The vehicle then ground its way up to a gravel car park on top.

Here they all climbed out and studied the view. It was windy and quite cool and Andrew breathed deeply at the sea air as he stretched. He liked the place. The lighthouse was a disappointment, being just a small square block with the light on top.

Adele looked at it and said, "Where does the lighthouse keeper live?"

Andrew shook his head. "I don't think there are any lighthouses with keepers any more. They are all automatic. It's cheaper," he explained.

This news disappointed Adele but she set to work enthusiastically with her camera. Andrew helped by pointing to various features and naming them. He found the view quite impressive. To the north the coast was rugged and he could make out Walker Bay and Mt Cook.

"Cooktown is on the other side of that," he explained.

Out to sea he was able to detect several of the small isolated reefs. He also noted a line of showers on the horizon.

We might be in for a wet bum! he thought.

But what really held his attention were the old wharf and the conical island beyond it. He carefully studied it but was not impressed.

Not a very good location for a port, he decided. *Too exposed to the winds and sea.*

There was a short breakwater but he felt sure the wharf had only been usable in calm weather. He tried to picture a large ship manoeuvring between the island and the rocky point and shook his head.

Tina pointed to the horizon. "They're the Hope Islands, aren't they?"

Andrew looked and saw two grey flat discs on the sea. They were partly obscured by some rain showers. A glance at his map confirmed they were.

"Yes," he said. "They are about twenty kilometres away."

Tina looked, then said, "I wonder where that mine got to?"

Andrew shrugged. "Don't know. Drifting on the current, I suppose."

"The idea of a live mine drifting around where a ship could hit it and innocent people get killed really bothers me," she said.

Andrew could only agree. The idea made him feel anxious and slightly sick. But there was nothing they could do about it so they went back down the hill. Andrew walked with Adele, partly because he disliked being in a vehicle in such circumstances but also because he was just enjoying the view and the fresh air.

At the bottom they went left along a narrow dirt road which ran on a bench cut on the lower slopes of the grassy hill. To begin with he could not see the old wharf because there were large clumps of bushes and the road had several bends in it. Even halfway along there was another big clump of bushes that hid the wharf from view.

Just down to the left was the beach but it was a litter of small stones and seaweed and did not look very attractive to Andrew. And once again he noted the outcrops of black rocks sticking out of the small bay.

No, not a friendly place for ships at all, he thought.

At the seaward end of the grassy hill the road joined another that came steeply down the front of the hill. The road down the hill was deeply eroded and was obviously rarely used. At the landward end of the old wharf there was a flat area with room for vehicles to park. Sticking out into the sea was an artificial stone breakwater with a rough roadway along it. This led to the rusting remains of the wharf. This was of steel construction but was missing much of its decking.

Cousin Sandy, Uncle Jack and young Bart were already out there fishing. Cousin Sandy came back and busied himself sorting out fishing tackle and bait. Most of his attention was to Tina, who blushed and looked a bit annoyed. Seeing this made Andrew feel jealous and he noted Carmen looking both sardonically amused and peeved.

There were not enough rods for everyone so Andrew selected a hand line and took himself out to explore what was left of the wharf. One by one the others followed until they were all perched on the rocks or on the rusting ruin. To Andrew's annoyance, Cousin Sandy seated himself next to Tina and began explaining to her how to use the equipment. To add to Andrew's sense of envy, Tina appeared to be responding to Cousin Sandy's attentions. Feeling distinctly miffed, Andrew moved to the very end of the old wharf and sat down.

Having studied the disused wharf Andrew settled to the fishing. As he sat there his attention moved to the water. In close the water was clear and did not look very deep. Andrew knew this could be an illusion.

It must be deep enough for large ships to tie up here, he thought. The notion that the port could only be used at high tide did not make sense.

There were fish there, lots of little ones. Only occasionally did a larger one appear and even those were hardly worth the effort. Certainly none of any consequence came anywhere near Andrew's dangling hook. He could see it quite clearly, the lure drifting back and forth with its fins waving gently in the current. Nobody else seemed to be having any luck either as there were no eager cries indicating a catch. After half an hour Andrew was bored. He drifted into daydreams and sat staring out to sea.

Suddenly, Adele cried out: "Ooh! Oh, what is that?"

Andrew looked where she was pointing just near the wharf but saw nothing but waves. Then Adele said, "Was that a shark?"

"Something big anyway," Andrew's father said.

This got Andrew's full attention and he stared at the sea. Just for a second he fancied he saw a large shadow flit across a patch of sandy sea bed below him but he wasn't sure.

Carmen said that it was highly likely and they discussed sharks and then other denizens of the deep. Andrew did not join in the talk but he listened. He knew he held some highly superstitious notions about the creatures that inhabited the ocean and as a diver had seen many of them. He had no desire to see any more, much less meet them closer up.

They won't get me, he thought. *No way I'm going swimming in there.*

He also knew it was the 'stinger' season in the Coral Sea, those months during the hottest time of the year when deadly jelly fish were prevalent.

The group settled to fishing again. For Andrew boredom set in. He felt comfortable enough as the wind was counter-acting the effect of the sun and there were enough clouds to give some shade. The rain showers persisted out on the horizon but did not seem to have moved any closer to the coast. He yawned and fell to pondering how he might win back Tina's affection.

While he fished Andrew snuck many covert glances at her and knew that he still wanted her to be his girlfriend. It was while he was looking at her that Tina made the first catch of the day. Her eyes lit up and she cried out, "Got a bite!"

She stood up and began to play the fish, reeling it in a bit at a time. As she did, Andrew could only admire her. Seeing her happy, laughing face, brown hair fluttering in the wind and her jutting bosom he was again struck by her sheer aliveness and desirability.

I wonder? he thought.

Then his pleasure was spoiled by Cousin Sandy coming to stand next to Tina. He kept giving advice and offering to help in a way that made Andrew want to grind his teeth.

Smarmy bastard! he thought, but Tina declined any help and reeled the fish in on her own.

The fish was only about 40cm long, a coral trout, but it was the first catch of the day so they all came and admired it and Adele took a photo. As Tina held the fish up, her face alight with pleasure, her eyes met Andrew's and he could not help smiling at her happiness. She smiled back but he put this down to her being pleased with her catch.

After soft drinks and some biscuits, they returned to their places and resumed fishing. Then Cousin Bart hooked a reasonable sized whiting and hauled it up. As Andrew watched the fish flicking and spinning on the end of the line, he felt both peeved that he hadn't caught anything and sorry for the fish.

Carmen moved to the outside of the breakwater and quickly hooked a mackerel. That caused her father and Cousin Sandy and Tina to move there as well. Andrew was tempted to follow Tina, but a sense of surly grievance kept him where he was.

I don't really want to catch a fish, he told himself.

He did not enjoy watching the creatures struggle to breathe and then lose their lustre after they died. But being a normal hypocrite he did enjoy eating fish!

For form's sake he reeled in his line and cast it again, throwing it as far out as he could. Then he settled to watch again. He had a drink of water and then felt the need to do a pee. He looked around but the closest piece of cover was a good two hundred metres away. This was the clumps of bushes beside the entrance road on the seaward side of the hill. There appeared to be no other cover anywhere on the seaward side of the hill.

At that moment, he saw a person walking along the side road going towards the clumps of bushes. It was Tina. That checked Andrew as he thought she might be going there for the same purpose he had in mind. But as she vanished from sight among the bushes Andrew saw Cousin Sandy put down his fishing rod and start making his way back along the stone breakwater.

Where is he going? Andrew wondered.

Horrible suspicions that he might be sneaking off to secretly meet up with Tina sprang into his mind. A spurt of jealousy caused Andrew's emotions to seethe as he watched Cousin Sandy reach the shore and then turn right to walk along the side road towards the clumps of bushes.

Surely not? he thought, grinding his teeth with emotion as he did.

Cousin Sandy vanished from view and a scan of the beach and hillside showed no sign of Tina anywhere else.

Have they gone to meet? he wondered, now sick at heart.

For a couple of minutes Andrew sat there, torn between rage and despair as he realised he really cared for Tina.

I've got to know, he told himself.

So he put down his fishing reel and set off towards the shore.

Chapter 28

JEALOUSY

Jealousy was Andrew's main emotion as he strode along the rough stone roadway to the shore. But there was concern for Tina mixed in there as well.

Did they arrange to meet or is Cousin Sandy just bothering her? he wondered.

At the shore he turned right and hurried along the old road at the base of the hill. It only took him two minutes to reach the first clump of bushes. At that, point a slight bend in the track and the bushes took him out of sight of anyone at the old wharf or at the vehicles. The track was muddy and had long grass on both sides.

As he passed a second large bush, Andrew came suddenly upon Tina and Cousin Sandy. They were standing facing each other and Andrew was both relieved and concerned to see that Tina was not smiling. When he came striding into view, she frowned. Cousin Sandy turned and scowled as he heard him approach.

Without waiting, Andrew said, "Are you alright, Tina?"

Tina nodded but did not smile. "Yes, thank you Andrew."

Cousin Sandy put his hands on his hips. "What are you doing here?" he snapped.

Andrew wanted to say *Making sure Tina is safe,* but because he did not want to annoy her he said, "Just going to the toilet."

Cousin Sandy curled his lip and gestured on along the track, "So go on then."

Andrew hesitated but could not think of anything to say that would not provoke a possibly unpleasant situation so he gave a faint smile and walked on. Embarrassment was now added to a feeling of self-loathing for having not spoken the truth. Feeling quite upset, he continued on for another hundred metres, almost to the junction of the road to the lighthouse. Here he found a place among another clump of bushes and relieved himself.

Then he hesitated again, hurting from jealousy and his own negative thoughts. But after several minutes he could only shrug and start walking back to the wharf. As he approached the clump of bushes where he had seen Tina and Cousin Sandy, he tensed, ready to speak his mind. But instead he heard raised male voices and was puzzled.

As he approached, he saw that Cousin Sandy was facing his younger brother Bart and was pointing back towards the wharf and saying, "Mind your own business, little brother! Now piss off!"

Andrew saw that Tina was standing to one side looking quite anxious. At his appearance she looked relieved. She said, "Don't argue, you boys. It isn't that important. Anyway, I'm going back to my fishing. Come on, Andrew."

With that she stepped out beside him and started walking. Cousin Sandy gave Andrew a look of thunder and Bart looked angry, but Andrew didn't care: Tina had chosen to walk with him.

Even if it was only to escape an unpleasant situation, he told himself.

"What was that all about?" he asked.

"I just went to the toilet and Cousin Sandy followed me and was trying to use his charm to impress me, then his little brother turned up," Tina explained.

"What did he want?" Andrew asked.

"He likes me and he is jealous of his big brother I think," Tina answered.

Hearing that made Andrew even more jealous and concerned. But he managed to mutter, "Well, I understand why they like you."

Their eyes met briefly and Tina shook her head and said, "Oh Andrew! Don't make it any harder just now, please."

Andrew could not work out what she meant by that but sensed she was hurting. Rather than make things worse he said nothing more. Back at the old wharf they separated and returned to their respective fishing spots. As Andrew picked up his fishing tackle, Carmen gave him a raised eyebrow, but he just shrugged. Out of the corner of his eye he saw Cousin Sandy and Bart walk back to rejoin them.

Fishing went on. Andrew caught nothing and became sun burnt and bored. He found it a relief when his father called them all to the vehicles to have lunch. This was sandwiches and soft drinks and was eaten standing in a group. Uncle Jack and Cousin Sandy both had beer in an eski and they drank several bottles.

Carmen, Tina, and Adele went into a huddle and then later walked off along the side track. The others talked for a while but Andrew stayed out of it as he kept getting hostile looks from Cousin Sandy and did not want to cause an incident. Instead, he went back to fishing.

But he paid no attention to the fishing line and just sat and either daydreamed or brooded. He knew from the pain in his heart that he really cared about Tina and that he wished she was still his girlfriend. And he was jealous and feeling rejected. It even hurt just to watch her and the other girls come walking back.

All in all he did not enjoy the fishing trip and he was very relieved when his father announced it was time to pack up. As the gear was loaded into the vehicles, Andrew looked at Tina and she noted this and gave a frown and shook her head in irritation. That made Andrew feel even more rejected and he was careful not to look in her direction again.

* * *

The drive back took only half an hour. Andrew sat in the front and stared moodily out. The map and the scenery held no interest for him. It was only after they had passed the gap between the Black Mountains and his father began slowing down that he really became aware of where he was.

His father said, "We are just calling on Grandma Cynthia. I will give her and Bert this fish I caught."

Both vehicles turned in and were parked. Everyone climbed out to be met by four dogs. These barked and then just wagged their tails once Grandma Cynthia and old Bert appeared. Hellos were said to Grandma Cynthia and to old Bert. They insisted that everyone come in for afternoon tea. Andrew just wanted to get home but out of politeness he said nothing and followed the others in. Uncle Jack, Cousin Sandy and Bart joined them as well.

Inside the small house it was very crowded but seats were found for everyone and they settled to chatting and admiring the fish. Tea, coffee, and biscuits were provided, and Andrew hunched in a corner feeling bored and depressed. The minutes seemed to drag by. Then Grandma Cynthia said to Carmen, "How would you girls like to collect the eggs?"

"Yes please, Grandma," Carmen answered at once.

She, Tina, and Adele made their way outside. Andrew wasn't interested so he remained seated. But the girls were only gone for a minute before there were cries of alarm from outside and Adele came hurrying in.

"Quick! There's a big snake in the chook house!" she squeaked.

There was a general stir of excitement. Old Bert pointed next to Andrew and said, "Grab the shotgun behind that door, boy. Quick!"

Andrew stood up and reached behind the door and took hold of the gun. A glance showed him it was unloaded.

"Ammo?" he queried.

"On the bench there," Old Bert replied, pointing.

By then he was hobbling towards the door. The others crowded out as well. Uncle Jack put out his hand for the gun.

"Give it to me," he said.

"I will be right," Andrew replied.

After a boring day of failure he wanted to do something. Stubbornly he shook his head and kept a grip on the gun. Uncle Jack shrugged and Cousin Sandy sneered. Both went out. Andrew followed, carrying the gun vertically as he walked to the bench. Several shotgun cartridges lay there in an open carton so he snatched two up with his free hand and went out the back door.

Uncle Jack said, "You be careful with that gun boy. You should let one of us have it."

Andrew again shook his head. "I am a quartermaster gunner in the Navy Cadets. I have been trained to use guns safely," he replied.

Cousin Sandy sneered and said, "Navy Cadets!" in a jeering tone, but he made no attempt to persuade Andrew to hand the gun over. Instead, he just stood on the back veranda with Bart and watched. Andrew did not load the gun but walked across to the fowl run to where the girls were standing in an excited group at the gate. Grandma Cynthia, Old Bert, and Andrew's father and uncle joined them.

By this time Andrew was feeling both excited and very self-conscious. His heart was going and he was afraid that he might make a fool of himself.

"Where is it?" he asked Carmen.

She pointed to the fowl house. "It slid in there."

Andrew eyed the structure. It was about 3 metres square and had walls of either corrugated iron or chicken wire netting. The roof was corrugated iron. Inside were half a dozen laying boxes and five rows of roosts. Cackling and frightened hens were fluttering in the far corners of the run and in the chook house. But there was no sign of any snake.

"What type is it?" he asked.

Carmen shrugged. "Don't know. We only saw the end of its tail."

"You all stay back out of the way," Andrew said.

His father supported this and urged everyone to move back. There was then a debate about whether to shoot the snake or not, it being illegal to kill snakes except in certain circumstances.

Grandma Cynthia ended that by saying, "I don't want snakes around my house or eating my hens. Shoot the thing."

So Andrew slid a cartridge into the breech and snapped it shut, feeling very self-conscious as he did. He was very careful to keep the gun pointing away from any of the people who had now spread out along the front fence of the fowl run.

Old Bert called, "You watch out young fella. There are some real poisonous snakes around here. We get Death Adders two foot long."

"It wasn't a Death Adder," Tina said.

"Doesn't matter. It might be a Taipan," Old Bert answered.

The thought of being confronted by a Taipan got Andrew even more anxious and he gripped the gun with sweaty hands as he walked slowly forward to the fowl house. He had heard stories of how aggressive cornered Taipans could be, of them striking fast and repeatedly.

I would not survive multiple Taipan bites, he thought anxiously. But to his concern there was no sign of any snake.

Andrew scouted around the outside of the fowl house but could see no sign of any snake. He looked at the roosts and beams supporting the roof but saw nothing.

"It must be in one of the egg boxes or behind a hutch," he said.

There was only way for it. *I have to go in,* he told himself.

As he edged in the doorway, gun muzzle leading, he heard several people say, "Be careful!" but the only voice that registered was Tina's. She was genuinely concerned.

Finger on the trigger Andrew looked into each of the six egg boxes. Still no sign of any snake. He poked the barrel into the two hutches with their hanging strips of cloth but no slithering reptile appeared. By now he was feeling particularly anxious.

Behind one of the boxes? he wondered. Cautiously he stepped forward and leaned over to look behind the boxes. Still nothing. *Perhaps it has slid out through some gap?'* he wondered.

"Andrew!" Tina screamed. "Above you!"

A spasm of sheer terror coursed through Andrew as he glanced up. To his absolute horror he found himself staring into the snake's eyes at a range of only a few centimetres! The snake was up among the rafters and its head was the only bit showing. He saw its beady eyes and then its forked tongue flicker and its jaws start to open. Terror and training took over. In an instant the gun muzzle was up and he pulled the trigger.

Bang!

To Andrew's horror, the snake seemed to suddenly leap down on him and start to wrap its coils around him in a quivering, slithering mass. He yelled in fright and scrambled to get out of the way, groping at the squirming coils that were around his neck and down his back. In his panic he stumbled and fell heavily, rolling in the chook filth.

Even as he sprang to his feet, knocking egg boxes and roosts flying and banging himself against the side walls, his mind raced: could he reload the gun? Was the gun any use?

Its barrel is too long to be able to aim it back near me, he thought.

At the same instant he realised that the snake, though several metres long, was actually a python of some sort. That calmed his worst fears but he was still almost hysterical with fright.

Then the snake slid off him onto the ground and he looked down. To his enormous relief, he saw that his first shot had blasted the head clean off the reptile. It was still writhing and squirming but they were plainly only its death throes. He edged away from the thing, his heart hammering and his breath coming in great gulps.

At the door of the fowl house both Carmen and Tina met him. Tina cried, "Oh Andrew! Are you alright?"

Andrew nodded, not trusting himself to speak as the reaction shook him.

Then he heard Cousin Sandy's voice, his tone sneering and mocking. "Huh! Only a rock python!"

At that, a whole mix of emotions swamped Andrew: anger at Cousin Sandy; relief at being safe; regret at having killed a harmless snake; and pleasure that Tina was there and caring.

Grandma Cynthia thanked him and Old Bert took the gun. Andrew looked back and saw that the snake did not look as big and felt both foolish and guilty. It was actually only about three metres long and he knew pythons grew three times that size.

Cousin Sandy annoyed him even more by saying, "You bloody drongo! You've wrecked the roof."

Andrew looked up and saw that the shotgun blast had blown a hole about ten centimetres in diameter in the corrugated iron. That made him feel both foolish and annoyed.

"Sorry Grandma," he said. "I'll fix it."

"No you won't. These others can do that. You come can have a bath and change of clothes," Grandma Cynthia replied.

"Yeah, good idea!" Cousin Sandy cried. "You pong!"

Hearing that both angered and pleased Andrew. *He's jealous that I did the job, and that Tina was worried on my account,* he thought.

Cheered by that thought Andrew allowed himself to be led back inside to the shower. Grandma Cynthia provided him with a clean shirt and shorts.

"They belonged to one of my boys. You can bring 'em back some day."

"Tomorrow, when I come back to fix your roof properly," Andrew answered.

He quickly showered and changed, the shame at having soiled himself on the chook poo adding to his embarrassment and guilt. While he showered a temporary patch was placed over the hole and the dead snake removed. Adele took photos of it and when Andrew came out she looked at him with eyes shining with adoration. Cousin Sandy kept sneering and all in all it was a very mixed-up boy who was driven back to the Lions Den.

Once there, his mother had to be told the tale and she was horrified and then amused. Andrew blushed and tried to make light of things. Then his emotions received another twist when he went out to the front and discovered Cousin Sandy sitting talking to Tina. Jealousy again became his dominant emotion.

To offset this was amusement that Cousin Bart kept trying to impress Tina as well and wouldn't go away when his big brother told him to. And Adele now became very obviously attentive to him, talking cheerfully and looking hopeful. That embarrassed but also lifted Andrew. It was a relief when Uncle Jack, Cousin Sandy, and Bart said their farewells and drove off. Andrew took himself to his room to relax and think.

To take his mind off things, he worked at painting and assembling a couple of the cardboard buildings. In the evening after tea his jealousy received another jolt when Cousin Sandy returned to flirt and talk with Tina. The only good thing was that Andrew's mother clearly did not approve of this and while she did not give Cousin Sandy his marching orders before closing time she made sure that either she or one of the other girls was always with them. Seeing Cousin Sandy trying to pretend he was happy with this gave Andrew some satisfaction, but even so it was a fairly unhappy lad who took himself to bed.

That night there was more rain but not a storm. Andrew slept fitfully, his mind crowded with dreams and half-awake ponderings about girls, snakes, and life.

* * *

The following morning the routine kept them all busy for the first couple of hours. There was nothing planned for the day except that Andrew had made arrangements to go over to Grandma Cynthia's after lunch to repair the roof and egg boxes properly. He was civil to Tina when he saw her at breakfast but then kept busy.

It was while he was raking up the mangos out the front that things started to happen. A vehicle came from the direction of Rossville. As it slowed down, Andrew saw that it was Barry's Land Rover. It pulled up nearby and the passenger door opened. Out jumped Little Terry, face alight with happiness. Then the door slammed and the Land Rover accelerated off towards Cooktown.

Andrew was surprised. "Hello, Little Terry. What are you doing?"

"Daddy said I could play with Big Boy today," Little Terry replied. He ran over and gave Andrew a hug.

Tina and Adele had heard the vehicle and come to look as it was well before opening time.

"Who is Big Boy?" Adele asked.

Tina smiled and replied, "Andrew."

"Is he?" Adele answered with a mischievous smile. "How do you know, Tina?"

Tina went red and so did Andrew. Having been Tina's boyfriend for more than a year meant they knew each other very well and had experimented with almost everything lovers did.

She said, "Because this little man is obviously a little boy."

"Oh, I see," Adele answered.

Then she giggled at the double meaning and gave Andrew another mischievous grin. This obviously nettled Tina but before she could reply Andrew's mother and father appeared.

"Who was that?" his mother asked.

"Barry. He's dropped Little Terry off to play," Andrew explained, gesturing towards the faint trail of dust still hanging in the air.

"What a bloody cheek!" his father snorted. "He might ask!"

But the boy was there so Andrew said, "Come in Little Terry and meet these girls."

He was introduced to Tina and Adele but obviously wasn't interested. Carmen's appearance got him to smile and then he said, "Can we've play farms down river?"

"Good idea. Come and see what we've made for you, Little Terry," Andrew said.

He led the little boy to his room and showed him the cardboard buildings. Little Terry was both fascinated and thrilled. His reaction really pleased Andrew. He carefully packed the completed buildings in a box, along with the cowboys and Indians and the farm animals. Then he changed into his bathers and the two walked down to the river.

The model buildings were a great success. This time Andrew set up his own farm so that the 'town' could be in the middle. A 'road' was marked out with 'fence posts' and each boy set up their own farmhouse and fences. While they were doing this the three girls arrived, also in their bathers. At the moment when they did Andrew was laughing and helping Little Terry round up an escaped toy bull and he looked up and saw Tina watching him. Being caught playing like a little boy caused him to blush with embarrassment, but Tina smiled gravely and said, "That is really good of you, Andrew."

"He will make a good father," Adele added, giving him a meaningful look.

Andrew blushed some more and his mind raced. *Holy Moses! Is that what Adele has in mind?* he wondered.

She certainly had in mind winning his attention and affections as she knelt down and asked if she could join in the game. Andrew could only nod as he found himself staring down the cleavage of her one-piece bathers.

Holy Moses! They are bigger than I thought, he told himself.

From then on, he was hotly aware of Adele's hopeful smile, big glasses and seemingly bigger boobs.

"Can we play too?" Carmen asked.

Little Terry said yes, so each girl marked out a farm and got to work. With the three girls to help more farms were quickly constructed until the whole sandy river channel was covered.

While they were doing this Andrew found Tina kneeling facing him. The front of her bathers sagged open and he found himself getting an eyeful of those delectable big boobies that he remembered so fondly and which had got him into trouble. The sight sent his heart rate up and his mouth went dry with desire. He looked up and found himself looking into her big brown eyes. For a few seconds he looked into them while wondering if she was annoyed at him so obviously looking. But she didn't seem to be and he thought there was just a hint of regret in her gaze. It dawned on him that maybe Tina was jealous of Adele and was trying to compete. But he shook his head.

Nah! She has dumped me, he told himself.

Little Terry then gave him more food for thought. Andrew took out some of the plastic Indians and put them down. Little Terry's immediate response was to turn a cowboy with a rifle to face them and then he yelled, "Bang! Bang!"

Andrew was so surprised he said, "Do you know what guns are, Little Terry?"

Little Terry nodded and said, "Yes. Mine daddy and his friends they has got lots and they shoots them off all the time."

Before Andrew could ask more a voice spoke from up on the riverbank, calling: "Well, hello all. How are we today?"

It was Cousin Sandy. Andrew felt both embarrassed and annoyed. Then his jealousy returned like a hot wave as Tina stood up and went to talk to him. Little brother Bart appeared also.

Cousin Sandy said, "I'm not going to play little kids games. Come and have a swim you girls."

The implications of that made Andrew blush but he stubbornly stayed kneeling with Little Terry.

Carmen helped by saying, "What would you like, Little Terry?"

"Mine would like swim, then play cowboys some more," Little Terry answered.

So they stood up and made their way to the water downstream of the rapids. Andrew came last, seething with annoyance and jealousy at the way Cousin Sandy was so obviously making a play for Tina. Thus he saw clearly what happened next. Cousin Sandy waded in beside his brother and pushed him over, then laughed. Next, he turned and splashed water on the girls, making them shriek and try to get away. More jeering laughter pursued them.

Cousin Sandy ran after Tina and grabbed her around the waist and went to duck her. Tina pushed at his hands.

"Stop! Let me go!" she cried, a half-smile on her face.

But Cousin Sandy did not. As she squirmed out of his grasp he reached out and grabbed her again. This time his right hand grabbed at Tina's left breast.

"Stop that! Leave me go!" she cried, annoyance now plain on her face and in her voice.

Jealousy and frustration fuelled mounting rage in Andrew. He ran forward into the knee-deep water and as Tina broke free he shouted at Cousin Sandy.

"Leave her alone!"

"Mind yer own business, ya jerk!" Cousin Sandy replied, ignoring him and trying to grab Tina again.

Andrew slammed into Cousin Sandy with both hands, pushing him over. Cousin Sandy went down in a huge splash. His head went under and he floundered for a moment before struggling to his feet. With water streaming off him, he sprang angrily at Andrew. Before Andrew realised what he intended, Cousin Sandy swung a punch that connected with Andrew's head.

Stunned, he went down.

Chapter 29

HERO!

Andrew went under water, half stunned from the blow. But he still had enough wits about him to roll away before scrambling to his feet. He at once put up his fists. Through eyes filled with drops he saw Cousin Sandy swing another punch. By a convulsive twist he was able to dodge it and in return drove his own right hard into Cousin Sandy's stomach.

As Cousin Sandy doubled up, Andrew stepped forward to thump him with a left upper cut, only to have Carmen grab his arm.

"Stop it Andrew! Stop it!" she cried.

Tina also pushed in and then Adele. Cousin Sandy straightened up with difficulty, gasping for breath and furiously angry.

"Bastard pushed me over!" he shouted.

"Because you were groping Tina!" Andrew yelled back.

"I was not!" Cousin Sandy angrily denied.

Everyone looked at Tina and Andrew saw a look of pain cross her face. Then she shook her head and said, "Don't fight, please."

Cousin Sandy scowled and muttered that Andrew would be sorry, but he subsided and swam off downstream for twenty metres. To Andrew's distress, Tina went with him. Carmen turned him the other way and she and Adele stayed with him. So did Bart and Little Terry.

Little Terry was all excited and clearly on Andrew's side. "That was a good thump you give him," he chortled.

Bart nodded. "Serve the pushy bugger right!"

"That's enough talk like that," Carmen said.

She stood to examine where Andrew had been punched. So did Adele and he found himself staring at her thighs while her bosom accidentally bumped his face. But he found her cloying attempts to win his attention wearing. He knew what he wanted: Tina.

But how do I win her back? he wondered. He was worried she might think him a brute and a bully for pushing Cousin Sandy over and punching him.

The swim was not a success, but after a while Cousin Sandy waded ashore and walked off up the bank, scowling and muttering that he needed a drink. To Andrew's relief, Tina did not go with him. So the group returned to playing farms. Bart joined in unasked and spent most of his time making big eyes at Tina. As Bart was younger than her by several years, his actions did not annoy Andrew so much.

It was Bart who suggested that the Indians should attack the settlements. Andrew wasn't sure about introducing such ideas to Little Terry but the little boy cried with delight and said he knew what they meant.

"Mine have seen it on the movies what Daddy gets," he explained.

So a battle took place. That did not please Andrew as it led to arguments about who was shot and when and the only way to defuse these was to allow himself to lose. From experience with Graham Kirk and his friends, he knew that rules and dice were the only fair way to play such games. He explained this but it did not stop a second battle. This time he insisted that the Indians start from further away and they agreed on weapon ranges. To improve his chances, Andrew began constructing a timber stockade made of twigs driven into the sand side by side. Both Tina and Adele moved to help him, so he was further tormented and distracted by the sight of their almost bare bosoms close to his face.

The fort was a real success and sand castles were suggested. "Next, time," Carmen said. "It's time for lunch."

Lunch was in the dining room. While they ate, Cousin Sandy scowled at them from the bar where he was drinking beer and eating sandwiches. To Andrew's relief, Tina sat with her back to him and seemed to ignore him.

After lunch they all went to the veranda and set to work making more buildings and a fort out of the cardboard that had been purchased in Cooktown. Andrew also showed Little Terry the hundreds of Napoleonic soldiers and he was thrilled.

"Can mine play wiv them?" he asked.

"Sure," Andrew replied. He settled to painting more details on the French Imperial Guardsmen.

While they did this, Cousin Sandy sat further along the veranda. He continually cast them dirty looks while talking to two stockmen. Tina appeared to ignore him and helped paint a model saloon. That pleased Andrew as well.

Then Barry returned and took Little Terry away. Little Terry did not want to go and began to wail until his father scowled and raised his hand. The little boy went instantly silent.

Barry said, "Say 'Thank you'."

"Thank you. May I come and play again?"

Andrew nodded. "Sure Little Terry," he answered.

With an uneasy feeling he watched as the little boy meekly hurried to the Land Rover. *That poor little kid is scared of his dad,* he thought. The idea that Barry might beat the little boy crossed his mind and made him feel sad.

At 2pm Andrew's mother drove him and the girls over to Grandma Cynthia's in the 4WD. To Andrew's chagrin Cousin Sandy and Bart followed in their car.

"He shouldn't be driving after drinking alcohol," Andrew said.

His mother agreed. "You are right, but I didn't know they were going to, so I can't stop them now."

At Grandma Cynthia's they all examined the fowl house and discussed the snake. Once again Andrew felt both embarrassed and guilty. Cousin Sandy, who had joined them, sneered, "Big man! The hero who shot the harmless python!"

"That's enough, Sandy," Tina said.

That shut him up, but Andrew saw his mother look from one to the other, sensing something was wrong but not knowing what. To defuse the tension, she said, "Andrew, you fix the fowl house. While he does that we will help Grandma weed her vegetable garden."

Grandma had an extensive vegetable garden on the slope down to the creek at the back of the house. Even Cousin Sandy got roped in (With evident bad grace!). Andrew had brought tools with him and helped by Old Bert he got a ladder and climbed up to cut away the damaged iron. A new patch was nailed over it. Andrew then climbed down and carried the ladder back to the rear of the house near the woodpile.

As he leaned the ladder against the wall, he heard cries of alarm behind him and then a scream. He looked around to see Cousin Sandy racing up the slope, leaping garden beds when he could and crashing through them when he could not.

"Pig!" he yelled, fear evident in his every action.

Andrew looked and momentarily froze in alarm. Down near the

bottom of the garden were his mother, Grandma Cynthia, and the three girls. On the creekbank only twenty or thirty paces from them was a large wild pig. It was big and black and obviously a feral boar. Andrew could see its tusks and had heard and seen enough over the years to know that it was a truly deadly creature.

All the women began backing up the garden. Tina was the closest to the pig. Andrew took one look and then acted. Terrified that she be injured or killed, he dashed across to the woodpile and snatched up the axe that was there. Gripping it firmly he raced down the slope, leaping the bed of vegetables as he ran. As he covered the ground his heart was gripped by dread. He knew that if the pig attacked it would rip and rend the girl's flesh and even bite and tear. Tina being harmed he found too horrible to contemplate.

"Run!" he shouted. "Get up a tree!"

But there were no trees nearby and the pig was snorting and scraping up the leaves and dirt.

It's going to attack! Andrew's instincts told him.

Bounding over the last vegetable garden, cabbages, he came to a gasping stop in front of Tina even as the animal launched itself forward. Through eyes that seemed to be seeing everything in a narrow misty tunnel Andrew hefted the axe.

I will only get one go, he thought grimly.

His whole body tensed as he measured the distance. The boar charged at a truly frightening speed, so fast it almost mesmerised Andrew. It all seemed to happen in the twinkling of an eye. With a cry that was part shout and part sob he sprang forward and swung the axe in a massive side swipe.

Thunk!

To Andrew's immense relief, the blade connected. But he had no time to see what damage he had done. Twisting and springing aside he flung himself out of the animal's path. He did not quite manage this and he felt a sharp stinging blow on his left leg. But the survival part of his brain told him that he was not knocked over and still had a chance.

As he landed, he looked around through eyes red with terror. Where had the pig gone? Then he saw it. The pig was down, and it was writhing and scrabbling among the cabbages.

I must have hit it, he thought in amazement.

He had. And his amazement increased when he saw what the axe blow had done. The pig's skull had been cleft in two, leaving a neat cross section of bone and brain. As Andrew raised the axe for another hit, his mind told him it was not needed. The animal was plainly dead and had stopped moving.

Stepping closer he bent and studied the damage with horrified fascination. An aroma of blood and smelly fur filled his nostrils making him feel ill. From behind him he heard someone retching. A glance back revealed Adele vomiting while held by Carmen. Tina stood there wide-eyed, hands clasped to her bosom.

"Oh Andrew, you saved us!" she cried.

Adele looked up, wiped her mouth and cried, "My hero!" and ran over to hug him.

That really embarrassed Andrew, who was now feeling very queasy and shaky himself. He kept hold of the axe with one hand and hugged Adele with the other. As he did, he looked over her head and met Tina's gaze. A look of hurt crossed her face. That was enough to make Andrew let go.

By this time he was shaking with emotion; appalled at having killed an animal in such a brutal way; immensely glad he had saved the girls, and himself. He met his mother's eyes and saw them filled with concern and relief.

He was about to speak, to express his sorrow and disgust, when Cousin Sandy yelled from up near the house, "There's another one!"

Andrew looked and saw a second pig, as big as the first and this one was a sow. He estimated it as weighing more than him and it looked very agitated.

I've just killed its mate. Will it attack me? he wondered.

Old Bert yelled something about guns and Andrew glanced back in time to see Cousin Sandy snatch a rifle from the old man. It was another old ex-army .303 bolt action. As he walked forward, Cousin Sandy worked the bolt to place a bullet in the breech.

Andrew opened his mouth to warn Cousin Sandy not to shoot because he and the women were in front of him but before he could speak Cousin Sandy raised the rifle to his shoulder and fired. The shot snapped past, and Andrew felt himself go cold with fright.

He yelled angrily, "Don't shoot till you are past us, you idiot!"

Cousin Sandy scowled and clumsily re-cocked the rifle, hurrying down the garden as he did. Andrew was not impressed, fearing an accidental shooting far more than a wild animal.

"Watch where you are pointing that thing; and keep your finger off the trigger!" he snapped.

"Don't tell me what to do, Mr Know-all Hero!" Cousin Sandy snarled back.

He stopped next to Andrew and aimed again. The pig was still there on the other side of the creek and it was looking even more agitated.

Bang!

"Missed!" everyone said together.

Cousin Sandy swore and re-cocked he rifle. The pig snorted and ran around in a circle and then set off up the far slope at a trot.

Bang!

Missed again! Andrew's fingers twitched to take the rifle. "Let me try," he cried.

Cousin Sandy ignored him and fired a fourth time.

Bang!

Missed again.

"Let Andrew have a go," Tina called.

Cousin Sandy swore again and then angrily thrust the rifle at Andrew. Cousin Sandy was plainly humiliated and furiously angry.

"Alright Mister Expert Navy Cadet, you do better!" he snarled.

Andrew re-cocked the rifle and snuggled the butt into his right shoulder. As he raised the sights he saw that the pig was now over a hundred metres away, right near the top of the slope. It stopped and looked back.

Now! he thought.

Through his head ran the words of his Navy instructor: bring the sights up onto the target, take the 'First Pressure', breathe in, half out, as the sights come back up onto the target hold your aim and squeeze the shot.

Bang!

The wild pig fell flat. Then it began to twitch and scrabble at the grass and leaf mould. Andrew was both amazed that he had hit it and sickened that it had not died instantly. Without waiting, he dashed down the slope and across the creek. All he wanted was to put the animal out of its misery. As he approached it, puffing up the slope, he re-cocked the rifle and held it ready.

Close up he was sickened by what he had done. The shot had punched through the pig's head, tearing out chunks of blood, bone and brain on the other side. Blood was trickling out of its nostrils and mouth and it was looking at him with one eye as it scrabbled to get up. To end it, Andrew aimed at where he thought its heart was and pulled the trigger.

That did it. The animal convulsed and then lay still. By then Andrew was trembling with reaction and disgust. *I am not a hunter,* he thought.

Sadly he unloaded the rifle, turned and walked back down the slope, and into another emotional drama.

His mother let out a cry as he approached and then ran towards him. "Oh Andrew! You are hurt!"

Andrew remembered the first pig catching his leg a glancing blow. Now he glanced down, and nearly fainted. There was a gash at least ten centimetres long in the front of his right calf and blood was streaming from it!

They were all fuss and concern then. Old Bert took the rifle from him, Andrew remembering to tell him it was unloaded but not on safe, Grandma Cynthia thanking him and saying that those two pigs had been terrorizing her for weeks, Adele hero-worshipping; and Tina and Carmen helping his mother to staunch the flow of blood while they urged him up the path.

"It's the doctor for you," his mother told him. "This will need stitches and a tetanus shot for sure," she said.

"Sorry about your garden," Andrew said to Grandma Cynthia.

"Oh, think nothing of it. Those pigs have been digging it up every night for weeks," she said.

Adele piped up, "You didn't do as much damage as Sandy did when he was running away!"

"I was not running away! I was going to get a gun," Cousin Sandy cried indignantly.

"Pity you couldn't use it when you got one," Old Bert commented.

Cousin Sandy gave him a look of hatred and for a second Andrew feared he would hit the old man.

Carmen diverted him by saying, "If you hadn't drunk so much beer you might have been able to shoot straighter."

Cousin Sandy glowered at her too, then said, "Well if that's how you feel! Come on, little brother!" He turned on his heel and stalked off. Bart cast several wistful glances at Tina and then followed.

Andrew's mother called after them, "You shouldn't be driving if you've been drinking. It's irresponsible."

To that, Cousin Sandy made a rude reply that got Andrew ready to punch him again, but his mother held him back.

"Let him go. He is just bad mannered. Let's get you to the doctor."

The leg was bandaged at the house and then Andrew was helped into the vehicle. By then the wound had begun to throb and sting but he was not really concerned. He was more upset over the violence he had inflicted. His mother phoned the hospital and was advised that they had no doctor.

"He is on call but is at his private surgery at the moment, so they said to go straight there," she explained.

So they did. Half an hour later Andrew was helped up the front path to the doctor's surgery by Carmen and Adele. Tina followed behind looking unhappy. The doctor's receptionist met them at the door. She knew the story from the telephone and said, "Ah! Here's the wounded hero. Doctor still has a patient in with him. Bring him through to the next room so I can wash the wound ready."

Andrew blushed at being labelled a hero but he also sparked up on seeing the doctor's receptionist. She looked to be about thirty and was very smart and attractive and exuded a sort of warmth and sex appeal that he could not define but could sense. Added to this was a delicious aroma of scent that helped him relax.

Once they had him on a couch in the next room, she said, "It's alright. I'm not just the receptionist. I am also a trained nurse and the doctor's wife. I will look after him."

The doctor's wife proceeded to clean the wound. At the same time she reassured him and got him to tell her what had happened. He was in the middle of this when the doctor came in. He was a portly man in his forties and Andrew thought they made an unlikely couple. But the doctor was brisk and efficient. Within minutes a local anaesthetic had numbed the wound and the doctor quickly stitched the wound. Then he administered a tetanus injection. That hurt most of all but Andrew determined not to flinch with the doctor's wife watching.

"It's not deep," the doctor explained to Andrew's mother, "But he should take it easy for a couple of days and keep the dressing dry. I will see you in a week to take the stitches out."

No swimming! Andrew thought with dismay. Half of his anticipated pleasures melted at those words.

Then it was back to the Lions Den and bed. Once he was lying down and alone reaction really set in and he shook and shivered and pondered the nature of life and the real world. He also thought hard about Tina and Colleen. Andrew felt reasonably sure that Cousin Sandy's pursuit of Tina was not going well.

But that doesn't mean Tina will have me back, he thought gloomily.

At dinner time he was feted as a hero by the miners and then everyone trotted out their own wild pig stories and assured Andrew he was 'Bloody lucky'. He was irritated that both Carmen and Tina still seemed to respond to the miner's flirting. He was also bothered by Adele's open hero worship and clinging attentions. This was obviously causing problems between her and Tina and he wished she would give up. But he didn't have the heart to tell Adele that she had no chance.

Then there was the embarrassing incident of the phone call. As Andrew lay on his bed after dinner Tina came in and said in a very frosty and formal voice, "There is a phone call for you. Some girl."

Andrew blushed and wondered who, even as he silently cursed her for phoning while Tina was there. He limped out and Carmen handed him the phone with his mother and Adele and Tina all watching.

"Hello?" he said.

"Oh Andrew! It's Colleen. I hear you have been a real hero today, fighting wild pigs and saving your sister and your mother," she said.

Andrew blushed as he noted all the eyes on him, Tina's looking like hard glass. "Yes, I did. Who told you?"

"Never you mind. I have my spies," Colleen replied with a laugh. Then she said, "Are you able to come to town tomorrow? What are you doing for New Year?"

"I will try to," Andrew replied.

He wanted to talk to Colleen, to pour out his feelings and desires, and to make plans but he felt very constrained and embarrassed with all the others within earshot. Trying not to make it too obvious he turned away from them and lowered his voice.

"We are coming to town tomorrow about three o'clock. Where can we meet?"

"Do you know where the Botanical Gardens are?" Colleen asked.

"Yes, I do," Andrew replied, his heart leaping with hope.

The ideal place! he thought.

"I will be there for one hour, between three thirty and four thirty," Colleen said.

"I will be there, you can count on it," Andrew promised, his heart hammering wildly with mounting joy.

They settled a few other details and then Andrew put the phone down. As he did, he caught Tina's eye. She appeared to sniff and then turned away.

Oh well, he thought. *If you don't want me then others do.*

Andrew limped to his room to daydream and fantasise. Only later did he realise how little he had comprehended just who else wanted him, or what a test of character and conscience he was about to be submitted to.

Chapter 30

CONSCIENCE

Andrew slept fitfully. Bad dreams full of sharks and wild pigs and madmen with guns kept waking him. So did the throbbing of his wound. He lay awake fantasising about his meeting with Colleen. Then he had another bad dream in which he was with a girl (Adele? Daphne? He wasn't sure) and they were going to have sex but somehow they didn't and then Tina arrived and he couldn't find his pants. And he woke up sweating.

He also woke up thinking, *New Year's Eve. I will see Colleen today!*

With that happy thought he took himself to the showers, to find that his wound ached and he had to be very careful not to wet it. Showered, shaved and dressed he took himself to breakfast, and to his first test of conscience. Tina was there and at the sight of her he felt quite guilty. Then he rationalised it by remembering that she wasn't his girlfriend anymore. But the pain he felt made him uncomfortably aware that he wished she was and he knew he still loved her.

Chores followed and then Andrew sat on the veranda painting cardboard walls for a fort. The girls did not join him and he did wonder a couple of times where they were. But it was a hot day and a busy one. Vehicles kept coming and going and the bar was busy from opening time on.

At about 10:30 Andrew was interrupted by Irish who gestured behind him. "Tis the doctor's wife; says she has come to change your dressing," he said. Then he gave Andrew a peculiar look and added softly, "She's in a funny mood and looks to be half pickled already. So... so... well. well, there are stories."

But he got no further as the doctor's wife had reached them. She was carrying a shoulder bag and a medical kit, and a glass of some alcoholic drink. Muttering and giving Andrew odd looks Irish withdrew, shaking his head as he did.

The doctor's wife was dressed in a plain cotton frock and slip on shoes. Her hair was a mass of golden curls and her face looked clean and fresh. But it was the expressions that crossed it and the look in her eyes that got Andrew wondering and worrying just what Irish had been hinting at.

"Hello Andrew. How's the leg today? Can you walk?"

"Yes ma'am," Andrew replied, putting out his leg for her to look at.

"Oh good!" she murmured as she knelt to examine it.

As she did, the front of her dress sagged open and Andrew was surprised to see that she was not wearing a bra and that he was able to see all of her breasts. Compared to Tina's they were quite small, but the sight still had an electrifying effect on him.

"I just want to check that there is no infection," she added, taking gentle hold of his lower leg.

Her hands felt warm and soft and her touch was certainly soothing, but combined with the frequent glimpses of her breasts also quite arousing. Andrew found himself staring into a pair of wide blue eyes with what he thought was a faraway look in them. Her lips parted slightly and for a second he thought she was going to kiss him.

"You are a good-looking young man," she said. "And this leg looks fine. Would you just take a few steps to show me how it works before I change the dressing?"

Andrew did not remember anything from the doctor about changing the dressing and he was puzzled. Then he caught a whiff of some sweet-smelling alcohol on her breath and he put her strange behaviour down to too much drink. But he did as she told him. As he limped a few paces along the veranda he noted Irish and another man watching them from along at the bar. That gave him the unpleasant sensation that something was going on that everyone else knew about but which he didn't understand.

The doctor's wife then proceeded to remove the dressing. After that she cleaned the wound, muttering in a husky, silky voice that there did not appear to be any infection and that was good. During all of this, Andrew tried hard not to look down the front of her dress but she seemed not to notice. As she re-dressed the wound her hands did a lot of stroking and touching. That bothered Andrew a bit but he found it soothing as well as arousing.

When she had finished the bandaging, Andrew expected her to leave but instead she quite surprised him by saying, "I think I will stay for a swim. Would you please open the gate and then show me where to park?"

Andrew could not see why she could not open the gate for herself, but the thought crossed his mind that because she was the doctor's wife maybe she thought she was some sort of 'upper class' person who was used to having servants do things for her. Part of his mind told him that was nonsense as she was doing the receptionist's job as well, but he prided himself on being a gentleman.

And she certainly looks and acts like a lady, he told himself.

So while she went to her car he limped along the length of the veranda past the bar. As he did, Irish and his drinking partners all grinned and Irish even winked and said, "You'll be in like Flynn, Boyo!"

What did he mean by that? Andrew wondered as he stepped off the veranda.

Vaguely he remembered that there had been a movie star named Errol Flynn, but he did not know much about him, so he shrugged and made his way to the gate. He swung it open and the doctor's wife drove through. She then waited for him to close it and to show her a shady tree she could park under.

Then, as he bent down to talk to her through the car window, she quite stunned him by saying, "I want to do some nude sunbathing. Can you show me a place where I can do that please?"

Nude sunbathing! Andrew's mind felt like it was exploding.

His eyes met hers and he noted the rapid rise and fall of her breasts through the thin cotton dress. The memory of them now got him quite aroused. Part of his mind told him to get out of there quickly and he licked his lips with anxiety and looked quickly around. But he was also a red-blooded male and here was a challenge with a bit of titillation built in.

So rather than being sensible he nodded and mumbled he could show her a place. Into his mind flashed the sandy beach where he and Daphne had enjoyed their fumble. Anxiety and guilt caused him to glance up at the side of the hotel, wondering if his parents or sister were watching. But there was no sign of anyone so he limped on to the trees beyond the lodges. There he was out of sight of the hotel and was able to breathe easier.

The doctor's wife parked her car and climbed out with her shoulder bag and towel. She gave him a smile that set his heart and hopes racing and then walked over to him.

"Which way?" she murmured huskily.

Before he could answer, Andrew had to swallow as his mouth had gone quite dry. He pointed along the riverbank and said, "This way."

"Lead on," she told him. She then stumbled and Andrew wondered if she was drunk.

She is certainly acting a bit odd, he thought. He was scared now, but also fascinated and hoping for a bit of a glimpse of naked female flesh.

With his heart beating quite fast, for he now understood that he was getting himself into a possibly unusual situation, Andrew led the way west along the riverbank. They went past the swimming hole and on through the jungle for 200 paces until they came to the small beach at the next bend. By then Andrew was quite horny and worried lest the doctor's wife see this.

"How about this?" he said, indicating the small beach with its second overflow channel and patches of shade.

The doctor's wife clapped her hands with delight and cried, "Oh just the spot! Very nice! Nobody will disturb us here, will they?"

That 'us' rang an alarm bell in Andrew's mind and he said, "They shouldn't. Nobody much comes here. Anyway, I will go back along the track out of sight of here and stand guard for you if you like?"

To Andrew's shocked surprise, she shook her head and replied, "I'd rather you stayed here with me."

"But... but... but you said you wanted to... to... sunbathe nude," he stammered, his mind reeling with the possible consequences of her suggestion.

She smiled and nodded. "That's right. Wouldn't you like to see me naked?" she asked.

Andrew could only nod. Then he goggled as she peeled off her frock in one swift movement to reveal that she wore no underwear! She had a nice body, very shapely and tanned and with long legs. The sight made his fingers twitch and his hands go sweaty as lust surged through him.

Before he could react, she stepped forward, took his head in both hands and gently kissed him. As she did, she brushed her nipples across his chest. Andrew felt the fires of desire at the same time as he smelt the alcohol.

Gin or something, and she smokes, he thought.

"It's alright," she murmured. "I won't tell anyone."

Andrew knew he was scared and knew he was looking doubtful as she stepped back, granting him a full view of her naked form. She whirled her towel out and bent to lay it flat, granting him a wonderful view. Then she lay down and said, "Join me."

This time Andrew managed to shake his head. "I'd better not," he said.

"I'd like you to," the doctor's wife murmured huskily.

That sexy voice seemed to grate around inside his skull, weakening his resolve and making his heart palpitate.

"You should undress too."

"I wouldn't want to offend you," he replied, still staring and quite unable to believe his eyes.

She laughed and shook her head. "I'm a nurse, remember. I see naked men all the time, and I'll bet you look good with no clothes on. You won't offend me." Then her eyes slid down to his front and she added, "Besides, I can see that you really like me, so show me what you can do."

"I... I can't." Andrew gasped as the full implication of what she was suggesting burst on him.

"Can't, or won't?" she said, her expression hardening a little.

As she did, she writhed her lower body, scissoring her long legs to give him tantalising glimpses that sent the lust surging in his veins.

"Shouldn't," he said.

At that, the doctor's wife pouted. "I want you to. I want you to make love to me. You are the first real man I have met in this place."

Andrew groped for the right answer. Part of his mind rang with warning bells, about pregnancies, diseases and jealous husbands. But he found the first two excuses were frail branches to cling to.

She is a nurse and a doctor's wife. She won't get pregnant and she will know all about sexually transmitted diseases.

The other warning was the old proverb about 'Hell hath no fury like a woman scorned'. *She could cause me lots of trouble if I don't please her,* he thought fearfully.

He silently cursed himself for being such a weakling and a fool as to have allowed himself to be lured into such a situation.

But what a situation! Andrew had never had sex and here was a grown woman who was no innocent young virgin offering him!

And she won't get pregnant or tell, his lustful mind cried. What an opportunity!

"You mean you want me to do it with you?"

"Yes."

Temptation rose in a dark flood and Andrew found he was panting and feeling driven to comply. But there was also the fear, and the tiny voice of his conscience.

It is wrong. I shouldn't do it, he thought.

Then an image of Tina filled his mind and with it a surge of guilt. In a desperate attempt to save himself he shook his head and said, "You are a married woman. You are the doctor's wife."

At that, she laughed aloud and then sneered. "Doctor's wife! Now there's a joke! If the fool noticed me and gave me what I needed I wouldn't drink so much, or need to ask."

"I'm sorry, but I still don't think I should," Andrew said. "I really want to. I mean, you are very beautiful, and I would love to... to make love to you. But I've never done it and I do want to, but I don't want to cheat on my girlfriend."

"Girlfriend!" she muttered. "Of course a young man as good looking and brave as you would have a girlfriend." Then she went all pensive and a tear trickled out of her right eye. "I'm sorry. I didn't think. Of course you mustn't cheat on your girlfriend. But if you change your mind, just give me a call and I will teach you all about it."

Andrew hopped from foot to foot feeling relieved, extremely horny and guilty. He was also ashamed of himself for not being man and doing it, and for making weak excuses. He gestured back the way they had come. "I will just wait back along there to warn you in case anyone comes."

The doctor's wife stood up and put her arms around him. "Oh, you are such a gentleman. Thank you, and please forgive me. I just need it."

She kissed him and pressed herself against him in such a way that his resolve almost melted. But she did let go and waded out into the shallow water, casting him sad smiles as she did. Seeing her out-thrust breast and her beautiful curve of hip and thigh caused Andrew another sharp surge of desire and a stab of regret. He knew he would carry that wonderful image to his grave.

Fearful lest he weaken again he turned and walked quickly away. He found a small clearing about 50 metres back and sat down, his emotions a maelstrom of conflicting arguments. For the next half hour or so he sat there, wracked by doubt and lust. The whole time he was gripped by desire and was fearfully tempted. And he felt driven by the doubts of a young man: Was he normal? Could he do it?

What if I am no good? he worried. It was all torment.

As he wrestled with his conscience, Andrew came to the sickening discovery that he was not dealing with a simple issue of right and wrong. He realised that a major part of his choice may have been motivated by fear. There was not only anxiety over his possible performance but a whole raft of fears at different levels. Near the surface was fear of being found out, of trouble with parents and Tina. Deeper down was fear of what the doctor might do if he found out.

Doctors could do horrible and painful things and it could never be proved they did it with intent to harm, he mused.

And that took him to an even deeper level of fear. He agonised over how he would be able to look people in the eye (The doctor, his parents, Tina) if he was a sneak and a cheat. Then his fears moved to the religious level and the words 'Thou shalt not commit adultery' pounded in his brain. Terrifying images of hell fire and damnation rose to cause him to break into another sweat.

Am I just a coward? he wondered as he contemplated all these causes of fear.

But he knew that the deepest fear he had was of losing his own self-respect. Amid the swirling doubts it came to him as an absolute certainty that his decision was right. This knowledge stiffened his resolve and calmed him.

But then sounds reached his ears that sent his anxiety soaring. Voices: girl's voices! It was Carmen, Tina, and Adele. They came walking along the foot trail and Andrew stood up, torn by indecision. When they saw him they stopped in surprise.

Carmen asked, "Andrew, what are you doing here?"

Andrew blushed, knew he looked guilty and blushed some more. He stammered and gestured and did not know what to say. Finally he said, "I'm stopping anyone going along here because... because the doctor's wife is having a swim."

"Doctor's wife? Swim?" Carmen queried.

"She... er... she is... she wanted to swim with... with nothing on," he explained.

Tina walked on a few more paces. Andrew wanted to stop her but did not know what to say and did not dare try to restrain her. She glanced through the trees and then nodded. As she turned back towards him her face was hard.

"She is there, lying on a towel in the nuddy."

Andrew flushed with shame. "I... I haven't been peeking. I... er."

Carmen shook her head sadly and said, "So how did you get here?"

"She asked me to show her a place. Then I left her," he explained. He knew he was blushing and knew it sounded lame.

Tina gave him another hard look and walked back the way she had come. Adele looked very hurt and turned to follow her. Carmen again shook her head sadly and said, "I think you should come back to the hotel."

Andrew could only nod and follow, feeling thoroughly ashamed of himself. He did not want to meet Tina's eyes and yet he did not think he deserved such censure. Defiance and anger took the place of guilt and he acted as though nothing had happened. Back at the hotel the girls went off to Carmen's room so Andrew returned to his painting on the veranda. It did not help his composure when Irish and another beery yokel came sauntering along and grinned at him.

"How'd it go. Boyo?" Irish asked.

"How did what go?" Andrew replied, acting innocent but knowing he was blushing again.

Irish winked and said, "Did you give the poor woman nurse the injection she needed?"

Andrew shook his head. "I just showed her the swimming hole."

"Is that all you showed her? Oh well, pity. They say opportunity knocks but once and that yer never catch up on the ones yer miss out on," Irish replied.

That made Andrew even more embarrassed but also angry. "Excuse me," he said.

Burning with embarrassment he stood up and walked off to his room. Once there he closed the door and flung himself on his bed. To his added shame he began to weep. For the next hour he lay there, wracked by guilt, shame, doubts and lust.

He was roused from this by Carmen. She knocked and poked her head around the door. "Lunch time. Andrew."

"Thanks," Andrew replied, trying not to sniffle.

"You alright?"

"Yes. I didn't do anything wrong," Andrew answered, but more forcefully than he meant.

Carmen nodded. "I didn't think you had," she replied.

"Tina obviously thinks I did," Andrew said.

Carmen looked thoughtful. "Do you still love her?"

All Andrew could do was shrug and then nod. Carmen sighed and shook her head and said, "Then she might just have been jealous."

"Why should she care?" Andrew cried.

"I am sure she still likes you," Carmen answered. "Now come and have something to eat. We are going to town soon remember."

Andrew had forgotten and into his mind leapt images of Colleen and the planned meeting. But what Carmen had just said about Tina just added to his confusion. Feeling very mixed up, but also excited at the prospect of being with Colleen again. he went to the dining room.

There he acted normal and was polite to Tina and Adele. From the shy, anxious little smiles Adele gave him. Andrew was sure she wanted to have a relationship with him.

And she is jealous, he thought.

It occurred to him that if he suggested going for a swim in the nude to Adele, she would be willing, and that she would probably let him do whatever he liked. But he shook his head and knew with certainty that he did not love her and would never do such a thing.

At 2pm they climbed into the car. Once again Andrew's mother was driving, and his father and Irish were staying to mind the pub.

"Like leaving Dracula in charge of the blood bank!" Andrew's mother commented.

His father had suggested that they could stay home for the New Year celebrations but his mother had countered by pointing out that the young people need a bit more excitement and fun than just listening to a bunch of drunks. "There will be other young people and there might even be fireworks," she said.

And it was the thought of one of those other 'young people' that had Andrew gripped by anticipatory excitement as they drove to town.

But how will I get away unnoticed to meet Colleen? he worried.

Chapter 31

PASSION

On arrival in town, Andrew at once set about implementing his plan, such as it was. He had decided to brazen it out and be vague.

"I am going for a walk around town," he announced as they got out of the vehicle in front of a house.

"Why?" his mother asked.

"To get away from all these girls," Andrew answered.

Carmen laughed and said, "More likely to meet some other girls!"

That caused both Tina and Adele to frown and his mother to shake her head. "Not until you have said hello to Aunty May and Uncle Tom. And you will join us for tea."

"Yes Mum," Andrew answered.

He knew the others were suspicious but he didn't care. So he went in and met a middle-aged couple who were not really an aunty and uncle but were cousins of his father's. While there he also learned that there was to be a party for the 'young people' here that evening and that his mother would allow them to stay as there would be no alcohol or mischief allowed.

Andrew then very self-consciously took his leave. He found that awkward to do as Carmen obviously did not approve, Adele was looking unhappy, and Tina? Exactly how Tina felt he could not fathom as her face looked neutral.

Anyway, she dumped me! he told himself. But his defiant rationalisation did not ease his conscience and he went out feeling unsettled and unhappy.

Only as he walked along the street and thought about his coming meeting with Colleen did his temper improve. 'Tryst' was too strong a word for what he planned but he vividly remembered her kisses and the feel of her shapely young body firm against his and that got him aroused and hopeful.

I might get a bit more than a few kisses, he mused.

To his concern, he found his mind being continually swamped by images of the doctor's wife and he was unable to control his body's reactions. Luckily the streets were mostly deserted so he hoped nobody could see his aroused state. But it was not just his physical arousal that bothered him. He went over and over in his mind what had happened down by the river and what might have been and then went through all the arguments for and against.

The result of his agonised debating was that he was still sure that he had done the right thing. But he was quite anxious about what might happen between him and Colleen.

She isn't married; and she seems warm and willing, he mused. Hot even, but probably an innocent young virgin. *In that case I won't do anything serious,* he told himself.

It was just after 3pm when Andrew reached the Botanical Gardens. With half an hour to kill he decided to do a detailed reconnaissance. The place appeared to be deserted and turned out to be bigger than he remembered. There was a sports ground as well and he circled that uphill and came to the gardens from the back. A notice indicated a walking track to Finch Bay, and he thought about that.

It is a really nice place. I could take her there, he considered.

After a study of the layout he sat in the shade where he could see the road but was not visible to passing cars. As the minutes passed he began to perspire, both from the tropical heat and from anxiety. Mosquitoes also buzzed and bothered. Anxiety built as the appointed time came closer.

Then he saw her. Colleen came walking down the grassy footpath on his side of the road. She wore a straw hat, a yellow halter neck top and short white shorts that showed off her shapely legs to perfection.

God, she is beautiful! Andrew marvelled as he watched her turn into the gardens.

He was already aroused from thinking about the doctor's wife, but as Colleen came closer and he saw the way the front of her skimpy halter neck top shivered and moved he felt a surge of desire. His hopes shot up even higher when she hurried across to him and without a word flung her arms around his neck and kissed him, pressing herself hard against him.

As their lips parted, Andrew gasped and said, "You are the most beautiful girl in the whole world."

He saw that she was panting as though she had run a race. She smiled coyly at his compliment, and said, "I was worried you would not be able to make it."

Andrew had been a bit anxious lest she be offended by him being aroused but now she kissed him again and pressed hard against him. Before he knew it, his own hands were sliding up and down the silky-smooth skin of her back and sides and then over the back of her tight shorts. Her response was to press harder against him.

After kissing passionately for a few minutes they drew apart. Andrew stared into her eyes in delighted wonder, the sheer romance of the situation gripping him. But as he kissed Colleen again, Andrew could not help contrasting her with Tina. A twinge of guilt bothered him, and he shook his head and told himself that it was alright.

Tina dumped me, so I can meet other girls, he told himself.

For a few minutes they indulged in some heated petting and Andrew could only marvel at his luck. They kissed some more and Andrew wondered just how far he dared try to go. Colleen certainly seemed very willing and he began to very carefully and gently experiment by kissing her in different ways while gently running his hands over her back and sides.

Then she slapped at her leg and the spell was partially broken. "Bloody mosquitoes!" she said.

Andrew realised he was also being bitten and used his free hand to slap at more. He also realised they were both sweating in the sultry heat. Colleen complained of more mosquitoes biting her bare back. To deal with them he turned her around and hugged her from behind, being very careful not to touch her in the wrong places.

Suddenly she swore, and for a moment Andrew feared he had offended her. But then he looked up and followed her gaze. A truck full of council workers had turned into the driveway only 50 paces away.

Oh blast! Andrew thought.

He swore again when the truck came to a stop and four men in orange work shirts climbed out. "I hope they aren't going to stay," he whispered. But they obviously were. The men lifted down a lawn mower, whipper snippers and other tools.

Colleen muttered her disappointment. "Oh! One of them is Dad's friend, Billy. I mustn't let him see me. If Dad learns that I have been sneaking off to meet a boy he will ground me."

Andrew and Colleen were partially hidden by bushes but they now moved right behind them and she quickly looked around for a way to leave without being seen. Her attention was focused on the side of the gardens nearest the town but Andrew noted the sign he had seen earlier that indicated the walking track to Finch Bay.

"What about that?" he suggested.

"That will do," Colleen said with a nod.

After a quick glance towards the men, who were now starting the mover and cutting at plants with shears, she set off at a quick walk. Andrew followed, looking back from time to time. Not that he was worried about being seen as he was sure none of the men knew him.

The walking track was just a narrow sandy trail through the thick bush. It was easy to follow and apart from going uphill for a short distance presented no real problems. The main concern Andrew had was the occasional twinge and dull ache in his wound. But to be with Colleen he felt he was willing to risk any injury.

"You will like Finch Bay," Colleen said.

Andrew did not tell her he had seen it a couple of days earlier so as not to spoil her pleasure in showing him. But he could not help imagining a romantic fantasy in which he was the hero rescuing her from pirates back in the days of sail. He pictured them running along the trail while holding her hand and then having to turn and use his sword and pistol to fight off pursuing…?

He reconsidered. *They can't be pirates in a town. They must be… er… Spanish soldiers in crimson coats. I have just rescued her from imprisonment in the town and now we are fleeing to the beach along this jungle path. There will be a boat from my ship waiting on the beach,* he daydreamed.

Through the trees he began to get glimpses of the ocean and he pictured an old square rigged sailing ship anchoring off the bay, a row of cannons poking out of its gun ports. A glance over his shoulder allowed another short daydream.

A minute later they came out on top of a steep slope above the beach and were greeted by a fine cool breeze. Colleen stretched and sighed.

"Ah! That is better. That will keep the mosquitoes away!"

They ran down the sandy path to the narrow beach and stopped at the edge of the sea. Andrew looked both ways and smiled. His mental image of the boat and cutlass armed seamen waiting to take them off vanished and was replaced by the urgent reality of the here and now. There was not a soul in sight and he was instantly eager to resume his passionate exploration of Colleen. So apparently was she as she swung round and hugged him. They kissed again. Her kissing was so fierce and heated that Andrew wondered just how far they might go.

They moved into the shade of a tree at the back of the beach and leaned on some rocks to help them keep their balance while they kissed. To help himself cool down, Andrew undid his shirt, which was wet with perspiration, and hung it on a bush. Colleen did not seem to mind and slid her hands over his bare skin and complimented him on his muscles. For several minutes they clung to each other, kissing and petting until Andrew was fearfully aroused. Now he was gripped by the sheer wonder and mystery of the experience, and he savoured every delightful moment.

This must be real love!' he told himself.

But the wonder was tinged by anxiety about how things might develop, and the potential for very serious consequences if they went too far, or if they did something foolish in the heat of the moment.

Colleen was obviously thinking along the same lines as she stopped kissing and said, "Sorry if I have led you on, but I don't want to do anything. I'm not ready for that yet."

Andrew was both disappointed but at the same time mightily relieved. "I agree," he said. "We must be truly in love."

Colleen smiled and nodded, then said, "Thank you. You are wonderful."

That was pleasing and Andrew relaxed and kissed her and they hugged each other tightly again.

Suddenly he went stiff from fright.

Voices!

They were coming from behind the bushes further along the beach near where Andrew knew the steps down from the car park were. He looked but could not see anyone. He turned back to kissing Colleen.

Then the voices came again, louder this time, a male voice and a girl's voice.

Tina's voice.

And she was not happy. "Stop it! Let me go!" she cried.

The male muttered and swore and Andrew could not make out what he said except for the words 'teasing bitch!' Tina then cried out in pain and called again, loudly, "Let me go! Stop it or I will scream!"

The male laughed and said in a jeering voice, "Scream all you like. Nobody will hear you here."

By this time Andrew had let go of Colleen. She was looking anxiously along the beach and then at him. He said, "Tina is in trouble."

Tina screamed. Andrew did not wait. He stood up and ran along the beach. He didn't have far to go, only 25 metres. Into view burst Tina. She ran down the beach with Cousin Sandy chasing her. She wore shorts and a shirt which was partly unbuttoned and he wore only shorts. Cousin Sandy caught up and grabbed her arm then roughly hauled her back so he could try to kiss her.

Andrew shouted, "Let her go!"

As Cousin Sandy turned an astonished face towards him, Andrew cannoned into him and knocked him flat. In doing so he lost his own balance and staggered on along the beach. As quickly as he could, Andrew turned and braced himself for a fight. In doing so he faced back along the beach and saw that Colleen was clearly in view. She looked anxious and frightened. To add to Andrew's dismay, he was sure that Tina had seen her.

Cousin Sandy came up snarling and swearing, fists flailing. "You turd!" he screamed. "Mind your own business!"

Andrew was scared because Cousin Sandy was older and bigger, but he was also angry and determined. One glance at Tina's anxious but relieved face was enough to add steel to his determination. As Cousin Sandy came hammering in, Andrew coolly endured a couple of wild punches and then struck back. The punch had all of his pent-up emotion behind it and took Cousin Sandy hard in the face. It knocked him flat on his back.

For a few seconds Cousin Sandy lay on the sand, a look of stunned surprise on his face. Then he shook himself and warily moved to get to his feet. Andrew moved Tina behind him and allowed him to.

Then he said, "Clear out, and leave Tina alone, or else!"

Anger and hatred blazed in Cousin Sandy's eyes but he made no further attack. Then his eyes widened and Andrew knew he had seen Colleen. Andrew glanced back and saw that Colleen now had moved a few paces towards them. Tina also glanced at her and a look of hurt crossed her face. Without a word, Cousin Sandy turned and stalked off along the beach and up the steps out of sight.

Andrew turned to face Tina and took her in his arms. She hugged him strongly, her whole body trembling. He stroked her hair and said, "Are you alright?"

She placed her head on his bare shoulder and shuddered. "Yes," she whispered. Then she added, "Thank you."

Then she went stiff and eased herself away. Andrew saw that she was looking over his shoulder and guessed she was watching Colleen. A wave of regret and embarrassment engulfed him and he bit his lip and could only mumble and gesture. Colleen walked over, her face red with embarrassment. She had Andrew's shirt and handed it to him. Blushing furiously, he slipped it on and began buttoning it up. As he did, he heard a vehicle start up and then its engine roar before it sped away.

Tina looked white and shaken and very upset. She said, "Thanks. I had better be going now."

"You aren't walking back to town on your own, not after that," Andrew said.

"I will be alright."

"No! We will walk with you," Andrew insisted.

He was in an emotional boil over all that had just happened but there was no way he was going to allow Tina to be at risk. Colleen looked unhappy and he thought he had probably done his dash there, but he also knew he didn't care.

Tina is the one, he thought.

Tina suddenly realised that half her shirt buttons were undone and she blushed furiously as she did them up. But she did not argue when Andrew and Colleen started walking with her. It was all very embarrassing at first and she did not want to talk about the incident. Nor did she ask how Andrew and Colleen came to be there.

It is pretty bloody obvious what we were up to! Andrew thought ruefully.

He said, "He was attacking you. You should report him to the police."

But Tina shook her head. "No. It was my fault. I shouldn't have allowed him to drive me here. Anyway, he didn't do... do anything."

Andrew did not agree but Tina would not change her mind. They made their way across the car park and along the dirt road. This had mangroves on the left and the thick scrub of the hillside on the right. As the road curved to the right, the surface changed to bitumen and the swamp on the left became paperbark and pandanus, a very unpleasant looking place to Andrew.

Certainly no place for a girl to be walking alone, he thought.

They came to the Botanical Gardens and Andrew exchanged a wry glance with Colleen. The council workers were still there and one was working near the bushes they had hidden behind. It was very hot and sweaty by this as there was almost no breeze in the lee of the hill and the sun was blazing down.

At the first intersection a moment of crisis arrived. Tina started turning left and Colleen kept walking. Andrew looked from one to the other.

Colleen pointed and said, "I live along this way."

For a few seconds he was torn by indecision. Colleen resolved this by saying, "I will be alright. You take her home."

Andrew moved the couple of paces to be able to speak to her privately. Confused and concerned about Tina, Andrew glanced at her and saw her look at them. A hurt look crossed her face before she turned away and kept on walking. Andrew felt an instant stab of doubt and realised he had probably made a mistake.

To Colleen he said, "But... but you shouldn't."

Colleen shook her head and replied, "This is my home town. I walk here all the time and we are in town now. I will be fine. Besides, if Mum and Dad see me walking with a boy I will get into trouble. Don't worry about me. You walk her home."

Andrew nodded and swallowed, very conscious that Tina was now fifty paces away. He felt torn between wanting to be with her and wanting to please Colleen. "But... er... will I see you again? Maybe tonight?"

Colleen shook her head. "I don't think so." A look of pain crossed her face and tears misted in her eyes. She reached forward and placed a hand on his cheek. "You are in love with Tina, aren't you?"

Andrew felt his chest tighten up and his own eyes go misty. Through a choked-up throat he croaked. "Yes. But she dumped me and doesn't love me."

Colleen shook her head. "I think you'll find she does. Anyway, you try."

"But what about us?" Andrew asked, feelings of confused misery threatening to choke him off.

Again Colleen shook her head. "It wouldn't have worked. I mean, you are a wonderful guy, and I really like you and I love being with you, but we aren't really suited, and there is the religion thing too. Mum and Dad won't approve."

Andrew was quite shocked and hurt. He glanced towards Tina, who was now a hundred paces along the street. In his heart he suspected Colleen might be right but it still hurt. He nodded dumbly, aware that he was fighting back tears and not wanting to have that happen in front of the girls.

Colleen said, "Goodbye Andrew, and thank you." Then she quickly kissed him on the cheek and hurried away.

In a state of numb misery Andrew watched her go. Then he turned to follow Tina. It took him two blocks of fast walking to catch her up. When he did, he said, "Sorry about that."

Tina shrugged and bit her lip and he saw that she was looking upset as well. "None of my business," she replied.

Andrew wanted to tell her he loved her, wanted to ask for another chance, but his tongue seemed to be frozen. He rationalised that it probably wasn't a good moment so said nothing. The pair walked in silence back to Aunty May's house. The whole time Andrew felt miserable and as though his heart would burst. At the front gate he made a feeble attempt to persuade Tina to complain about Cousin Sandy but she just shook her head and refused to discuss it.

They went inside and she acted as though nothing unusual had happened. Andrew felt he had no choice but to comply with her wishes so he sat and watched TV and pretended everything was normal.

What can I do? he wondered miserably.

Tina seemed to be ignoring him and then she went to a back room with Carmen and Adele. Andrew remained slumped in a chair. He felt quite battered in his emotions. But he was still hopeful.

Maybe I will get a chance at the celebrations tonight? he thought.

Chapter 32

NEW YEAR'S EVE

For the remainder of the afternoon Andrew sat and pretended to watch TV. For most of that time he did not see Tina or the other girls and when they did appear she ignored him and appeared quite normal. There were showers and a change of clothes ready for the night's festivities. Andrew still took particular care and changed into long pants and a nice casual shirt. He still had some hopes of making it up with Tina.

But how? That was his problem. He simply could not decide on a plan and the obvious option; of simply telling her how he felt, he was unable to summon the courage to do; or at least he might have if she had ever been alone. But there was no way he was going to risk the humiliation of a rejection with someone else listening.

At 7pm they left the house and drove down to the 'Sovereign' Hotel in the main street. Here they went to the dining room and had dinner. The food was very good, but Andrew would have preferred a hamburger from Colleen's cafe. He thought the meal very good but quite expensive, but his mother waved the notion away.

"We don't do this very often. So relax and enjoy it," she said.

For Andrew, the worst thing about the dinner was sitting almost opposite Tina. Only occasionally did their eyes meet and when they did a look of pain seemed to darken hers and she would immediately look away. It upset him but also made him a bit resentful.

She could be a bit more friendly and grateful, he thought, remembering the fight on the beach.

Dinner took nearly an hour. When it was finished they all went outside and strolled along the street. By then it was dark but the street was well lit with party lights. The town appeared the busiest that Andrew had ever seen it. There were lines of cars parked outside the hotels and halls and plenty of people walking up and down the footpaths. The sound of music and singing melded into the general medley of noise.

But walking did not help Andrew settle. Tina seemed to make a point of avoiding him, always staying with Adele or Carmen between him and her. She did not speak to him at all and he became quite resentful and annoyed at that. One of his responses to this was to look at all the pretty girls they passed. He was hoping to see Colleen but did not.

Andrew became even more angry, but for quite a different reason, as they passed the middle pub. Outside the hotel was parked Barry's Land Rover and sitting in it was Little Terry. Andrew stopped and spoke to him to cheer him up. The sight so angered Andrew he felt like going into the bar and telling Barry what he thought of him.

"We should report him to the police," Carmen said. "It is child abuse."

Andrew's mother said she thought it was against the law but wasn't sure. "If we see a policeman we will tell him," she added.

But they didn't and Little Terry was soon forgotten as they approached the cafe. Andrew kept glancing towards it, hoping to see Colleen while also hoping that Tina would not notice. He failed in both aims and castigated himself for being a failure and a fool.

After walking two blocks they crossed the street and strolled back on the river side of the road. This took them right past the front door of the cafe. There was still no sign of Colleen but sitting outside were Cousin Sandy, Bart, and Cousin Jean, along with other young people. When Cousin Sandy saw Andrew he scowled but said nothing. Andrew gave him a hard look in reply, not caring if there was another fight.

They also encountered some of the younger miners, including Simon and Tim. They latched on to the party and started flirting with the girls. To Andrew's annoyance, the girls responded. Seeing Tina smiling and laughing at silly jokes by Simon really made his blood boil and he dawdled behind.

There were plenty of drunks at the hotels and as they passed the middle pub again there was the sound of breaking glass, shouts and yahoo noises and then loud swearing and raised voices. It all fizzled out quickly enough but that annoyed Andrew as well. He disliked drunks intensely.

They came to a hall or shop which was open and had some sort of display of clothing and jewellery inside. The others all went in and Andrew followed. But when he saw what it was, and noted his mother chatting to several of the women there, he went back outside and stood leaning on a rail, looking down into a park and brooding.

Happy girl's voices attracted his attention and the next thing he knew Kristen and Daphne were slapping him on the back and giggling.

"Hello sailor! All on your own?" Kristen asked with a laugh.

Andrew looked around and saw that there were at least five girls, some much younger but one dark-haired one with a ponytail who looked older. There were also several youths and boys. He was about to say he was with people when he glanced through the window and saw Tina. She was talking to Simon and smiling.

"Yes," he replied.

"Come with us then," Kristen said, linking her arm through his.

She snuggled against him, her right boob pressing nicely against his left arm. On an impulse Andrew allowed himself to walk with her. Daphne took station on his other side. The group set off along the footpath.

"Where are we going?" Andrew asked.

"Down near the wharf," Kristen replied.

As she did, Andrew caught a whiff of beer and his suspicions were confirmed, but he was so mixed up he did not care.

It was a very happy group that strolled along. Their conversation was a mixture of silly jokes and sexual innuendos that got Andrew hopeful but also made him blush. They also embarrassed him somewhat by calling out loudly to people on the other side of the street or waving to passing cars whose occupants they knew.

Down near the cannon their calling out led to a utility with two youths in it pulling up. The youths looked to be 'ringers' in their early twenties.

"Hiya chicks! What ya doin'?" they asked.

"Lookin' fer a bit 'o fun eh?" Kristen replied.

"So are we. We can give yer a bit of fun," one of the stockmen replied.

Andrew did not like the way the conversation was going and wished the two youths would leave but he was even more shocked by Kristen's next comment. "Cost ya," she said.

"Oh yeah? What?" the youth asked, while leering at her.

"Got anything to drink?"

"What ya want?" the youth asked.

Kristen named several alcoholic drinks. The youth said, "We got some bourbon. Billy here will go back and get the other stuff if you girls promise to stay here."

They did and the youth lifted several bottles of alcohol and a carton of beer out of the cab. As he did, Daphne and the girl with the ponytail let out loud shrieks.

"Sssh!" the youth cautioned. "The cop shop is just over there."

Andrew had forgotten that but he now glanced that way and felt unreasonably guilty. There was no sign of any police but the lights were on. The group walked across the park in under the trees beyond the cannon.

"This will do," Kristen said.

She sat down and the youth joined her. Andrew was left standing and feeling foolish. He wondered if now was not a good time to leave, but Daphne took his hand and said, "Sit, Andrew."

Foolishly he did. So did most of the others but a couple wandered away. The youth named Billy got back in the ute and drove off. Kristen was handed a bottle of beer and she took a big gulp and then leaned over and gave the youth a kiss on the cheek. He got all keen and put his arm around her waist and drank some beer himself. Bottles were handed to the others. Daphne took one and then went to hand one to Andrew.

"Here you are, Andrew. Get that inside you," she said.

"No thanks," Andrew replied.

"Why not? Don't you drink?"

"My mum might smell it," he answered in what he knew sounded a lame excuse.

"Oh poor little mummy's boy!" the youth jeered.

Kristen quaffed more beer and said, "Go on, Andrew. Don't be a wuss."

Andrew felt really torn. Daphne leaned over to give him the bottle and as she did, she got bumped and spilled beer down his front.

"Oh sorry!" she mumbled.

To save the argument, Andrew took the bottle and she laughed and sat back to drink.

By now Andrew was feeling very uncomfortable and contemplating slipping away. Only the fact that Daphne now had her arm around his shoulders and was pressing against him kept him there, hopes rising. They went up even more when Daphne gave him a drunken, slobbering kiss on the side of his face. The others all drank joked and laughed and the youth began kissing Kristen.

Billy returned with several more bottles of spirits and another carton of beer. By his weaving walk it was obvious he had been drinking. As he placed these down Billy saw the cannon nearby.

"Oi! Here's that bloody cannon. I've always wanted to fire this bastard."

"Why don't ya, Billy?" Kristen said with a teasing laugh.

His friend laughed and said, "Pity it's not pointed at the bloody cop shop. We could give those mongrels a wakeup call if she was."

"Near enough," replied Billy as he leaned on the cannon and squinted along the barrel.

He then staggered back to his ute and rummaged in the back. After a couple of minutes he made his drunken way back to the cannon and stood at the muzzle, muttering and chuckling. Andrew watched, puzzled and unable to see clearly in the semi darkness.

The other youth called out, "What ya doin', Billy? Come and have a pash with one of these chicks. They're real scrumptious."

"In a minute. I'm gunna fire this bloody cannon first," Billy replied.

"How ya gunna do that?" the youth queried.

Billy chortled and held up his hands. "One of these sticks of gelignite we got for blastin' tree stumps."

"Ya mad bastard! You'll bring the cops," the youth answered.

Alarm bells now rang in Andrew's brain. What particularly appalled him was the thought that too much explosive could burst the barrel of a gun and he had such a strong feeling for the old gun that he stood up and called out, "Don't! You could burst the barrel."

"So what?" Billy sneered. He kept preparing the explosive.

Andrew went over to him and said, "Please don't. It could wreck the gun."

"Please don't! Who the hell are you tellin' what to do sissy boy? Piss orf before I belt ya," Billy retorted. With that he used his cigarette to light the length of fuse sticking out of the stick of gelignite.

"Don't!" Andrew cried, and tried to grab the fuse.

Billy snatched it angrily away from him and attempted to shove it down the muzzle. Andrew pushed his hands away and again tried to pull the hissing fuse out. Billy swore and then punched. Andrew did not have time to react. The blow took him full in the side of his head and he went down, striking the other side of his head on the barrel of the cannon as he did. He fell to the ground, stunned but still just conscious.

Then he heard Billy swear and yell, "Christ! I've dropped the bastard! Run!"

There were cries of alarm and people began jumping up and running. Even in his fuddled state Andrew understood the danger and he managed to drag himself upright. For a terrible second he nearly blacked out and he had to cling to the cannon as waves of nausea and dizziness swept through him. Then fear gave him strength and he clawed his way back around the breech of the gun and went staggering off across the lawn, trying to keep the gun between him and the fizzing explosive.

KA-BOOOM!

The blast stunned Andrew and blew him flat just near the monument. As he lay there, his ears ringing and waves of dizziness sweeping through him, he heard the ute start up, along with loud screams and cries of alarm.

I'm not dead anyway, Andrew thought, flopping face down as acrid smoke wafted over him and dust and leaves fluttered down.

The ute accelerated away with a screech of burning rubber. Voice's yelled and several vehicles braked to a stop nearby. Boots pounded across the road and onto the lawn. Strong hands grabbed Andrew and rolled him over. He looked up and in the light of the street lights he saw it was a policeman, the same big sergeant he had met before. Only then did it dawn on him that perhaps he should have run away.

"Got you!" the sergeant cried. Then his expression changed to one of concern. "Are you hurt?"

Andrew shook his head and then spat sand and grass out of his mouth. "No, I don't think so," he croaked.

"Good. Stay here," he said, then yelled to his partner, Constable Hauser, to call an ambulance.

He hurried across to the cannon and inspected the smoking hole in the turf. A police car came along the street, siren wailing and lights flashing. It pulled up and two constables got out. The sergeant (Sgt Bull, Andrew now remembered) called to them to secure the area and to keep the sightseers away. He then returned to kneel next to Andrew.

"Collins isn't it, the navy cadet whose family is looking after the Lions Den?" he asked.

Andrew nodded. *Bloody hell, he's got a good memory!* he thought.

"Andrew Collins," he said. He gingerly felt the side of his head which was feeling numb but starting to throb and hurt.

Sgt Bull studied his head and then looked grim. "Okay Andrew, what do you know about this?"

"Some bushie named Billy, he drives a ute. He came along and said he was going to let off the cannon. He went to shove a stick of gelignite down the barrel and I stopped him," Andrew said.

"Billy?" Sgt Bull said. He glanced up as a policeman came over to him. "Billy with a ute. That could be Billy Hayter, couldn't it?"

The other policeman nodded. "Billy Hayter it will be. Was his mate Toby with him?"

"He had a friend. I wasn't introduced. I had never seen them before. We were just walking along and they pulled up here," Andrew explained.

"It will be him. I saw the ute drive off," Sgt Bull said.

The other policeman bent down and looked grim. "Lot of alcohol scattered around over there sergeant. A group having a party. You know anything about that boy?"

For the first time it dawned on Andrew he might be in real trouble, and that he could get others into trouble. He hesitated to frame his answer and realised that was a mistake as both policemen noticed it.

He said, "I was with a group of boys and girls. We were just walking past. The two men in the ute had the alcohol."

"Were you drinking?"

"No sergeant."

"Smells like you were," Sgt Bull said.

"Daph... er... er... one of the girls spilled some on me," Andrew replied, then mentally kicked himself.

"Girls? What girls?" Sgt Bull growled.

Andrew bit his lip and shook his head. "I'd rather not say. I don't want to get anyone into trouble."

"Very noble of you!" the other policeman said sarcastically. "I'll bet it was that Kristen Cummings and her mate Daphne Fairweather."

Sgt Bull nodded. "I've seen that pair with Collins here. We will ask them. Send a car round to their houses now to check with their parents."

By now a fair crowd had arrived and the area was lit up by the headlights of the cars. One of the policemen kept the crowd back but when Andrew's mother saw him and cried out she was allowed past. Tina, Carmen and Adele were also allowed past. They hurried over and knelt down.

His mother took hold of him. "Oh my poor boy. What has happened to you? What was that explosion?"

Andrew explained how he had stopped the man placing the gelignite in the cannon. Sgt Bull wanted to know why he took such a risk and Andrew got all embarrassed and explained that it was because it was an historical navy cannon and he did not want to see it destroyed.

At that moment, the other policeman came over and held out a girl's handbag. "Found Daphne Fairweather's bag, Sarge."

"Daphne?" Andrew's mother queried.

Andrew blushed and felt anxiety and guilt surge because Tina was next to him. Sgt Bull then dropped him right in it by saying, "He was with some of the local girls, Mrs Collins."

A hurt look crossed Tina's face and she bit her lip. Andrew hurriedly said, "We weren't doing anything mum, just walking along."

"Weren't doing anything?" Carmen said.

She reached out and wiped her fingers on Andrew's left cheek and then held them in front of his face. He saw they were smeared with lipstick.

"So what's this then? And how did it get here?" she snapped.

Having his sister act like that really stung and hurt. Andrew struggled for an answer and was further embarrassed when Sgt Bull said that it was possible the girls had been drinking alcohol and that they were under age.

Andrew's mother turned to him and said, "Oh Andrew! You weren't drinking alcohol, were you?"

"No Mum!" Andrew cried.

Sgt Bull shook his head. "He may have been, Mrs Collins. We will have to check on that. But here is the ambulance and we need to get him to the hospital for a check-up. You may go with him. Constable Smith, you go with this lad. I will talk to you later young Collins, so don't leave town."

Andrew's mother said, "I need to get our car. Carmen, you and Tina go with Andrew."

Carmen said yes but to Andrew's dismay Tina said she'd rather not and she walked away, her eyes wet with tears. Instead, Adele offered and went in the ambulance with him. As he sat down inside Andrew looked out and saw Tina in the crowd. She looked very upset, and he could only bite his lip and shake his head.

What a fool I am! he thought. *I have really done my dash with Tina now.*

Chapter 33

THE NURSE

Andrew did not want to go to the hospital. After that morning's episode (Was it only this morning?) he did not want to meet either the doctor or the doctor's wife. But there was no possible excuse he could think of so he made no protest. He went in the ambulance with the policeman, Carmen, and Adele while Tina went in his mother's car.

It was just on 8pm when they reached the hospital. Being New Year's Eve they were busy with a range of minor injuries, mostly from drunks injuring themselves falling over or fighting. To Andrew's dismay even at the hospital they had heard of the cannon incident and to his embarrassment and annoyance he found himself being treated to some sideways and very curious looks.

He was even more distressed to find that Tina did not come in. *I have really mucked things up now!* he thought miserably.

So he sat there among the drunks and sick children with his ears buzzing and his head throbbing. His fingers told him that an egg-sized lump had developed on his right temple.

Where I hit the cannon, he remembered.

His anxiety about meeting the doctor, or worse, his wife, grew by the minute until he was quite apprehensive. But when he was called in at about 8:45pm he was met by a very pretty nurse in her early twenties. She had wavy brown shoulder-length hair and a pair of 'doey' brown eyes full of sympathy. Her face was a classic heart shape and she had lips that just needed to be kissed. Her body was very nicely curved and Andrew felt his pulses speed up at the sight, and smell, of her. She exuded a most delicious perfume and he shook his head at his own weakness.

No wonder I am not winning with Tina. I fall for every pretty female I see, he thought.

The nurse's touch was so soothing that Andrew instantly relaxed. She gently wiped his face and head and then checked his arms and legs.

"Any bruises on your body?" she asked.

The thought of this particular nurse examining his body got Andrew's heart rate right up. Very pretty, she had a lovely soft voice as well and Andrew was lulled into relaxing. Thus, when the doctor did arrive, he was somewhat off guard. It was the same doctor and Andrew felt an instant spasm of guilt and then curious shame.

Does he know what his wife is like? Andrew wondered.

Lurid images of the doctor's naked wife increased his embarrassment. Being close up to the man as he examined him, Andrew could only speculate what his inadequacies might be that drove his wife to drink and worse.

Then the doctor alarmed him more by saying, "You seem very anxious about something. Anything the matter? Your heart rate is very fast."

As the panic surged through him, Andrew looked up and met the nurse's smiling eyes. He forced a grin and, on an impulse, said, "My heart is beating so fast because your nurse is so beautiful."

At that, she opened her mouth in pleased surprise and then snorted, "Oh! Don't get too fresh, young man! I am the one who will give you any needles, don't forget."

But she wasn't offended. Andrew could tell. He managed a grin in reply and the doctor just 'hummpf'd' and went on with testing his skull to check for fractures.

"Did you go unconscious?" he asked.

"No sir," Andrew replied, still lost in admiration for the nurse, who had now blushed prettily.

"Hmm! There doesn't seem to be any serious damage, just bruising. We won't keep you in, but if you feel at all nauseous phone at once and come in. Now, since you are here let me take a look at your leg wound," the doctor said.

Andrew put his leg up and the doctor bent to look at it. As he did, he said to the nurse, "He is quite the hero this young man. He is the lad who saved Grandma Cynthia and three girls from two wild pigs, fighting them off with an axe. Killed one of them, which is when he got this."

All Andrew could do was blush while the nurse cried, "Oh yes! I heard about that. So he's not only brave, he is handsome as well."

The doctor laughed. "Steady on, nurse. Hmm. You've changed this dressing I see," he said to Andrew.

That confirmed Andrew's suspicions that the doctor had no idea what his wife had been up to that morning, and he experienced a spasm of what he knew was fear. In reply he could only grunt. The doctor did not appear to notice and continued with his work. When he had finished, he got the nurse to re-dress the wound. As she did, Andrew was able to study her up close and knew that he liked the look and scent of her.

She is very nice, he thought.

When the wound was re-dressed he was ushered out. As he went past the nurse, he whispered, "Sorry. But you are very pretty, and very nice." He was surprised at his own bravado but she smiled and said a gracious thank you for the compliment. "See you again," he said.

"Maybe," she replied.

But there was no time for more as the policeman was there and said they must now go to the police station. This time Andrew went in a police car with Carmen while Adele went with his mother and Tina in their vehicle. Seeing Tina sitting there and not looking or smiling got Andrew all dejected again.

The next hour was unpleasant. Andrew sat in an interview room with his mother and was questioned by Sgt Bull and Constable Smith. This time he told the whole embarrassing story and was subjected to a breath test for alcohol. This returned a negative which eased some of Andrew's anxiety. But having a relatively clear conscience he wasn't worried about the police or the cannon. It was Tina and his relationship with her that weighed on his mind.

As they came out of the interview room there was another unpleasant incident. Coming the other way, handcuffed and held between two policemen, was Billy the Drunk. As soon as he saw Andrew, Billy shouted at him, "You bloody dobber!"

Sgt Bull confronted him. "Don't be daft, Billy! We didn't need anyone to dob you in. Half the bloody town saw you do it. I saw you do it! Now shut your gob and go quietly into the cell."

Billy muttered and grumbled but stopped his accusations. One of the policemen tugged at his sleeve and said, "Come on, Bombardier Billy."

Then, just as they were about to walk out of the police station, a constable behind a desk held up a phone and called, "You are Mrs Collins from the Lions Den? Your husband wants you urgently."

That got Andrew all anxious but it turned out that there had been some sort a drunken fight between some stockmen and the miners. Two of the miners were hurt.

The policeman said to Sgt Bull, "I have the other car on the way already and the ambulance is on its way. But this gentleman here," he gestured to a middle-aged man sitting on a nearby bench, "is the mine manager and wants a lift to go and deal with his own people."

The mine manager stood up and said, "Sorry. I'd drive if I could but I've been drinking so I can't drive and none of my people are around."

Andrew immediately thought of Simon and Tim and experienced a spurt of jealousy. His mother said, "We can give you a lift. I think we have had enough excitement for the night."

Carmen did the maths and shook her head. "We won't all fit, Mum. One of us will have to stay."

Andrew really wanted to go home and lie down ('Crawl into his cave to lick his wounds,' was how he worded it) but nor did he want one of the girls left alone in town for possibly several hours, not even at the police station.

He said, "I will stay."

There was some discussion but finally his mother said, "Alright. I will take the girls home and come back for you. In the meantime I will see if you can lie down at Aunty May's."

A phone call established that this was possible. As she put the phone down his mother said, "That will be alright. Aunty May says there are a few young people there having a bit of a party so you won't be alone."

So Andrew was driven there, to discover that the young people included Cousin Sandy and his little brother. For a moment Andrew considered refusing and saying that he would wait at the police station, but then he realised that explanations would be needed. Reluctantly he went in and tried to pretend everything was fine. Cousin Sandy was sitting in a corner and apparently trying to chat up a skinny young blonde. He gave Andrew a very covert hostile glare but did not say anything, and Andrew was led through to a back bedroom and allowed to lie down.

The door was closed and he heard his mother and others talking outside. The topics were obviously the gelignite at the cannon and the fight at the pub. After a few minutes, the door opened again and his mother looked in.

"It is alright, Andrew. Your cousin Sandy has said he will give you a lift home. He assures me he hasn't been drinking and will bring you home just after midnight."

Cousin Sandy! Offering a lift! Alarm bells rang in Andrew's throbbing head but then he shrugged. *Maybe the fight wasn't as bad as I thought? Maybe he doesn't care, or wants to get into mum's good books because of Carmen?*

Unable to fathom Cousin Sandy's motives, Andrew shrugged and made no protest. His mother wished him well and closed the door.

Andrew lay back in the semi-darkness and tried to relax. When he thought about it, he realised it had been the most emotionally exhausting day he could ever remember.

First the doctor's wife, then Colleen, then Daphne and the cannon, he mused.

In spite of his exhaustion he became aroused and that got him feeling guilty and anxious as well because the fantasies were not all about Tina but included the doctor's wife and Cousin Jean and Colleen. It was all very testing and confusing for him.

He drifted into a doze and an hour slipped by. Aunty May roused him from this when she popped her head around the corner to check how he was. As Andrew sat up, he heard noises that indicated even more people had arrived for the party. After assuring Aunty May he felt better he got up.

"I need to go to the toilet," he explained.

Andrew made his way out into the lounge room and stopped in surprise. Cousin Sandy was now standing leaning on a door post but he was no longer talking to the skinny blonde. Now he was busy using his charms on the pretty nurse who had tended Andrew a few hours before. The nurse saw him and a happy smile spread across her face.

"Oh hello again! How do you feel now?' she asked.

Andrew smiled back and said, "Fine."

As he did, he noted Cousin Sandy trying to keep a grin on his face while his eyes glinted malice. *I hope he doesn't impress her too much,* Andrew thought. *She is much too nice for the likes of him.*

Andrew went on to find the toilet. Then he returned to the lounge room and found a seat near the door through to the kitchen. There were at least a dozen young people present and despite the earlier protestations about no alcohol Andrew saw that nearly everyone, including Cousin Sandy, was drinking. Most of the people there appeared to be a bit older than him, but he did note Cousin Bart sitting in a corner looking glum.

Having no wish to talk to him, Andrew stayed where he was and chatted to a dark-haired girl whose name was Susan. But he found his eyes continually drawn back to the beautiful nurse. Cousin Sandy was still trying to impress her with his usual 'charm' but she did not seem to be responding.

Good! Andrew thought, having no wish for the nurse to be subjected to an attack like the one Tina had suffered that afternoon.

Several times the nurse met his gaze from across the room and the second time she raised an eyebrow, to which he daringly returned a smile. He had no real intent to impress her, but he did think she was admirable.

A check of the time showed Andrew it was nearly 11:30. *Not long to go and I can go home*, he thought.

But he was feeling increasingly 'out of it' at the party as most were older and he was too tired to feel like being friendly. The party was beginning to assume the course of such events with people becoming more and more drunk and the music being continually turned higher, causing the people talking to talk louder. To get a bit of fresh air and to escape the noise which was making his head throb, Andrew got up and strolled out the back to a patio, laundry area facing the back yard.

He had only been there a few minutes, breathing the cool night air, when the pretty nurse appeared beside him.

"Hi," she said. "I'm Lynn, and you are Andrew."

Andrew was quite surprised and found it hard to say anything. But she was so close their arms touched and he could smell her (and some sort of alcohol, gin was it?).

Curious about her accent he said, "Are you English?"

"Yes. And you are the best thing I have seen since I came to this place," Lynn replied.

To Andrew's surprise she leaned forward and gave him a kiss on the mouth. It was slow and gentle and he was able to gaze into her lovely soft eyes while she did it. In wonder at his good fortune he put his arms around her and kissed her again. She tasted and felt delicious and he experienced a surge of desire such as he had never known.

They parted and stared at each other and Andrew thought, *I could fall in love with her, if she wasn't so much older!*

It got him worrying that she had not guessed his real age. But desire took hold and they came together again in a long, passionate kiss.

To be rudely interrupted by an obviously jealous Cousin Sandy. "You sneaky little bastard! Stop kissing my chick, you little turd!" he yelled, waving a beer bottle towards him.

Lynn answered before Andrew could. "I'm not your chick! And I will kiss who I like, so leave us alone."

Cousin Sandy sneered and shouted back, "What are you, you silly bitch, a cradle snatcher?"

"Don't call me names, you peasant! Leave us alone," Lynn snapped.

By now Andrew had moved to confront Cousin Sandy but he wasn't fast enough. Cousin Sandy lashed out. In his attempt avoid the blow Andrew tripped over a bucket and fell heavily on the lawn. Cousin Sandy jeered and stepped in to kick him. The kick struck Andrew in the thigh before he could roll aside. But Lynn stepped between them and shouted at him to stop it.

Other people appeared and Cousin Sandy stepped back, then swore and turned on his heel. As he went back inside, Andrew scrambled to his feet, and said, "Sorry about that."

"Who is he?" Lynn asked.

"My Cousin Sandy, I'm ashamed to admit," Andrew replied.

Lynn frowned and said, "What did he mean by accusing me of being a cradle snatcher? How old are you?"

Andrew felt his hopes crash and he blushed with shame. "Sixteen," he replied. "I'm still at school."

"Oh what a pity!" Lynn cried. "We could have been great together. Sorry."

"My fault for flirting," Andrew said. He felt a surge of genuine regret and sensed that, but for the age difference, he might have found 'the one'. "I'd better go," he said.

Something about Cousin Sandy's comments made him anxious. With a wry smile and a whispered 'thanks' he left Lynn and walked through into the lounge room. He arrived just in time to see Cousin Sandy going out the front door with a tipsy Cousin Jean in tow!

Cousin Sandy slammed the door. Andrew sensed what was about to happen. He hurried across the room and wrenched the door open, in time to see Cousin Sandy, Cousin Jean, and Bart hurrying through the front gate and across to their vehicle. Before Andrew had even reached the gate they had climbed in and the engine was started.

"Hey! You said you would give me a lift home," Andrew called.

Cousin Sandy shook a fist at him. "Get stuffed! That's twice in one day. You owe me, Mr Bloody Goody-goody Hero! You can bloody walk home!" he shouted.

With that he put the vehicle in gear and accelerated away. Andrew's last image of them was three hostile faces glaring at him. The vehicle vanished down the street, leaving him alone on the footpath.

What do I do now? he wondered.

Chapter 34

STUBBORN PRIDE

Outside Aunty May's house it was very quiet. Andrew stood in a state of exhausted shock and stared along the deserted street wondering what he should do. Three options immediately sprang to mind; two sensible and one not so. The sensible options were to go back inside and telephone his parents and get them to pick him up; with the variation of sleeping the night at Aunty May's and then getting himself transport home. The less sensible option was to try to hitch-hike.

But Andrew did not want to go back inside that house. He was ashamed of having led Lynn on and did not want to put her to more embarrassment. There were other people there who had seen him and Cousin Sandy clash and he did not want to provide them with opportunities for behind-the-hand sniggering.

I will hitch a ride, he told himself. In his heart he knew this was a potentially risky choice as there was a high probability that any driver might have been drinking alcohol, it being New Year's Eve. But he shrugged. *It isn't far and it's a good road,* he rationalised. But in his heart he knew he was being silly and that it was really his hurt pride that was making the decision.

Shouting and singing from the house and from houses along the street made him think it might be midnight but the noise died down. *Not New Year yet,* Andrew thought, knowing that there would be noises right across the town at the stroke of midnight. A glance at his watch showed him it was still fifteen minutes away.

He gave a shrug and set off walking west along the street. A few blocks and a few minutes later he was on the main road out of town. All was still quiet except for some distant singing and music and the odd barking dog. A car went past, but into town.

At least it's cool, he thought, noting that the sky was clear and that the moon was well down to the west and only a half-moon.

By midnight he was on the outskirts of town and past the airport turn-off. He knew it was midnight without looking at his watch because a tumult of shouting and banging on cooking utensils sounded from many of the houses and several safety flares or rockets shot up from the estuary.

People shouldn't do that, he thought, knowing it was against the law to use flares or rockets except in genuine cases of distress. But he also knew that some people took the opportunity to use up flares whose 'use by date' had been reached.

Then he smiled and thought of the gelignite. *Now is the time for Billy the Blaster to let it off,* he thought. He was glad he had saved the old cannon but knew he had been very lucky.

The noise died down and Andrew resumed walking. He kept glancing back to see if a car was coming but the street remained deserted. Not wanting to stay near the houses with their barking dogs he kept on walking. Then he thought he needed to be at a safer place on a nice long open stretch of road before he tried to flag down a car so he kept on over the pass at the western end of Mt Cook. The road wound on down the other side in a wide curve and only after he had passed the turn-off to Walsh Bay did he pause again.

To his surprise he found it was nearly half past midnight and not a single car had passed in either direction. *This is the Mulligan Highway, the main road to Cairns,* he thought. *It is always busy. There must be traffic.*

But there wasn't. The road remained deserted and the only sounds were from the wind in the trees and insects. He decided to keep walking as there was no bus stop or seat and he did not feel like sitting on the grass because of snakes and for fear of dirtying his good long trousers.

As he trudged along the still curving road he worried about leaving without telling Aunty May. Then he shrugged. *Too late now. Anyway Lynn and some of the others saw me leave. Oh, I wish a car would come along!*

One did a few minutes later, just as he reached the start of a very long straight stretch of road. Andrew put out his thumb, but the car just raced past without even slowing down. That shocked him and he felt quite angry and then downcast.

Blast! Oh well, never mind. There will be another one along in a few minutes.

But there wasn't, not even in the next fifteen minutes. During that time Andrew kept walking, mostly out of habit. During that time he crossed

Meldrum Creek and now found himself in the middle of an extensive area of Ti-tree swamp. The place had looked spooky enough in daylight but now, with the moon almost down and casting long shadows through the large paperbarks that stood in the marsh it looked positively eerie.

Rather than stop in such a place he continued on, perspiring now as there was no breeze. The moon went down and it became even more creepy. Andrew's imagination began to work. He tried to channel this by thinking about girls but the situation was a bit too real and he could not hold the mental focus. He found he was afraid of snakes and kept thinking that crocodiles might lurk in the swamp. Someone (Graham Kirk?) had told him that snakes slid onto the bitumen roads at night for the warmth. That idea got him straining his eyes to check the road ahead.

Just before 01:30am Andrew rounded a bend and found himself at the Annan River Bridge. The two bridges, old and new, stretched before him 300 metres long. Every other time Andrew had been past there had been people fishing, mostly from the lower, old bridge. But now the place was deserted. On both sides was mangrove swamp. For a few minutes Andrew stopped and sat on the concrete kerbing of the new bridge. But no cars came past and mosquitoes and sandflies began a vicious assault. Also he could hear noises in the mangroves: sinister plops and splashes and squelching sounds and his imagination instantly converted these to huge crocodiles slithering towards him.

It was too much for him. Memories of that terrifying night in the mangroves at Bowling Green Bay crowded his mind. The thought of all those monster saurians so close, coupled to the insect attacks got him up and walking. It took him a conscious price in courage to walk across that long bridge alone in the darkness, with the wide river and its evil mangrove shores on both sides, the water lapping close at high tide and making sucking and splashing noises that made his hair stand on end. His rational mind told him there was no way any crocodile would ever climb up onto a concrete highway bridge, but it was late and very dark and in the starlight the sounds were enough to scare him.

He did not actually run, but by the time he reached the far end of the bridge Andrew was panting and perspiring and had thoroughly scared himself. Then he found he dare not stop. There was a mangrove swamp beside the causeway at the end and that actually was a dangerous place to sit and rest so he kept on walking.

The mosquitoes and stubbornness kept him walking. On both sides of the road was a fairly dense paperbark forest of mostly small trees and Andrew wasn't sure if it was swamp or not, and he was not going to investigate. So fear of crocs added to his desire to be away from that area. Then 2am came and went and still there was no end to the scrub and no car went past.

The first vehicle was a big semi-trailer. Andrew heard it long before he saw the loom of its headlights above the trees, but it was coming from the wrong direction. All he could do was wave as the big truck roared past towards Cooktown. The sound of its passing soon died away, leaving only the crunch of his own shoes on the bitumen and the odd insect or bird noises to be heard.

The bird noises did not help as the main ones were curlews and the mournful, eerie cry made him feel distinctly conscious of being very alone and now a long way from anywhere.

You a bloody stubborn idiot! he told himself.

But what to do? Just sitting down did not appeal but by this time he was feeling tired and bone weary and his wound was starting to throb. A headache added to his woes and he was starting to feel very thirsty.

Common sense told him to stop but fear would not allow it. So he trudged on. By 02:30am he estimated he had walked 10 kilometres.

How far is it from Cooktown to the Lions Den? Thirty kilometres, or is it thirty two? Surely a car will pick me up soon? he thought.

Hopefully, he trudged on. Another hour and five more kilometres brought him footsore and weary to a change of country. The vegetation opened out on the right to normal savannah woodland and the beginning of hills. On the left the vegetation was more scrubby and an old, disused road went off into this. Andrew tried to picture the map and decided he was near the abandoned 'Green Hills' homestead.

The turn-off to Archer Point should be just up ahead, he thought.

That seemed to be a desirable location to reach so he stepped it out. By this time he was thirsty, footsore and had the beginning of chafe on the inside of his thighs. But he stubbornly kept on.

There must be a car soon!

Ah! A vehicle engine! But the sound was coming from his left. He looked that way and saw the loom of headlights off in the distance above the trees.

Must be coming from Archer Point, he decided.

Fishermen going home, but were they going to Cooktown or the way he wanted to go? Just in case they were going his way Andrew increased speed to a jog to try to get to the junction before the vehicle.

In the end it was apparent that he wouldn't make it so he sprinted. But that did not work. He was too worn out and could not keep it up for more than a couple of hundred paces. Slowing to a gasping fast walk he hurried on. Then his spirits rose.

"It has stopped at the junction," he muttered.

Relieved, he continued to step it out. Near the junction the highway made a long curve, so Andrew could not see the vehicle until he was close enough to detect the road signs. In the starlight he saw a large truck with a canvas canopy over the tray. Then sounds of people unloading metal objects came to him, followed by the murmur of voices. By then Andrew was only about thirty of forty paces from the truck.

Suddenly his nerves went all a-tingle. *I know that voice,* he thought.

Out of caution he slowed to a quiet walk. The voice, a man's, came again quite clearly. The man said, "Okay Wes, that should do. Let's hope no stupid people try to move it or pass it."

Jan the South African! Andrew thought.

Instantly he was both alert and afraid. There was no way he was going to approach him and Wes on a lonely, deserted highway in the bush to ask for a lift. Biting his lip with anxiety Andrew stopped and moved to crouch behind a bush in the long grass beside the highway.

His caution was immediately rewarded when he heard Wes give an evil sounding chuckle and say, "They will regret it if they do."

What on earth are they doing? Andrew wondered.

He peered through the screen of vegetation but could not see clearly in the starlight. He was now scared that his own breathing might be audible to the two men and he tried to calm it. Sweat trickled out of him and he bit his lip. Then he saw one of the men, Wes he thought, appear beside the truck and climb into the cab. From the sound of a door closing Jan had climbed in the other side but the men's conversation was lost in the roar of the motor being started. The truck's headlights were turned on and it started moving. Andrew crouched further into the long grass in case it turned towards him but it swung out to the left and accelerated away from him.

Only after the tail lights had vanished and the sound of the truck had died away did Andrew move. There was something so unusual and suspicious about what the men had been doing that he was alert for trouble. Very carefully he crept forward along the verge of the highway to look at the road junction.

The Archer Point road had been closed off. A barricade and ROAD CLOSED sign blocked it completely. These appeared to be normal Main Roads or Council signs and Andrew wondered if they were meant to be there.

Why would Wes and Jan block the road in the middle of the night? he wondered.

It struck him as odd, but he could think of no explanation. Besides they were gone and he was very tired and thirsty.

I'm nearly halfway. I may as well keep going, he thought.

So he did. His watch told him it was just coming up to 03:30am. Anxiously he felt his dry tongue and wondered if he was getting the beginnings of heat exhaustion. But he was still perspiring so he decided he could keep going.

When I stop sweating, I am in trouble, he told himself. Knowing the first place he might get water was at Trevethan Creek and that was about another 5 kilometres motivated him to push his tired muscles and chafed limbs on.

Still hoping a vehicle might come along he plodded on, his head aching and his leg wound a dull ache. Forty minutes of steady walking brought him to the turn-off to the Mt Amos Road. By then he felt utterly worn out but made himself plod on for another kilometre to Trevethan Creek. Here he followed the old road down to the creek bed. After a few anxious minutes studying the water in the starlight he decided it was too shallow for crocs.

And anyway, it is fresh, he told himself.

Very cautiously, his heart beating with fear, he knelt and scooped up some water to test it. It was cold and fresh and tasted wonderful. He sighed and drank his fill, then rinsed his face.

But he did not linger. Fear of crocs and snakes had him across the old bridge and trudging up the other side in a few minutes. Feeling temporarily restored he stopped when he got to the highway again and looked around.

Four thirty. Bloody hell, it will be daylight soon, he thought. Gloomily he decided that there was little chance of a car coming along at that hour. Now another worry began to nag him. *I don't want mum and dad to know I have been this silly. I need to be back at the Lions Den before they wake up,* he thought. But how far was it; and could he do it in time?

His shivering, trembling leg muscles told him to keep moving. *If I stand still or sit down, I will freeze up or get cramps,* he thought.

He pushed his aching muscles into action and resumed plodding. As he did, he tried to work out how far he had come and how long it might take him to finish. Ahead of him he could now clearly see the bulk of the Black Mountains and that cheered him up.

Not too far, he thought.

But it was and long before he reached them, as he was passing the turn-off to the water supply pump station, he noted the sky to the east going grey. It was 05:20am and full daylight by the time he reached the saddle between the jumbled piles of black granite of the Black Mountains.

I'm not going to make it in time, he thought gloomily as he limped on. This changed to *I'm not going to make it at all!* by the time he was opposite Grandma Cynthia's house fifteen minutes later. He considered turning off and staying there to telephone later but stubborn pride pushed him on. *I've come this far I may as well walk the whole bloody distance,* he decided.

So he grimly plodded on, ignoring the growing agony of chafe and the sharp little stabs of pain from his leg wound. His whole body seemed to be a mass of aches, pains and sweat by the time he reached the turn-off to Helenvale at 05:50am.

Now Andrew really had to push himself. "Four K's to go," he told himself. "Come on weakling! You can do it!"

It had become an article of personal pride that he now walk the whole way, and if a car had come along he would have refused a lift. But none did and he limped the distance in 50 minutes. It was 06:45am with the rising sun already searing him as he rounded the bend at Mungumby Bridge.

Am I too late? he worried, blinking sweat from his eyes as he strained them searching for any sign of movement at the hotel. The family was usually up at 06:30am to get the miners away after breakfast but he did not know if they were working on New Year's Day.

It is a public holiday, he told himself hopefully.

As he limped the last hundred paces, heart hammering with exhaustion and anxiety he saw no-one. The front doors were open and Irish was asleep on the veranda couch but there was no sound of movement from inside and no miners in the dining room.

I might be lucky, he thought.

He began tip-toeing along the veranda towards his room.

But his luck was out. Carmen appeared at the next door and said, "Andrew, where have you been? We were just going to phone the police. Mum! Mum! He's here!"

Oh blast! Andrew thought. *Now I will have to explain it all!*

Chapter 35

STORMS

Andrew's mother appeared, all anxious and concerned. His father followed her out, then Tina and Adele. All Andrew wanted to do was sit down so, with a groan, he slumped into a chair.

His mother stared at him appalled. She said, "You look terrible! Where have you been? You didn't sleep in your bed."

"I just got home," Andrew answered, wishing they would leave him in peace as his muscles were starting to tremble.

"I didn't hear a vehicle," his mother replied.

"I walked," Andrew answered, tired, sore, and very irritable.

"Walked! Walked from where?" his mother demanded to know.

"From town," Andrew said.

All their faces showed surprise. His father spoke first. "From town! But that is more than thirty kilometres!"

"Thirty-two I think," Andrew said.

He was now feeling every one of them and tears of exhaustion and frustration were forming at the back of his eyes. With an effort he held these back, not wanting Tina or Carmen to see him cry.

His mother shook her head and said, "But... but you were supposed to come home with your cousin Sandy? Didn't he bring you?"

Andrew shook his head. "No. He left without me."

"But why?" his mother asked.

A multitude of images flashed through Andrew's mind: Colleen, Tina and Cousin Sandy at Finch Bay; Lynn the Nurse. His eyes met Tina's and he saw the anxiety in them. But his mother expected an answer.

"We had a bit of a falling out," he said.

It was a lame answer and his mother was not satisfied. "Falling out? What sort of falling out?"

His father made a face and said, "Over some girl, I suppose."

Vivid images of kissing Nurse Lynn swirled in Andrew's head. But Tina was there and he could only shake his head, not wanting to say anything. To his surprise and relief, Tina now spoke.

"It was over me," she said.

Andrew saw all their faces turn to stare at her. Carmen's lit up with hope and Adele's crumpled with defeat. Carmen said, "What happened Tina?"

"Sandy took me for a drive, to Finch Bay. Then he... he... he tried to do things... things I didn't want. Andrew stopped him and they had a fight," she answered. As she did, her eyes met Andrew's and misted up.

"Did Cousin Sandy hurt you Tina?" Andrew's mother asked.

Tina shook her head. "No, but I thought he might and... and he wouldn't stop... stop doing what I didn't want."

"Finch Bay?" Carmen said. "What were you doing there, Andrew? Did you follow them?"

Andrew felt his stomach turn over and Tina's anguished gaze met his. He swallowed and shook his head.

"I had taken another girl there for a walk," he muttered.

His mother frowned. "What other girl?"

"Colleen," Andrew mumbled.

His father grinned but his mother kept frowning. "Oh you silly boy! You shouldn't sneak away like that. I wondered where you had gotten to."

Tina said, "It's alright Mrs Collins. If Andrew hadn't been there, I might have been... er... er... He saved me!"

With that she let out a sob and hurried away in tears. Carmen glared at Andrew and hurried after her. Adele hopped about in indecision for a few seconds and then followed.

Andrew's mother looked hard at him and then shook her head. Then she said, "So if that happened in the afternoon, why did Sandy say to me that he would give you a lift home?"

Andrew squirmed and did not know how to answer. Finally he said, "We had a little disagreement after that," he muttered.

"What disagreement? Over what he did to Tina?" she queried.

Andrew met his father's eye and said, "I cut him out. He was trying to win on to the pretty nurse from the hospital and I thought she was too good for him. So I... er... I."

"You what?" his mother demanded to know.

"Talked to her and then we had a kiss, and Cousin Sandy saw us," Andrew answered defiantly.

His mother was astonished. "You mean the nurse who treated you at the hospital?"

"Yes Mum. Her name is Lynn."

"But she's years older than you!" his mother cried in astonishment. "Oh heavens Andrew, what has got into you? It seems to be a different girl every day. You will get into trouble."

His father chuckled, grinned and then said, "Enjoy it while it lasts son. You are only young once. It's good to see you are a chip off the old block!"

Almost at once he realised he had made a mistake as Andrew's mother rounded on him and began scolding him for putting bad ideas into a young boy's head. Andrew took the opportunity to slip away and left them to it. But he had to chuckle.

Good old Dad! he thought. *Maybe he was a bit of a lad when he was younger?*

Andrew limped to his room, acutely aware of sobbing and sympathetic girl's voices from the next room. His heart positively ached for Tina in her distress but he did not dare try to go there now. Instead, he collected his towel, toilet bag and a change of clothes and hobbled to the shower. After showering, shaving and changing he felt better but still exhausted. He was hungry but did not want to face his mother again so he had a big drink of water and went to his room and lay down.

Sleep claimed him within minutes, broken by agonising cramps in his calf muscles. He woke sweating and thirsty and had another drink before lying down again. This time he had difficulty falling asleep and lay there dozing and thinking. He did sleep and it was lunch time before he stirred again. Feeling very muzzy and irritable he made his way to the toilet and then washed his face. Then he hesitated. He was hungry but did not particularly want to face anyone. So he went back to his room and lay down.

The stifling heat woke him first. As he lay on his bed sweating under the fan he heard the grumble of thunder off to the west. *Going to be a storm,* he thought.

At that moment, Carmen knocked and put her head in the doorway. "Lunch is ready," she said.

Andrew followed her along the passageway towards the front veranda. Just before they got there, she stopped and faced him.

"Andrew, stop hurting Tina, please," she said.

That stung him. Tiredness, sore muscles and a bad headache all added to his irascibility. "I'm not doing it deliberately!" he snapped angrily. "I love her!"

"Funny way to show it, sneaking off to meet all these girls," Carmen retorted. She was angry too and put her hands on her hips.

Guilt added to Andrew's anger. "All what girls?" he demanded.

"You know perfectly well! Ever since we got here it's been a different one every day. There was that Daphne you snuck off with along the river; the one who kissed you on the cheek last night in case you've forgotten; and there is Cousin Jean that you've been getting all hot and excited over. And yesterday it was the doctor's wife down the river with no clothes on."

"I just showed her a place to... to swim in private," Andrew replied, blushing furiously.

"And yesterday you snuck off to meet pretty little Colleen. Tina told me you were both down the beach half undressed."

"I did not sneak off. We just met by arrangement and were minding our own business!" Andrew replied. He was so angry now he was almost shouting.

"Oh yeah? So, did her parents know where she was?" Carmen snapped.

That jagged at Andrew's conscience fuelling his defiant anger. "Lucky we did anyway. At least we were there to save Tina from that odious toad, Cousin Sandy. That cost me a thirty kilometre walk!"

Carmen nodded. "I know. And Tina is very grateful. She thinks you are wonderful and I know she regrets having dumped you. But now you've hurt her again. What's this about you kissing some nurse last night?"

Andrew's brain grappled with the 'she regrets having dumped you' but he was too upset to take it in. "I did too! I told you about her. She was very nice, thank you. And why not? Tina dumped me so I think I am free to play the field," Andrew said.

"Well, she is upset by it," Carmen said. "Every time she looks around she sees you flirting with some other female. I wish you wouldn't. It hurts her."

"I don't mean to! I love Tina!" Andrew cried.

"Do you really?"

"Yes! If all this has shown me anything it is that I want Tina, not those other girls. They are all very nice but she is special," Andrew replied.

Carmen frowned. "So why don't you tell her?"

Andrew shrugged and let out an exasperated breath. "Because the time has to be right or she won't believe me!" he answered.

At that moment, Tina stepped around the doorway behind Carmen. Her face was streaming with tears. "The right time is right now," she croaked.

"Tina! I… er… Tina!" Andrew croaked.

Carmen slid aside and pushed Tina forward. "Kiss and make up you two. I'm sick of this," she ordered.

Andrew stepped forward and put out his arms. Tina slid into them, her face turned up. Andrew was so choked up that for a few moments he was unable to speak. Tina helped by sobbing out, "I'm sorry! I didn't mean to eavesdrop. I was just sitting on the veranda with Adele and I couldn't help overhearing. Oh Andrew, I really regret dumping you!"

"I don't," Andrew replied. At that, Tina's mouth opened and she looked anxious so he hastily added, "It allowed me to find out that you are the best, the one I really love."

"Oh Andrew!"

With that they kissed and held each other tight, watched by an ecstatic Carmen who was crying and smiling at the same time. Then Andrew almost spoiled it by voicing his impish thought, "And it was fun too!"

"Andrew!" Tina and Carmen called together.

"Only joking! Let me kiss you again," he said.

Tina made an impish face and pretended to be coy. "I don't know if I should. Too much of anything is bad for you. Anyway it is lunch time. We mmmffff!"

Andrew stopped her talking by kissing her again. Her resistance crumpled and he gripped her tight. They were interrupted by his father who stuck his head out and said, "What's this, a different one today?"

"Father!" came Andrew's mother's voice as she looked to see what was going on.

But when she saw it was Tina she beamed with pleasure and allowed them to finish before ushering the whole group in to eat. As they walked in Andrew held Tina's hand. As he did, Irish and a man he thought was named Rooney stuck their heads out of the bar. Irish grinned and gave a 'thumbs-up', causing Andrew to grin and blush.

At the dining table Andrew and Tina sat side by side. For most of the meal Andrew held Tina's hand under the table and kept looking at her and smiling. It just felt so good and so right that he was bursting with pleasure and satisfaction.

After the meal they moved to the veranda. Andrew sat beside Tina wanting to hold her and to talk to her. But instead they sat and watched the storm roll over them. Lightning flashed down onto the mountains and then rain blotted out the view. It was a torrential downpour and was so heavy on the corrugated iron roof that conversation was only possible by shouting. The temperature dropped ten degrees in as many minutes and Andrew enjoyed the feel of the cool spray blowing in on him.

The storm only lasted an hour and then the sun came out. By then Andrew was feeling exhausted and much as he wanted to be with Tina he excused himself and went to his room. She insisted he rest and said, "I will be alright. I've got my friends to talk to."

She and the girls went off and Andrew lay down under the fan. To his surprise he found it was soon sweltering hot again and he felt sweaty and uncomfortable, even under the fan.

He dropped into a doze, to be woken at 3:30pm by Tina. She stood there smiling down at him and when he rolled on his back and held up his arms she came to him, half lying on him while they kissed. It felt very nice and Andrew quickly became aroused. Out of habit his hands began to caress her back and sides but when he slid them across the side of her left breast he had a sudden flashback to the incident that had resulted in his being dumped.

"Sorry," he whispered.

At that, Tina seized his hand and folded it over her breast. "It's alright! I like it too. You can if you want to."

He did, and he did. That got them both hot and excited and confirmed in Andrew's mind that Tina was the one and that he was very lucky. They were interrupted by Carmen telling them to come up for air and to come and have afternoon tea. This was served on the veranda and again Andrew and Tina just sat side by side and kept looking at each other and smiling. The main topic of conversation was the fact that another storm was rolling in from the west.

Towards the end of the meal, a vehicle pulled up and Andrew's dad had to go and serve in the bar. It was Barry and out of his Land Rover jumped Little Terry.

He rushed over to Andrew and said, "Mine daddy said I can ask you if we can play?"

"Sure Little Terry, but there is going to be a storm. We can't go down the river."

"Where can we play?" Little Terry asked.

"Here," Andrew answered.

So he led Little Terry to his room and collected the model soldiers, animals and houses. He also collected some dice. While he was doing this there was a massive crack of thunder and they both jumped. Little Terry looked scared but then smiled when Andrew did. The two boys sat on the floor of Andrew's room and set out the models and began to play.

They were joined by all three girls. Carmen and Tina joined the boys on the floor but Adele remained watching from the bed. Andrew could tell she was hurt but at the same time pleased for him and Tina. The game went on happily right through the storm. Andrew was too happy to care and barely noticed his sore muscles and tiredness.

It was at about 5:30pm that Barry appeared at the door. He stood there, leaning on the doorpost and watching for a minute before he said, "Come on, kid. Time we got home. I want to get across that river in daylight."

Little Terry didn't want to go but one scowl from his father had him standing up and looking scared. He turned an anxious face to Andrew and said, "Can mine play with little people again?"

Andrew smiled and nodded. "Sure, Little Terry. It is always a pleasure."

"Thankoo!" Little Terry said as Barry grabbed his hand and pulled him out of the room.

Carmen shook her head. "That man shouldn't be driving. He sounds drunk."

She got up and followed him out. Andrew, Tina and Adele did likewise. It was only when he was out on the veranda that Andrew realised just how bad this second storm was. The thunder and lightning had stopped but the wind had got up and the rain was bucketing down.

Andrew saw that his father had intercepted Barry and was

remonstrating with him. "You shouldn't be driving. You've had too much to drink."

"Mind yer own bloody business," Barry answered. He shoved Little Terry out into the rain and snarled, "Get in the Rover kid!"

Little Terry didn't want to, but to Andrew he seemed more scared of his father, so he did as he was told, getting soaked in the process.

Andrew's father shook his head. "It is my business. I could go to court and the pub could lose its licence if I let you," he replied, obviously struggling to retain his self-control.

Irish and Rooney both joined in, both pleading with Barry. "Don't be daft man! It ain't safe, 'specially in this weather," Irish insisted.

He reached out to grab Barry's sleeve. Barry snarled at him and wrenched himself free. "Keep yer bloody hands off me!" he shouted.

Waving an angry fist at them he stumbled out into the rain and wrenched the door of his Land Rover open. The watchers could only shake their heads as he started the engine. There was then a grinding of gears and two failed attempts to get moving before the Rover at last backed out. With a roar of its motor it sped off towards Rossville and was soon lost to sight in the driving rain.

"Bloody fool!" Andrew's father muttered. Shaking his head he went back into the bar, saying, "And no more for you two either, not if you are driving home tonight."

Tina, who had snuggled up against Andrew in the cool wind, shook her head and said, "Poor little boy!"

Which was exactly what Andrew was thinking. He almost said, 'Our kids won't have that problem' when he realised what he was thinking.

I'd better not let her think I am that serious! he told himself.

It was time for dinner by then and several of the miners appeared so the intimacy of the occasion was lost. Andrew was called to help serve in the dining room. But at every trip he exchanged smiles with Tina and she seemed to glow with happiness.

Their state of euphoria lasted into the evening despite the miners getting noisy and drunk and the arrival of some tourists who wanted a late meal. To Andrew, it seemed that all the world was now right, and his emotions swirled with happiness and fond memories. Throughout all of this the storm continued, making conversation difficult and resulting in the TV being turned right up.

Irish and Rooney had dinner as well and Irish kept grinning at Andrew and winking at Tina. This became irritating after a while and Andrew was happier when Irish finished and took his leave.

"I'll be off now," he announced.

"You sober enough?" Andrew's father asked.

"Yes your honour!" Irish replied, saluting as he did.

He gave Andrew a last wink and vanished out into the rain. Andrew met Tina's eyes and smiled again. The miners all cheered and raised their glasses and teased Simon who gave a good-natured toast.

"Besides, there are still the beautiful Carmen and the delectable Adele!" he cried, raising his glass to them. The miners then began singing.

This did not bother Andrew too much as he was still walking to the kitchen and back carrying plates and food. Thus he was just coming into the dining room with two plates laden with roast beef and potatoes when Irish appeared again at the front door. He was soaked and looking very agitated. Once glance at his face told Andrew there was a problem.

Irish stood dripping in the doorway, pointing off to the south. He cried, "There's been a crash! Barry's crashed his Rover at the bend and I can't find either him or the little boy."

Chapter 36

SEARCHING

Little Terry missing! Andrew thought.
Dread clutched at his heart, and he felt an immediate urge to rush there to look. But there was a ten minute delay while phone calls were made and people changed into old clothes and collected hats, raincoats and torches. Andrew did not wait for his parent's vehicle but went with Irish in his. Tina and Carmen came with him, despite their mother not wanting them to go.

It was raining so heavily that Andrew was wet even before he got into the vehicle. As it drove along the road it had to proceed at a crawl because the windscreen wipers were unable to clear the water quickly enough. Just staring into that blinding downpour was enough to make Andrew feel sick with apprehension.

This increased to near despair when they reached the bend and parked. As he got out and saw the crashed Land Rover tilted over against a tree beside the road Andrew felt so ill he wanted to vomit. The Land Rover had obviously come off at the bend, skidded and gone down over the bank. Luckily it had not rolled and had rammed the tree head on.

It only took a few seconds searching with the beam of his torch for Andrew to see that there was no-one inside the Land Rover. Fearing the worst, he directed the torch beam on the dashboard and windscreen and then on the seats and floor. He was looking for blood but did not say so as the girls and Irish had now joined him. To his relief, there was none.

With four torches they were able to search the immediate surrounds within another minute. Andrew moved to the barbed wire fence beside the road but still saw no sign of either Barry or Little Terry. Three more vehicles with eight miners and with Andrew's parents arrived and joined the search. One vehicle and two miners were sent to ask at the two farmhouses back in the big clearing and on the lower slopes of Helenvale Hill. Two miners began searching the bush on the lower slope of the hill near the accident. Andrew crawled under the fence and scouted along the edge of the jungle for a few minutes.

Then an idea came to him and we went back to tell it to Irish and his parents. "They might have walked on along the road to their turn-off, trying to get home on foot," he suggested.

"Good idea Boyo," Irish agreed. "We will go and look and search the road both ways while we do."

So the miners were split into two teams: one searching beside the road back towards the pub, and the other on towards the turn-off. Andrew, Carmen, and Tina went with Irish in his vehicle and his parents and Adele and another miner followed in theirs. The miners were in an angry mood and Andrew overheard some muttered assessments of Barry such as 'the bloody fool!' and 'drunken idiot!' Andrew could only agree but Barry's possible fate did not bother him. It was Little Terry he was worried about.

It took only a few minutes slow driving to reach the turn-off. Andrew saw that the wire gate was open and the dirt track had been churned up by big vehicles. The search vehicles were parked and the group proceeded on foot along the side track. First Andrew looked for footprints in the slush but could not decide if there were any or not. So he moved slowly along the track. Already he was dreading the worst and thinking about the river. He could hear it even before they reached the jungle. Tina walked with him, clinging to his left hand and looking very pale in the torchlight.

It was very dark inside the jungle and the dirt vehicle track was very muddy, churned into two deep wheel ruts by the big truck. *Wes and Jan,* Andrew thought, remembering the truck he had seen them driving.

That reminded him of their odd behaviour at the Archer Point turn-off the previous night. It also made him aware of his stiff muscles and chafing but he just thrust them out of his mind as irrelevant trivia.

The group sloshed and slithered its way down the cutting in the steep riverbank and came to water, even before they came out of the trees. Unable to go any further Andrew shone his torch out at the river and felt icy dread clutch at his insides. In the beam of the torch all he could see was a raging torrent!

Andrew felt Tina grip his hand tighter and she cried, "Oh my God!"

Irish stopped beside them and stared in horror. "Oh bejaysus! I hope that drunken idiot didn't try to wade across that, not with the little boy and all," he said.

Andrew's parents and Carmen joined them and they too stared at the rushing floodwaters. Andrew's father shook his head. "Nobody could cross that on foot. It wouldn't be possible even in a big vehicle. They would just be washed away," he said.

A horrible idea came to Andrew. "What if he did try and they did get washed away. They might be clinging to a tree in mid-stream or be hurt and on the bank further downstream."

All their torches were directed on the jungle beside the track. Andrew's father shook his head again. "Maybe, but we can't push through that in the dark."

"Oh Dad! Yes we can. It won't be easy, but we must try," Andrew cried. A feeling of sick desperation fuelled his determination to look. He began to push his way into the undergrowth.

His mother cried out, "Oh Andrew, don't!'

"I've got to, Mum," he yelled back, raising his voice to make himself heard above the rattle and roar of the rain on the leaves and the swirling flood in the river.

"But there might be snakes and centipedes and things," she called.

"There probably are. I will be alright," he called back.

"But there will be leeches and creepie crawlies and you could get bitten or hurt," she wailed.

It was the leeches that did it. Andrew smiled and said, "Yes Mum."

His father pushed into the thick scrub on his right. "You just keep away from the water Andrew, and watch out for a flash flood raising the level," he cautioned.

"Yes Dad. And you watch out for the leeches and Ow!"

A spiky bush jagged him and tore his raincoat. Andrew didn't care. He just backed off and went around it. Tina came along beside him and so did Carmen, leaving Irish and Mrs Collins at the side track.

Andrew's father called to them, "Go back and wait at the vehicles. We will only go as far as the power line crossing."

The group now moved slowly, keeping in line with Andrew right on the edge of the floodwaters. As this was still inside the jungle, and he could not see any of the trees he knew grew in the bed of the river, he was not happy, but it was better than not looking at all. There were lots of spiky plants, many more than they seemed to have encountered in daylight, including some of the 'wait-a-while vine with its vicious barbed tendrils. But none of that stopped them and they moved steadily downstream.

It was like a scene from a nightmare to Andrew. The soaked clothes and wet leaves on his face and down the back of his collar meant nothing to him. It was the brown, swirling waters in among the trees that appalled him. The narrow beam of his torch lit up only small strips of the darkness and at every step he dreaded finding a drowned body. From time to time he got glimpses of the river through gaps in the foliage and that was sight that chilled his heart as well. It was just raging foam and swirling white in the blackness. The thought of trying to swim in such a maelstrom made him shudder with apprehension.

It took them thirty minutes to move the few hundred metres to the powerline crossing and even before they reached it they saw torches ahead. That sent hopes temporarily up but when they reached the people with the torches Andrew saw it was two policemen in their raincoats and hats. One was Sgt Bull, and he briefly shone his torch to identify them.

Then he chuckled, "Good to see you young Collins. Any cannons along there?"

"No sergeant," Andrew answered. He wasn't in the mood for humour but it did help.

They searched a bit more but the bank in that area was mostly covered with a thick tangle of lantana and wild raspberry with its horrible long thorns so they soon gave it up. By then Andrew was bleeding from a dozen scratches and his raincoat and clothes were torn. He felt exhausted and sick.

Sgt Bull called them together. "This is no good. We will have to try again in daylight. My torch is going flat anyway."

Andrew did not want to give up but commonsense prevailed and he trudged out to the road with the others, holding Tina's hand. The rain had eased by then to just showers and drizzle and when told that the weather forecast was for isolated thunderstorms the next day he felt more hopeful. For the next half hour he and Tina stood with their arms around each other while they waited for the searchers to come in and report.

But there was no sign of Barry or Little Terry. Vehicles had even been to Wallaby Creek and Rossville to check at houses there in case they had walked that way. The river seemed to be the best, and worst, option.

"We will start again at First Light," Sgt Bull said.

Andrew and the others trudged back to their vehicles in the drizzle and mud. By then they were all cold and even though Andrew felt driven to keep searching he could see it was no use. Reluctantly he went with the others back to the hotel. When he got there, he was amazed to find it was nearly 10:00 o'clock. The girls were hurried in to hot showers while Andrew's mother got him to help make hot drinks for everyone. While these were drunk there was a lot of discussion about where Barry and Little Terry might have gotten to. Sgt Bull outlined his search plan for the next day and then arranged for accommodation.

There was a bustle of preparation during which Andrew had a hot shower and changed into shorts and T-shirt. On the way back to his room he met Tina at the door of Carmen's room. She wore only light cotton pyjamas and he could tell that she wore nothing under them. The sight infused him with urgent desire, but he was so overwrought that he could hardly think straight. Without even thinking he took her in his arms. She hugged him and they kissed.

Between kisses, she said, "It will be alright, Andrew. We will find them tomorrow."

"I feel so sorry for that little boy," he replied. Tears sprang to his eyes but he blinked them back and, with choking emotions, he kissed her again. "I wish we were spending the night together," he whispered.

"Oh, so do I! But I'm sorry, you will have to wait," Tina replied.

"Wait for what?" Andrew answered with an impish grin.

Tina blushed and giggled, then kissed him again. "You know perfectly well, you naughty boy!"

Andrew become aware that both Carmen and Adele were in the room and watching the whole performance. Blushing with guilt, he saw his mother appeared in the passageway.

She said, "Come on you children, get to bed! You can save that for another time. You need some sleep if you are to be any use tomorrow. We are getting up at four thirty remember."

"Yes Mum," Andrew replied.

He and Tina exchanged loving smiles and he kissed her again, not caring that his mother and sister were watching. It just felt right. They obviously thought so too because neither made any comment after he released Tina and moved to his own room. After a series of 'good nights' he went in, only to get a sharp reminder of Little Terry and his plight. Scattered across the floor were the model soldiers, some 'dead' and others still 'marching' in their ranks.

Andrew sighed and shook his head sadly. But he was too tired to pack them away. Instead, he just swept aside those that lay in the path from the doorway to his bed. Then he flopped onto his bed feeling utterly wretched and exhausted.

For a time he lay there, his mind a mix of emotions in a swirling contrast: delight over Tina and despair over Little Terry. But after a while tiredness overtook him and he slipped into a restless nightmare-fractured sleep. The nightmares were the usual ones, the boat shrinking until he was on a small surfboard and then slipping off into deep water with a strong current; deep water full of shadowy and threatening things.

But mingled with the images were ones of a raging flood in the darkness and of being hunted by evil men.

* * *

Andrew woke to find himself blinking in the light. Tina was there and she bent over and kissed him.

"Sorry to give you a start," she said. "But it is time to get up."

Andrew reached up and hugged her too him, kissing passionately. "Oooh! I know what I'd like to do," he said.

He could feel her almost bare skin under her thin pyjamas. With a sigh he gently stroked her. Tina squirmed out of his grasp. "Later. We have to find Little Terry,' she said.

Little Terry! Andrew had forgotten. His whole mood changed instantly and he slid out of bed, stepping on more model soldiers as he did. He kicked these aside and told Tina to leave so he could get dressed. She did so and a few minutes later, dressed in shorts, shirt and joggers, he met the girls in the kitchen. His parents were already there and dressed and had obviously been up longer as they had food and hot drinks in preparation.

Andrew was sent to rouse the miners and the policemen, who had been given one of the lodges to sleep in. He also roused Irish and Rooney who had been sleeping on the veranda sofas. As they straggled into the dining room they were given hot drinks of tea, coffee or cocoa and hot toast.

When all were assembled Sgt Bull outlined his plans. Two were to go to the Wallaby Creek area and to Rossville to check again if Barry had walked there with the little boy. The constable was to go downstream to the pump station to ask the attendant to watch the river and then to town to follow up the possibility that Barry had got a lift back to town on one of the several vehicles that people remembered having gone past the pub in that direction the previous evening. He was then to muster the local SES and bring them out. Two miners in a 4WD were to go to the vehicle track leading to Barry's shed and were to cross if it was deemed safe, to check at his shed.

"I will go to the station and then down to the highway bridge across the Annan," Sgt Bull said. "We will work our way upstream to Mungumby Creek." He then looked at Andrew and the girls. "I would like you kids to search the riverbank between Mungumby Creek and Barry's Crossing. Do not try crossing that river. There has been no rain during the night and it has gone down a bit but do not try anything foolish."

"What about us?" Andrew's father asked, indicating himself and Andrew's mother. Sgt Bull said, "I want you to stay here as the Search HQ and to provide food and drink for the search parties. Until the SES arrive with more hand-held radios we don't have good coms so each group needs to keep checking back here on progress."

"I will still search the road between here and the crash," Andrew's father said.

Sgt Bull nodded. "Yes, do that, and get the neighbours to search their properties as well. OK, let's move!"

It was 0530 by then and fully light so the various search parties split up. Andrew collected a couple of broom handles to poke the long grass with and also some garden secateurs and a water bottle, then he and the girls went out the front. They turned left and walked along the road northwards to the mouth of Mungumby Creek. By then all the other groups had driven off.

As they reached the first place where they could see the river Andrew saw that what Sgt Bull had said was correct. The river was significantly lower and not nearly as fast.

Not a flood anymore, just higher than normal, he thought.

He even thought it would be possible to safely cross if the level dropped much more. He looked up and saw that there wasn't a cloud in the sky. The sun was just lighting the top of Helenvale Hill by then and already the temperature was rising.

Andrew and the girls began searching back upstream along the riverbank. But this was easier said than done. That part of the riverbank was steep and dropped into deep water and the bank was covered by a thick tangle of long grass, weeds and lantana.

The perfect home for snakes, Andrew thought, which was why he had brought the broom handles. The secateurs were to cut a path through the lantana.

And he was right. Within fifty paces he saw the tail of a snake slither off into the weeds. "Snake!" he cautioned, pointing to where it had gone. "Olive brown colour," he added.

Which meant it could be almost anything, from a harmless tree snake to a deadly Taipan! To scare the thing away he flailed at the weeds and long grass with the broom handle. Then he inched slowly along. Adele wanted to turn back but he assured her that the snake would be long gone.

The thick tangle so slowed them that it was nearly six thirty before they had covered the 500 metres from Mungumby Creek back to the swimming hole behind the pub. There had been no sign of either Barry or Little Terry, which was a relief.

When they reached the walking track, Carmen pointed up it and said, "Let's go up and check if there has been any news."

"Good idea. I need to go to the toilet," Tina agreed.

Andrew wanted to keep searching but agreed it was a good idea. So they went up to the pub and found both parents in the kitchen. There was no news of any sighting so they were given drinks and more toast and went to the toilet. During all this Andrew fretted lest a body wash past while they were not watching. He knew this was irrational as hours of darkness had gone by but he still felt distressed. A deep feeling of anxiety and apprehension gripped him, only lightened by Tina's presence and obvious love.

At 07:30am they returned to the riverbank and began working their way upstream from the swimming hole. This was easier as they knew this part of the river and being rain forest there was less undergrowth. The problem was being able to see out through the leaves to search both banks of the river and the trees and snags in the stream.

Of necessity they moved at a slow walk and Andrew found it an emotionally harrowing experience. Not only was he expecting to find the little boy's drowned body, he had seen drowned people before, but there were the other memories, of Daphne half naked, of the nude doctor's wife, of kissing Colleen, of the presence of Tina. On top of that was his exhaustion from the previous few days and the sore muscles and chafing that still bothered him.

But none of that would stop him searching so he slowly pushed his way through the vegetation as close to the bank as he could get, looking in every dark hole, backwater and under every snag. The girls followed: Tina, then Carmen, and Adele last.

It took them two hours to move about one kilometre until they were behind the second farmhouse. There was then the unpleasant business of cutting a path through the wild raspberries and lantana under the powerline.

When they reached the vehicle track along the powerline, Andrew said, "This is where we searched to last night."

Carmen nodded and said, "I wonder if any of the other search parties have found anything?"

"We had better find out," Andrew said. He did not really want to walk all the way back to the hotel but could not see any alternative. So he led the way left along the vehicle track to where it joined the Rossville Road. This was right near the bend where Barry had crashed.

As luck would have it, they found two men with a flatbed tow truck busy winching Barry's Land Rover onto it. After saying hello, Andrew asked if Barry or Little Terry had been found.

One of the men shook his head. "Nope. Not that we know of. We have just come from the pub and they had no news. Sgt Bull told us to collect this vehicle and take it to the police station."

Andrew nodded. "We will keep searching then. Can you please tell them at the pub we are looking along the riverbank here?"

The man agreed to do that, so Andrew led the girls back to the riverbank and continued searching upstream. As he moved slowly through the rainforest he noted that it was thickening up and that there were lots more spiky plants and the first clumps of wait-a-while.

"This is the area we searched last night," he reminded the girls.

"I can see why it took us so long," Tina replied.

Carmen swore and muttered, "And why it hurt so much! Ow!" She unhooked a wait-a-while tendril and backed up.

Progress continued slowly. Then 11:00am came and went. "We might get this done by lunch time," Carmen suggested.

Because the river level had dropped Andrew made his way right along the edge of the water and even began wading out through shallow areas to look at stands of small trees and snags in the stream bed. By now they were all sweating and he stopped several times to drink from the river. Once he heard snorting noises and froze in fear as a large wild pig appeared on the other bank. But the pig did not hear him and went snuffling off into the trees.

At about 11:30am they rounded the bend near Barry's Crossing. A hundred metres below the crossing Andrew noted a small island studded with a thicket of small trees.

"I will just check this," he said.

Without waiting he waded through thigh deep water across to the island. It was just pebbles and water-rounded stones with the trees growing from among them. The trees had been bent by the flood and were now festooned by flood debris: sticks, grass, leaves and a few logs.

While he searched there the three girls stood on the bank and watched. Andrew heard the sound of a vehicle engine up among the trees on the other bank. He looked that way hopefully, but also with some anxiety.

I hope they aren't going to try and cross, he thought. *The river is still up and they could be in trouble.*

But it was quickly apparent that the vehicle was going to try and cross. Down the bank and out of the tunnel of vegetation appeared a large green truck with a canvas canopy on the back. Driving it was Wes and sitting beside him was Jan. The truck slowed and eased into the river. To Andrew's relief, the vehicle seemed high enough to be above the flow and it roared and churned its way across. Andrew did not particularly want to speak to either Wes or Jan but knew they had to ask if they had seen Barry or Little Terry so he yelled to Carmen to try to speak to them.

Carmen waved back and the girls began hurrying along under the trees to try to reach the truck before it had crossed. But Andrew saw they would be too late. The truck drove up out of the water, pushing a wave ahead of it. With water pouring off it the truck went into the muddy cutting and started grinding up the slope. As it did, its engine roared and Andrew saw mud being flung back from its rear wheels. Then the truck stopped, backed up and tried again.

It is bogged, Andrew thought as he picked his way through the small trees and over the logs towards the top end of the small island.

At that moment, the sound of a second vehicle reached Andrew's ears. It was another large truck and it came down the far bank and into the water without even slowing down. As it began churning its way across it pushed up a huge bow wave. Andrew saw this coming and jumped up on a log and clung to a tree to avoid being washed away. He also saw Jan appear at the back of the first truck, waving his arms and shouting. Andrew had expected to see Barry driving the second truck but now saw that the driver was a man he had never seen before, middle-aged, unshaven, dressed in blue overalls. Beside him was a second stranger.

The driver appeared to ignore Jan's signals and kept the truck moving fast. He could obviously see the other truck bogged and blocking the cutting because as the second truck burst from the water with its engine roaring it swerved, bounced across the rocks there and went straight up the steeper bank to the left of the cutting. There appeared to be a gap in the trees there and that was obviously where the man wanted the truck to go. As the second truck went up the slope, water cascaded from it. By then the three girls were so close they had to scuttle back to avoid being splashed.

But the slope was too steep and the truck was in the wrong gear. It came to a slithering halt, its wheels churning the muddy leaf mould. Then it rolled back down. The driver obviously jumped on the brakes as the truck slithered backwards and then came to a halt with a savage jerk as the rear wheels struck the rocks in the stream bed.

There was a loud bang and other minor crashes and the tailgate of the truck flew open and the canvas canopy was flung apart as ropes broke. Out of the back cascaded a dozen or more heavy boxes. The boxes were painted a dark green colour and had printing and markings on them. The boxes crashed onto the rocks and two of them burst open right in front of the girls. Out of the boxes spilled automatic rifles.

Andrew stared at the rifles in amazement. *Those are military rifles,* he thought. *Now what on earth is going on?*

An instinct warned him that this was trouble, and he began hurrying along the little island to join the girls, who were standing staring in astonishment at the pile of guns.

He was not the only one to hurry. Jan appeared at the back of the second truck. The moment he saw the girls he stopped shouting abuse at the driver and pulled an automatic pistol from the waistband of his shorts and cocked it. Then he pointed it at the girls and shouted at them to put their hands up.

The moment he saw this Andrew knew it really was big trouble. *They aren't drug smugglers,* he thought, *they are gun runners!*

Either way he sensed it was deadly serious. At that moment, he was still 50 metres away and wading in knee deep water. He stopped and looked around, wondering what the best course of action might be.

As he did, Wes appeared beside Jan and he saw Andrew. He grabbed Jan's left arm and pointed. Jan's mouth opened in surprise and then he pointed his pistol and yelled, "Hey you! Get over here with your hands up!"

Oh my God! Andrew gasped. *What should I do?*

Chapter 37

HUNTED

Andrew's mind raced. *What will Jan do to us?* he wondered. In a flash his mind told him what he would do if he was a criminal: kill any inconvenient witnesses. And Jan had been a mercenary in Africa.

He is certainly a killer! Andrew thought. *Surrendering to him is not going to save the girls,* he told himself.

And the girls were now undoubtedly prisoners. The passenger out of the second truck had now climbed down and held a rifle and Carmen, her face frozen in horrified disbelief, was raising her hands. Tina was looking shocked and Adele still had a foolish smile on her face.

As Jan called again other thoughts flashed through Andrew's brain; the result of training as a quartermaster gunner. *That is only a 9mm pistol. He isn't likely to hit me at that range.* Even as he thought this, Andrew started to turn away.

Jan yelled again: "Stop, or I shoot!"

Andrew believed him but he did not stop. Instead, he threw himself headlong into the knee deep water and began swimming underwater, downstream with the current.

Crunk!

Andrew heard the bullet strike the water but did not see where. But the shot had the effect of galvanizing his limbs with fear and he swam like a mad thing, breast stroking frantically. He could not keep it up for long and the desperate needed to breathe finally overcame the terror of putting his head above water. Cringing with fear he broke surface and gulped air, at the same time trying to dash the water from his eyes to see where he was going.

Crack! Thump!

This time Andrew saw the bullet strike just to his right front and he experienced a spasm of pure terror. But it did not stop him. *I must escape!* he thought. So he ignored Jan's screams to 'stop or else!' Seeing a clear channel ahead Andrew ducked under and resumed swimming.

As he did, his mind continued to turn over options. One thing was clear to Andrew: Jan could run along the bank faster than he could swim underwater.

I must get out, he told himself.

So next time he surfaced he made a point of glancing back. What he saw and heard did nothing to calm him. Jan had snatched the rifle, some sort of bolt action sporting rifle, off the other man and was yelling to the other crooks.

It was what Jan said that really chilled Andrew. Jan screamed, "Jake, guard these three bitches. Get them to reload the truck and then tie them up in the back. Wes, get a gun and follow me. Fred, go and get Barry and Johno. And get the dogs! We have to catch this little mongrel or the game is up. I will chase him."

Dogs! Andrew thought, horrifying images of bloodhounds swirling into his nearly panic-stricken mind.

He stood up and tried running but the water was waist deep now and he only floundered a few steps before his terrified mind told him to duck before Jan used the rifle. He went down, just in time. The water boiled around his head and he felt the concussion of the bullet striking. In a frantic spasm of arm strokes Andrew dragged himself down until he was scraping the sandy bottom. His only consolation was the knowledge, from watching the *Mythbusters* on TV, that he was safe from a high velocity bullet while he was underwater.

Andrew was swimming into deeper water now but that also meant that the current was slowing down. His eyes saw the gloomy shadows of deep holes and the snag he had noticed. During his brief attempt at running he had noted a big tree which had fallen into the river on the far bank. It was not the bank he wanted to be on. Home and friends and help were on the right bank, but so were Jan and Wes, and they were even now dashing after him. So for the moment the left bank appeared the safer option.

And there was the snag. Andrew knew he was taking a deadly risk and his whole being squirmed at the thought of it but he also sensed that any hesitation would be more surely fatal.

Jan won't let me live after trying to shoot me, he thought.

So it was all or nothing. As Andrew swam in behind the fallen branches and vines, he swerved in close to the bank and broke surface. A glance showed that he was, for a few moments anyway, hidden from Jan and Wes but he was immediately confronted by a physical barrier he had not considered and which threatened to bring his whole plan undone. The tree had fallen because the bank had been undermined by the floodwaters. This had left a vertical cliff of about three metres of crumbling soil.

Faced by this Andrew nearly gave up, but the sound of voices over on the right bank got him moving. *Go fast or you are dead!* he told himself.

There were trailing vines hanging in the water and he grasped one and hauled himself frantically up, walking up the slope and using his arms more than his feet to drag himself up.

As he reached the top he heard a shout, "There he is!"

A terrified glance over his shoulder showed him Jan stopping to raise the rifle butt to his shoulder. Andrew used all his strength to flick himself up over the lip and onto the flat ground.

Crack! Thunk! Thump!

Sound of the bullet; bullet striking the tree; sound of gun going off, Andrew's mind told him as he yelped in fear.

A wave of hot and cold terror surged through him. The bullet had come so close he now had absolutely no doubt of Jan's murderous intent.

Driven by sheer terror and the instinct of self-preservation Andrew crawled frantically away into the rainforest, desperately trying to keep trees between himself and Jan. Jan tried one more shot but it hit a tree beside Andrew, causing him to flinch and cringe.

Then Jan shouted, "Wes, you stay on this bank. Whatever you do don't let the little bastard get to one of those houses or to the pub. I will cross over and hunt him. Tell Johno to join me. Keep in touch by radio."

Radios? Andrew thought. He risked a peep and now noticed that both Jan and Wes had small hand-held radios clipped to their shirts. *Oh hell!* he thought.

Then Jan went running on along the bank, looking for a place to cross without swimming.

I must get ahead of him, Andrew thought.

So he broke into a run, first heading deeper into the forest and then heading north along the bank but keeping at least fifty paces back from it so as not to expose himself to being shot by the men on the other bank. Luckily the vegetation was dry rainforest with very little undergrowth so he was able to run fast. The worst aspect was the ground litter of dead leaves which seemed to crunch very loudly as he trod on them. Minor life-threatening perils such as snakes he just thrust to the back of his mind.

At every second he expected to hear a shot or Jan yelling but none came so he ran on. Very quickly he began to puff but with his life in mortal peril he pushed himself to keep moving. But his haste led to a bad stumble. Gasping in fear and unfitness he scrambled to his feet and brushed the leaves off as he started running again. As he did, he heard Jan's voice behind him. Jan was calling to Wes across the river and sounded to be about a hundred metres back. Just far enough to be out of sight in the forest but deadly close if the country opened out. So Andrew ran even faster.

Then skidded to a stop. In a small clearing ahead were six wild pigs! *Not just one!* he thought in dismay. In desperation he again considered the river as a sanctuary. *A sow and her piglets and a huge wild boar!*

He knew that a sow defending its young would be absolutely deadly. And the pigs had seen him! And Jan was close behind! There was nothing for it but to keep running.

Andrew dashed towards the riverbank, just visible as a lighter area to his right. The pigs began snorting and squealing and running around. As he passed each tree Andrew glanced for the next one that might provide a haven in case he was attacked. He saw the baby pigs go into a mad rush, luckily away from him. But the big boar and the sow held their ground and were snorting and pawing at the leaf mould!

Suddenly, Andrew burst out of the trees into a clearing on the riverbank. A glance showed him he was almost opposite the bend where he had brought Daphne to, and where the doctor's wife had gone nude sunbathing. But it was not a naked female standing on the sandbank, it was Wes! Wes saw him at once, shouted and threw up his gun.

Andrew swerved and ducked.

Crack! Bang!

Missed! his mind told him. And Wes was yelling and Jan calling back from behind him!

Just as Andrew regained the cover of the forest he heard Jan's rifle go off. For an instant he feared he had been seen, and he almost soiled himself in terror. But then Jan was shouting, "Bloody pigs! Bloody hell!"

There were two more shots, each slightly further away. Andrew did not hesitate. He bolted. At every step he knew he was now getting further from the river and from the hotel because the river curved away to the east. A sense of despair began to form like lead under his heart.

I've been cut off! Where should I go now? he wondered.

Worse still the ground was rising and the bush turning to savannah woodland. Andrew considered turning right and following the river, hoping to sneak across to reach the hotel but knowing there was an enemy waiting near there and another close on his heels made that a very risky proposition. As he ran Andrew pictured the map in his head.

Maybe I can reach the cattle station homestead? he thought.

Then another idea came to him. Only a few kilometres ahead of him was the Mulligan Highway. It was two or three kilometres, he couldn't remember for sure.

But the highway bridge is where Sgt Bull said he was taking his search party. Maybe I can get to him; or even just flag down a car on the main road and get a lift to a house or to Cooktown? he thought. The more he thought about it the better the plan seemed to Andrew. *It is not what the crooks will expect,* he told himself.

And it would certainly spread their forces very thin. So he gave up trying to reach the hotel and kept on going north.

He very quickly began to regret that decision but once made he stuck to it. The main reasons for regret were the slope got steeper and steeper and the bush became very open. Andrew found he was on a small range of hills. He had seen them before from a distance and had noted them on the map but found the reality much bigger and harder to climb than he had expected. Not that they were big, only a few hundred metres high, but he was now gasping for breath and getting a bad stitch. Reluctantly he had to slow to a gasping plod.

I hope Jan is not as fit as me, he thought.

He kept looking back, fearing to see his pursuer appear at any moment. In doing so he was dismayed to note the roof of the hotel and the houses beyond it, all clearly visible in the distance beyond the dark green line of the river, and all getting further away at every step!

By the time he reached the top of the hill Andrew was gasping and sweating so much he feared heat exhaustion. His heart was hammering fit to burst but he did not dare slow down. With an effort of will power he urged sore and tired muscles into action again. To begin with he ran along the crest of the ridge, cursing the blazing sun as it was too high overhead to give any real idea of direction. But navigation was no real problem. From the moment he had reached the upper slopes he could see the peaks of the Black, Trevethan Range.

I am heading too far to the west, he thought.

So he headed down a spur that ran in a more northerly direction. There was another range of hills a kilometre or so ahead and he thought the highway went around the right hand end of them. But as he got lower down the hills became hard to see, hidden by the trees. Down on the flat there was waist high long grass and that was more scary to run through. There was no possibility of going slow enough to see snakes or to give them time to slide out of his way. All he could do was depend on speed and luck.

Several small creeks caused him delays. The first he cursed because of the time and effort wasted in negotiating its steep banks but at the second he took the opportunity to have a big drink, after pausing to survey the country behind him to be sure that Jan was not close on his tail.

Can he track me on the dry hills? he wondered. Through the long grass it was more likely as he was leaving a very obvious trail of trampled grass. *But dogs will be able to!* he thought.

After a big drink and a check of his watch (*Good lord! 12:50pm. Where has the time gone?* he thought) he hurried on. Ahead of him a dense wall of greenery indicated a large watercourse and he wondered if he was off line. But when he reached it ten minutes later, still with no sign of pursuit, he saw it was not the river. It was large creek with steep banks which were lined with jungle.

He slid down the bank, paused to gulp more water, then scrambled up the other side, hauling himself from tree to tree. A large goanna was disturbed and went scampering up a tree but Andrew had no time for wildlife. He found himself on a wide, grassy flat with the eastern end of the hills in front of him. Even better, at the base of the hills, was the highway! When Andrew saw a car go speeding along it toward Cooktown he cried out with relief.

"Nearly safe!" he told himself.

But he was too exhausted to run. All he could do was limp, gasping and perspiring, his wounded left leg now throbbing painfully. It took him nearly ten minutes to limp across that flat. When he got to the highway he threw himself down in the shade of a tree and sucked in air.

He was waiting for a car or truck. But another ten minutes went by and no vehicle appeared. *I will look silly if Jan catches me because I am just sitting here hoping,* he thought. *If Sgt Bull is at the Annan River Bridge I should go there,* he decided.

Andrew knew the bridge was to his right so he stood up on trembling legs and began hobbling along the highway in that direction. All the while he kept a wary eye on the thick vegetation of the creek line to his right for any sign of his pursuers. As he walked he sweated as there was very little breeze and no clouds. The bitumen was so hot it was half melted and sticky to walk on and seemed to radiate the heat in waves. This caused a shimmer in the distance.

As the minutes and the hundreds of metres walked went by, Andrew became more and more worried. It was soon obvious he was further from the bridge than he had thought. Just as disturbing was the fact that not a single vehicle came from either direction. The only good thing was the hills on the left got lower and lower.

I am sure the road goes around the end of the next spur, Andrew told himself.

He trudged on around a curve to the right. The road ran straight for a few hundred metres and then curved left out of sight. More worrying was the fact that the creek line on his right was now right beside the road and if Jan came out of it he would have very little warning.

A noise. *Is that a vehicle?* Andrew wondered.

By now his throat was parched and he was feeling the beginnings of heat exhaustion. It was. Around the bend in front of him came a green Land Rover. Andrew stopped walking and waved his arms. The vehicle was going the wrong way but he didn't care. Then, as the Land Rover came out of the heat shimmer his eyes focused and his heart seemed to stop. Sitting in the passenger's seat was Jan!

Shock and disbelief held Andrew for a few seconds, during which the Land Rover covered most of the distance towards him. Then he let out a sob of disbelief and dismay and ran. Sheer terror sent his aching muscles into overdrive as he sprinted up onto the dry, rock strewn ridge on his left.

The ridge was low and the going fairly easy and as Andrew reached the crest he glanced back in time to see the Land Rover brake to a halt and Jan clamber out, rifle in hand. Then Andrew was over the crest and bounding down the other side, to be confronted by the realisation that he had made an appalling mistake. Stretching right across his front was the gorge of the Annan River!

The gorge was several hundred metres wide. Both sides were very steep, often cliffs. These were not high as cliffs go, only twenty of thirty metres but still precipitous and largely bare of cover. But it was the river bed below that was the real obstacle. It was a jagged jumble of black rock. Worse still the river cut through this rock in a twenty or thirty metre deep cleft that was too wide to jump. Off to the right was a waterfall over which the river was thundering in a welter of spray. Above that was a jumble of seething foam and rapids. In the far distance Andrew glimpsed the concrete highway bridge but he knew he had no hope of reaching it over those rocks, not with Jan on the ridge above him. Downstream of the falls the river plunged out of sight into the dark cleft, to reappear far downstream in swirling dark pools surrounded by steep rock slopes and huge, jagged boulders.

There seemed no way to escape but Andrew did not give up. He slid and bounded down the steep, grassy slope to the black rocks in the river bed and went scrambling frantically over them.

Crack! Wheeeee! Bang!

A bullet struck the rock he was climbing onto, throwing stone chips into his face causing him to flinch so violently he nearly lost his balance. But fear drove him on. He scrambled up onto the rock and jumped recklessly off the other side. He landed heavily on a flat rock but pitched forward and slammed his nose into the next stone. It was a numbing blow and he felt blood trickle but he did not stop. After pausing to get his breath and to check the next move he scrambled up and over another boulder in a single slithering movement.

Another shot echoed around the gorge and the bullet ricocheted off the rock beyond him. Andrew dropped down behind another boulder, gasping and crying at the pain in his hands and knees from the heat of the rocks. By now he knew he was almost at the end of his strength and his whole emotional system was nearing hysteria and collapse. Absolute terror gripped him and flight was his only plan.

For a few seconds he crouched, whimpering and sobbing behind the boulder and then cautiously raised his head to peek around the end of it. To his horror he saw that Jan was standing on the skyline in a position where he could see right along the gorge both ways for hundreds of metres. But worse still, climbing down the slope and heading towards Andrew was the other man from the Land Rover, and he also had a gun!

Jan is going to pin me down and that fellow is going to find me and kill me, Andrew thought.

In desperation he looked around. Five paces away was the deep cleft. A single glance showed it was much too wide to jump. And it was so deep he could not see the bottom. But he could hear the water swirling and roaring in it and further downstream he could see horrible black water swirling in a large pool.

Oh my God! I'm trapped! Andrew thought.

Chapter 38

DESPERATION

Andrew stared at that potential whirlpool of death and swallowed. The swirling water was full of logs and sticks and the deep, dark water looked like anything could lurk in it. By anything he meant crocodiles but did not want to articulate the thought. But to stay was certain death, quite apart from the fact that he was baking in the blistering heat on the exposed rocks.

"Die if I stay, might die if I jump!" Andrew told himself.

It seemed a hell of a choice and all quite unreal. But there was nothing unreal about that man with the gun who was now at the bottom of the slope and starting to pick his way carefully across the jumbled rocks.

If I wait I am done for! Andrew told himself.

Realising that the more he thought about it the more scared he became and the more he hesitated, he forced himself to spring up and run forward.

Before he could have stopped himself he had jumped. As he went over the edge the view sent a paralysing spasm of pure terror through him. It was a long way down! And the water looked black and evil. Even as he fell he noted that the water was swirling like a giant washing machine and it was full of flood debris, sticks, and several logs. The drop was so big his mind had time to register all of this and for fear to wash through him, as well as thoughts of regret that he was about to die.

He narrowly missed one of the logs as he punched deep into the water. The impact hurt but Andrew barely noticed it as he was so full of fear. Even before he had stopped sinking he had his eyes open and was thrashing with his arms and legs to try to surface. He broke surface near one of the logs and grabbed at it to help him float while he got his bearings.

The knowledge that the man with the gun was making his way towards the cliff top above kept Andrew in a state of desperation. He found he was disoriented and that sent a surge of panic through him. The black rocks were sliding past and it took him several seconds to note that he was actually going around in a circle.

Then, just as he worked out which way to go, his heart received another jolt. A large centipede was crawling along the log, amid dozens of big red ants. The scuttling insect crawled onto his hand even as he saw it. Horrified and so distressed he could barely think straight Andrew flicked it away and started swimming. But his aim was poor and the centipede landed on his shoulder. This time he screamed but this was lost as the current caught him and sucked him under.

The outlet from the 'washing machine' was a narrow gap through which the water poured in a small waterfall. Andrew went down this completely out of control. More fear coursed through his veins till he felt sure he must die just from heart failure. He was tumbled over and over and his cheek struck a rock with a near stunning blow.

If I hit my head and get knocked out I will drown! he thought, adding a whole new dimension to his fear.

Being a trained diver Andrew was a very good underwater swimmer, but he had a pathological fear of drowning. Frantically he struggled to break free of the current and to swim up to the light. But he kept rolling over and found it hard. The effort of holding his breath began to turn to an agonising pain. He knew he was approaching that horrible moment when he must breathe regardless, and that it would be water, not air.

Swim with the current, he told himself.

He knew that the river widened out into a large pool further downstream. So he struck out in a desperate side stroke. Within seconds he felt better. The current grew less and eased its grip and he was able to stay facing upwards. At once he propelled himself to the surface. He broke surface and gave a mighty gasp, then looked frantically around.

I am in the big pool, he thought. Now terror returned in force. *I must swim across it and around behind those rocks before the man with the gun reaches the top of the cliff or I am dead,* he told himself.

In desperation he started swimming across the pool. As he did, he kept glancing back, dreading to see the silhouette of the gunman. But he was winded and could feel his strength ebbing fast. As exhaustion set in his feelings of panic increased.

The pool seemed huge but he told himself it was only about 50 metres across. The rocks at the far side seemed to stay as far away as ever and he sobbed with fear. Then the current sped up as the pool narrowed and the rocks seemed to slide towards him. Now they were only ten metres away.

Andrew glanced back, and saw movement on top of the cliff. Immediately he sucked in a deep breath and lifted himself in preparation to dive. Suddenly spray deluged him and he knew it was a bullet striking the water right beside him. The concussion hammered at him and he flinched and threw his hands up. Partly this was instinct and partly training as it helped him slip under.

Stay under! Stay under! he told himself.

With his eyes blurry in the horrible muddy water he started swimming underwater in the direction he thought the outlet to the big pool was. But it was hard to do as the water was so murky and dark. His main guide was the current.

Swim with the current, he told himself.

Then the current really had him and he again lost control. He knew there might be another waterfall or a set of rapids as the river went around a slight bend but he could do nothing to stop himself. All he could do was pray that he wasn't dashed unconscious on the rocks. Once again he was tumbled over and over, his head even coming out of the water several times, but not long enough to get a breath. As he came up the next time, he heard what he thought were the echoes of a rifle shot.

They are still shooting at me, he thought.

Then the tumbling stopped and Andrew came to the surface, spinning around in a backwater behind the rocks on the left side of the river. A glance showed him he was at the top end of a reach a hundred metres long that ended in another narrow cleft. The reach had almost vertical rocky sides in most places but there were a couple of small sandy beaches in places.

I could get out here, Andrew thought, looking up the steep slope. *But it is the same side that Jan and the other man are on.*

He saw that he was hidden by the steep rocks from the men where he was at that moment. But the cruel dilemma was that to cross to the other bank he would have to swim into their view. He only hesitated for a few seconds, deciding that the other bank gave a better chance of survival.

If I can get up that cliff, they will take a long time to get around to the other side of the river, he decided. Besides, there were people living on that side: Grandma Cynthia and further downstream the people at the pump station.

So he struck out downstream using a side stroke that allowed him to keep looking back. By hugging the bank he was able to stay in 'dead ground' from both Jan and the man until he had covered nearly 50 metres. As he swam he recovered his breath and studied the rocks and slopes to plan his next move. He saw that just before the next cleft on the other bank there was a small beach on the right. It was tucked in behind a rocky spur. From this a steep gully led up the slope. The gully reached almost all the way to the top of the line of cliffs walling in the river on that side. The upper slopes were not really cliffs, just very steep slopes covered in some grass and a few trees. There was not much cover so he knew they would see him go up it.

If I don't keep slipping. It looks pretty loose stuff, he thought anxiously. But it appeared his best chance. *But I mustn't get washed past those rocks or I will be in another set of rapids.* He did not think he could survive another tumble. *I am getting very weak,* he told himself.

From experience he knew he could swim 50 metres under water, and he estimated the distance at less than that. So it was now or never. After another glance back he sucked in a deep breath and dived. Using his best side stroke he struck out across the pool, trying to stay deep. As he did, he was chilled by another terrifying thought. The pool was so deep that bottom was lost in murky blackness.

I am below the falls. This is the lower Annan. There are crocodiles in this part of the river.

The thought galvanized him with fear and he found a new reserve of energy. Swimming as fast as he could he kept on across the river. At every second he imagined the mighty jaws clamping onto a leg or foot; the ghastly teeth crunching through flesh and bone; the death roll and drowning as he was mangled!

Andrew swam so fast he ran into the rocks hard. Luckily his hands took the blow and he was able to stop his head striking the rock. Then he had to instantly decide, left or right? He opted for left and hauled himself along the rocks. Now he was running out of air and struggling to stay under. The rock curved the way he wanted it to and he felt a current pulling him and he knew he was in a backwater.

Unable to stay under any longer he surfaced right against the rock, then sighed with relief. He had made it!

I am in the right place, he thought.

For the moment he was hidden behind the outcrop of rocks. He thankfully dragged himself up the tiny beach and stood on trembling legs in the cover.

While recovering his breath he looked up and decided he could climb the rocks. It was as he had thought. It would be the last ten metres of open slope above the rocks that would be the hardest and most dangerous.

And he knew he dare not wait. A peek around the rocks showed him this. Walking along the ridge top opposite was Jan, a tiny silhouette two hundred metres or so upstream. But within a few minutes he would be opposite the gully and able to see into it.

Then I will be like a fly on the ceiling as I climb up, Andrew thought.

So up he went, muscles trembling from overexertion. It was easy enough, just climbing from one foothold to another with plenty of handholds and the slope not too steep. The real worry was staying hidden behind the ever-diminishing rocky outcrop. And then the gully ended and all there was the steep, grassy slope. Andrew had hoped to sneak over the crest unseen but there was no fold in the ground to allow this so he took a deep breath and went scrambling up, now depending on speed.

Almost as soon as he broke cover, he heard a shout and knew he was seen. Another spasm of terror urged him up. But the slope had a lot of loose pebbles and sand and his gym boots began to slip. In desperation he scrabbled for a firm foothold while grabbing at the grass and then small trees and bushes to haul himself up.

Crack!

A shot smacked past his head so close he felt the wind of it. It struck the ground almost in his face and flung sand and stone chips into his eyes. Blinking and sobbing with fear Andrew kept on going. It wasn't far but the top seemed an impossible distance away. Another bullet stuck the slope to his right.

The other man. He's not as good a shot as Jan, Andrew thought.

Then the slope was easing and the skyline coming closer by the frantic second. Another shot cracked past but Andrew was now running and dodging and it missed. Suddenly he was on the skyline and he kept going, throwing himself flat and rolling down the other side, even as yet another bullet cracked past.

Safe! For the moment! But would Jan or the other man risk swimming the river?

They could do it, Andrew thought. *I had better keep moving.*

But he was winded and shaking so violently that he had to rest for a minute. While he did he studied the lie of the land and took stock of the situation. He also shook his head and thought, *Kirk can have this army business of crawling around the ground and being shot at! Give me the navy any day.*

He noted that he was at the top end of some small gullies that ran parallel to the river, but which obviously joined it further along. Beyond them a few hundred metres away was a fair-sized hill. The hill was covered with savannah woodland.

I think Grandam Cynthia's is on the other side of that, he told himself. He saw that to climb directly up over the hill would be foolish. *I will be seen, and they can move to head me off,* he thought.

So he set off going northwards, keeping in the gullies. As he did, he risked several peeks over the crest from behind trees or bushes. It was as well that he did because he saw Jan stride back across the skyline on the far side of the river.

He is going back to his Land Rover. They will try to get around ahead of me, Andrew thought. *Can I get to a telephone before they do that?*

The situation was taking on all the worst aspects of a living nightmare for Andrew and he knew he was exhausted. But necessity drove him one. He started walking as fast as his overstretched and sore muscles would allow.

But other problems now crowded in to make things worse. The gullies were steep and rough and very wearing to cross. And down in them there was no breeze and the midday sun turned them into a blazing hot reflector oven. So he sweated and blinked salt from his stinging eyes. Chafing and cuts both stung as well and his whole body seemed to be throbbing aches and pains.

As he gasped his way diagonally up the side of a hill Andrew shook his head in near despair. *I will get heat exhaustion next!*

But he struggled doggedly on, angling around the lower slopes of the hill. This meant crossing half a dozen gullies and each one became a cruel test of character as he went down and then had to haul himself up the other side. Sweat trickled and his breath came in gasps and his muscles trembled and ached.

I can't go on much longer, he thought.

Collapse from heat exhaustion became a real possibility as he stopped sweating and knew he was very thirsty. To try to get at least a cooling breeze, Andrew began angling slowly up the side of the hill, He thought he was now far enough from where he had climbed the cliffs, at least a kilometre, that he would not be seen by the other man.

Even if he did swim across to follow me, he thought. But he doubted if he had.

There was a slight breeze. But even better, as he climbed higher, Andrew saw away out to the west a long line of dark storm clouds rolling in his direction. The clouds stretched right across the horizon. Beneath them was a solid curtain of rain. There was no thunder or lightning so he looked forward to a drenching from cool rain.

Ten minutes later Andrew reached the crest at the northern end of the hill. Ahead of him appeared Mt Simon, the large black mountain on the western side of the pass. Below him to his right front he glimpsed Grandma Cynthia's and the highway. He estimated that it was about a kilometre away.

But can I make it in time?

By then the advancing storm front had reached the range of hills across the Annan Gorge. The rain looked even heavier, and Andrew licked dry lips in anticipation.

It should get here in a couple of minutes, he thought happily.

But his pleasurable anticipation changed to dismay and then fear within a few seconds. A massive bolt of lightning suddenly struck down out of the roiling black clouds. The jagged bolt hit the hills just across the river. Even before the booming echoes of the strike had ended several more lightning bolts struck down. Andrew's brain had time to think that the sudden change to a thunderstorm must have had something to do with the clouds crossing onto the rocky hills from the flat plainland beyond. Then he was moving.

A wave of cold air engulfed him along with the first patter or raindrops. But it was not the air that chilled him, it was fear. He was amazed at the speed at which the storm was moving and appalled at its sudden violence. The black clouds rolled overhead and he watched the watched the wall of heavy rain sweep across the gorge towards him. Even as it reached him he was enveloped in dazzling light. Even before his brain could say 'lightning' and the fear kick in his heart seemed to stop as a massive crack of thunder almost stunned him.

The bolt had struck the hill close behind him and even as the spasm of terror kicked in he began running. *You are right up on top of a big bare hill. Get off it!* he told himself.

Almost sobbing with fear he fled down the slope. Even as he did he was engulfed by the heavy rain. It came in a cooling, drenching downpour that made it hard to see.

Then another heart stopping crack of lightning close behind him made him run faster. Then he changed his mind and skidded sideways. Just ahead was a rocky outcrop with a small overhang on the side of it.

I will shelter there, Andrew thought.

He flung himself into the tiny space, only to find it already occupied! Two grey wallabies, eyes wide with terror, sprang up and scrabbled to get out. Then they scampered and bounded away down the slope.

They gave Andrew another fright but then he hunched in the tiny space, his own heart palpitating with fear as another lightning bolt struck somewhere up the hill nearby. Rain still drenched him and he knew he was half protruding from the pitiful cover. He was also torn by the knowledge that the longer he stayed the more he was in deadly peril from the men. To add to the cruel dilemma, he wondered if the rocks really provided any protection from the lighting.

Or will they attract it?

To add to his terror, a lightning bolt struck a tree only about fifty metres from him. At that moment, he was looking right at it and the result caused him to gulp in fear. The tree was an ironbark. Andrew had never seen a tree actually struck but was now stunned and appalled. Even as the brilliant light all but blinded him he saw the tree explode. A great shower of jagged splinters flew in every direction. Some of these even struck him, luckily without causing serious injury. The whole top of the tree disintegrated into a shower of leaves and splinters.

Panic had Andrew out of his cover and running in a second. Terrified, he bolted down the slope. Low ground became his desired location.

I must get to the cover down in the valley, he thought. But as he ran he found himself baulked by a barbed wire fence running across the slope. *Steel attracts electricity,* he thought.

Even as he did he was brought to a terrified standstill by another bolt of lightning. This struck down onto a steel fence post only twenty or thirty metres to his right front in a sizzling flash. The steel fence just vaporised before his eyes. Then the thunderclap and shock wave knocked him flat.

Oh my God! I am going to die! he thought.

His heart hammering wildly he sprang up and bolted. In a second he had leapt the fence where it had collapsed and went on down the hill, dodging around the trees and sobbing in fright. More lightning bolts struck the hill behind him to speed him on. Then they began to sizzle and crack down onto the Black Mountain ahead of him. He decided that the dense trees along the creek line at the bottom of the hill offered the best option.

Or Grandma Cynthia's if I can make it!

He could just see the farmhouse through the rain and noted it was only a few hundred metres way. So he ran on, soaked and shivering from both cold and fear. Thankfully he reached the line of trees along the creek and dashed down under them. The creek was already flowing knee deep but even as he reached it he changed his mind.

The farmhouse, he told himself.

It was only two hundred paces away up the slope through an orchard and vegetable gardens.

So he dashed up the other side of the creek and out of the trees, only to skid to a stop in horror. Jan and the other man were standing on the front porch of Grandmas Cynthia's!

Chapter 39

CRUEL CHOICES

Andrew gaped, then turned and flung himself back among the trees, slithering and scrambling on the soggy leaf mould. With his heart palpitating with fear he peeked back from under cover. As he did, he wondered how he had not noticed the dark green Land Rover parked near the side of the house. The heavy rain made it difficult to see but he knew that was what had saved him. The two men were standing with their backs to him while talking to the old couple at the front door.

Damn! What do I do now? Andrew wondered. *I can just wait until the men leave and then go to the house,* he thought.

But that option was almost immediately scotched when Jan turned and made his way to the Land Rover. As he got in Andrew saw him using a radio. Then he started the vehicle up and drove back towards the highway. The other man, still carrying his gun, vanished inside.

Andrew shook his head and thought, *I can't sneak up without taking a terrible risk. And besides, it will place Grandma Cynthia and Old Bert in danger.*

So he thought about other options he had. Two choices occurred to him: re-cross the hills and go to the pump station a few kilometres away; or go to the highway which was only a hundred metres to his right and try to thumb a lift. In his exhausted state the highway seemed a better option.

But I have to do it without them seeing me.

Carefully he slid back down into the cover of the creek bed. Once there he paused to have a drink, gulping greedily at the flow until he felt better. As he rinsed his face, he realised that the thunder and lightning had all moved east onto the main part of the Black Mountains and that the rain was already easing.

The storm will be over soon, he thought. That was no good as the rain gave him both cooler weather and water and also some cover.

After refreshing himself Andrew looked at his watch. With a shock he saw it was now nearly 2:30pm. But for the first time he could afford to relax.

Dogs won't be able to track me after all that rain, he thought. It occurred to him that he could easily hide and wait till the crooks were gone. Then he shook his head. *No I can't. They have Tina and Carmen as hostages. I must get help.*

With a stifled groan Andrew forced his stiffening muscles back into action and began creeping east up the creek. Within a few minutes he came to the end of the trees and had the highway in sight. He saw at once that it was a poor choice of location. The highway ran straight for over a kilometre and where the creek reached it was all open grass.

The other side of the farmhouse is a better spot, he thought.

He knew that the creek the other side of the farmhouse, the one where he had shot the pig, joined this one just to the west of the house. So he turned and made his way back down the creek. Ten minutes later he was at the junction of the two creeks. Cautiously he made his way eastwards up the other creek. It was not as deep and had fewer trees along it so he kept getting glimpses of the fowl shed and the house. Wondering if he had made another mistake, he crept on till he reached the bottom of the vegetable gardens.

Here he lay flat and scanned the creek bed and the back of the house. He also had another drink. There was no sign of the crook but he knew the man could be watching so he continued on hands and knees, talking great care to remain out of sight of the house. After fifty metres the creek became deeper and the vegetation thickened up. The creek flowed through jumbles of rocks and boulders now and that got Andrew anxious.

Grandma Cynthia said there were lots of Death Adders in these rocks, he remembered.

Another five minutes of creeping and crawling had Andrew crouched in a culvert at the highway. After another careful look around, he crept up the steep embankment through waist high blady grass. He saw that he had been right. To his left, the highway curved off to the right to cross the pass between Mt Simon and Black Mountain. Directly in front of him was the towering jumble of Black Mountain. For a minute Andrew stared at the massive jumble of black rocks. Then he shook his head.

I hope I don't have to try to escape over that pile, he thought.

To his right was the long straight, allowing him plenty of distance to observe approaching vehicles. The rain had now eased to a light drizzle so he could see the whole length of it clearly.

Now all I need is a car, he thought.

Fretting with impatience he lay in the grass and weeds and watched. But ten minutes crept by and no vehicle appeared. Andrew became more and more anxious. Thinking about what the men might be doing, or might have already done, to Tina and Carmen made him ill with apprehension.

They will kill them for sure, he mused.

But would they do horrible things to them before they did? It was a sickening prospect.

The sound of a vehicle reached his ears and Andrew looked hopefully to his right. Yes, a vehicle. Then his eyes focused on it. It was a large green truck.

Is that the crook's truck? he wondered.

Because of his doubts he did not dare jump up to flag it down. As it got closer, he became sure it was one of the crook's trucks and he cursed his luck. Then he became extremely anxious, wondering if he had been seen because the truck began to brake.

To his dismay, the truck came to standstill almost directly in front of him. The back wheel was so close he could almost reach out and touch it. With his heart hammering with fear Andrew hunched lower in the weeds, sweating with anxiety.

If a man gets out of the cab on this side, he must see me! he thought.

The idea caused him to break into a sweat of anxiety. Then Andrew got another shock. From close behind him came a man's voice!

Out of the corner of his eye, Andrew saw that it was the man from the farmhouse. He had both a gun and a radio and was hurrying through the long grass beside the creek. At first, Andrew thought he had been seen and he tensed ready to fight desperately. But then it became obvious he had not been seen as the man stepped out onto the highway only ten paces to Andrew's right and went on around to the other side of the truck and began talking to the driver, who had remained in his cab.

By peering under the truck Andrew could see the man's feet. He could also overhear the conversation. The truck driver asked, "Have you caught that boy yet?"

The man replied, "No. He's on this side of the river somewhere. The boss told me to wait here to try to stop him calling the cops."

"What ya gunna do when you catch him?"

"Shoot the little bugger. He's given us too much trouble," the man said.

"What about the old people?"

"Boss said to shoot them too if I have to," the man replied.

On hearing this Andrew was appalled. It also confirmed his worst fears and stiffened his resolve. The man went on to say, "Anyway. I've only got to keep him away from a phone for a few more hours. After tonight we will all be out of here."

"Amen to that," the truck driver said.

He then began asking about a man Andrew had never heard of. As Andrew considered what he had overheard, another thought came to him. *I wonder if this is the truck that got bogged?*

It looked muddy enough. Then an even more disturbing idea came to him: What if Tina, Carmen and Adele were tied up in the back? The thought that they might be just there was more than he could stand.

I must check, he thought.

After another glance to confirm that the man was still talking to the driver, Andrew stood up and in five paces was behind the truck. He knew he was taking a risk of being seen in the rear vision mirror but he just had to know. The canvas canopy was held down by the usual roped loops hooked under metal brackets and it was the work of a moment to undo one and lift the canvas. He stuck his head up inside and squinted into the dark interior.

For a few seconds Andrew could not see anything but then his eyesight adjusted to the gloom and he saw that the back was almost completely full of wooden boxes. From the green colour and markings he decided they were more rifles. But no sign of the girls. His hopes crashed and he shook his head in sick despair. He pulled his head back out and prepared to creep back into the long grass.

But as he did he heard a vehicle coming fast from the other direction. It began slowing down and Andrew bobbed down and looked under the truck. His heart gave a lurch when he saw it was Jan in the green Land Rover. Andrew tensed ready to scuttle into the grass but then heard footsteps heading along the side of the truck. For an instant Andrew considered the desperate expedient of knocking the man down and trying to get his gun to fight it out. But sanity and fear of Jan both prevailed.

I must hide! he thought.

The only place he could reach without being seen was up in the back of the truck. As quickly as he thought of it he acted. His foot went up onto a metal bar and he heaved himself up under the canvas and over the tailgate. For a moment he caught his shoulder on the canvas, but he wriggled and it came free and he slid as quietly as he could onto the floor of the tray.

Just as he did the man reached the back of the truck and the Land Rover braked to a stop. Jan's voice yelled, "Get back to that bloody farmhouse, Ken. Jake, you get moving. See you there with the last load. Ken, I will pick you up on the way past in an hour or so."

The men called assent and the truck's engine roared to life. Andrew heard the man walk past the back of the truck. He was muttering and did not sound happy but he just walked on into the grass. The Land Rover accelerated off towards Helenvale and the truck began moving towards Cooktown. Andrew lay wedged between the tailgate and the boxes and sighed with relief. Safe, for the moment!

I will jump out as soon as we round the next bend, he thought.

The truck ground its way up over the pass. Andrew got ready to jump, but to his dismay the truck increased speed until it was obvious he would be badly injured if he leapt off. All he could do was stay aboard and hope.

I must get off before they reach their destination, he thought anxiously.

The truck sped up as it went down the other side of the pass. Andrew tried to picture the road as he travelled along. Having walked all of it he could picture it but he was also able to peek out through the loose corner of the canopy flap. The truck drove on towards Cooktown across the flat country past the pump station turn-off, then crossed Trevethan Creek and continued on past the Mt Amos turn-off. For another five minutes it raced along the highway at a hundred kilometres per hour.

Then it began slowing and turned off the highway and came to a stop. Andrew risked a peek and it confirmed his thoughts.

The Archer Point turn-off. Are we going to Archer point? he wondered.

The driver got out and did something, then climbed back in. The truck drove forward a few metres and stopped and the driver climbed out again and walked back past the back of the truck. Andrew peeked through the gap in the canvas and saw that the man was putting the ROAD CLOSED sign back across the side road.

Then Andrew got another heart-stopping shock. As the man walked back towards the cab he swerved and came over to the back of the truck. For a second Andrew feared he would be found but the driver just swore and hooked the canopy rope back on its bracket. Still muttering he returned to the cab and the truck moved off.

As the truck rattled along the gravel road Andrew's mind raced. *Archer Point! Is that where they have taken Tina, Carmen and Adele?* he wondered. And how to save them? *Should I jump out and make my way to Cooktown to get the police?* he thought.

Then another frightening idea came to him: what would happen when the truck reached is destination? Presumably that would be the gun runner's lair and he would be in the middle of them. He pictured the canopy being opened by the crooks and him being found, trapped by his own stupidity!

I must get out, he thought.

But easier said than done. The truck was driving fast and the road was rough. Dust was swirling into the back and Andrew had to continually fight back the urge to sneeze. He slid his arm down outside the tailgate and pushed at the rope holding the canopy. But the man had done some sort of knot and it was much tighter. It took Andrew several very anxious minutes to work the knot loose and then slip the rope off its hook. Then he saw that he could not possibly jump out without a strong probability of injuring himself.

I will have to wait till the truck slows down, he thought.

It did a few minutes later and he crouched ready to spring out. He even had the canopy held right up out of the way before he saw he was crossing a bridge. *Can't jump here,* he thought. Then he got a horrible shock. As the truck rumbled off the bridge (Esk River he remembered) a man with a rifle stepped onto it! Luckily the man was looking the other way and was lifting a barricade and road sign back across the bridge. Andrew immediately pulled the canopy back down and sat down again while his heart recovered from the shock.

He knew they were more than halfway to Archer Point. *We will be there in a few minutes,* he told himself. That got him wondering where the crooks were going. *Up one of those side roads probably, maybe to a deserted beach?* he decided. But the truck had picked up speed again so he was still a prisoner. He began to really fret about being captured. *And then I am dead!*

The truck sped on along the dirt road and with every kilometre Andrew became more anxious and more determined.

I've got to risk it, he decided.

Once again, he lifted the canopy and nerved himself to leap out. But he knew it was going to really hurt. What bothered him the most was the thought that he might break his back and be unable to go to get help.

If that happens the girls are done for!

Then the truck slowed again and Andrew recognised the place. *We are going to cross that deep dry creek near the beach,* he thought.

Knowing he was unlikely to get a better opportunity, he climbed out and clung on with his feet on the bottom of the tailgate while he hooked the canopy rope back on. He was still not finished this when the truck ground down the steep slope to the dry creek bed and then turned to drive up the other side. As it began the ascent, Andrew dropped off the back, landing lightly on both feet. His next move was to throw himself sideways onto the sand and to roll away to the left.

Within seconds he was behind a tree and the truck had gone up the slope, leaving a haze of dust in its wake. Andrew crouched under cover and looked warily around in case there were more crooks. He was now getting paranoid about how many there seemed to be. When silence had settled and he was satisfied there was no-one nearby he turned and walked away up the dry creek bed. This was out of sight of the road as the creek did a sharp bend at that point. But he knew he was leaving footprints so he went slowly and brushed them out. Then he sat in the cover of a bush fifty metres from the road and tried to decide what to do next.

Andrew found he was now presented with some cruel choices: to go back and to try to get to Cooktown; or to go on and try to rescue the girls. Common sense said go back but his emotions said go on. In his head he totalled up the distances. To walk back to the highway was about 10 kilometres.

And I have to go cross-country, or I risk stumbling into their vehicles; and I have to detour around that guard at the Esk River Bridge, he thought.

And once at the highway he had to get away from the turn-off before he tried to flag down a car.

I can do it, he told himself. A check of his watch showed him the time. *Ten to four!* he thought in astonishment. *I have been on the run for over four hours.*

It seemed more like four days. He applied maths to the problem.

Twelve kilometres, cross-country at perhaps 3kph meant 4 hours to reach the highway. *That is 20:00, then another half hour or hour to get to Cooktown.*

Into his mind came the memory of that long, lonely road at night and he wondered gloomily if there would be any vehicles. *Must be. Anyway it has to be risked.*

Then another thought came to him. *It will be dark by the time I get the cops. It will be a big help if I can find the crook's hideout and can give the police a map of the layout.* It was a skill he had watched Kirk and the Army Cadets do on an exercise and it had impressed him then. *I am only a kilometre from the beach so they can't be far,* he thought.

But that would add a couple of hours to the times. For a few more minutes he agonised over the decision. And the more he thought about it the more sense it made to be able to take definite information to the police.

I will do a reconnaissance, he decided. *Then go and get help.*

Chapter 40

THE DEVIL AND THE DEEP BLUE SEA

Having made his decision Andrew forced himself to his feet. He felt exhausted, bruised, battered, frightened, thirsty, and hungry, but also very determined.

I have just regained Tina's love. I am not going to give up just because it hurts, he thought.

He set off walking through the scrub, keeping about 50 metres from the line of the road. There was plenty of cover, too much in places as he encountered tangles of lantana and prickly weeds that he had to detour around. Along the way he crossed a rough vehicle track going north. It was one of the places he had expected the crooks to hide but even a casual glance showed that no vehicles had been along it for a long time. He reached the base of the mountain behind Archer Point and went to the south of it, still keeping near the road. There were more thickets of lantana and scrub but ten minutes of steady movement had him in sight of the ocean. For no reason he could articulate that cheered him up and he sniffed the sea air.

From his memory of the fishing trip he had a vague hope that there might be campers at the beach or even a boat but another five minutes of cautious sneaking forward showed him an empty bay and no sign of any camps or vehicles under the trees. Nor were there any of the crook's vehicles visible.

So where did they go? he wondered.

To answer that, Andrew crept down to the road at the point where a track went off to the south along the back of the beach in Walsh Bay. The wheel tracks of heavy vehicles all went on east towards Archer Point.

Archer Point? he wondered. He had imagined that smugglers would use a secluded cove or a hidden mangrove creek.

For a couple of minutes he studied the lie of the land. It was as he remembered it. The lower slopes of the mountain were all grass with almost no cover. Nor was there much cover beside the beach, which turned into a straggly patch of mangroves and then rocks. The only safe

376

way forward was about a hundred metres back from the roads on the lower ground where there were clumps of bushes and outcrops of rocks.

Andrew checked his watch and saw that it was already 16:40. That worried him. *I have wasted nearly an hour since I got off the truck,* he thought. As quickly as he safely could, he set off through the long grass and bushes towards the low hill that overlooked the old port. *I should get a good view from up there,* he reasoned.

As he moved, he kept continually scanning for any sign of movement, either by people or vehicles. But all he saw were distant sea birds. It took him 15 minutes to cover the 300 metres to the low saddle at the back of the hill and another five to creep up to where the road to the lighthouse crossed over. As he went up the back of the hill he was very conscious that he must be visible to anyone coming from the same direction as him so he kept crouching down and looking back. There was also the possibility of a watcher in the vicinity of the lighthouse, now higher up to his left. But he saw no sign of any movement or vehicles there. He strained his ears for the sounds of any vehicles but found the strong sea breeze was interfering with that.

Andrew went across the road at a low crouch just to the left of the turn-off to the flat area on top. Almost at once the whole horizon opened up ahead of him. Then, step by step he was able to see more of the sea and of the bay below him. The rocky island with the little lighthouse came back into view and then the tip of the old wharf.

Two more steps revealed to Andrew a man standing out on the old wharf. This appeared to be piled with heaps of boxes. At that, point Andrew went down on his hands and knees and began to crawl.

I've found the crooks! he thought. *But where are the girls?*

Andrew crawled right to the forward lip of the hill top. From there the situation became clear. The old wharf had been given a temporary timber deck and this and the breakwater were stacked with piles of boxes, most covered by dark coloured tarpaulins. Parked with its back to the old wharf was a large green truck with a canvas canopy. Nearby, on the parking space between the end of the hill and the old wharf, were two more large trucks. Two men were sitting near them. To Andrew's surprise one of them was Barry.

So where is Little Terry? Andrew wondered. But there was no sign of the girls. *Maybe they are still in one of the trucks?* he conjectured.

It was obvious to Andrew that the smugglers were planning to use the old wharf. What really surprised him was the quantity of cargo stacked ready to load. There were places at the foot of the hill, including the access road, that Andrew could not see and he wondered if the girls were there. But it was too risky for him to try to creep any further forward.

Not enough cover and one of those men might spot me, he thought.

Shaking his head with regret at not finding the girls he decided it was time to head back to get help. His watch said 17:20. It would mean a lot of night movement but he decided he would risk moving along the road in the dark. So he turned and started crawling back off the crest.

But he hadn't gone five metres before he heard a vehicle. It was coming from the land side and fast. Andrew flattened himself in the grass just in case. It was as well that he did because a few seconds later the green Land Rover roared up to the turn-off and swung onto the open space only ten metres from him. It stopped and out of it climbed Jan and the man who had been at Grandma Cynthia's. The man had his gun, radio, and binoculars.

As both men walked over to the back of the hilltop near the road junction, Andrew heard Jan say, "You stay up here on guard, just in case any busy-body snooper or fool of a fisherman should get past the guard."

Jan then strode back to the seaward side of the hill top and stared out to sea. Andrew lay flat in the grass, sweating with fear and trembling in every muscle from tension and over-exhaustion.

Blast! he thought. It was very obvious that to try to go back the way he had come was now impossible. *I can't possibly sneak across all that open ground without being spotted by this bloke.*

A careful look towards Archer Point showed him that there was no reasonable chance of sneaking off in that direction either. From where the guard stood he could see all the landward approaches to the hill. It dawned on Andrew that he was trapped.

I am caught between the devil and the deep blue sea! he thought.

Having realised his position Andrew just lay low. He was trapped but still alive. *And they have no idea I am here. Maybe I can still do something?* he reasoned.

So he lay there, shivering and scared while Jan stood nearby talking on his little radio and looking out to sea. *What is he looking at?* Andrew wondered.

Very cautiously he screwed his head around and looked out to sea. Within seconds he had spotted what he expected to see: a shape out on the horizon.

A ship, and heading this way, he noted. He had assumed that the smugglers would be using a fast launch so was surprised. *But then, considering the amount of cargo they have there they will need a ship,* he reasoned.

To Andrew's great relief Jan went back to the Land Rover and got in. After starting it up he drove off. This time he turned right and drove down the hill.

He is probably going to the wharf, Andrew guessed.

He was right. A minute later he heard the Land Rover drive past below him. The access road was hidden from him but the Land Rover reappeared at the parking area near the trucks. It was parked and Jan got out and began talking to the three men.

Without Jan standing nearby Andrew was able to safely slither a few metres further from the clearing. He went left and down behind some rocks. Here he was able to stretch out and relax.

I will wait till it is dark, then sneak away, he decided.

There was plenty to occupy him as he lay there. To begin with there was the approaching ship. But there were also his physical and mental states. His body began suffering cramps and muscle spasms and he experienced frequent bouts of shivering as his over-taxed muscles reacted. He was thirsty and very tired. But worst of all he was deeply distressed.

Where is Tina? And where are Carmen and Adele? he fretted. *And what horrible things might have been done to them?* Love, care and jealousy combined to torment him, making him deeply angry at the men.

The sun went off Andrew and he saw with a shock that it was nearly 18:30. By then the ship was close enough in for him to note that it was a rusty old coaster with two masts and its superstructure at the stern.

Something familiar about that ship, he thought.

He was right. When it was only a few hundred metres offshore it slowed and turned side on to reveal that it was the old freighter that had been arrested by the HMAS *Armidale*.

Hmm. Commander McDowall was right, they were up to something fishy, Andrew thought.

379

The ship lowered a motor boat which then acted as tug to help swing its stern towards the shore. The ship then dropped an anchor and proceeded stern first towards the wharf.

He has dropped a kedge anchor to help haul himself out again if the wind and tide are against him, Andrew thought, noting the wave pattern that was coming inshore. The wind was dropping but he noted that the tide was coming in.

It was dusk by the time the motor launch had carried a line to the wharf. The ship was eased in and tied up. Gangways were placed across onto the temporary planking. Andrew noted that the ship already had its hatch covers off. The motor boat helped push the ship against the wharf and was then secured outboard and the two men in it climbed aboard up a rope ladder. As soon as the ship was secured, men began carrying boxes up the gangways, to be passed down into the hold.

The last of the sun went off the distant heights of Mt Finegan and Andrew decided it was time to start creeping away. But even as he started crawling he heard the sound of another vehicle coming from inland. So he lay under cover and peeked around the side of a rock. He glimpsed the canopy of another large truck as it went over the back of the hill. Then he heard it slow down and turn right onto the wharf access road. Another glimpse of its canopy showed briefly just near the bushes where Andrew had found Tina and Cousin Sandy during the fishing trip. It came to a stop in the parking area.

Out of curiosity Andrew moved back to his vantage point to look. What he saw made him gasp and his heart started hammering and tightening up with apprehension. Climbing out of the back of the truck was Tina! A guard covered her with a gun, but Andrew was relieved to see that as far as he could tell Tina's clothes had not been torn or damaged.

Maybe she is alright? he thought.

Carmen and Adele climbed down to join Tina. Jan strode over and spoke briefly to the guard and pointed to the ship.

Oh no! Andrew thought. *They are being put on board the ship!*

They were. The three girls were marched aboard and vanished out of sight into the superstructure. Andrew was dismayed. He had pictured the police rescuing the girls, possibly from a hostage situation, but on dry land.

How can they rescue them now? he wondered. Then another awful possibility struck him. *At the rate these men are loading those boxes this ship will be gone long before daybreak.*

Once again Andrew did the time calculations, allowing 5 hours to reach the highway and one more to contact the police. *Then one or two for them to react. And I can't leave here till it is fully dark, which is about 19:30, or that guard will spot me. That makes about eight hours minimum; say between 03:30 and 04:00 before the cops arrive. That is nearly daylight. I'll bet that ship is planning to be well away from the coast before then.*

But what to do? Andrew again faced an agony of decision making. He was helped by noting that even Jan was helping load boxes. Then the guard was called down the hill as floodlights were turned on over the working area. The guard also began carrying boxes.

If they are that short of men, will they waste a man guarding the girls; or will they have them locked in a cabin or storeroom? Andrew wondered, which gave him the germ of another idea that rapidly crystalised into a plan. *I will get aboard and use their radio to call for help, then try to free the girls,* he decided. He knew it was foolish and potentially fatal but having found Tina and his sister he felt compelled to try to save them.

But how to get aboard? *I will have to swim and climb up that rope ladder from the motor boat,* Andrew decided.

That seemed the best plan as it meant approaching from the side away from where the men were working. Anywhere else was too risky. But it had the huge disadvantage from Andrew's perspective of requiring him to swim in the sea at night. He had done so before on a number of occasions and had found it a truly terrifying experience. Now he just gritted his teeth and tried not to think about it.

Navy Clearance Divers do it all the time and they don't get eaten by sharks, he told himself.

It was as dark as it was going to get by then, which wasn't very dark. Between the half-moon and the ship's working lights the whole area seemed to be lit up.

I will just have to hope that nobody is looking, he thought as he began climbing slowly down the grassy hillside.

It took Andrew five minutes to edge his way down the slope to the access road. He reached it near the bushes where he had confronted Cousin Sandy and Tina and the memory caused him a spurt of jealous anger. But the bushes provided good cover and he slipped across the access road and carefully made his way down the rocks beyond to the beach.

For a minute or two he crouched in the shadows of the rocks there and studied the scene. The sea looked like rippling silver in the moonlight but he reasoned that it would look different from another direction. The wind had dropped almost completely and the waves were only a few centimetres high, almost ideal for what he intended. Knowing how difficult it is to swim in footwear he sat and removed his boots and socks. These were placed neatly under a bush. Then he stood and stared at the ship for a few frightened seconds.

With a sigh he forced himself to move, "Come on you coward! You are just putting it off because you are scared," he told himself.

He was too. He was terrified. And the water was cold. And the sharp and slippery rocks hurt his feet and were painful to walk on. As he waded cautiously in he shivered and flinched. When it reached his thighs he stopped, shivering with overexertion and fear. With another effort of willpower he resumed wading and then, as sharp rock hurt his toes, slid in to begin breast stroking.

Within seconds, Andrew was hyperventilating and sobbing with fear. He had the horrible feeling that at any second some huge set of teeth would grab his feet as they dangled down. The urge to draw them up was all but irresistible. It took all of his resources of courage to keep on swimming out into that dark ocean.

Stop being silly! You are being irrational, he told himself as he battled with the urge to turn back. But then he remembered that Carmen or Tina had said they had seen a shark right in this very bit of the bay. *And I saw something big in the water,* he remembered; the image of that flitting shadow rising like a spectre to grip his throat and chest.

But he kept on swimming. Other considerations began to take over. A wave bigger than usual splashed into his face, making him cough and splutter. He tasted the salt and that reminded him just how thirsty he was. And the effort of swimming was taxing his tired muscles, and he could feel his energy draining away.

I hope I don't get a cramp, he thought, knowing how over-worked his muscles were. Fear of possible drowning came to equal fear of being attacked by some denizen of the deep.

And the moon did not help. It made every wave a small silhouette and most of them had a triangular shape that set his heart leaping with fear in case it was a shark's fin. Despite this he swam out for at least a hundred metres before he changed direction and began to swim towards the ship. It was at least two hundred metres away and Andrew began to wonder if he had miscalculated his own strength. Several times he stopped swimming to tread water or float to get his breath back. But the fear was too great.

I must get aboard, was how he put it, to mask his own shame at being such a coward.

As he approached the ship Andrew saw that the side away from the wharf was mostly in shadow and there was only an occasional glimpse of the men. They appeared to be all working at the forward hold and there was no sign of any lookouts or guards. Hoping that this was so, he kept on swimming. The ship appeared closer and closer by the minute, but the swim was hard work.

Suddenly, when he was only a few metres from the ship, Andrew got a fright that seemed to stop his heart. He swam onto something floating just on the surface that was hard and rough and scaly!

Shark! No crocodile! his already frightened mind screamed.

To his horror, the thing bumped hard against him, and he grabbed at it to fend it off.

Then he got an even bigger shock. The object he was clinging to was the mine!

And the thing he had grabbed was one of the projecting horns, the detonator that caused the mine to explode!

Chapter 41

TRAINING TELLS

For several seconds Andrew clung to the mine, frozen with fear. As the first wave of shock wore off, he tried to back away, only to make another terrifying discovery. The mine was all tangled in an old fishing net and this had snagged his left foot. With his heart hammering in his choked-up throat Andrew ducked under and carefully untangled himself. He then pushed himself away from the mine. Once free he noted that the netting appeared to be snagged to the ship somehow.

The current or waves could push this thing against the ship's side at any moment! he thought.

It was a horrifying prospect and raised another cruel dilemma: having called for help and rescued the girls should he somehow warn the crooks?

First things first, Andrew told himself. *First try to call for help.*

Having decided that he looked up to check no-one was watching, then breast stroked along the side to the motorboat. Getting aboard it was easy. Years of reboarding capsized sailing boats gave him the experience. This, coupled with fear gave him both the skill and the strength to haul himself silently aboard.

For a few seconds he lay there, sighing with relief and letting the water drain and dribble off him. As he waited he looked anxiously up at the ship's rail above him. A shudder went through him as he imagined getting caught. But then he got to his feet and made himself go up the rope ladder until his head was just level with the deck. Here he paused to look both ways. The deck was deserted and mostly in shadows.

Now that he was out of the water Andrew felt much more confident. Ships were something he was very familiar with and some of his courage returned. He even became excited. Coupled with his determination to rescue the girls it gave him the strength to go on. Instead, of climbing over the rail onto the deck he stood up on the rail and reached up to grab handholds on the next level. Having found firm holds he clambered up the outside of the superstructure and hauled himself up onto the next deck. This was the boat deck behind the wheelhouse and bridge.

Andrew did not expect to find anyone there but just in case he crouched under the lifeboat and looked carefully. A shiver ran through him, partly from the feel of the cold steel deck under his wet, bare feet, but also from fear. Only a few paces away was one of the doors leading into the wheelhouse. That was his first objective.

The radio should be in there, or in a cabin leading off it, he reasoned from his knowledge of various ships.

The wheelhouse was in semi-darkness but just in case there was a man on watch Andrew first peeked cautiously over the window sill of the door. No-one was visible but he could not see all of the space without going in. Very quietly he gripped the door handle and opened the door. Then he poked his head around the corner to look. Nobody.

"So far so good!" Andrew muttered.

He slipped through the door and quietly closed it behind him. Then he checked the layout. It was a very conventional if somewhat old-fashioned set-up with the binnacle and steering in the centre front. To starboard of that were a radar display and echo sounder, then a chart table. To port was what Andrew sought, a radio set. And it was switched on. A glowing diode on the console told him that.

Wishing that he had some sort of weapon, just in case, Andrew padded across to the radio, noting as he did that the layout was as expected. A companionway at the rear led down a lighted stairwell into the superstructure from behind the captain's chair and another door on the far side of the wheelhouse led aft onto the starboard boat deck.

Next, Andrew stepped forward and looked down at the well deck. *A ship like this should have a crew of about half a dozen at least,* he reasoned, totalling up captain, mate, a couple of engineers, the cook, bosun and a couple of deckhands. But this was plainly no ordinary merchant ship. *They are gun runners and smugglers so they are liable to act like pirates. If get caught I am food for the fishes,* he thought.

He shuddered with fear and then breathed deeply to calm himself. For a few more seconds he watched the men busily lowering boxes into the forward hold. The well deck was lit up by the overhead lights so Andrew could see them very clearly. They were a rough looking lot and among them were Jan and Barry and the other men of that gang.

"Get on with it. No time to lose," Andrew told himself.

But it took a conscious act of bravery to turn away and move to the radio. For a few seconds he studied it and then nodded with relief. It was an ordinary marine radio of the type he had often seen at Navy Cadets and on the Kirk family ships. Sucking in deep gulps of air to steady his racing heart he clicked the frequency to the one he knew the RAN used for its patrol boats.

That should get a quicker response than the normal marine radio, he reasoned.

Then he spoke, knowing he could be precipitating his own death if he was caught in the act. "Mayday! Mayday! Mayday! Calling the navy. This is the M.V. *Kanar Matu*. Mayday! Mayday! Mayday! Archer Point, over!"

He released the 'transmit' and listened. There was a pause and then some static crackled before a voice answered. "This is HMAS *Armidale*. Say again Motor Vessel calling Mayday at Archer Point, over."

Andrew could not believe his luck. *Armidale!* he thought. He quickly repeated the message. HMAS *Armidale* answered at once and Andrew went on, "This is Navy Cadet Andrew Collins. I am on board the MV *Kanar Matu* at Archer Point. The ship is a smuggler loading guns and the crew do not know I am on board. But they have three girls prisoner on board. At the old wharf at Archer Point are six men with trucks and a Land Rover who are loading guns and ammunition onto the ship. Send the police at once, over."

This time when the radio answered it was a different voice. "This is the CO of *Armidale*. Confirm your identity if you can."

Andrew smiled with relief. "Sir, this is Navy Cadet Andrew Collins. I was on board your ship when we discovered the old mine on Hope Island. You are Lieutenant Commander McDowall. Your XO is Lieutenant Forster. One of the girls who is being held prisoner by the smugglers is Navy Cadet Tina Babcock who was also on that voyage with us."

Lt Cdr McDowall then asked Andrew a number of detailed questions about his ship and ship's company, all of which Andrew was able to answer instantly. Apparently convinced that the call was not a hoax Lt Cdr McDowall then got Andrew to explain the situation in detail.

Then he said, "Now Cadet Collins, you get off that ship and somewhere safe until we arrive, over."

"Yes sir," Andrew answered, even though he had no intention of obeying. Then another worrying thought came to him and he said, "Sir, that old German mine we found, the one that floated off Hope Island. It is here, drifting in the bay and I think it is snagged to the ship by an old fish net, over."

"Roger, now get off the ship and somewhere safe. We will get things rolling, over."

"Yes sir, out!" Andrew answered.

Shuddering with relief he breathed out and then in. A feeling of intense satisfaction surged through him. *That was the easy bit. I have warned the authorities and the navy are on the way. The smugglers won't get away. Now I have to save Tina and Carmen,* he thought. But where were they? *Someone below,* Andrew reasoned.

To check on the smugglers he stepped to the front of the bridge and again looked down at the well deck. The men were still hurrying back and forth loading the boxes and none even glanced up at the wheelhouse.

They are all busy, so this is my chance, he thought.

Andrew padded over to the central companionway and began sneaking down it. As he did, he was engulfed by the 'ship' smell he was so familiar with, that compound odour of salt, rotting marine organisms, paint, diesel fumes and human smells.

At the bottom he found himself in a companionway that led fore and aft with cabins, store rooms, the galley to starboard and a large eating mess to port. Logic told Andrew not to waste time on this deck.

This is where the crew live and eat, he told himself. *The next deck down is a better bet.*

The squeak of a door hinge sent Andrew scuttling over under the long table. The door was the one that opened out onto the well deck and through it came two men. From under the table Andrew stared at them with horror, his heart hammering with fear and his mouth dry. One was Jan and the other was a big man with a black beard. Both went to the stove in the galley and the bearded man handed Jan a cup and then poured what Andrew supposed was coffee into it.

Jan thanked 'Blackbeard', and while he also poured a cup said, "What do you think we should do with these girls; sell them into the white slave trade or just get rid of them?"

Blackbeard took a gulp of the coffee and then shook his head. "Nah, just get rid of them. We will keep them as hostages until we are near Bunga Lunga and then throw them over the side. A length of steel wire rope should take them to Davy Jones's Locker very nicely. The boys can amuse themselves with them until then."

Jan grunted and drank his coffee. Blackbeard then finished his and said, "Heads are just there. Come on, I want to be under way by midnight if I can."

He then went back out and Jan went to the toilet. Andrew remained crouched in his hiding place, quivering with fear and sickened and appalled at the callous way the men had discussed the girl's fate. The thought of Tina and his sister being so abused and then being subjected to such a horrible death made him ill. But it also steeled his determination.

I must find them, he thought.

He remained in hiding until Jan came out of the toilet and went back outside. Only after the door had been closed did Andrew crawl out and look around.

Directly below the steps he had come down was another companionway leading below so he scurried around to it and went padding silently down. As he got lower, he bent double to peer along the corridor that was revealed to him. It was as he had expected: more cabins and storerooms, and another set of steps leading down to what the noise and smell told him must be the engine room. The sounds of the huge diesels and pumps, generators and the fans that ventilated the ship made it difficult for him to hear. No-one was visible so he stepped off the steps onto the second deck and looked both ways.

Right beside the stairs on the starboard side was a door. Andrew stepped across and tried the handle. The door opened at once to reveal a musty storeroom full of what looked like carpenter's stores and tools. Disappointed but hopeful Andrew moved to the next door aft of that. This was a steel door and was locked. That was good sign so he tried the handle again, then knocked as loudly as he dared on the door.

"Tina! Tina! Are you in there?" he called.

To Andrew's relief, she answered. "Yes! Oh Andrew! Is that you?"

"Yes. Is Carmen with you?"

"Yes, and Adele. Oh Andrew, get us out," Tina cried.

"I will. I just need to get a key," Andrew replied.

Then a sixth sense made the hair on his head prickle, and he glanced over his shoulder, just in time to see a bearded man raising his arm to strike him down!

The glitter of the descending knife caused Andrew to give a convulsive jerk and to spring aside. Even as he did, his mind took in the appearance and identity of the unshaven ruffian holding the knife. Black eye patch; one ear missing, scarred face, a steel hook on the other arm, and wooden 'peg leg', he noted.

Ben Silver! Long John Silver! Andrew thought.

Andrew was just quick enough to avoid the deadly blow. He sprang back and looked frantically around for either a weapon or a means of escape. Long John Silver staggered and clutched at a fire extinguisher in an attempt to regain his balance. As he did, his eyes widened with recognition.

"You! You little bastard!" he screamed. Then he launched himself into another attack, the knife this time sweeping up in a deadly scything arc toward Andrew's stomach.

He means to kill me, Andrew thought.

He was surprised, but then he wasn't, to find Long John Silver on board the ship. They had met half a dozen times over the last few years and each time Long John had been up to no good as either a pirate or a smuggler. By a frantic jump backwards Andrew caused the knife to miss but in doing so he cannoned into the stairs and badly bruised himself.

Long John Silver swore loudly and then began to yell for help. That set Andrew's already racing heart hammering even faster.

I must get away, he thought.

But he reasoned that to turn his back on Long John Silver to try to get up the stairs would be fatal. Instead, he danced sideways, causing Long John Silver to hobble and shuffle around to keep facing him. Then Andrew did something he was not proud of but which the desperate situation seemed to demand: he grabbed the fire extinguisher off the wall and flung it at Long John's peg leg.

The heavy fire extinguisher struck only a glancing blow but Long John's attempt to avoid it put him off balance and Andrew followed up by rushing in and pushing. Long John crashed over backwards and his knife went flying along the corridor away from both of them. For an instant Andrew considered trying to jump over Long John to get the knife but he knew he would not be able to bring himself to stab the man so instead he turned and fled up the stairs.

Straight into the clutches of a hairy bear of a man!

Andrew glimpsed him just before a stunning blow pounded into the right side of his head. As he fell at the top of the stairs, Andrew felt a huge hand grip his arm. Then he was punched again. The blow sent him reeling on the edge of unconsciousness.

The big bear of a man yelled, "Hey Cap'n Hayes, come an' see what I caught!"

Failed! Andrew thought, thinking of how close he had come to rescuing the girls. Then fear flooded in and he could not get his knees to function and nearly lost control of his bowels as Long John Silver came stumping up the stairs, knife in hand and murder in his enraged eye.

Long John made a lunge at Andrew but Big Bear heaved him easily out of reach. "Take it easy Long John, wait till the cap'n has spoken to him," he said.

"I will murder the little bastard!" Long John screamed, waving the knife wickedly close to Andrew's face.

At that moment, the captain, the big man with the black beard, hurried through the door, followed by Jan.

"What the devil is going on?" the captain asked angrily.

Long John Silver stabbed the knife towards Andrew, causing him to flinch and fear for his left eye. "I caught this little bugger sniffin' around the cabin where them girls is locked up."

Jan cried out in disbelief. "You! How the devil did you get here?" He turned to the captain. "This is the little mongrel we were chasing."

Long John Silver butted in and cried, "Let me kill 'im, Captain Hayes sir. I got a score to settle with the bit o' toad dung. It was 'im an' his sister what done all this to me." He gestured to his eye and ear and then held up his steel hook.

Andrew nodded with grim satisfaction. *We did too,* he thought remembering those adventures: the eye on Endeavour Island after he had knocked him out and taken him prisoner; the leg when he was rescued from the wreckage of a trawler in Bowling Green Bay after a cyclone; the sword scar on his face and the ear in another sword fight in the Whitsunday Islands the previous July; and most recently the hand, blown off during a fight over buried treasure in Bowen last September holidays.

Even though he was in mortal fear it gave Andrew savage satisfaction to see his enemy aroused, so he said, "We did too, captain. You want to watch out, Long John. What will you get chopped off this time?"

Long John's response was to lunge at him but Captain Hayes held him back. "Back off, Long John. Wait till we have questioned him. Then you can have him. Now, did he set those girls free?"

Long John Silver held up a set of keys that were hooked to his belt. "No, Captain sir, I got the keys right here still."

Captain Hayes turned to Andrew and said, "How did you get aboard this ship?"

"Swam," Andrew replied. With his damp clothes he thought that was obvious.

"How did you know about this ship?"

"I didn't, not until I saw you sail in and anchor," Andrew replied.

His mind was now racing with a story that might keep him and the girls alive. *Do I tell them that I have warned the navy or not? If I tell them will they hold us as hostages? Or kill me out of spite?*

Jan now asked, "But how did you know to come here? Last I saw of you was when you crossed the Annan River Gorge."

Andrew made no answer to this so Captain Hayes nodded and Big Bear twisted his left ear so hard he feared it might be torn off.

"Speak up boy! The cap'n he asked you a question."

Andrew remained stubbornly silent so Big Bear hit him and then slapped his face. Still he would not answer. Jan shook his head and said, "Don't keep hitting him. Thumping just dulls the senses. We will find out what he is really afraid of and then hurt him badly if he doesn't tell."

That sent a chill through Andrew but the next suggestion made him feel like throwing up. Long John Silver said, "We could do things to those girls he was trying to rescue. You know, rape 'em and mutilate 'em and so on. I know he really cares about his sister, so that should loosen his tongue."

"You evil filth!" Andrew cried. But he knew he was beaten.

I can't let that happen, he thought, but there was also the doubt that even after he had talked such unspeakable atrocities might still be inflicted on Carmen and Tina. It was too horrible for his mind to bear so he said, "You may as well give up. The police are on their way."

"How the hell do the police know?" Jan snarled, grabbing Andrew's shirt and forgetting his own advice while he punched him in the mouth.

This broke one of Andrew's molars on the right and sent an agonising stab of pain through his head but he still managed a smile of triumph.

"Because I told them," he replied.

For a second so much hatred flared in Jan's eyes that Andrew feared he would be killed there and then. But Captain Hayes shouted at him, "How did you do that? When did you do that?"

"Hours ago," Andrew lied. He did not say how.

Captain Hayes glared at him, obviously unsure whether to believe him or not. "Who is this kid?' he snapped.

"Just a schoolkid whose parents are running the Lions Den hotel during the holidays," Jan replied.

Captain Hayes looked puzzled. He turned to Long John Silver and said, "So how come you have tangled so badly with him, Long John?"

"He's a bloody navy cadet," Long John answered, glaring at Andrew.

Captain Hayes appeared to blanch. "Navy! Christ! Has he told the navy too?" he shouted. He grabbed Andrew and shook him violently. "Have you told the navy about us, kid?"

"Yes, so you may as well give up now, and let us go free. It will make things easier for you at your trial." It was a slim card to play but he was clutching at straws now.

"How could he do that?" Jan queried.

"Radio!" Captain Hayes shouted. He turned and went thundering up the companionway to the wheelhouse, Andrew heard a loud blasphemy and then the captain slid back down the stairs, his face back with rage. "The smart little bugger has used our radio! But he wasn't clever enough to remember to switch it back to the frequency it was on. Damn you!" he shouted, waving his fist in Andrew's face.

Then he turned to Jan and said, "We have to get going. There will be a patrol boat sailing from Cairns as quick as may be. We need to be in international waters by daybreak. Get your men off the ship. Stop loading!"

"But we have a deal! You can't just cut and run!" Jan argued.

"Deal be damned! Bosun, get the men to stop loading and get the ship ready to sail. I want to be under way in fifteen minutes."

The two men continued to argue but Mister Bear, the bosun, handed Andrew into Long John's eager grasp and went forward shouting men's names. Long John Silver jabbed Andrew in the ribs with his knife, and said, "Don't try anything silly, cully."

Captain Hayes said, "Don't cut him, cookie. We might need them

C.R. Cummings

as hostages. Now come on man, get your men off the ship!" He began herding a still protesting Jan forward.

With that Andrew played the last card he could think of. "Captain Sir, don't move your ship. It might be blown up."

"Blown up? Blown up by what?" Captain Hayes demanded to know.

"A mine, a World War Two German naval mine. It was laid by the surface raider *Pinguin* in 1941. It is floating just near your ship. If you move the ship it could strike it and cause it to detonate."

"World War Two mine! Are you crazy?"

"No sir. We found it a couple of weeks ago on Hope Island but it floated away before the navy clearance divers could blow it up. I saw it when I was swimming out to your ship."

Captain Hayes frowned and looked as though he believed him. Then he shook his head. "I don't believe you. Anyway, a mine that old won't go off."

"It might," Andrew answered, trying to remember the details he had heard.

"Maybe, but I have to take that risk. And if it does blow this ship up you will go up with it. Put him in with his little girl friends Long John," Captain Hayes instructed. He then turned and shepherded Jan out through the door onto the well deck.

Long John leered at Andrew, and said, "Down below, me bucko! If there is a mine you go down with the ship."

At the thought of being trapped inside a sinking ship, Andrew almost collapsed as terror flooded through him.

No! How can I avoid that? he wondered.

393

Chapter 42

PINGUIN'S MINE

Terrifying images of being trapped underwater in the wreck of the *Merinda* flooded through Andrew's mind. It was more than he could face and he began to sob.

In desperation he cried out to Long John Silver, "But there is a mine. I can show it to you!"

"Crap! You are just trying to fool me," Long John Silver replied.

"I'm not! I really did see it. Come out on deck and I will show you," Andrew begged. He was crying now, the fear all but overwhelming him.

"You just want to try to escape," Long John Silver retorted. "Now get below!"

He was right of course. Andrew could see through the door and the tantalising glimpses of possible freedom and the wafts of fresh air all filled him with a desperate desire to get outside. Long John Silver began to lose patience. He pricked the knife into Andrew's ribs and snarled to get moving. But Andrew feared the knife less than drowning so he clung on to the railings and pleaded to be allowed to stay on deck.

Long John Silver dug the knife deeper, drawing blood and threatening to shove it right in if he didn't move. Andrew clung to the rail in terror and shook his head. He knew he was sweating and was ashamed of his loss of courage but could not help it. He heard shouted orders and saw a gangway pulled aboard. Then a man cast off a mooring line.

"They mustn't! The mine is snagged on the ship somehow," Andrew wailed.

Long John Silver lost his temper and struck him a savage blow to the side of the head with the end of the knife handle. He did it so quickly Andrew had no time to react. Half stunned he sagged at the knees and nearly fell to the deck. A vicious kick in his left knee accomplished this and he screamed and then let go with one hand. Long John Silver immediately hammered his other hand with the knife handle and then shoved him hard. Andrew lost his grip and found himself being dragged by one arm which was twisted up behind his back.

He found himself being dragged down the stairs and another wave of panic surged through him. In desperation he snatched at a railing and at the same time lashed out with his feet. Long John Silver swore as he was hit. His reaction was to hit back and then to stab with the knife. This took Andrew in the face, the point driving in to strike bone just above his right eye. Blood at once began to trickle down into his eye, making him blink.

A spasm of rage coupled to Andrew's fear gave him the strength to grab Long John's arm. At the same time he went into a frenzy of kicking. Long John screamed in anger and let go of the rail with his steel claw and grabbed at Andrew's throat with it. Both began slipping and tumbling down the stairs. Andrew did not dare let go of that wrist that was holding the knife, the point of which was aimed at his left eye from only a few centimetres away. Panic surged as Andrew strained to hold the knife off.

He is stronger than me! he thought. And the steel claw was digging into his windpipe choking him!

Desperation produced an idea his father had taught him. Taking the risk that his right arm was strong enough to hold the knife away for a few seconds, he let go with his left. He then used this to grab the little finger of Long John Silver's knife hand. Knowing his life was at stake, Andrew yanked this as hard as he could, and kept on twisting. Long John screamed as the little finger broke. His hand flew open and the knife went bouncing down the stairs, making a metallic tinkle as it did.

Long John Silver went berserk. He screamed in pain and rage and tried to choke Andrew with the metal claw. But while the steel of the claw was strong it could not exert enough pressure and Andrew grabbed at that arm with his own left. The two rolled and tumbled further and suddenly Long John let go and let out a shrill scream of agony. Andrew broke free and fell flat on the deck at the bottom of the stairs.

Frantic to escape he wiped blood from his eye and rolled over. He was just in time. During the struggle on the stairs Long John Silver's wooden leg had poked through between the treads and been twisted almost off. Now Long John was free and on his feet, looking wilder than ever. His little finger was sticking out at an odd angle and was definitely broken but he was still able to stump around on the peg leg. And the knife was right at his feet.

Andrew hesitated to dive for it and then realised he had made a mistake as Long John Silver bent and scooped it up. He had difficulty holding it in his injured hand but it was still a deadly weapon. He advanced and Andrew backed off. He glanced behind him looking for another way out and saw that there was a closed watertight door at the end of the flat. But could he get to it and open it in time? And did it lead anywhere or was it just the door to a storeroom or cabin?

While he was thinking this, breathing heavily and blinking blood away Andrew became aware that the engines had changed their note to a deeper tone.

We are under way, he thought. A distant clanking sound told him that the anchor chain was being wound in by the capstan. *The ship is moving! We could strike the mine!* he thought.

Once again, the terror of being drowned clutched at his heart and throat. But to escape he had to get past Long John Silver who was slowly advancing while muttering murderous threats. There was no doubt in Andrew's mind that this time Long John would kill him if he could, no matter what his captain had said. Andrew found he was trembling violently and sweating heavily. Fear seemed to paralyse him.

The corridor was too narrow to be able to dodge past Long John so Andrew decided he must risk the door behind him. There were no other fire extinguishers or similar items he could use as a weapon. As quickly as he could, he turned and ran the ten paces to the door. With hands all a-fumble with feverish haste he began heaving the locking bars open. But a glance over his shoulder told him he did not have the time. Long John Silver was stumping towards him, knife at the ready.

A feeling of defeat mingled with desperation. Andrew braced himself for another hand-to-hand knife fight, knowing that this one would be to the death.

KAA... BOOM!

A shattering explosion made the whole ship leap and quiver. The motion was so violent that both Andrew and Long John Silver were flung up to strike the deckhead and then they fell back down onto a deck that was vibrating so hard they were bounced around. Andrew had struck his head but was still conscious.

The mine! he thought as he made frantic efforts to get to his feet. He yelled, "The mine! We have hit the mine! I told you there was one!"

He saw that Long John Silver was face down and scrabbling to pick up the knife which he had dropped. Fear and fury fuelled Andrew and he sprang forward. By the time he reached Long John, the pirate had grabbed the knife. Instead, of grappling with him Andrew seized the hair on the back of Long John's head and in desperation slammed his face into the steel deck. Andrew was so afraid that he hammered the pirate's face and head against the deck three more times.

To his relief, Long John slumped unconscious and the knife dropped from his hand. Andrew stood up, chest heaving, appalled at what he had done.

Have I killed him? he wondered as he saw blood flow across the deck from the pirate's face.

A sudden lurch caused Andrew to stumble and he nearly lost his balance. Through blurry eyes he saw with horror that the deck was at an odd angle.

We are sinking! The ship is rolling over! he thought.

All his fears of being trapped in a sinking ship welled up to make him panic and he bolted along the corridor to the steps.

Only as he set foot on the treads did he remember Tina and Carmen. It was enough to make him pause and study the situation. He realised that he was hyperventilating so much that he was dizzy.

"Calm down! You want to be an officer in the navy. Officers don't act like this. Get a grip on yourself," he said.

With an effort of willpower he paused and while gripping the rails made a more objective study of the situation. *If I am a damage control officer, I will have to face this,* he thought.

The concept of dying with dignity crossed his mind, as did a fleeting image of a story he had heard about the officer on the *Titanic* who had kept the stokers working because they needed steam to run the generators for electricity for the radio, lights, and winches, even though he knew it meant all their deaths. With a conscious effort of willpower Andrew steadied himself. Then he wiped sweat and blood from his eyes to clear them. The ship was listing, but not very much. But the engines had stopped and already the lights were flickering and growing dimmer.

Running on battery power, he thought.

Feeling suddenly calm Andrew turned and walked over to the door where the girls were imprisoned. He called loudly, "Are you alright?"

Tina answered. "Yes, but Adele has lost her glasses and Carmen has hit her head. Please get us out."

"I will. I just need the keys," Andrew replied.

The ship gave a sudden shudder and a distinct lurch, but the other way, righting itself. *I'd better hurry,* he thought. So he walked along the corridor to where Long John Silver lay. By then Andrew was feeling quite detached and relaxed. To his relief, he noted that Long John was breathing. It was a snorting, snuffling sort of sound but breathing. Andrew picked up the knife and quickly used it to cut through Long John's belt. Then he slid the key ring off. He slipped the knife into his own waistband just in case, then turned to go.

But he found he couldn't just walk away. *The mongrel will drown,* he thought.

With a sigh, he bent and grabbed Long John's shirt collar. With strength he did not know he had Andrew dragged the unconscious pirate along the deck to the bottom of the steps. This resulted in a long smear of blood but Andrew felt quite unmoved by it.

He turned and walked to the door. Selecting a likely looking key he attempted to insert it into the keyhole. As he did, the ship gave another shudder. This was followed by a series of loud crashes and bangs somewhere forward. The deck lurched and quivered and the whole stern took on a sudden tilt aft. From inside the cabin came yells and a hysterical scream. Andrew staggered and was thrown against the bulkhead, bruising his shoulder.

With difficulty Andrew remained on his feet. *I had better hurry,* he thought.

He tried the key. It did not fit so he flicked it aside and inserted the next likely looking one. Still no good. Then the lights went out and a waft of acrid smoke tickled his nostrils.

This is not looking good, he thought as the deck tilted once more to port.

A dim light glowed overhead allowing Andrew enough light to see by. He inserted a third key. It fitted. Carefully he turned it. There was a click and to his relief the handle worked. He swung the door open. Tina was there, holding Adele and shaking her. It was Adele who was doing the screaming. When she saw Andrew, Tina let go of Adele and ran to him.

He hugged her tight and said, "You are safe, and I love you."

"I love you too!" Tina cried, tears of relief streaming down her face.

Carmen appeared beside her. "Well done, brother. Are we safe?"

Andrew nodded. "Well, sort of. Let's get Adele up on deck."

As he said this the ship gave another lurch and heeled even more to port. For a second Andrew feared it was going to roll right over but it steadied itself with a massive shudder accompanied by the gurgle of rushing water. Andrew released Tina and hurried her across to the bottom of the steps. Carmen followed with a sobbing Adele.

Tina stopped and pointed at Long John Silver. "What about him?"

Andrew left a sudden rush of guilt. He had been going to leave him. "Help me get him up the steps," he said.

"Companionway," Tina corrected.

Andrew grunted and grinned. He grabbed Long John's left arm and Tina took his right and they struggled up the steps with him. Carmen helped with his feet, hampered by Adele who kept trying to push past her. For a few seconds the limp pirate jammed between the railings. Andrew feared that he had made a mistake but gave a furious wrench and Long John came free. Angry that the pirate might cause the death of the girls Andrew dragged him up by brute force, not caring if it injured him further or not.

Once up on the next deck, Andrew dragged Long John along to the door leading to the well deck. This was open and he was able to step over the coaming and then lift Long John out as well. Andrew dropped him there and then stared in amazement. Most of the ship in front of him was sticking up at a most peculiar angle and he realised that the blast from the mine had buckled the deck upwards and almost cut the ship in two. The masts had fallen and the open hatches were covered in a tangle of steel wire ropes.

Tina, Carmen, and Adele crowded out beside him and stared wildly around. So did Andrew, but more in dismay. It was dark, the ship's lights having failed, but he could make out enough in the moonlight to realise that the situation was not what he had thought. He had pictured the ship being almost alongside the wharf and in quite shallow water but the wharf was nowhere to be seen. He strode across to the starboard rail and looked aft. To his astonishment, he saw that they were at least a hundred metres from the wharf.

Carmen joined him and took in the situation at a glance. "We need lifejackets, or a life raft," she said.

Andrew pointed upwards. "Boat deck," he said.

Without waiting he hurried aft to where a companionway led up to the back of the wheelhouse. By then the ship was listing so badly he had to put one foot on the deck and the other on the bulkhead. Carmen, Tina and Adele followed him. He went up the steps three at a time. At the top he turned left and raced aft, slipping and ending up on his hands and knees as he did. There were some empty chocks and davits.

Where that motorboat came from, he surmised. Beyond them were two white cylindrical containers close against the railings.

"Life raft," he said.

Carmen joined him and they both began wrestling with the clips that sealed the end on the container. The lid flew off and he grabbed at the bulky package inside. As he did, the ship gave another lurch that threw them all to the deck. Tina went sliding away to port but Andrew grabbed her leg and hung on.

Just as Andrew changed his grip to help her up the ship suddenly heeled. Adele screamed and Carmen cried out in alarm. "We are capsizing!"

Andrew hooked his right arm through the railings and heaved Tina up. She grabbed at the railing and he was able to let go of her and reach across to help Carmen with the life raft. Even as he did so he felt the ship start sliding under. He jerked out the safety pin and pulled at the catch to inflate the rubber raft. Suddenly the dark, roiling water swirled up and engulfed him.

It was so sudden and so cold that Andrew lost his grip on the raft. He tried to swim up and realised from the pain in his ears that he was still going down. With a shock he discovered that he was snagged on the wreck.

I am being dragged down! he thought.

Once again, panic began to surge as fear of drowning gripped him.

Chapter 43

OLD SHIPMATES

Andrew struggled violently, his whole being screaming in terror at the idea of drowning. Salt water gushed up his nose making him cough and want to vomit.

Hold your breath! his mind cried. Then his diver training kicked in. *Calm down and find out where you are caught,* he told himself.

By this time he was deep under water and in total blackness. All he could do was feel with his hands. Within seconds he found that the pocket of his shorts was snagged on a bolt head. He wrenched it free, ripping the material in the process. Immediately he began floating up. In the black water there was no visible reference but he was calm enough to allow himself to rise. Once he had the direction he was able to use his arms and legs to accelerate the rate of ascent.

A greying overhead indicated the moonlight and Andrew even glimpsed blurry bubbles. He added to these, exhaling air to have his lungs empty and ready for a fresh breath as soon as he broke surface. When his head bobbed out he immediately gulped in fresh air and began treading water.

Gasping with relief, he looked around. His eyes stung from the salt but he squeezed them shut and then wiped them and looked again. Nearby was a boiling maelstrom that indicated air escaping from the sinking wreck.

I need to get away from that in case pieces of flotsam come shooting up, he thought.

So he turned and began breast stoking away, all the while looking for the life raft and the girls. He saw the raft almost at once. It was only ten metres away but he had to swim as hard as he could to reach it. In fact he nearly didn't make it as it kept drifting away.

Must be a breeze, he thought.

By the time he grabbed at the looped rope around the outside his arms felt like lead and he was panting hard. Andrew was about to heave himself into the life raft when it occurred to him that the girls might have trouble reaching it too. So despite his fears of sharks and other sea creatures, he stayed in the water, holding the raft and calling out.

To his intense relief, Tina answered him and she came splashing towards him with one arm helping support Adele. Andrew swam side stroke to meet her, towing the raft behind him. He then helped push her aboard while holding Adele. Tina then dragged Adele on board.

Andrew looked around, worried that Carmen might have got sucked down with the ship but in answer to his calls she came swimming out of the darkness and was heaved aboard. It was then Andrew's turn. Tina and Carmen took an arm each and lifted and a moment later he slid into the soft bottom of the life raft.

"Oh, thank God!" he sighed.

For several seconds he lay there, panting and shivering but glad to be alive. Then he raised his head.

"What was that?" he asked.

"Someone calling for help," Carmen replied.

Andrew moved to a kneeling position and looked out. Up until then he had not given a thought to the possible fate of the crew of the ship. *At least one of them has survived,* he thought. Anxious lest the man drowned, he scanned the surrounding sea.

It was Tina who spotted the man. "There!" she cried, pointing.

Andrew looked and got a brief glimpse of an arm and a head against a shimmering, moving backdrop of silver and black waves.

"Here!" they yelled.

"Help!" came the faint, gargled reply.

"He will never catch us. This breeze is pushing us faster than he can swim," Carmen said.

Oh bugger! was Andrew's response. "In we go, Car." he said. With that he lowered himself back into the water. Carmen did likewise and so did Tina. Andrew called, "Adele, you keep watching him and give us direction. Okay, tow the raft."

By holding the rope around the outside and kicking with their feet the three of them were able to move the raft against the wind. It was slow work but the man managed to swim closer and in a couple of minutes they met. As they did, Andrew recognised the survivor.

Oh bloody hell! Long John Silver!

Tina and Carmen were pushed aboard and they hauled Long John

Silver out of the water. While they did Andrew felt for the knife. But it was gone.

Bugger! Defenceless, and with a pirate on board, he thought.

He was dragged aboard and moved to face Long John Silver. When the pirate recognised him, he stared and then swore.

"Doo! Off all da flooffy luck!" he cried.

"You can always leave," Andrew retorted. "Now sit still and don't give us any trouble or we will chuck you over the side."

He could see that Long John's face was all swollen and bruised and his nose appeared bent and misshapen. He did not seem to have much fight in him.

Carmen said, "How did you hurt your face?"

Long John shook his fist at Andrew and said, "Thiff barfdurd smashed my fafe into da deck. He bwoke my nove."

Andrew put his clenched fists on his hips and said, "And I'll break your bloody neck if you give any trouble. Now shut up!" Long John subsided muttering into the bottom of the raft.

Tina looked from one to the other and said, "Do you know him, Andrew?"

Andrew gave a short laugh. "Yes, and so does Car. We have been shipmates of a sort several times. He is a thief and a pirate called Ben Silver. His nickname among the pirate fraternity is Long John Silver."

"What else!" Tina replied.

"Keep a weather eye on him and don't trust him an inch," Andrew said. "It was him who gave me this." He indicated his now stinging cut above his eye. "The mongrel tried to kill me with a knife."

"Was that the fight we could hear?" Carmen asked.

"Yes," Andrew agreed. At that, his emotions boiled over and he began to tremble and was unable to speak.

Tina hugged him and said, "Oh Andrew! You really are the bravest. You are a real hero! My hero!" She kissed him and held him tight.

That made Andrew even more emotional but all he could do was hold her while tears of exhaustion trickled down his cheeks.

It was Carmen who broke the spell. "What are those lights?" she asked.

Andrew looked where she was pointing and for the first time really noticed the shore. Up till now it had been a vague part of the dark background but now he saw that the hills were sharply silhouetted against the starry sky by the setting moon. On the hill above the old wharf lights were appearing. Most were vehicle headlights but some were flashing blue and red.

"The police!" he cried. "Oh, I hope they have caught those mongrels."

"What mongrels?" Tina asked.

"The smugglers; Barry and Jan and so on," Andrew replied.

Carmen said, "Did you call the police?"

"Yes, well, via the navy," Andrew replied. He then explained quickly how he had swum out to the ship and used the pirate's own radio to call HMAS *Armidale*. On hearing this Long John Silver muttered and swore.

Tina said, "But how did you find us?"

Andrew replied, "Tell you later. We need to get this tub ashore. Try paddling." By this time they had drifted several hundred metres further out to sea. Andrew noted that it was only a gentle land breeze but decided there was probably an outgoing tide to help it. But the combination was too strong for them and they were soon gasping for breath. It was painfully obvious they were even further away from the area where the lights were. They tried yelling but it was quickly obvious that no-one on shore could hear them. Carmen suggested swimming again but Andrew refused.

"No. We are not risking anyone's life when we are quite safe. We will wait till daylight."

So they sat and told each other their stories. Adele started by asking Andrew if he had blown up the ship. Andrew was astonished. "No, it wasn't me. I'm not that good! I was trying to save you, not kill you. It was that old German mine." He then described the old mine. As Tina had also seen it on Hope Island this was accepted. There was then a discussion about sea mines and how many had been laid along Australia's coast during World War 2, and by whom.

Next, Tina and Carmen described how the crooks had tied them up and made them prisoner. It was obvious to Andrew that the girls had been terrified, but he did not tell them what he had overheard the crooks say they would do to them.

I will tell them when we are all safe ashore, he decided.

Andrew then told them how he was chased by the crooks. When he described how he had jumped into the Annan Gorge and then hitched a ride on one of the smuggler's trucks the girls were full of admiration. Tina hugged him tightly and that made him even happier.

Carmen said, "So if that horrible Barry was driving one of the trucks then Little Terry must be at his shed across the river."

"I hope so," Andrew said. It was only one of the nagging worries he had.

The others were whether Grandma Cynthia and Old Bert were safe; and what his parents must be thinking. *They must be worried sick,* he thought.

That took them to midnight and by then Andrew estimated they were at least a kilometre offshore and that they had drifted northwards another kilometre or so.

Adele was really worried and said, "But what if we drift out to sea and nobody finds us? We will die of thirst."

Andrew shook his head. "No, the prevailing wind should push us ashore tomorrow. We will probably end up on one of the beaches just south of Cooktown."

As he said this, he realised he had blundered as it conjured up images of the incident at Finch Bay. His words obviously had the same effect on Tina as she gave him an anxious look. To reassure her he squeezed her hand and smiled.

He then went on to describe how he and Graham Kirk had floated for 18 hours after a floatplane crash. "We just drifted northwards until we were picked up," he said.

It had been one of the more terrifying experiences of his life, but Carmen then reminded him of the other two times they had been adrift in the ocean. The most recent had been in April out on the Great Barrier Reef and Andrew shuddered at the horrible memories.

Their desperate struggle for survival was discussed and then they described to Tina and Adele all the adventures in which they had encountered Long John Silver. He was a reluctant listener and from time to time swore or added some of his own information.

"I'll get even one day," he vowed.

"Only when you are an old man and they let you out of jail," Andrew retorted.

They fell silent at about 2am. Exhaustion claimed Andrew and he slipped into a fitful doze with his head on Tina's shoulder. He woke with a start after a bad dream in which a huge shark was about to grab his dangling feet while he was swimming in the sea at night. For a few moments he sat there shivering and disoriented. Then he remembered where he was and looked around.

Andrew immediately sensed that something was wrong. A glance revealed what it was. Someone was missing from the raft, Long John Silver! For a moment Andrew feared that he had cut the girl's throats from the way they were slumped in the raft but then Tina stirred and he saw that Carmen was breathing normally.

Andrew looked at the dark sea and then at the shore. He noted that they were now several kilometres north of Archer Point. The flashing light from the lighthouse was clear to see.

How far is to the shore? he wondered. He tried to estimate the distance and decided it must be at least a kilometre. *Surely he didn't try to swim that?* he wondered.

Tina woke up and asked him what was wrong. Their conversation woke the others. Carmen stared at the distant shore and said, "If I was facing years in jail I would risk swimming ashore. We risked swimming to the wreck on Longbow Reef remember."

"Yes, but we had wet suits and personal flotation devices; and we were dead if we didn't," Andrew answered.

Tina hugged him and said, "You swam several hundred metres in the sea at night to rescue us."

"That was different. I was trying to save you," Andrew replied. The memory got him all choked up with emotion.

Tina added to this by kissing him and saying, "I'm glad you did. I love you."

Andrew could only blush and enjoy it. They sat and bobbed slowly along on an almost calm sea until the sky began to lighten to the east. Dawn crept slowly over the sea and Andrew felt much better. He was even happier when he detected a tiny dark spec on the southern horizon. The spec was throwing up tiny puffs and white and he knew it was a bow wave.

Twenty minutes later, as the sun came up, there was no doubt. It was a navy patrol boat. They cheered and waved, but the jubilation turned to dismay when the patrol boat, now identifiable as *Armidale*, turned inshore while still several kilometres away and headed for Archer Point.

"They haven't seen us," Carmen said.

"They don't even know we are out here," Andrew replied. Suddenly he felt depressed and very, very tired and sore.

Tina knelt and began unzipping the small pouches on the raft. "This thing should have survival and signalling gear," she said. It was one of the lessons they learned at Navy Cadets and was part of every safety briefing whenever they went for a sea ride on a navy ship. She rummaged around and then grinned. "Here we are, a mirror and some flares. Andrew, you use the mirror while Carmen and I use the flares."

The flares were fired and Andrew flashed the mirror. A few minutes later they saw the Patrol Boat suddenly turn in their direction.

"They have seen us!" Adele cried happily.

Then all they had to do was sit and wait. Ten minutes later the *Armidale* hove-to a few metres to windward of them. A row of faces peered down at them from the railings and the bridge. Andrew saw Lt Cdr McDowall and waved.

"Hello sir. Here we are."

"Where's the ship?" Lt Cdr McDowall asked.

"At the bottom of the sea sir. She hit that old mine we found and it blew up and sank her," Andrew answered.

A look of astonishment crossed Lt Cdr McDowall's face and he cried, "The Devil it did! By Jove, you must remind your friend not to sit on the old rusty ones in future."

They were helped up over the rail of the Patrol Boat by strong hands backed by grinning familiar faces.

"Hello Matey, taken to playing Robinson Crusoe, have you?" asked a seaman whose face was familiar but whose name Andrew had forgotten.

"No, pirates," Andrew replied. He stepped down onto the Patrol Boat's deck and experienced an intense feeling of being safe and at home.

I will make the navy my career, he decided.

The bearded Chief Bosuns Mate grinned and shook his hand. "Welcome aboard, shipmate."

"Thanks Buffer," Andrew replied. He hurried on for fear that the tears forming at the back of his eyes would embarrass him by trickling out.

He made his way to the bridge, followed by the girls. As he arrived Andrew noted that there were a Rear Admiral and a captain also present. Unsure what to do he came awkwardly to attention. But before he could introduce himself Lt Cdr McDowall said, "Sir, meet Cadet Petty Officer Andrew Collins. And this is Cadet Leading Seaman Tina Babcock. And I've seen this young lady before but she wasn't on our most recent voyage." He indicated Carmen.

Carmen came to attention and said, "Midshipman Carmen Collins, sir. I start at ADFA next week."

The Rear Admiral raised an eyebrow and said to Lt Cdr McDowall, "You know this band of ruffians, I see?"

"Yes sir. They are old shipmates," Lt Cdr McDowall replied.

At that moment, Andrew almost burst with admiration and hero worship.

One day I will be a naval officer, and captain of my own ship, just like him, he vowed.

Chapter 44

ENDS WELL

The patrol boat returned to the waters off Archer Point. Aided by Andrew and the depth sounder they soon located the sunken ship and marked it with buoys. There was a police Land Cruiser at the old wharf and a boat took the Rear Admiral, Captain and Lt Cdr McDowall ashore to look at the stacks of boxes still littering the area. While this was done Andrew was examined by a navy doctor who had been brought along 'just in case'.

The navy doctor put two stitches in the cut in Andrew's eyebrow and told him he had been very lucky. "If the point of the knife hadn't dug into the bone it might have slipped down and cut the optic nerves behind the eye, blinding you."

Andrew shuddered and shook his head. "I broke the pirate's nose," he replied, then briefly described the fight with Long John Silver.

"You have certainly accumulated some bumps and bruises, not to mention a good collection of scratches," the doctor replied.

Andrew knew that. His whole body seemed to ache and itch and he felt utterly drained and so tired he could hardly keep his eyes open.

"It's been a very busy few days," he replied.

Once his wounds had been tended, Andrew was put to bed in the sick bay. Tina sat with him, smiling contentedly while holding his hand. Carmen brought him a mobile phone and handed it to him.

"Mum," she said. Andrew found it hard to speak to his mother as his throat choked up with emotion.

"Sorry for causing you so much worry, Mum," he croaked.

"Oh Andrew! I am so proud of you," his mother replied. Then she sniffled and so did he. Finally she said, "We will see you at the Cooktown wharf in a couple of hours."

Another half hour went by before the senior officers returned from the wharf. The Rear Admiral came to see Andrew in the sick bay and shook his hand. "My word, young fella, you have done a mighty job from what I hear. But for you all these guns and grenades and so on would have caused untold death and misery. At least two countries owe you a great debt."

Andrew felt very self-conscious under the gaze of so many important people. He shrugged and said, "Oh I don't know, sir. Maybe the mine would have sunk the ship anyway?"

"Oh you are being too modest! You had radioed us long before then. If the mine hadn't got her we would have caught her the next day. She certainly wouldn't have reached her destination," the Rear Admiral said.

"Where was that sir?"

"Bunga Lunga," the Rear Admiral replied.

Andrew nodded. He knew that Bunga Lunga was one of the tiny island nations of the South Pacific out past Vanuatu and the Solomons.

He said, "Did the police catch all of the crooks, sir?"

The Rear Admiral shook his head. "No. They got some of the ship's crew and some of the truck drivers, but I haven't heard if they have rounded up the whole gang yet."

"Did they catch Long John Silver, sir?" Andrew asked.

"No, your old shipmate has either drowned or is hiding in the scrub," the Rear Admiral replied.

Andrew did not know if he was glad or sad at that news. *I just hope I never run into him again,* he thought.

He said, "Where did the guns come from, sir?"

The Rear Admiral looked thoughtful and then said, "I can't tell you that, I'm afraid. But there are a damned lot of them. Anyway, you rest there and we will take you off to Cooktown just as soon as we have put an armed party ashore to help the police guard the loot."

The Rear Admiral and the other officers left. Andrew and the girls discussed the news and then waited. It took another hour for all the arrangements to be made. During this time they were fed a very welcome breakfast. By then helicopters were circling the area and it was obvious the incident was world news. The Patrol Boat then got under way and proceeded to Cooktown. This took another hour.

During the last part of the trip Andrew and the girls stood on deck and watched the scenery. It was a lovely sunny day and the coastline looked very pretty. As they passed Finch Bay Andrew had some twinges of guilt and regret.

Colleen is a nice kisser! he thought.

Then he hugged Tina and was glad they had rediscovered their love. She looked up at him, eyes sparkling and they tenderly came together and kissed, until some of the sailors began teasing them with, "Oi, Oi!"

Andrew's parents were waiting on the wharf, along with a football scrum of media. Andrew had been briefed by then to say nothing to them so he just ignored the reporters and cameras and pushed through them to where his parents waited. There was a tearful reunion for him and Carmen.

Then his mother said, "I don't think I am going to allow you pair out of the house anymore. Every time you do you get into some awful adventure that makes me age ten years."

Sgt Bull was there and he took them all to the police station. Even though Andrew now felt exhausted again the police insisted they be interviewed. This took several hours and it was midday by the time their statements had been signed.

As they went to leave Andrew said, "Sgt Bull sir, have you caught all the crooks yet?"

Sgt Bull shook his head. "No, we have five men off the ship but not the captain and his mate, or your friend the cook with the peg leg. As well we have arrested six of the truck drivers. They tried to leave the area but there are really only two roads south from Cooktown and they have been picked up at either Daintree River or Mt Molloy. There is only one of them yet to be accounted for and that it Barry Philby, the local man whose property they were using."

"Barry! Did you find Little Terry, his son?" Andrew asked.

"No, we didn't," Sgt Bull replied.

Andrew felt his chest tighten with anxiety. "So where is he? Have you searched Barry's property?"

Sgt Bull nodded. "Yes we have; and we have officers there now. We have found three more sheds hidden in the jungle. But the little boy is definitely not there."

"So where is he? Oh no! He must still be lost," Andrew cried.

A horrible feeling of dread gripped him, and he felt the urge to rush out to look for Little Terry.

"Or dead," Sgt Bull added, further fuelling Andrew's fears.

"We must go and look!" Andrew cried.

His mother shook her head. "Lunch first, and then bed for you."

"Mum! I couldn't lie down knowing that Little Terry is still missing," Andrew cried.

"You will! If need be I will get the doctor to give you a sedative," his mother replied firmly.

Carmen gave a chuckle and added, "Or the doctor's wife!"

Andrew blushed and tried to avoid Tina's eye. His mother said, "Doctor's wife? What has she got to do with it?"

Carmen shook her head. "Nothing, Mum. Just a joke. Come on, let's eat and then go home. Then we can plan a search."

Of course they went to the cafe in the main street to buy lunch. With apparent inevitability Daphne and Kristen were sitting outside with some of the local youths and Daphne gave Andrew an odd look that caused him to blush again. With equal inevitability Colleen was inside with her mother. She gave Andrew a sad smile and came around the counter. Andrew thought for a moment she was coming to him but instead she went to Tina.

"I've heard a bit of what happened to you guys," Colleen said. She then gestured to Andrew and went on, "Andrew has been a real hero again, I hear."

Tina nodded, her face vaguely hostile. Colleen said, "He loves you, you know. So don't you throw him away or I will have him."

Colleen's mother looked surprised and cried, "Colleen! What are you saying? Do you know this boy that well?"

"Yes Mum; and I mean it. And I don't care what you or dad say," Colleen answered. She them stepped over and kissed Andrew on the cheek. "Good luck, Andrew. You love her properly. And Tina, you love him properly. He deserves it."

Colleen then turned and hurried from the shop, her eyes filling with tears. Andrew was both embarrassed and pleased. The only thing he could think of doing was turning to take hold of Tina to kiss her. She responded and he noted that her eyes were wet as well.

Carmen broke the silence by cheering and clapping. Andrew did not care. He just looked deep into Tina's eyes and whispered, "I will!"

She melted into his arms and they kissed again before stepping apart. Andrew's father clapped him on the back and grinned. His mother looked pleased and Colleen's mother smiled but looked puzzled.

Food was ordered and Andrew thankfully eased his aching and weary body into a chair. He was hungry and quickly devoured a hamburger and a milkshake. When they had eaten, they made their way out to the vehicles.

As they got in, Carmen said, "Dad, who is minding the pub?"

"Irish."

Carmen shook her head but smiled. "Oh Dad! We have warned you about leaving Count Dracula in charge of the Blood Bank!"

That eased the tension but it returned as they drove home. Andrew fretted, when he wasn't dozing. Anxiety about what had happened to Little Terry now dominated his mind. Along the way Andrew found that every stretch of road now brought vivid memories to mind. Then, as they crossed Trevethan Creek and the Black Mountains came into sight, another horrible thought came to him.

"Grandma Cynthia and Old Bert, are they alright?" he asked.

"Yes, we called in on the way to town," his mother replied.

Andrew described the threats he had overheard and his mother was appalled. "What horrible men! I knew that Jan character was a bad egg!" she cried.

As they drove past Grandma Cynthia's, Andrew pointed to the spot where he had climbed into the crook's truck. His mother was appalled at the risks he had run. But Andrew shook his head.

"It got me right out of their search area, Mum. They had no idea where I had gone then. Besides, I was sure it would lead me to finding Tina and Carmen; and it did!"

A few minutes later they pulled up outside the hotel. Irish and several of the locals came out to greet them and there was a noisy ten minutes of talking and back-slapping. All Andrew wanted to do, despite his bone weariness, was to go and look for Little Terry and he said so very firmly.

His mother shook her head. "Not until you have had a shower and changed into clean clothes and had a bit of a rest. We will get organised while you do that. You girls do the same. We have to wait for the police and the SES anyway. So go!" she ordered.

Andrew saw the sense in what his mother was saying so he limped along the veranda to his room. The girls followed. As he turned into the corridor, Andrew felt extremely anxious.

I hope Little Terry hasn't drowned, he thought.

To him it was a ghastly way to die and the thought of the innocent little boy struggling in the swirling flood in the dark and then sucking in water instead of air was horrible.

For a few seconds Andrew felt so nauseous that he became dizzy. He paused to lean on the wall because the door to his room was closed. Carmen put her hand on his shoulder. "You okay Andrew?' she asked.

Andrew nodded. "Yes, just feeling worried about what might have happened to Little Terry."

He then turned the knob and opened the door. Then his heart skipped a beat and he stood open-mouthed. Sitting on the floor playing with the model soldiers was Little Terry!

"Little Terry! You are safe!" Andrew cried.

He rushed in and hugged the little boy. His heart felt as though it would burst with happiness and he wept with joy.

The girls heard him and came crowding in, crying with happiness and patting and hugging each other and Little Terry. The commotion attracted Andrew's parents and then Irish and the others. There was a lot of relieved chatter. Andrew's father at once went to telephone the police and to cancel the SES search party.

Andrew sat down beside Little Terry. "But what happened Little Terry? You left here in your dad's Land Rover and it crashed up the road. We went and looked for you half the night and again yesterday but couldn't find you," he said, while thinking: *Was it only yesterday!*

Little Terry looked very anxious and had to be reassured that he would not get into trouble from his dad. He said, "After daddy crashed the car he told me to sit in it and wait while he went to get a friend to help. So he walked off. Then I got really scared and I got out and tried to follow him. But... bb... but it got really scary and I thought... thought (sniffle) that there was m... m... mon... monsters f... following m... m... me!"

With that he burst into tears. Andrew comforted him and felt really sorry for him, imagining what it might be like to a little boy alone in that storm. After Little Terry had calmed down he told them that he had fallen into a ditch while he was running and had then got caught on a barbed wire fence. When he got free of that he could not find the road again and had wandered around until he blundered into some cattle. He thought they would eat him or gore him with their horns so he ran away, into another barbed wire fence. He crawled under this and into the edge of some jungle.

"I was really scared and I could not move," Little Terry explained, showing the scratches from the fence and the jungle. "And there were big pigs snorting close by so I hid behind a big tree. I must have gone to sleep. When mine woke up mine heard water and as I needed drink I went and found the river. Then I got a good idea. I knew we played farms beside the river so I walked along until I found where we played and then I came up here. I couldn't find anyone so I lay on your bed and went to sleep."

Andrew was amazed. "And you've been here ever since?"

Little Terry nodded. "Mine been playing wiv little people. I hope you don't mind?"

He looked so anxious that Andrew thought his heart would break. He said, "Of course not Little Terry. They are for you anyway."

Tina said, "But what did you eat?"

Little Terry shook his head. "Nuffing," he muttered.

Andrew's mother cried in dismay. "Oh you poor little mite! You must be starving. Come to the kitchen and we will feed you up."

She took Little Terry's hand and led him out onto the veranda. Everyone else followed. As they walked along the veranda Andrew began worrying about what might now happen to the little boy. They were just reaching the door of the dining room when a police car came racing along the road from Mungumby Bridge. It pulled up near them and Sgt Bull and another policeman climbed out.

Andrew's mother led Little Terry down under the mango trees and said, "Didn't you get our message sergeant? Here he is, safe and sound."

Sgt Bull shook his head, then looked around. "No I didn't. So the little boy is safe? Good. Sorry, I have come about another matter." He turned and said to the constable, "Bill, back the car up out of sight behind that shed at the end of the pub."

That intrigued Andrew. He was even more curious when Sgt Bull said, "They haven't arrived yet? Okay, I would like all of you people inside and out of sight please. Go quickly." He ushered them into the dining room and would not answer questions. "Just stay in here please."

At that moment, another vehicle appeared from the direction of Mungumby Bridge. Andrew could just see through the front door and saw that it was a white 4WD. He also noted Sgt Bull reach back and unclip his pistol.

What is going on? Andrew wondered.

The white 4WD stopped in the middle of the parking area and out of it climbed Dave Philby. He went around to the passenger door and opened it and reached in. Next moment he hauled a person out onto the ground. Andrew gasped when he saw it was Barry and he was tied up.

As soon as he saw this, Sgt Bull drew his pistol and walked out through the front door. Andrew looked at Barry, who was whining and begging to be let go. The sight was enough to make Andrew feel nauseous.

Then he thought, *Little Terry shouldn't see his dad like this.*

He turned and called, "Mum, take Little Terry to the kitchen and feed him some chocolate ice-cream, please. Quickly!"

His mother understood at once and nodded and did so. Andrew then turned back to watch. He was just in time to see Dave drag Barry to his feet.

Dave faced Sgt Bull and said, "This piece of shit who calls himself my brother arrived at my place and wanted me to hide him. From what I heard on the radio I gather he is wanted for various crimes including kidnapping the girls here and for being part of a gang of crooks smuggling guns."

Sgt Bull stopped a couple of paces from Barry and said. "That is correct. Thanks for bringing him in."

Dave shook his head angrily as he untied Barry's wrists. "I didn't bring him in because of that but because he can't tell me where Little Terry is. The selfish bastard has lost his little boy and couldn't be bothered to keep looking for him."

Dave then shoved Barry towards Sgt Bull. Barry staggered a couple of paces and whined, "It wasn't like that! I had to go or the gang would have done me in! You mongrel! Call yourself a brother and you shop me to the bloody coppers! You are the shit!"

With that Barry lost his temper and flung himself at Dave, punching and kicking. Dave stepped back and put his fists up then stepped in and drove his right fair into Barry's jaw. Barry went down hard and Dave stood over him.

He said, "Call yourself a father! You are nothing but a miserable failure of a human being. Here sergeant, you can have him!"

Sgt Bull and the constable rushed forward and quickly handcuffed Barry and bundled him off into the police car. Dave saw he had an audience and strode up onto the veranda. "Sorry about that. Bit of family business. But when he told me he had crashed his Land Rover and left that poor little boy alone in the dark near a flooded river I just saw red. Then not even to go looking for him the next day!"

Andrew stepped out. "It's alright, Dave. We have found Little Terry. He was hiding here."

Dave's eyes lit up and he cried, "Where is he? Is he alright?"

"Yes. He's in the kitchen eating ice-cream," Andrew replied.

Dave strode through the dining room and into the kitchen. Andrew and the others followed. He was just in time to see Little Terry's face light up.

"Unca Dave!" he cried. He scrambled down off the stool and ran to Dave's arms. For a minute or so they just hugged each other.

Then Dave stood up and said, "Your daddy won't be back for a long time. Do you want to go home to Mummy?"

Little Terry's face instantly changed to a look of anxiety and he shook his head fearfully. "No!" he whispered.

To Andrew that was one of the saddest things he had ever seen, and he returned Tina's hand squeeze in sympathy. But what happened next made up for all of it.

Uncle Dave said, "Would you like to live with me?"

Little Terry's face lit up and he flung himself into Dave's arms again. "Yes, Unca Dave!"

His heart nearly bursting with happiness Andrew turned to look at Tina. She smiled up at him and hugged him tighter. Instinctively they came together and kissed.

When they came up for air, Tina whispered, "And don't forget you promised to love me properly!"

He looked into those lovely big brown eyes and then studied the enigmatic 'female' expression on her face.

Anxiety returned. *What does she mean by that? Does she mean physical love as well? Is she going to let me do it?* But he did not dare ask, just felt irritated. *Does she expect me to know what she is thinking?* he wondered as they kissed again.

Author's Note

This novel is a work of fiction. The names, characters and incidents portrayed in it are the work of the author's imagination. Any resemblance to actual persons, living or dead or events is entirely coincidental. The locations, except for the smuggler's hideout and Mt Penniless, are real and are described as during the author's most recent trip to the area. The location of the smuggler's hideout is fictional and placed in that area for convenience. As far as the author is aware, no person who has lived, or is living, in that area has ever carried out any illegal activity.

Note that the first edition of this book was written in 2005 and no attempt has been made to update the setting. Please just enjoy the story.

Enjoy more C.R. Cummings stories

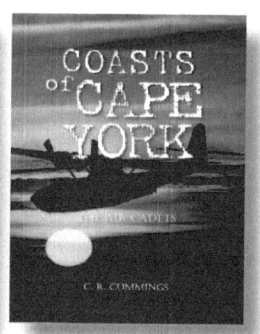